THE BEST
AUSTRALIAN
STORIES
2 0 0 6

Edited by
ROBERT DREWE

Published by Black Inc.,
an imprint of Schwartz Publishing Pty Ltd

Level 5, 289 Flinders Lane
Melbourne Victoria 3000 Australia
email: enquiries@blackincbooks.com
http://www.blackincbooks.com

ISBN 1 86395 270 5

THE BEST
AUSTRALIAN
STORIES
2 0 0 6

Contents

Introduction

Robert Drewe

So, what *is* a short story exactly? Well, it's a powerful thing. As an art form it can even aspire to beauty and perfection. Beautiful or not, however (and some might argue that for a riveting anecdote *inspired craft* is a more accurate fit than *art*), a good short story has a sharper force and focus than the novel. Apart from its heightened narrative tension, the well-told short story seems to speak to something deep in our souls. Curiously, it can set up a need in us we weren't even conscious of before we began to read – and then somehow fulfil it. How miraculous is that?

What the well-told story and the gifted storyteller accomplish, and have done since the ancient fireside tale, is to strike a chord whereby an essence of our own lives is extrapolated. You could call it the recognition or *wow!* factor. For just a moment we can make some sense of the tempestuous human journey towards oblivion.

An important literary form then, wouldn't you say? It's gratifying that many readers would seem to agree. *Best Australian Stories* is now an established annual best-seller. Its success gives the finger once again to those pessimists in book and magazine publishing who lost confidence in the saleability of short stories two or three decades ago.

That was then; this is now. I must say I find such pessimism unwarranted and wrong-headed. My personal experience as a writer of two short-story anthologies, and an editor of three, has been rewarding enough to keep the wolf, if not from the front gate, at least from my family's door. Whatever the current publishing shibboleth might be, it's not readers who are averse to stories.

Writers themselves, of course, have never tired of the genre. Interestingly, as some of the traditional homes of the story have closed their doors in this country, new Australian literary magazines and journals have sprung up which better reflect the taste of the more imaginative contemporary writer and reader.

Griffith Review, the *Sleepers Almanac*, *Heat*, *Verandah*, *Page Seventeen*, the *Monthly*, *Making Tracks* and *Coastlines* (the last two anthologies from writing students at the University of Technology, Sydney, and Southern Cross University respectively) have all made impressive strides recently. These newer journals, as well as the old established *Meanjin*, *Overland*, *Westerly* and the *Bulletin* summer reading issue all had an influence on my story selection for this anthology, as did the *New Yorker*, *Granta New Writing*, in London, and *Southword*, in Dublin, sources for three of the stories.

All told, thirty of the forty-four stories came from those journals, the remainder resulting from my inviting submissions from around the country. About half the total selection came from well-known writers, but one of the gratifying aspects of producing this book was discovering people previously unknown to me, including several young writers published here for the first time.

I hope the anthology reflects the diversity I was seeking. Readers will find great variety within. Here in abundance they will find contemporary life in all its anxiety – a subject shunned of late by the Australian literary novel, with its obsession with the past and the bush. They will find urban stories and rural stories. They will find humour and fear and poetry and cryptic suppressed narrative and biographical colonisation. They will perceive influences from abroad, chiefly recent American, but also European and Asian. At the very least I hope they will find that Edgar Allan Poe's simple definition of a short story, a narrative that 'can be read at one sitting', properly applies.

This was my selection guide: that the story in question should achieve an effect that made it hard to encapsulate or summarise.

It should have a resonant and mysterious quality – what the English writer William Boyd calls 'a complexity of afterthought' that couldn't be pinned down or analysed. I decided at the outset to look for genuine, complete-in-themselves stories rather than chapters of unpublished novels.

I received hundreds of submissions for this book, including many multiple submissions and some entire books of stories that a single editor, working alone in a narrow time frame, could never hope to read in their entirety. Many good stories missed out, not because they lacked quality but because the book required a certain literary balance and, of course, necessarily reflects my own taste. I like to see an adventurous, quirky story leavening the mood. I could have produced another two anthologies with the material I received. My heart goes out to these writers, even to those who will never speak to me again.

I should point out that *Best Australian Stories 2006* has already made some sort of postal history at Chris and Evan Connick's General Store and Post Office (*'For Honesty and Courtesy'*), the only commercial building in the tiny Northern Rivers hamlet of Tintenbar, New South Wales, where I kept a post office box to cope with the flow of entries. To this good-humoured and patient couple, I apologise once again for over-running their store counter with parcels of short stories for six months, an occurrence which actually suggested to me a sort of Borgesian short story itself.

I would also like to acknowledge the invaluable editorial assistance of Caitlin Yates, the publishing manager at Black Inc., and, especially, to thank the publisher, Morry Schwartz, without whom *Best Australian Stories* would never have been born, much less thrived.

Robert Drewe
Tintenbar, 2006

Like the World's an Armchair

Paddy O'Reilly

Norm Stevens Snr tells me I'll never get that truck off my land. He says it's too old, been there too long, the hoist will try to lift the thing and it will break apart into red stones of rust.

'Leave it,' he says. 'Let it rust away. One day you'll look and it won't be there anymore.'

He gives me a sideways glance.

'Like husbands,' he says. 'You look away and when you look back they're gone, right?'

'Right,' I say.

'So have you heard from the bastard?' he asks.

'Nope,' I say.

'And you're getting by all right? For money, like?'

'I've got more money now than when he was here.'

We both laugh.

'Now Loretta, you know I can take the kids for a night if you need some time off.'

'I might take you up on that,' I tell him. 'I've got a prospect. A biker, but a nice one, not a loser. On a Harley, no less.'

'A Harley?' he says, raising his eyebrows. When he raises his eyebrows the crusty skin on his forehead wrinkles and he always reaches up to touch it.

'You should have that looked at, Norm,' I say.

'Yeah, yeah, and I should give up the spare parts work and get out of the sun too.'

His arm gestures around his junkyard. Some of the machinery is so bent and broken you can't even tell what it used to be for. Right in the centre of the yard is a lemon tree, the only greenery in sight. It always has lemons. I'm sure I know what Norm does to help it along, but I don't ask. He's got four guard dogs too, tied up around the yard, vicious snarling things that he feeds by tossing them hunks of sheep carcass. As if anyone would want to steal any of this crap.

'Well, I'd better pick up the kids,' I say.

I don't want to pick up the kids. I want to send them to an orphanage and buy myself a nice dress and learn to live like I used to, before I turned into the old scrag I am now.

'Don't you worry about that truck,' Norm says, patting me on the arm. 'It'll just go back into the land.'

I get into the car and do the three tries I need to do before the engine will fire. I should have that looked at, I think. There's half a kilo of sausages on the seat beside me and I realise they've been sitting in the sun for half an hour already. When I unwrap the paper and have a sniff there's a funny sulphur smell. They'll cook up all right, I tell myself, and I gun the Holden and screech in a u-turn onto the road. I can't get used to this huge engine and every time I take off I sound like a pack of hoons at Bathurst. It's three-thirty already and Jake and Melissa will be waiting at the school gate when I get there, ready to jump in and whine about how everyone else's mum always gets there before I do. Maybe I'll drop them off at the orphanage.

At the school gate Melissa and Jake are both standing with their hands on their hips. I wonder if they got that from me. Old scrag standing with her hands on her hips, pursing her thin lips, squinting into the sun. You could make a statue of that. It would look like half the women in this town. A bit of dust and a few plastic bags swirling around its feet, the tail lights of the husband's car receding into the distance. They should cast it in bronze and put it in the foyer of Centrelink.

'Mum, we have to have four sheets of coloured cardboard for the project tomorrow.'

'Alright.'

'And me too, I have to have a lead pencil and I don't want bananas in my lunch anymore. They stink.'

'Alright.'

As I steer the great car down the highway towards home I have a little dream. I'll arrive and swing into the driveway and there, sitting right next to the veranda, will be a maroon shiny Harley. I won't even dare to look but out of the corner of my eye I'll see a boot resting on the step, maybe with spurs on it. Then I'll slowly lift my head and he'll be staring at me like that actor, George Clooney, the gorgeous one, stared into J.Lo's eyes in that film and I'll take a deep breath and say to him, Can you hang on five minutes while I drop the kids at the orphanage?

A bag of lemons is sitting on the veranda. Norm must have left them while we were at the newsagents.

'Who left these?' Jake says.

'Norm,' I say.

'How do you know?'

'There's oil on the bag.'

I bought Norm a cake of Solvol once. Delivered it to the junk-yard all wrapped in pretty pink paper with a bow. He rang up to thank me.

'I think you're insulting me,' he said.

'It's for your own good, Norm.'

'You're a minx,' he said. 'If I was thirty years younger …'

'Fifty more like,' I told him, 'before you'd get those paws on me.'

When the kids are finally settled in their rooms doing their homework or maybe downloading porn from the Internet, I get on the phone for the usual round of begging.

'Are you coming to the meeting tomorrow?'

'Oh Loretta, I'm sorry, I completely forgot. I've made other plans.'

I can imagine Helen's plans. They'll involve a cask of white and six changes of clothes before she collapses onto the bed in tears and starts ringing her friends, me, asking why she can't find a man, is she too old, has she lost her looks. It helps to actually leave the house, I often remind her.

'The Grade Three teacher's coming. And Brianna's offered to mind all the kids at her place. She must have hired a bouncer.'

'He's told you he's coming?'

'Yeah, he left a message on my machine,' I lie.

So Helen's coming. I herd up seven others with more lies and false promises, then I put the sausages on. Sure enough, the sulphur smell fades when they start to burn. I used to like cooking quiche and fancy fried rice and mud cake. Gourmet, like on the telly, the boyfriend boasted to his mates. Then we get married and it's, Listen darl, I wouldn't mind a chop for a change. Now the kids think gourmet is pickles on your sandwich. They won't even look at a sun-dried tomato. Last time I tried that Jake picked them all out of the spaghetti sauce and left them lined up like bits of red chewed meat on the side of the plate. Gross, he said, and I had to agree, seeing them like that.

Standing at the stove, rolling the sausages in the pan and stirring the potatoes in the boiling water, my face warms up in the steam and it's time for another fantasy moment. The pudge has magically fallen from my hips and I'm wearing a long, slinky silk dress. I'm in the function room of the golf course, tossing my newly blonde-streaked hair and full of ennui or some other French feeling at these boring wealthy men crowding around me. Then there's a draught from the doorway and I don't even have to look back – I can hear the jingle of spurs.

The meeting's in the small room at the Neighbourhood House because the Church of Christ had already booked the large room. We're sitting pretty much on top of each other, trying to balance cups of tea and Scotch Finger biscuits on our knees, except for Maxine, who's supposed to take the minutes. I thought I'd made it up, but the Grade Three teacher has come and Helen's paralysed with excitement and terror. She's wearing enough perfume to spontaneously combust and in this tiny room the smell's so overwhelming that Maxine has to swing the door open. Then the noise from the meeting next door starts up.

'Yes!' they all shout. 'Yes! I do, I do!'

'Well, I don't,' Maxine says, and she swings the door half-shut so that we're dizzy with perfume and still listening to the frantic clapping of people being saved next door. Maxine shrugs.

I give the list of apologies, which Maxine writes down, and I welcome everyone who's come, introducing the Grade Three teacher in case the others don't know him. Helen's gone pink and glistening like a baby just out of the bath. She'll have a seizure if she's not careful. I can't see the attraction. The Grade

Three teacher's five-foot-four, stocky, and always says At the end of the day.

'At the end of the day,' he says when I introduce him, 'I am totally committed to this cause.'

Just in case, I look down at his feet, but no spurs. I read out the list of agenda items.

'Do we have to do all this agenda crap? And the motions? I motion, you motion. My Mark's doing motions you wouldn't believe and I have to be home before nine for if I need to take him to Emergency.'

'Yes, we do,' I say, 'because we're trying to be bloody official. And as you well know, Emergency in a town half an hour away closing at ten is one of the reasons we're here.'

'Oh, yes ma'am.'

I roll my eyes. Maxine rolls her eyes. For a minute I think of us all rolling our eyes like a bunch of lunatics in the asylum and I almost cheer up.

'Item one. I've written a letter to our local Member about the closure of the school,' I say, and I pause for the inevitable joke about members, which, to my amazement, doesn't come. 'We need everyone who has kids in the school to sign.'

'It'll never work,' Brenda says.

'Does anyone know how to drain the oil from a sump?' Kyleen pipes up.

Only another half an hour, I think, and then I can pick up the kids from Brianna's, drop them at the orphanage and drive straight down to Melbourne. With the experience I've got, I'll land a good job in a centre for adults with attention deficit disorder.

When I pull up in the Holden at Brianna's the kids run to the front door and they look pleased to see me. They're way too quiet in the back seat. They must have done something horrible.

'So did you have a good time?' I ask. I speed up to catch the amber light and the car roars like a drunken trucker. I can't make out exactly what Melissa says, but I might have heard the word fight. I think back. Were they limping when they got into the car? Was there blood? I can't remember anything like that so I turn on the radio and keep driving along the dark highway, listening to the soothing sound of a voice calling Race Seven of the trots, something I've learned to love since I found out the radio was stuck on this station.

'Mum?' Melissa says as we pull into the unsurprisingly Harley-free driveway.

'Yes, sweetie?'

'I don't ever want to leave this house.'

'I thought you wanted to live in a hundred-room mansion with ten servants and a personal homework attendant?'

'Nup.'

'Why's that, then?'

'Because Dad doesn't know we've got email now, and so he'll have to send a letter and if we're not here we won't get it.'

'Ah,' I say.

When we get inside they brush their teeth without a single protest and climb into bed.

'You OK, Jakie?' I ask as I lean down to kiss him goodnight.

'Brianna and her boyfriend had a big fight,' he whispers. 'I think he hit her.'

I kiss him twice, then again.

'I'm sure she's all right,' I tell him. 'I'll call her tomorrow. You go to sleep now.'

'I don't want bananas in my lunch.'

'I wouldn't dream of it. Bananas stink,' I say, and turn out the light.

Next morning as I'm packing bananas into their lunchboxes I realise I forgot to thank Norm for the lemons. I drop into the yard on the way back from the shops. He's down the back of the block with three other blokes, all of them standing in a line with their arms folded staring at the body of an old tractor. This would be the matching statue. Bloke standing, feet apart, arms folded, staring at a piece of broken machinery. No idea how to fix it. We could put Him and Her statues either side of the high-way at the entrance to town.

After they've stared at the tractor body in silence for a full ten minutes, Norm sees me and ambles up.

'Don't tell me you're going to sell something?' I say.

'Not bloody likely. Every month they're here with some new scheme for making money.'

'None of them happens to ride a Harley?'

He doesn't even bother answering, just nods his head at their banged-up ute on the road. We step inside his shed for a cuppa. The radio's on the racing station.

'Harlequin Dancer made a good run from fourth in Race Seven last night,' I say.

'You need a new car,' Norm answers, handing me a cup covered in grease and a paper towel to wipe it with. 'Sorry I didn't get to the meeting, luv.'

'It's not really your problem,' I say.

'Course it's my problem. It's everybody's bloody problem.'

We drink our tea. The three blokes wave as they pass the shed. There's a protest at Randwick in Race Two.

'I've got money on that horse,' Norm says. He turns up the volume.

'Which one?'

'The one that'll buy you a bottle of bubbly if it wins the protest. Long odds. Very long odds. Bring me luck, Loretta.'

The day's starting to heat up and blowies are banging against the tin roof of the shed. Norm picks up the trannie and holds it to his ear. I look out at the heat shimmering over the piles of junk and think about writing another letter, this time to the Prime Minister. Norm's touching his crusty forehead as he listens for the outcome of the protest. He must win against the odds sometimes, I think – otherwise why even bother betting?

Underneath the dust coating my feet and sandals, I notice a summer tan starting on my skin. I pull my skirt up to my thighs and stretch my legs out through the door of the shed and into the sun. Harley man might ride by, see these finely turned ankles sticking out the shed door and fall in love. Harley man. It's the way those blokes lean back on the bike that does it to me. Like the world's their armchair. Like they're waiting with their arms wide open for someone to fill the space between their lap and the handlebars. Or maybe it's just the bikes. I can imagine what it feels like to straddle the leather and rev the powerful engine. To strap on the helmet and the mirror sunglasses and the gloves and know you have the freedom to choose whatever and whoever you want. To look back and smile as you're leaving the latest town, the latest broken heart. I can see the surprise on Harley man's handsome face when I toss my newly blonde-streaked hair and throw my leg over the saddle. He looks longingly at me. You were good, I'd tell him, but he'd hardly hear over the deep throbbing of the bike's engine. You were real good while it lasted, lover, but I've got important letters to write.

Sleepers Almanac

I Feel So Strong

Venero Armanno

1.

If you can manage to keep yourself from becoming too anxious when you wake to discover someone using an electric power tool on your head, then it's safe to assume you're well on your way to making peace with your new circumstances. With a sort of odd sense of detachment I take note of the way these two attendants work methodically and fast, sawing my skull open and creating a lot of bone-dust as they go. Their Perspex goggles fog up with the fine spray but they don't stop until the job's done – out comes the brain.

The two boys handle it with plastic-gloved hands. I can hardly call these two individuals 'men' for they must be all of twenty years apiece, but they seem to be skilled apprentices in the little-discussed mechanics of a death's investigation. Their boss will come and check their work as soon as he finishes his coffee and Danish in the staff room, but he's got no need to worry: the intensity and curiosity in their faces is exceptional. They love their job. In fact, they make me feel special, though of course there's nothing much that's special about having dropped dead.

The extraordinary in this situation has nothing to do with them. Instead, it's my sense of pure sentience. Maybe it's like this for all fresh cadavers, I don't know. My body's well and truly fin-ished but my mind is as alive as it's ever been. Possibly more so, because I feel free from quotidian responsibilities. Nothing remains undone or half-done, as is usually the case in the ongoing frustrations of our daily lives. I don't have to fret about getting myself ready for work, finding a mechanic to fix that new knocking sound in my truck's transmission, buying groceries and eating more fruit and vegetables, or where and how will I go about getting some girl to sleep with me. All that's left, really, is to drift off into the white forever – but it doesn't happen.

Now these two young students of mortality and its limits carefully transfer my brain into a glass beaker. Awareness doesn't follow that slide into glass, no, it stays right here with my body. I guess this is where I am, then, attached to a corporeal self that was – for the most part, barring the encroaching decrepitudes of middle age – the fun part of me. A human body, but it's already inert, and will soon be rotting in the earth.

What a thought.

Back in primary school, the nuns believed they had a good grip on the mysteries of the great beyond. Heaven, hell, purgatory and limbo – each has its membership rules, though I remember hearing recently that the Pope, whatever his name is, might rescind the antiquated idea of limbo. Everybody will get to go somewhere; no one will go nowhere. This is good of him.

The nuns told us that there's no definite span of time defined for exactly how long the soul will remain with its body upon physical expiration. If the death is sudden and unexpected, stroke, car accident or gunshot, say, then it might stay where it is for a day or anywhere up to three or four. If the death is long and drawn-out, something like an octogenarian succumbing to a long bout of disease, then the soul will probably slide on out and be on its way almost immediately. In other words, it has been primed for departure and is absolutely ready to go.

Where the good nuns of the Holy Mother primary school got their information from I don't know, but everything they said was reinforced by the Christian Brothers at secondary school.

'Your flesh is weak,' Brother Connors told us in our first Religious Instruction class, 'but your soul is forever. That means this –' and he took a chunk of chalk and wrote a '1' on the board, then with a sense of theatre followed that number with zeros scrawled all the way off the chalk board. He went across all four walls of our schoolroom, then he went around again, and again, and again, and again, without stopping. The chalk was worn down to a nub. It took him the better part of the lesson to get all the hundreds and hundreds and hundreds of zeros he wanted. When the bell rang, he surveyed his handiwork.

'And even this will be the blink of an eye when it comes to the never-ending life God has blessed his children with,' he declared. 'Do you understand?'

Without warning, and with the force of an expert pitcher, he then hurled his chalk-nub at the side of the head of a boy named Lawrence English. Laurie was languishing at the back of the classroom picking his nose and staring at the pigeons cooing in the playground. The chalk hit him square in the temple. The boy started to cry.

'Well – try crying to the Lord.' A red, thick vein had appeared in Brother Connor's brow. 'Try crying to the Lord when your time comes.' In a whisper he added, 'So why not pay attention to your soul from now on? Can't you see it's the you that God is going to judge?'

We strained to hear that spooky whisper, and he terrified all the ten- and eleven-year-old boys in that room except for me. Why? I thought he was a clown. His sense of theatre was for the theatre of the absurd. He knew nothing. A year hadn't quite passed since the morning I went to wake my mother and discovered I couldn't. From that moment nothing much had the power to scare me, and certainly not a buffoon in a cowboy's black clothes, a white inverted collar yellowing with age, and with a zealot's belief in things that could simply not be proven.

Still, maybe I could have paid more attention. Maybe mad belief is proof enough of the existence of things: such as souls, eternity and the afterlife. I'm trying to remember if either the nuns or the brothers ever said what your soul was supposed to do while it was still stuck to its cadaver, or if there was a purpose to remaining so encased.

Whatever. Life – or maybe I should just call it existence now – never stops throwing challenges at you. Some are excruciating, some are just plain silly. This one seems more of the latter than the former, but I find myself in new terrain and I don't have a map. I don't know if I'm going to heaven, hell, in between, or even – despite the Pope's promise – absolutely nowhere. No matter. Whatever happens I'll face it down. I'm certainly not the first to be stuck in a situation like this; soon enough things will become clear. At the moment my biggest task seems to be to keep any rising apprehension and disquiet at bay. Which is of course a little more easily said than done: I'm all too aware that the most pimple-faced of the morgue attendants is idly using a sponge to wipe off the skull cap he's helped saw off. He's humming a tune. Tufts of my hair are matted and wet. He peers into the empty cave of my head and I also get a glimpse.

Let me tell you, there are some things you don't want to see, dead or alive.

2.

Another sterile room; time has passed. I've slept, at least in the metaphoric sense. It could be a day or two later, but these are the sorts of measurements that mean less than ever.

Today I've been dressed in the clothes the boys from the band put together out of my closet at home. They chose my usual look: black T-shirt, jeans and lace-up hiking boots. If not for the fact that my blood was pumped out and my brain extracted, I'd almost be my old self.

Here's a memory: the embalming fluid that went in had been cold and dry, like a wind whistling through my veins. After a while that wind died and the fluid set like concrete. Now there's a thoroughly unfamiliar sensation. Something's in my stomach and it isn't some delicious meal. Ah, that'll be my brain. The cavity in my head has been stuffed with surgical padding – a nice enough term that really means they've wadded up the inside of my skull with lumps of those paper towels you take from a roll to clean up your kitchen messes. Then, because even the most devoted necromancers like shortcuts, and this has become the conventional practice, the two morgue boys deposited my brain into the slit they'd made when they dug out my guts to see what was inside. Sewed up my head and sewed up the smile in my belly, all is well.

None of these physical misfortunes should mean very much, they should be as inconsequential as Father Time, but I seem to retain enough human frailty that I wish my regular GP, Dr Bailey, had said something like, 'Yeah, I saw this guy often. His heart wasn't going to last much longer. Had a balloon fitted eighteen months ago. I'm happy to sign the death certificate.' Instead, he'd come to see me on the morgue slab and declared, 'Lots of musicians around Max, better open him up and make sure this wasn't drug-related.'

It wasn't and now they know it.

I understand that my friends haven't arranged an open-coffin visiting session, so the stitching these two young apprentices made didn't need to be too perfect. No make-up required either. What I've got to look forward to is the bye-bye ceremony itself, at which time the coffin lid will be as tight as my sutures.

My mind, my glorious undead mind – or maybe I should give in to the nuns and brothers and call it my soul after all – tells me I should be cold on this table, but no, whatever sensation I have, none of it's really all that physical. Just the recollection of how things used to feel against my skin. Instead, I seem to be a floating ball of emotions and memories and moods. I'm not so anxious anymore, just sour. Sour because my veins have been filled with concrete, my skull has been stuffed with paper towels, in the place where glorious food and drink used to go I now have my dissected brain, and someone is using a dry razor, no shaving foam, to scrape the whiskers off my face.

I'm in a different place. It's no longer the morgue but a funeral home. The person shaving me is the other end of the spectrum to those apprentices. He's a wizened old man with a forest in each nose hole. What indignity to be toyed with by an individual who owns such fertile nostrils. Maybe he'll have an assistant in a slinky nurse's uniform, zip down just a little too much and a nice healthy cleavage. Maybe Father Concrete here dreams of allowing his hairy nose to rove over those merciless hillocks, taking in the perfume of young flesh after the iniquities of being the handmaiden to death day in, day out, no respite till Sundays.

No.

His assistant wears a green cardigan and is as old as he is. She has a limp, thanks to a titanium hip installed less than a month ago. Actually, she's feeling better than she has in somewhere between thirty and thirty-five years. I'm happy for her, yes I am – wish I could say the same for myself, really.

3.

Somewhere between thirty and thirty-five years: a black-haired hippie called Maree came to me right about then. So long ago but who'd ever forget? It was November 1973 to be precise.

I turned sixteen years of age on the twelfth of the month and was already something of a drummer by then, my jazz-drumming new stepfather teaching me just about everything I needed to learn. I met Maree at a friend's place while a little practice band I was in trashed surf music tunes with gay abandon.

The first days of being sixteen; I lost my virginity and betrayed my best friend, Joshua, at the same time. She was going out with him and he was foolish enough to bring her to the practice session, showing her off. Josh wasn't a musician, just one of the gang of useless teenage boys we all were, and he should have had the presence of mind to stay at home that day. He'd just discovered Dvořák and the cello; Maree couldn't get enough Hawkwind and drugs. We talked for about fifteen minutes. I was the only person she'd met who knew about a poet and performer named Bob Calvert, an American counter-culture figure she idolised. I only knew about him by chance. A couple of weeks earlier I'd stolen a new live Hawkwind double album from the local record store, and this nut called Calvert screamed maniacal lyrics and monologues all over the spacey music. To my jazz-trained ears it was all thoroughly unlistenable – but why tell a pretty hippie that?

Maree stood a little closer while everyone else talked about whatever. I was already dying for her to touch my cock. Soon enough, she did.

She left Joshua to eat his heart out, and in the way of selfish young boys I felt guilty for less than a week. By the second week, that troublesome lump of human metal of mine was raw with the quick furtive soundless fucks Maree and I had in my bedroom while my stepfather watched television in the lounge. I didn't feel so guilty about my ex-best friend anymore. Sex makes you heartless. It also makes you want more. When we weren't at my place, Maree and I had long horny sessions in her older brother Michael's borrowed flat.

We'd go for hours at Michael's place, at the same time working our way through his knee-high stack of LP records. There I learned about women, love-making and rock music. For the rest of my life, in my mind, the three would remain indivisible. *Led Zeppelin II* was perfect for the things Maree taught me, and we'd take a minute's break when the end of side one started ticking, then get going again with the wintry fervour of *Immigrant Song* at the start of side two.

Another break, what's next? *Who's Next.* We'd have it so loud Keith Moon's drum skins might as well have been my shoulders and back, as if he were wrenching his rolling beat out of my young muscle and flesh. We'd scream with Daltrey after that long synthesiser break in *Won't Get Fooled Again* and still not come. Eyeball to eyeball, staring straight into one another, we breathed each other's expirations and ground pubic bone against pubic bone. That's where the human soul starts, that's what we learned, in the raw aching pubis of sex-mad teenagers. Away from one another we were young, bored and stupid, but together the world was a long, loud song – with many more to come.

I'll ask her this from the coffin: 'Stick on another album from your old collection, won't you do that for me, Maree, if you're still alive somewhere? Bob Dylan said it better than me on that album *Blonde on Blonde* we used to eat each other up to: "Where are you now, Sweet Maree?"'

Of the two of us, she was the smarter and more well read. Maree introduced me to even greater pleasures by channelling Bobby Zimmerman, Marc Bolan and David Bowie. Her taste was eclectic. Alice Cooper was just getting big in Australia, so Maree would copy his death's mask make-up, wearing little pink hot pants and long silver boots with spiky heels. Somehow she'd have a fluffy feather boa to wrap around herself. She lived in op-shops, spent all her money on outrageous clothes. At sixteen she was already doing her own writing, and I'd take her raven hair in my fist and push my nose into her unshaved armpits, breathing the sweaty stench and silk of a poet.

Panting. Stop.

Then what?

Get shoved onto my back and Maree would say, 'Don't come. Do not come. Please don't,' and she'd grind her hips down into me. I only came as required. In his green days, a young man can do just about anything with his body. 'Whew,' she'd say. 'Fantastic. OK, another album.'

'You choose this time,' I'd tell her, 'I'm very busy.' Her fingers would leave wet fingerprints on Michael's much-adored record sleeves and vinyl. 'That one, *Billion Dollar Babies*, put that on.'

Naked, she'd crawl off on all fours, and while she was digging for it I'd take her from behind.

'I'm going to make it so loud,' I remember her telling me, her white rump in the air, her small breasts shaking and vibrating, flushed-pink face pressed down over her forearms. 'Wait. Stop for a second, let me get the needle down on this one, it's my favourite. Then you can fuck me all the way and you don't stop. You finish me off with Alice.'

Alice Cooper would sing, 'God/I feel so strong/I feel so strong/I'm so strong/I feel so strong,' and for the first time in my life I knew exactly what it felt like, tingling gooseflesh covering my body at the raw power my Maree had led me to.

More weeks and more months and more records devoured like meat. Michael was a hospital wardsman and kept strange hours. He didn't mind what his little sister was up to, so we had his flat all the strange hours we wanted. The only thing he asked was that we should sometimes vacuum his carpets. Small price to pay; I got to know that threadbare carpet well. Maree and I practically wore holes into it. He didn't want us to use his bed, and he expected that we would always restack his long players. Sometimes I'd leave a pot of soup on the stove for him, ready to heat when he came home to empty rooms still thick with sex. In those days I was already a pretty good drummer and an even better cook. It's not so bad to have an Italian stepfather: he had a quick temper but he loved Miles Davis and John Coltrane, strongly fla-voured food with a bottle of red wine, and an artichoke-based liqueur called Cynar that he had his friends in Italy send over by the carton. We fought like cannibals but I ended up following him in almost everything.

I'd like a drink now, truly I would, a nice aperitif of iced Cynar. They ought to serve it in heaven.

Anyway, if Maree and I could scrape some cash between us, sometimes we'd buy exotic stuff and she'd make her brother some special delicacy, leave it in a casserole dish in the oven for him. Ham hocks with canelli beans. Baked chicken breasts with rosemary and sweet potatoes. A dish she called Mongolian lamb.

For a hippie, she was quite a gourmet. In Brisbane in 1973 you had to try hard to find interesting epicurean ingredients; we weren't quite aware of it but we were in a complete cultural desert, and things wouldn't change for more than a decade. That didn't put Maree off. Thing was, the hippie era was already three or four years out of date anyway, so she could reinvent the sensibility in any fashion she wanted. She hated vegetarians, daisies and the acoustic guitar in the hands of any sensitive soul. The music of Simon and Garfunkel made her want to scream. The new era of sensitive singer-songwriters brought tears of frustration to her eyes. Poor James Taylor, Donovan and Elton John, they couldn't know what vitriol they inspired in one sexy, crazy, antipodean pseudo-hippie named Maree Kilmister.

I was crazy about her. Anything she did or said was fine by me. Whenever we cooked for Michael, which was often, it gave us a break from our sexual proceedings. We'd get back to the real stuff soon enough. Near the end of one of Maree's old favourites, Jefferson Airplane's *Surrealistic Pillow*, we'd start shaking one another like skeletons dancing over gravestones, and then we'd come, but it wouldn't be an explosion but a sort of melting, young bodies dripping like wax, disappearing from the flat, evaporating from each other's arms and visiting the stars.

Later we'd dab our knees with Michael's mercurochrome. He stole things from the hospital; his medicine cabinet was like a well-stocked Emergency Ward. Our generation believed it was only fair that the world should give us whatever we wanted, and we took it all like greedy young dogs.

Maree Kilmister, outlandish poet, never-ending pleasures.

That was 1973. Go on, try to tell me you had a better year.

from *The Dirty Beat*

Fox Unpopuli

Eva Sallis

Tasmania has been invaded from the north by a fox.

A pregnant vixen arrived by sea in the belly of the *TigerCat*. Photographs hit the front pages: uniformed wildlife experts point at the floor of the *Cat*'s hold. From Devonport to Hobart and from Swansea to Strahan, people talk of it, shaking their heads, wondering what will happen.

Even as the forensic experts go to work on the impounded vessel, the sightings begin.

A fox could do untold damage. A fox could gnaw at the heart of this country, suck it back to white gristle and shit it out in hairy scat. TASMANIA ATTACKED! the headlines cry, above pictures of the uniforms and an identikit of the fox. The army, the air force and the resources of Tasman Forest are brought in to hunt her down. No expense is spared. Twelve choppers, two from the air force and ten from Tasman Forest, pound the air above the city and the foothills.

Suddenly the fragility of the island and its unprotected borders are blinding. Suddenly the stark white trees of the deadlands in the centre seem more visible, sentinel skeletons with armbands of silver, *mementi mori* of some past great invasion.

The island is on edge, on the brink.

The bone-thin vixen (her own army squirming in her belly) is sighted in the suburbs ten times and missed ninety-nine. She is moving west from the port, sure and efficient as an armoured personnel carrier, eating sufficient native birds, lizards, insects, snakes, amphibians, rodents and marsupials to leave a trail of cleaned bones and to keep her babies fat. She passes rapidly through the yards, under fences, through rhododendrons and rose gardens to the denser gardens and the bush at the foot of Mount Wellington; and then, for a short while, she disappears. Troops eddy and lose direction and Tasman Forest special forces stop massing on the streets, scouring gardens with spotlights, and shooting rabbits, devils and quolls.

There is a lull.

It is winter and the land is shadowed, even sombre. The nights are long and the mornings and evenings end and begin at midday. The trim-edged woodpiles on which Tasmanians pride themselves (you can tell a lot about a person from their woodpile) slowly shorten as the wood fires puff without stopping. On a clear day, Mount Wellington looms over the smoking city, a white-haired old man contemplative over a campfire. The cold sea and the red icebreaker vessels in the harbour bring murmurs of the frozen Antarctic. Tasmanians gather in pubs and talk openly of the fox. The talk carries a bellyful of histories into the warm fug – past poisons and murders and losses: the dark things to be visited on this land.

For the first time, the greenies and the rednecks are united – this is an environmental disaster you can shoot.

Everyone has bitter words for Victoria, the home port of the fox. It's an act of insane jealousy, of war, of terrorism, to smuggle a fox to Tasmania. It was deliberate. Nothing good has ever come from Victoria. Melbourne, riddled with foxes, is a polluted wasteland. Melburnians are known to live in fear and lock their doors at night.

The *Examiner* runs stories daily and speculates on the clash between the fox and Tasmania's other carnivores.

PRAY THE DEVIL SAVES US, the *Mercury* screams.

The fox's apocalyptic wail shakes the air.

It is winter. She follows a tunnel pathway trodden through the undergrowth by many animals. Mountain ash loom in impeccable lines, up and away to the clear sky where their feathery leaves wave in thinner air. The light at the forest floor is dim, blue-green, pungent. Richly traced with the pathways of pulsing feather and fur. The mottled trunks glow a rimmed pink at dusk, the light dims to amber and the new smells still in the chilled air. The redolent stories of the night begin. Every thicket is laced with stories, filled with evening piping and shrilling. The birds give alarm uncertainly and the animals, despite themselves, stop and stare at the red stranger trotting up, smiling, to meet them.

It is winter but she shines and glitters rich red above the snow, rich red beneath the blue-frosted eucalypts. Rich red among the gaunt Huon pines and rich purple in the night shadows of the King Billys. Her ribs disappear even as her milk fills her undercarriage. Her masked face takes on a blue-black sheen and her whiskers lengthen.

Her cubs are larger at birth than any she's had before.

It is a muted spring on Mount Wellington. Bushwalkers find piles of white bones and old scat but no other sign of the fox. The special forces comment grimly on the nightly news. The experts are hopeful as each day lengthens and there is still no sighting. Maybe she died. Maybe the devils got her young. Maybe the 1080 baits Tasman Forest uses to protect trees from wildlife have got her.

The moss and lichen warm under her paws. She avoids the aridity of the cropped green carpet lands – the dead trees are too few for shelter. She and her family hug the sleek and shining pelt of grass and marsh-lands, the warm blood of plenty pulling them northwards. The sounds of wood ducks call them on until the crackle of bark birds, the tonk-tonk of linnets and the musk of potoroos draw them back into the woods; and then diamond birds in the white gums pull them to the mountains again.

In late spring the fox becomes visible again, almost. There are sightings of strange yellow eyes at night around Doo Town. Red hairs found on a fence near the Bay of Fires are sent to the Forest and then to Victoria for analysis. Footprints appear in the mud around dams and the forests seem hushed over leaf litter that buries the trail of bones. Electricity to a remote farm is cut, the wires chewed through; and then the quolls vanish. Greenies rich in fox folklore and mainland experiences are welcomed in redneck haunts, and rednecks with long genealogies of trapping and marksmanship speak at Greenpeace meetings.

Summer brings strange portents.

The weather stays grim and savage over Ben Lomond. The light of the sun hasn't been seen since the fox landed.

A jagged stone bridge, built by chained hands two centuries before, falls suddenly into the drain (once a river) beneath it. There is no explanation.

A record number of teenagers jump off forbidden things: for pleasure off Kings Bridge into the South Esk River; and to their deaths off the rim of the Tasman Blowhole into the raging sea.

She sits under a sizzling canopy. Leaves mottle the white-hot sun to a sliding shimmer across her fiery back. The cicadas rasp and sigh. The lichen clings like a pale dried skin to the rocks. The mosses are browned and crisp and the stalks of the grasses whisper against each other. She is above the fern line, a speck of red in this open, once-logged woodland. Below the hill she knows a wide river bends. She can smell the water, sticky and blood-rich, and she has tasted the abundance of water in the animals and birds. She surveys the forest, ears pricked for sounds of food stirring, but all she can hear now is the sound of her young at play and the distant mumble and footfall of cows. These trees and hollows have been licked clean. She can smell only fox stories and fading whispers of other trails. She doesn't rest long. They will be gone in a minute, leaving eggs in high nests to cool to a final stillness.

The beloved can hunt now for themselves, and the clan moves fast. Soon they will disperse.

The *Examiner*, 14 February:
TERROR STRIKES!
All doors are locked in Jericho tonight after an alleged sighting of a fox in the early hours of this morning. 'When I realised it might be a fox, I called the dogs off,' Harry Proctor, a local grazier, said today. 'You never know what a fox might do to my dogs.'

Jericho is the second town to have a scare in as many nights. Bagdad, just forty kilometres away, locked all doors last night after an unexplained wailing was heard by several Fox Emergency Line callers.

A young male fox ranges over a headland heath above a wild western ocean, eating as he goes. The wind blows over the land. He leaves small explosions of hot blue feathers scattered in the tea-tree brush and flecks of blood on the black rocks. He is too well fed to bother chewing lizard legs, beaks or birds' feet, so he leaves these too – tiny ciphers drying in the now brief midday sun.

A vixen stalks an eastern marshland. She is a small smokeless flame, licking through the reeds and grasses without so much as a crackle. She is seeking variety. She is bored with black ducks, bitterns, marsh snakes, egrets, pademelons, ibises, spoonbills, water dragons, skinks, rails, crakes, turbo chooks, banjo frogs, water rats, voles, mice, dunnarts and potoroos.

Her brother in the north wails his breathless cry to a chill moon. He is perched on a jagged tor, silhouetted above a cataract. A glittering city trickles out from far beneath him, curves in scattered glints and then spreads across hills and plain. The sheen of a wide river stretches towards the northern sea.

He has just killed twenty-three peacocks.

He is answered to the south-west and the south-east.

In March the light is tilting into shadow and summer is over. Before the winter comes and the mud bogs the trucks, Tasman Forest orders the logging of strips for wide roadways through the Cradle Mountain, Franklin-Gordon and South-West national parks. 'Without access, we cannot hope to win this war,' a spokeswoman says, staring unsmiling into the eyes of the TV viewers. 'God help us if we have to log more.'

Surveillance teams are formed in the autumn. Ultraviolet cameras are imported from the United States and set up at key locations in the forests, mountains, marshes and plains. Satellites are sent up from Woomera. Victorians advertise in the *Examiner* and the *Mercury* – 'Fine Fat Foxes Fought and Killed', and 'Seven at One Blow' – and the best Victorian fox killers are flown in by Tasman Forest.

As the hunters head for the hills, Tasman Forest runs community service announcements – *in the event of a fox emergency.* Get Foxed, a fox repellent invented by a feral and tested on devils, is an overnight sensation and spawns a thousand imitations. Prophylactics dominate the stalls at festivals and markets.

The trappers lay 50,000 neckers of the finest garrotte wire and 30,000 leggers, and set 10,000 spring traps with stainless-steel teeth and German-made trigger plates. They build 500 hides of mottled canvas at locations deemed most likely. Covered in Get Foxed, they man them for a week on army rations, Sako

222s sighted for long range cocked and ready. Just in case, they dig 500 holes with stakes at the bottom and cover them with leaf litter. They lay nearly fifty experimental designs, most coming from the fertile brains of Tasmania's writers, artists and bush philosophers.

The hunters return from the hills with enough meat to feed their dogs and cats for twenty years, but no fox. Not one. The fox is around the same size as nearly all the wildlife on the island and many different heads have fitted into fox-sized nooses. The fox has shown more-than-devilish cunning in its use of natural selection.

Tasman Forest introduces a curfew. Irreverent jokes about fox appetites are no longer seen as funny. A teenager caught sharpening the points of a McDonald's 'M' with red texta is expelled from school.

The island seethes with rumour and rising terror and the first evacuations begin.

The logging trucks clog both lanes of the Lyell Highway in a seemingly endless convoy, roaring with an excess of horsepower and enthusiasm. Going east laden with the freshly stripped carcasses stacked in the cradle of the horned trucks: *Eucalypti globulus, viminalis, dalrympleana, gunnii, delegatensis, regnans* and *johnstonii* (and the occasional *Lagarostrobos franklinii* or *Athrotaxis selaginoides*); and going west again, rattling and empty. Squashing enough fleeing wildlife to make the whole highway stink of carrion. They have bumper-stickers saying *The Forest Fights the Fox*. As winter begins the Foxies – a vocal minority of former greenies, assembling under the banned slogan *Better the Fox than the Forest* – become the most despised Tasmanians in recorded history. Prison populations rise to 10 per cent Foxies despite them being 0.001 per cent of the population overall.

The *Mercury*, 2 June:
HUONVILLE SAFE FROM FOX FRIGHT
Huonville can rest easy tonight, knowing that Tuesday's alleged fox sighting was a case of mistaken identity. 'We did think it was a fox, but it proved to be a Tassie tiger,' a relieved Bastie Turpin said today. And the brave orchardist has the carcass to prove it.

The *Mercury*, 30 August:
FOX CRACKS GORDON DAM
Alarming cracks appearing in the Gordon Dam wall have been linked to the fox disaster, as the State of Emergency enters its terrifying third month. 'The dam requires daily monitoring, maintenance,' Lieutenant Brett Grunie, Tasman Dams, said. 'We just can't spare the men to Operation Fox-Fire, but we have had to. It's disaster, whichever way you go.' So far Tasman Dams has no conclusive evidence of alleged Foxie involvement.

The *Australian*, 11 November:
TAS GOES 1080
Tasman Forest has put all its resources into the controversial final attempt to either kill or starve out the fox. The evacuated island will in its entirety be 1080'd and left for an unspecified period. During this time, the island will be off limits, except for specially trained miners, who will be safely underground.

Tasman Forest's Major-General Ippo Vaulter held a press conference this morning from his Melbourne base. 'Tasmania has lost Tasman Dams altogether. It is imperative that the brave Tasman Mines workers maintain some revenue for our battered forces and for repatriation. There is no scientific evidence of the foxes burrowing more than a metre into the ground.'

Rumour has it that some foolhardy Foxies also remain in hiding in the impenetrable deep south-west, most likely out in the open.

'These people are all wanted criminals,' the major-general said. 'We can't hold off the operation because there is an unconfirmed rumour that four or five of them have chosen to stay. There will always be fifth columnists and bleeding hearts. When the going gets tough it is the Forest that gets things done, not these tragically, culpably misguided criminals. They'll have a long wait. Our commandos will enter the zone in January to check for any sign of fox and to check that collateral odour has cleared.'

And if Operation Foxglove doesn't work?

The major-general is reassuring.

'In the unlikely event that Operation Foxglove is only partially successful, we will do everything we can to safeguard Tasmanians' wealth and preserve our unique way of life.'

He intimates that Tasman Forest would have to strip the fox of habitat. Clearing the south-west would also raise revenue for fox-proofing human environments and rebuilding a mines-based economy.

'Tasmania, I assure you, will survive,' the major-general guaranteed. 'It is bigger, older and richer than any of us can imagine.'

Bulletin

Ain't No Ordinary Ham

Will Elliott

Never did find out what Jimmy saw in that meat – Jimmy's a weird one. All I know is, he barges in and shouts: 'BORIS! We have just three days to eat this ham!'

Now, my name's Jake, not Boris, but Jimmy's never been too keen on details – they confuse him. You just gotta roll with the punches sometimes. Get this: he kicks open the door and staggers in with a giant knob of meat in his arms, holding it like a baby, oozing salty hamjuice down the front of his flannelette shirt and glistening pink, like he'd rubbed it all over with hair gel. He never said why we had three days – I guess he meant it was going stale. He lugs it to the kitchen and slams it down on the table with a grunt and looks at me with that look he gets when he's stirred, which can unsettle folks: kind of lets foamy spittle hang around his beard, lips peeled back, teeth bared like knuckles cocked ready for a fist fight. When he gets like that, you just gotta keep your cool and let him know you're on his team – but don't say it outright, you gotta *demonstrate*. 'Where in hell'd you get that meat?' I said, sounding mighty impressed, which was a mistake: he might've thought I wanted it for myself. Sure enough, he gets all defensive and throws his arms around it – and don't get me wrong, it was a mighty lump, quivering pink on the table like jelly, smooching ham slime over the daily paper (was glad I read the funnies already). He stands there like I meant the meat harm, which I did – we were gonna eat it, weren't we?

'Hey, what's cooking Jimmy?' I says, backing up to show I didn't mean no harm.

'Cooking?' he says, and looks all confused. Next he glances out the window and says, 'Go lock the door.'

'Why?' I says. 'You steal that meat?'

'Lock it!' he screams, so I shrug and lock the door, then drag the couch in front of it to kind of make the point he was yelling at me for no reason, then I put the small dresser on top of the couch. Jimmy missed the point. 'Good,' he says, nodding all grave like. 'Good thinking. I'll get the backdoor.' Like it was the most sensible idea in the world. Next thing he's bolting and chaining, wrapping a bike chain around the backdoor handle would you believe it, and looking for his hammer to board up the whole damn house. I watched all this wondering what the hell? Sometimes Jimmy gets in these moods where it's best just to let him spit it up and throw things around, and you just hide in the cellar till he's done. You know what people are like. Next day, you forget all about it.

So I went to the kitchen while he's slamming stuff around and mumbling about security and took a look at the ham. I've never seen a lump of meat like it, big and round as a rolled-up sleeping-bag. I poked it and a moist spot went under my fingernail. Next thing I know, Jimmy's right behind me, snuck-up like, and I screamed.

'What'd you say about the ham?' he whispered, creepy whisper. 'You touch it?'

'Yeah I poked it one,' I said all calm like. Times like this, you gotta put his attention back on the ham. I says: 'Look at it. This ain't no ordinary meat. Where'd you ...' Oh no, that wasn't the right question to ask yet – not till he knew I was on his team. 'Check it out,' I whispered, creepy like him, like it was hidden treasure or something. 'This is *big* meat Jimmy. Wonder what kind of pig this come off? More like a mammoth or ... shit, I dunno, some kind of *sea* monster.'

Jimmy's eyes went shiny and beady as that rat we caught in the microwave. He didn't answer, just gave this half-sigh, half-grunt and ran a palm down the side of the ham, smearing finger trails in the grease. Wasn't so sure I wanted to eat it after that – I've seen Jimmy's personal hygiene habits and he doesn't have any.

Supposed it'd be OK if we cut the edges off, like skinning an orange. Was about to suggest it when I heard Jimmy mumbling to himself, or maybe to the meat, I couldn't tell. His throat sounded hoarse and full of muck, almost like a man in a peep show booth trying to talk himself into enjoying the show. And what he said? I swear, it's not how he normally talks: 'Beats it by a fine line ... just a little, one section with no jiggles, no spaces to crawl into, no ... hand to hold ... could smack it like a cheer-leader's backside nonetheless ... no charges pressed ... she'd sing songs of love if I bought her the lips for it ... stuff 'em in my pocket at the butcher ... oh sweet glory ...'

He wasn't blinking, was kind of panting through the lips and a funny thought hit me that he was comparing the meat to ... nah, damn it, that made NO sense. He bought it to eat, not marry it, right? That's what he said when he came in, remem-bered it clear as day: *We have just three days to eat this ham.* What changed his mind? Whoever heard of a man falling in love with a ham? Anyways, I backed outta there, not sure what to say. He looked like he wanted to be left alone with it, so I left him to it. Can't say I felt real comfortable with the whole business.

So, I went to bed with no dinner because I wasn't too hungry after that. Couldn't sleep well either, cause I could hear Jimmy sometimes shouting at the ham, and could hear the floorboards creaking out there, which made me wonder what the hell he was doing. Must've dropped off around twelve, but at one a weird smell woke me up. Jimmy was in the room with me, just sitting there looking out the window with this real sad look on his face. The moon lit him up like a Halloween pumpkin. I screamed, but he didn't flinch or blink or anything. He says, 'You have to help me Boris.'

Enough's enough, I reckoned. 'Hey! I'm sleeping you fuck.'

He says: 'I can't stand her just ... sitting there. Not moving. Not talking. It's taking me over Boris. I need help.'

I wanted to clock him one, but there was a greasy shine over his face and beard, and I reckoned I knew why: he'd been rub-bing his face against the slab, I'd bet my thumbs, and he smelled salty. I didn't want that slime on my knuckles, so I just shook my head. Seen Jimmy do some weird stuff in my time – once he got up on the roof and wouldn't come down for a week, kept

screaming about earthquakes. He only came down when mag-
pies started swooping him.

'What you want me to do?' I says. 'How'm I meant to help? You
want to eat that damn meat or what? What's the story Jim?'

He looked out the window at the moonlight. I could just tell
he was thinking of boarding up the window, but whether to keep
folks out or keep me in, I couldn't tell. Then I backed up a step
and realised he'd called the ham *her*.

Kind of lost it. 'JIMMY!' I screamed. 'THAT HAM ... IT'S
NOT A SHE, ALRIGHT? NOT A SHE.' It was all I could think
to say. For a second it looked like I'd got him stirred, cause he
reached in his pocket and pulled out a knife – by God – and a
fork. Still looking out the window, he laid them across my sheets
where my belly was, and without a word stood and made a 'follow me' sign with his hands, all solemn like. It was like we were
at a funeral. So I follow him down the hall, out to the kitchen
where the meat pile was starting to stink the place up. There was
a chunk missing from around the top, looked like it'd been
gouged out with fingers. He'd eaten some then, which seemed
fine to me – that's how people and ham are supposed to get
along.

'So what do you want me to do?' I says, though I reckoned I
knew: he wanted me to eat it for him, God knows why, only he
couldn't bring himself to say it. Next thing he's crying like a
baby, sitting on the kitchen floor bawling, whole body lurching
around like he was being kicked. Didn't know what to tell him
– what was making him sad? He wasn't even drunk.

Enough's enough, I reckoned again, and said, 'I'm throwing
this out, you watch me.'

He says: 'NO.' I says: 'YEAH, FUCK YOU. IT'S GONE ON
LONG ENOUGH.' He says: 'SHE CAN'T BE NOTHING BUT
WHAT GOD MADE HER.' I says: 'WHAT'S GOD GOT TO DO
WITH IT? AND IT'S NOT A SHE JIMMY.' He called me insen-
sitive or some such, so I did what I had to: popped him in the
mouth. Thought he'd fight but he broke down again and cried
and said: 'TAKE IT, TAKE IT AWAY, I CAN'T DO IT BY MYSELF,
I'M LEANING ON IT LIKE A MAN WITH A CRUTCH, AIN'T
SPOZZA BE LIKE THIS, HELP ME BORIS FOR GOD SAKES
HELP ME.'

So I grabbed the ham and went to the door, but the damn thing's barred up and I couldn't get the boards loose. I set the meat down and Jimmy's had a change of heart all of a sudden, and he's running at me with murder in his eyes, yelling about me taking her away from him, and how everyone always took everything away from him, and how he wasn't gonna let it happen no more. I said fine, take the fucking meat and do what you gotta do, just leave me out of it OK?

Back in my room I could hear him blubbering, then an electric carving knife started up. Next thing there's a quiet tap on my door and I open it, and Jimmy's left a plate of ham slices out there on the floor. He'd cut 'em into the shape of tears, probably trying to make me feel guilty for something I couldn't quite understand, but they might've been quotation marks, I never really found out. You know what people are like. Some of 'em are lonely, I guess, and some of 'em had too much taken away and they get attached to things they probably shouldn't. Guess it makes you think.

In the morning the meat's all gone and Jimmy seemed to have pulled the boards loose from the doors and his coat wasn't hung up. There was meat slime all over the damn kitchen … I never knew ham could be so wet. Around then I thought I heard digging in the yard. I went to the kitchen window and saw someone had spit up some ham in the sink and left it there. Wasn't me, is all I know.

Out in the yard, there was Jimmy. He'd dug a hole with a shovel and the ham was lying in the dirt. Felt kind of sorry for it, and for Jimmy, who just stood there with his head down. Wondered what the neighbours would think. I watched him for a bit, whispering to myself, 'Come on Jimmy, you can do it.'

He stayed completely still for a while longer. I was rooting for the guy, you know, saying: 'Come on Jimmy, do what you gotta.' Must've been an hour before he gets down on his haunches and pushes the meat into the hole he dug, and starts raking dirt back over there. Made a big old lump in the yard, it did. He looked up at me through the window, and we met eyes for a sec, and he nodded his head. I nodded back to him – he did what he had to do and I was proud.

*

Few years later we were having a beer and I saw fit to mention the ham. Been anxious to talk about it, you know what people are like when they got wounds. But you just got to clear the air sometimes, you know?

'Hey, Jimmy.'

Jim looked at me. 'Yeah?'

'Remember that ham?'

Jim nodded. 'Yeah.'

'Where'd you get that ham, anyway?'

Jimmy shrugged. 'Found it,' he said, and as far as *that* conversation went, it seemed to be the end.

Griffith Review

Indelible Ink

Fiona McGregor

She was fifty-nine, rich, divorced for a year, and out alone on a
Saturday night. She told the taxi driver to head for the Cross;
she wanted to do something different, and she decided on the
bar where Leon had taken her as a treat the last time he had
been in Sydney. On reaching William Street, the traffic slowed
to a crawl and Marie looked out the window, fascinated by the
gaudy scene. A woman as big as a man stood out from the shadows of a building like a fruit-vendor, holding her enormous
breasts to the passing cars. A prostitute half her age and size
teetered past in spike heels to a companion propped against a
pylon, head lolling. They leaned against one another like slivers
of cardboard with fluff for hair, trying not to blow over in the
wind. A group of English boys lurched down the footpath shouting drunken songs. All of this had to be endured like a thicket
of lantana that had grown across the path, as the taxi struggled
onwards. The rawness of the street not two blocks from that
sumptuous bar with designer chairs and a billion-dollar view
amazed Marie. As the taxi paused at a red light, some Aboriginals
sauntered up from Woolloomooloo screaming with laughter
then stopped to stare directly through the window at her.

Inside the bar, safely seated in front of the view, Marie ordered
a Cape Mentelle white. It had been three hours since her last
drink: she swallowed the wine quickly and ordered another. The
man at the bar was staring at her. Tall and slim with thick grey

hair, he was picking peanuts out of a dish and tossing them into his mouth with a languid precision that Marie found sexy. She sat facing the view, watching his reflection. She turned to catch the waiter's eye, meeting those of the man at the bar in the elegant suit.

She tried to identify the colour of his eyes, the curve of his lips as he turned away and exchanged a word with the barman. She moved into their meeting, the first touch of his hand, the shape of him seated in the chair opposite, as the waiter walked back to the bar with her order. She went with him into the first months, the initial electric offering of bodies, discovery, compromise, the unravelling of pain and history as they gently conquered one another's children. They argued and reconciled, the months settled into comfortable silence. All of this before her drink arrived, thinking so far inside a life together that she only noticed at the last minute that the man was placing money on the bar and leaving, shattering an ancient intimacy. She sat there humiliated, friendless, staring at the city lights.

Drunk, exhausted. Floating over to the lift, leaning up against the cool mirror, floating out onto the street. The fresh air slapped her back to herself and she began to walk as though she had a purpose, somewhere to go. But where was she anyway, where was the taxi rank? This was Leon's territory. Leon would be taking her arm, urging her to forget her car parked on the other side of the city and take a taxi all the way home. She walked faster down the hill past a lump of rags in a bus stop that she realised afterwards was a human. My God, was he dead? Was he a he? Aren't there any bloody taxis on this side of the street? What a waste of time having lunch with Susan and accompanying her through two furniture warehouses, buying more things she didn't need, only to be told just before they parted that Susan couldn't do the Spanish course. Susan's calculated contempt for Ross and his young wife hovering in her ears like a malign whisper. Well, all of you can go to bloody hell. Marie stopped to face the oncoming traffic, headlights glaring, a car slowing to a halt the driver leaning over. It wasn't a taxi – he wanted to hire her. Flattered and frightened, she left the edge of the footpath and pressed herself against a shop window.

She found herself looking through the window of a tattoo par-lour, then, pushing the door open, tinkling a bell. Eddies of flash flew around the walls blurring into an ugly miasma inside which she felt somehow at home like a leper rightfully sent to quaran-tine. There were more designs in folders on the counter. A sort of aggression was pawing inside her as though she had set out that night to hunt and the prey still eluded her.

She flicked through the folders quickly then, reckless as a teenager, she was past the counter and inside a small room on a padded vinyl couch. She was actually unbuttoning her shirt in front of a strange man, hiding her face, her fear and excite-ment. Her heart rose and inflated to a large throbbing ball inside her mouth. She kept it shut. Face down now, her right bra strap pulled aside, the shopping, the bar, Susan, her family, everything disappearing into the small black moment of this whirlpool. The burly bearded man pulled on latex gloves. She heard the rip of a packet and the smell of isopropyl alcohol scoured her nostrils, her skin icy clean. How long had it been since the touch of a man? No, this was like being at the doctor's. A sudden desire to laugh hysterically surged in her stomach, then he gently touched a transfer to her shoulderblade and her body stilled.

'Want to check before I start?' He angled a mirror behind her and she twisted to see herself. Calm down Marie, it's just a little picture.

'That's good,' she managed.

'So what's the occasion?'

She would have seen a look of knowing bemusement on his face, but kept her eyes on the floor. She had to think. She looked at the pictures on the walls. Girl on a motorbike, Chinese dragon, rock band, some mass of green – maybe a rainforest. Photo-graphed body parts livid with fresh designs like the offcuts in a forensics laboratory. She had walked through the looking glass, shattering everything she had known. Sliced and swooning, she tried to think.

'My freedom,' she said. 'I'm free for the first time in almost forty years.'

'To your new life, then.' He pressed a switch and the iron began to whir. 'Ready?'

'Yes.'
The needles entered her skin.

From the mirror, the red rose stared at her slick and shiny as
though painted on with oils. Marie fetched her reading glasses
then removed the gauze pad, hanging by a piece of tape after a
long night's sleep. A sore heat radiated from the fresh tattoo, the
memory of pain a tiny glowing ember. In the ensuite in the morning sunlight, twisting to the mirror, she could see every detail.
The curl of crimson petals, the serrated leaves, three thorns, the
entire area raised red. And all the surrounding skin – tired, old,
damaged.

She hated her skin. Imported, unsuitable, over-reactive. It
kept no secrets. Everything transmitted, most things exaggerated. Spicy meals, daybreak tears, anxiety, embarrassment,
another long, hot day in the garden. Every ultraviolet hour of her
life was written across her skin, every drink taken. Her entire history roamed its galaxies of spots, scars and blotches. Marie
untied the belt of her dressing gown, removed it and hung it on
the back of the door.

Fearless, she appraised herself on this warm winter's morning,
naked in her bathroom. The breasts she had always considered
too large, sagging and drained, the belly loose with menopause
and childbirth. The short, thick legs, the swollen ankles she
hated enough to hide even in summer with socks and shoes. The
darker, mottled skin of exposed areas, liver spots creeping across
her hands. Like an old queen whose realm had survived the rav-
ages of decades, she sadly examined all that had invaded her.

Yet here, finally, was a scar she had chosen, a red rose cut into
her flesh gleaming like a beacon. She had planted her own flag
in her own country.

She washed the tattoo carefully under the shower then covered it in a layer of cream and a fresh gauze patch. A Bloody
Mary with breakfast, to settle her stomach, then a taxi to town
to fetch the car. A parking ticket was slipped like an invitation
beneath the windscreen wiper. Wearily, Marie got inside and sat
staring at the street. She reached into the glove box for a mint-
flavoured indigestion tablet, then thought about what to do for
the rest of the day, leaning back against the seat for the pleasant,

painful reminder of tattoo. She wasn't needed anywhere, she wasn't missed. She set off reluctantly in the direction of home then an arm came down out of the sky and turned the wheel and like a stormchaser Marie was speeding towards the hurricane, towards the parlour, where she chose a floral motif as an ankle-band. She signed the same piece of paper she vaguely remembered signing the night before.

She was able to look at the tattooist properly today. His beard was grey, what little hair he had was grey too. He was wearing a flannelette shirt and leather waistcoat and writing something into a large ledger with a cheap biro whose end had been chewed. Stuck on the corkboard behind him was a photograph of two toddlers perched on a huge motorbike, the tattooist holding the handlebars and smiling at the camera. His bare arms were covered. Imagine being nursed in those arms. If he had told her she had come to the wrong place she would have agreed and left immediately. She kept wanting somebody to wake her up, but she slept on through the alarm. Cautious, polite, the tattooist welcomed her into the back room. 'My first customer of the day!'

She supposed he saw all sorts in here. A cavalcade of criminals, sluts and rock stars sauntered through her mind. She wanted and didn't want to follow them, but they didn't seem to know where they were going. Not in here anyway. Marie changed the channel. She saw herself, lost but moving, moving again onto the couch.

'I hope I don't get another parking ticket,' she said, lamely.

It was cool and quiet in the shop. Sporadic Sunday traffic drifted past. How still these moments that change everything, hollow, pregnant, like the eye of the storm.

'S'pose you're happy with the rose then?'

'I love it.'

She could have been at a florist's. Practice for customer service at the nursery.

'You got a garden? You've chosen more flowers.'

'I do actually. A big one.'

'With roses?'

'No. I have a lot of natives. And a subtropical section all along the bottom.'

It hadn't even occurred to her; she hadn't even thought about it. She didn't want to think about it. She removed her shoe and sock then settled onto the couch and watched him swab the area to be tattooed.

'I don't grow roses,' she said. 'I tried once and they didn't take … never persisted.'

He wrapped the transfer around her ankle. 'You'll get some swelling after this. Don't go running around afterwards.'

How drunk had she been the night before? This wasn't the sensation she remembered – not the smarting that rang through her leg to her heart like an alarm. Her breakfast Bloody Mary wasn't sufficient for the ordeal. She forced her eyes open and, soothed by the dexterity and steadiness of his hand, watched transfixed, holding her quivering thigh as though her leg would leap off the couch of its own accord to flee the clawing pain. The man paused and scrutinised her face, wiping blood and ink from her ankle.

'You're bleeding a lot. You OK? Yes. Can you turn over?'

And the needles went in again, her heart banging furiously against her ribcage like a lunatic prisoner: what am I doing? why did I get a rose? Christ I can't stand this. To be able to stand, and speak and walk away half an hour later felt like a victory. She was flooded with energy.

How could she go home now? On such a sunny day, in an unfamiliar neighbourhood with its terraces and flats and narrow streets, the bitumen like a strip of black paint between gutters of colonial sandstone. The sweet reek of the season's first jasmine washed over her as she turned the corner. She smiled broadly at a couple walking past, the girl turning to look back at the ageing woman getting into a pale blue Saab.

Hobbled by folly, she drove aimlessly with her pristine right foot until she saw a café with white awnings and pine furniture. She felt like celebrating. She parked the car and went inside. Did they know? Could they see?

'I'll have a ham and cheese baguette, please,' she said to the waiter as though nothing had happened, 'and a glass of the Lehmann's Cab Sav.'

She longed to rest her swaddled ankle on the chair beside her.

Opposite, a well-dressed young man was reading the paper. On the front page, Marie saw the familiar image of a torture victim, naked and blindfolded, hands tied behind his back, curled on the ground by the boots of a soldier. The young man saw her looking and smiled over the newsprint then went back to his reading. So many people out there getting away with murder, day after day, so many bodies, so many crimes. And this, now, in her own smug heart, this pounding lust for taboo and severance, this blood seduction. Like coming home after a tryst with Jonesy in the boathouse to her husband and children. Serving dinner slick with lies and another man's sperm, drunk with orgasm. Full of love. This bliss, this murder.

The waiter placed the bill on her table and she saw the sacred heart tattooed on the inside of his forearm. Wreaths of thorns encircled the red organ, a drop of blood spilled down his wrist, all of it nestled in a bed of flames. So the bells had rung, the bets been laid, and she made her way back into the ring, terrified of fighting again, terrified of death equally if she reneged.

When she entered the tattoo parlour, there was nobody behind the counter. From the back room, the buzz of the iron and a fat white back reclining on the couch. The tattooist came to the counter and eyed her warily.

'I want another one on my right ankle.'

'Whoa,' he said.

She stood her ground with the arrogance of the initiate. And a woman who always had money to buy.

'Are you sure you don't want to wait a while and think about it?'

'I have thought about it. I feel unbalanced.'

Through the door she could see the owner of the back. A man in jeans with copious ginger-grey hair that gathered up his body to a bush around his face. He twisted his head around to look at her and grinned. His chest a blur of hair and old tattoos, the afternoon's work a lurid expanse down the inside of his forearm.

'I don't recommend getting so many tattoos so fast,' said the tattooist.

'It barely takes an hour.'

'And you shouldn't be getting tattooed when you've been drinking.'

She looked at him with amazed resentment. 'I had one glass of wine with lunch.' She said it quietly, conscious of her breath travelling through the air.

'Apart from the fact it's not a good state of mind to make decisions in, you bleed a lot more.'

How dare he speak to her like that ... a grubby tattooist.

'I'm not a teenager for God's sake.' She put the money on the counter.

'You'll have to wait.'

'How long?'

'Maybe an hour.'

'I'll wait.'

He sighed and picked up her money. Nobody paid beforehand. 'I'll do it this time then. But you're going to have to take a break after this, and think about what you're doing.'

He looked at Marie authoritatively. 'You might want the same design.' He opened a folder and pushed it towards her. 'Or you can choose a different one. Think about it.'

He turned to walk into the back room, stopping in the doorway. 'It's for life, you know.'

For over an hour she sat in the small waiting room plastered floor to ceiling with designs. She chose a slightly different floral band for her right ankle, based on lilies. She remembered Blanche, the inveterate art director, at her wedding, shifting an enormous vase of day lilies to a better position, her head tilted to one side. An hour later, seated beside her at the long head table, Marie saw a delicate track of yellow pollen smeared across Blanche's white neck. She was filled with a sorrowful pang and wanted to grab her daughter and tell her everything would be all right. But Blanche, flushed and gregarious, busy with her friends, seemed to be convinced that it would be all right anyway.

Night fell on the street outside and, as the alcohol receded, Marie's desire remained white and certain as a bone. She began to look through the pile of dog-eared magazines, hoping vaguely to find somebody like herself. A fried egg and bacon on top of a bald head, the knife and fork angled like flowers over each ear. A girl with an airbrushed stallion cantering across her back, sundry bikers wearing their totems with surly pride. Blanche reappeared briefly to scoff at the designs and Marie for once found herself in genuine agreement. All of them left her cold.

The next magazine was better. A Louis XIV sun shining on a plump shining chest muscle, its eye a pierced nipple. A Yakuza in a loincloth photographed full length, his entire body a floating world. Then yes, at the end, a woman older than forty. Well, probably only just, the photograph itself at least forty years old so the patchwork of bluebirds, hearts and sailing ships on her skin was as faded as the print itself. But nor was Marie a tattooed lady for exhibition in sideshows across the land; she could not picture herself among these people.

She was nowhere. She belonged to nobody.

She realised when the tattoo was completed that she didn't even know the tattooist's name.

Griffith Review

The Shed

Chris Womersley

1.

I still can't believe how quickly he took over, or how he did it. Incredible how the inevitable is hardly ever obvious. I found him one afternoon in the shed at the bottom of the garden. It was mid-winter, June or July. It was cold and wet. I remember the thick smell of damp earth. The clouds hovered low and it was dark by four p.m. I don't know how long he had been there – it might have been years. I wasn't really afraid of him, although I probably should have been.

The wife was gone by this time, of course. Packed up some weeks before and wandered into the sunset. Told me I'd had my chances. Told me she was unhappy. Told me it was the end. Just the usual things women will tell you.

2.

I confess I was drinking at this stage and the house was falling to pieces bit by bit. The kitchen was in ruins, cluttered with pans and plates and takeaway containers. The lounge room was vanishing beneath mountains of unread newspapers and biscuit wrappers. The brackish air in the bathroom had begun to take on a life of its own. There was a pile of dry shit in the hallway, which was odd because I had never owned a dog and couldn't even remember one being in the house. Some windows were broken and somebody – perhaps even me – had covered the spaces with cardboard that fluttered when it was windy. It was a large two-storey house but it smelt suddenly small, like some mangy cupboard.

The only place to be at times like these was in bed. I retreated from the rubbish and mayhem, room by room, until the bedroom that overlooked the backyard was the only vaguely habitable space. I climbed aboard the large, soft bed and hung on like it was a raft of some sort floating above the swell of bottles and butts and broken things.

And you can pretty much do everything you need to in bed: eat, sleep, dream, stare at the ceiling and jerk off to your heart's content. The television sat on a milk crate at the foot of the bed and at my right hand was a chair on which was scattered an assortment of reading material and odds and ends. And, of course, in bed one can drink.

And drinking – and I mean real drinking – is pretty much a full-time occupation. It's not just a glass of wine here and there, the odd long-neck after lunch. It's true that drinkers are disorganised and irresponsible and unreliable, but that's only concerning things other than drinking. A drinker might forget his daughter's birthday or be incapable of managing laundry, but his mind is crystalline when it comes to locating drink. When he needs to call in a three-year-old debt of twenty dollars or remember the Monday night opening hours of a bottle-shop on the far side of town.

When drinking, there is planning to be done, things to be considered, decisions to be made. Total destruction takes precision and concentration. It's not as haphazard as it looks. You can't buy takeaway alcohol easily at four a.m., for example, so one needs to be careful of running out at an inconvenient time such as this. Far better to run dry early in the morning – but not so early as to be caught empty-handed too long before business hours – so all that's required is a short trip to the pub down the road for your morning cask of wine.

Drinking is not a social event; it's an interior monologue. God forbid you should ever have to sit with others to get it done. Doing it is only half the work. There's thinking about doing it as well. It all takes time.

3.

I can't even remember why I went down to the shed in the first place. Probably looking for something to pawn or scrounging for empty bottles to sell. The only light was that of the late afternoon coming through the open door. Everything looked grey and furry. One wall bore the drawn shapes of garden tools, like the crime-scene outlines of murder victims. Grass was growing through the floor and vines curled between gaps in the walls. A light rain grizzled on the tin roof like an endless army of tiny feet. The shed smelt like all garden sheds, of dirt and oil and the bitter tang of fertiliser.

But there was something else. I was surprised to detect my own sharp smell, perhaps drawn out by the rain I'd staggered through to reach the shed. It was the machinery of my body, working vainly to expel the toxins I was pouring into it. I sniffed my armpits and yanked a handful of wet hair in front of my nose, but I was inured to myself. The smell was of something different, something muddy and fecund.

I stepped further into the gloom. An ancient handmower rested against a wheelbarrow, small packets of seeds were arranged on a wooden rack designed for the purpose. The desiccated remains of failed gardening enterprises. A battered paper kite hung in one corner.

I trailed some fingers across a dusty cardboard box of papers and books and reached out idly to caress a thick, squat roll of brown carpet standing on its end in the middle of the floor. To my surprise, it was not just wet, but warm as well. It moaned and turned around heavily. I found myself staring into a pair of dark, apelike eyes, framed by dank hair.

By now the rain had stopped. There were just the sounds and smells of our breathing.

4.

He sat in the kitchen, naked and wet. A grey puddle formed on the floor beneath his chair. The long hair covering his entire body was flat and black against his shiny, pink skin. He didn't seem afraid, and made no sound apart from the occasional low groan, which may have been of distress or satisfaction, it was hard to tell.

He sat with his round shoulders hunched and hands clasped loosely upon his lean and hairy knees. Although his bearing changed very little, those large, sooty eyes circled ceaselessly and took in the entire room. It was difficult to know what he knew. He took no interest in the tin of baked beans open on the table in front of him, although his nostrils flared slightly when it was first set down. By now it was night. There were just the two of us. The backdoor and kitchen windows were all open wide to rid the house of his stench, a thick stench I could feel on my skin.

I was drinking from a bottle of sherry and eating chips from the local fish-and-chip shop, popping them into my mouth one by one. They were barely warm, like the small, narrow corpses of recently murdered things. I sat watching him on the opposite side of the table. Despite his hairy, unwieldy torso and barnyard eyes, he looked like a man. He breathed like a machine, deep and even.

5.

He was still there two days later, but no drier. His wetness was apparently something that seeped from his pink skin. The puddle on the floor expanded and trickled away beneath the kitchen door. As far as I could tell, he had barely moved. I waved a hand in front of his eyes, I held up a piece of toast to his dark lips. When I tried to scare him by clapping my hands or banging two old cooking pots together, he just angled his head away and screwed up his round face a little. His body made a sticky sound when he moved.

What are you, then? I asked. His unresponsiveness was getting to me. What are you? Are you human? You stink like a fucking animal. You know that? You really stink.

He sort of looked at me with his watery, brown eyes and let out a rumbling groan, not of anger or frustration, but something darker and far more terrible. The sound vibrated in the air. I lit a cigarette and watched him. Smoke filled the small space between us. I drank.

6.

Some time later, the following day or week, he was gone from the kitchen. I wondered if I had imagined the entire thing, but on the floor was a shallow puddle, and closer inspection revealed several clods of long, black hair. I looked through a grimy window into the garden. It was still raining. The shed door was still open. I imagined him snuffling around in there with his long, articulate fingers and liquid eyes. I would wait until the rain stopped and the place had dried out and then I would close the shed door and set fire to it, with him inside. I could wait. What else was I going to do?

It was only late morning and I was already in ruins. I checked my alcohol supplies and was relieved to discover an unopened cask of wine and half a bottle of port that I had forgotten buying. I made a quick calculation. If today was Friday, then tomorrow was Saturday, which meant I could still buy something locally until late if I needed to. Perfect.

I cut the mouldy corners from some bread to make toast and even managed to find some coffee on the laminated bench under the window. The wife must have bought it before she left. I was suddenly, inexplicably, in good spirits. I ate my breakfast, shaved off several weeks' worth of thick beard and stood in the kitchen doorway to smoke a cigarette. Rainwater fell from the gutters and eaves like a trembling curtain. God knows why, but the world seemed suddenly full of possibility.

There comes a brief moment in every bender when you're able to see things for what they are – not just what you construct in order to be able to keep drinking – and this was that moment. It is always frightening. I saw the tatty garden dotted with empty bottles and cans, the sink full of broken, mouldy dishes. I saw the stains on the walls and the wreckage of furniture, the cold skulking in the sharpest corners of the house. I held a hand in front of my face. It was like a foreign object, the nails ragged and worn, like something you'd use to dig in the dirt.

I flicked my cigarette butt into the garden and went back inside. It was time to clean the place up, to try to get things together again. I walked into the lounge room. It was dim and musty. I opened the curtains and window and there he was, sitting on the low couch with those hands, as always, clasped gently between his knees. He looked up at me with a look of something like embarrassment and it was like the first time, just the sounds of our breathing in that small, enclosed space. We looked at each other. What are you doing? I yelled. *What are you doing?*

He didn't answer, of course. Made no sign he'd even understood. And then slowly, very deliberately, I picked up the telephone. I was going to call the police, call someone, the local loony-bin or something and get them to come and take this thing away, this thing that had taken up residence in my house. In my house. He watched me with those begging eyes as I did it, as I raised the plastic receiver to my ear. And I watched him watching me, just so he knew exactly what was happening, but when I put the receiver to my ear, there was no tone, no sound of any sort, just the humming silence of an unpaid bill.

The moment, it seemed, had passed.

7.

I woke up at some point in the day and waited. The bed smelt grey. Even from behind closed eyes, I could sense something was different but I was reluctant to find out what it could be. Whatever it was could wait. Things had moved beyond the point where I could reasonably expect them to actually get better. I could hear birds outside and the sighing of wind through trees.

When I opened my eyes, it was no surprise really. Just his dark eyes staring down at me. His body was still wet, and dripped slightly, although the terrible smell was gone. Either that, or I had become accustomed to it. We stared at each other for a long time, me lying on my back under a thin doona, while he stood slack-shouldered at the end of the bed. I'm sure we could have stayed like that forever, trading blinks, waiting for something to happen.

After some time I pushed the doona aside and swung around to put my feet on the cold, rough carpet. He stayed utterly still while I moved around the dim room and pulled on some clothes, although I knew in the time I staggered down the hall and through the front door onto the street, he had lumbered into my bed and eased himself beneath my covers.

Granta New Writing

Dangerous Shoes

Christine Stanton

'Sensitivity!' cries Donna. 'That's what I want us to be about.'
She cocks her head slightly to one side and makes a down-
pointing steeple with her hands at belly level. We all stare at
her, silent. It's too early in the morning to guess what she's
up to. It's too much trouble to argue with her, and it's too
cheeky of her to want us to stand round in a semicircle for this
meeting.

Donna puts a finger to her lips, as if we had broken into raucous, joyful clamour. Then she straightens up, raises the finger
and looks around, bobbing her head emphatically at each
person.

'I will be watching to see that *all* my staff's sensitivities develop
favourably,' she says. 'I know!' Her eyes widen, not quite spontaneously. 'Let's have a special greeting every week at assembly in
one of our students' languages!' she cries. 'Let's greet today's
New People in ...' She turns to the ancillaries. 'Where are they
from? What do they speak?'

'Nine Mainland Chinese today,' says Lily Li. 'All country
bumpkins, speaking very lousy Mandarin. And three Sudan
Africa boys. Merap's not here, so we're waiting for Immigration
to send around a Sudan Africa talker.'

'Well then, you can give today's assembly greeting in Chinese,
Lily.'

Lily Li shakes her head. 'Nothing doing extra from me,' she

says firmly. 'I'll be saying *"Ni hao"* too many times today, my tongue is already tired thinking about it.'

'Perhaps you and I can have a little counselling session later on today, Lily.'

'No way. Going to be too busy with the bumpkins,' says Lily Li.

Donna shrugs. 'Guess I'm the boss, so I need to make the hard decisions,' she says. She puts a forefinger to her lips and waggles it, and her head, at each person around the room.

She chants. 'Eeny, meeny, miney, mo, catch a, a – *tiger* by the toe, if he hollers let him go, eeny, meeny, miney – and you're mo, Owen. Pick a language. Greet us in it.'

Owen rubs his chin and chews his lips. '*Cymru am bith,*' he says at last. This is what Owen likes to shout when he is drunk and watching Wales chase a muddy ball to glory across a television screen. *Cymru am bith!* Wales forever! And fuck the rest!

'Thank you, Owen. Thank you for your willing co-operation,' says Donna. 'Is that a Balkan tongue?'

'No,' Owen growls.

'I can't remember us ever having any *Welsh*-speaking students,' says Winsome, frowning.

'Ah, but you never know when one might walk through that door and need the reassurance of a kind word, do you?' says Donna.

'These Sudanese, Lily,' Ari shouts across the room. 'Are they bumpkins too?'

Lily shakes her head. 'No, they're Baptists.'

*

Assembly is outside in the quadrangle today, at Donna's insistence, even though the clouds are knotting themselves into greasy bundles above the trees at the edge of the playing fields.

The English Unit students usually sit at the back of the high school's assembly. Even though they don't understand much of what is going on, it introduces them to a ritual they'll have to be part of soon, and gives them a chance to get a good look at their high school peers, without being challenged, *Whaddyalookinat-dickhead?*

Donna doesn't think Unit students should be exposed to the

crass brutality of the high school captain's plodding, polite address or have to cheer for sports wins, or listen to Principal Craig's harangues about 'Rubbish in the Creek Bed'.

'They don't need it. That is *too* Australian for them to cope with at this juncture,' says Donna.

So now we have our own assembly, distant from native contamination.

Donna has told Paddy to set up a microphone on a lectern at the top of the steps that lead down to the quadrangle. She has done this at very short notice, and in an imperious tone of voice.

'She's brave, you have to give her that,' says Owen, dryly.

Donna overhears part of this remark.

'Thank you, Owen, it's good to feel supported as team leader.'

'Yes, I was beginning to feel isolated on that point,' says Winsome.

'Oh, I'm supportive, too,' enthuses Clomper, even though she was overheard at lunchtime telling Craig that she, Janet McClomb, thought that charm bracelets were not all that, you know, *tasteful*, and what did Craig think about this?

Ari and Owen stand to one side of the lectern. They have lists of tasks to be done, behaviour to be avoided, and students to be lauded. Horrible has been seconded to hand out translated sheets of what Ari and Owen hope Donna will give them a chance to say to the assembly.

I stand on the other, far side, of Donna. I am holding a large, rolled-up poster.

Donna gazes over the rows of adolescents lounging and squatting on the ground below her. She says something into the microphone. Her voice comes out muffled at first, and then in a bellow, even though she has persuaded Paddy to stand by to help out if there are any problems with the PA system. She catches his eye now. He twiddles a few knobs.

Now no sound comes at all. Donna grasps the neck of the microphone in a stranglehold. The microphone whimpers. The students laugh. Ari attracts Paddy's attention, and bows his head, his hands together as if in prayer. Paddy grins and gives Ari the thumbs up. Paddy flicks a switch and signals to Donna to try again. She steps up to the microphone.

'*Cymru am bith!*' she shouts. 'That's "Hullo, how are you?" from Wales. Say it with me! *Cymru am bith!*'

A dribble of chorus follows her.

'Once more and all together!' she tries again.

The students open and shut their mouths, generating sounds, though nothing resembling any language on earth.

Donna looks down to where the new students are seated at the very front of the audience with Lily Li.

'Join in! We love you!' Donna yells at the newcomers. The microphone screeches in reply. The Africans giggle and the rural Chinese look at Lily Li and at the kids behind them for clues to what is going on.

Lily says something to them in Mandarin. The kids look dubious.

'Say it again!' Donna punches the air. The audience half mumbles, half silently mouths its way through Owen's rugby shout. Their words are swept away in a sudden rush of wind across the quadrangle; the Moreton Bay fig leaves on the far side of the science block smack together, and the microphone stand wobbles. Donna pauses, flushed and breathless, and wags a finger at the audience. The girls in the audience pay close attention to the finger, checking out her manicure.

'I can see I will have to get your teachers to show you how to greet one another from the heart,' says Donna. 'I have a lot of love in *my* heart.'

The breeze picks up a strand of Donna's pale streaked hair and plasters it firmly, diagonally across her forehead.

I've been standing just behind Donna, rocking from foot to foot, waiting my turn. Now I seize my opportunity, while Donna is concentrating on unsticking the hair from her forehead and trying not to get it entangled in her charm bracelet. I make a grab for the microphone.

Donna steps in front of me, holding out one arm to block the microphone. 'And because of how I feel about you all,' says Donna sideways to the audience, 'I have some special advice to give you today.'

'Is this about Dangerous Shoes?' I ask. 'Because *I'm* doing Dangerous Shoes. Stella asked me to.'

'I'm in charge here,' hisses Donna.

'Stella is responsible for Safety and Hygiene,' I say.

'So why has she inconvenienced me by taking an in-service today?'

Stella is giving a talk to new teaching graduates on 'Issues of Safety in the Playground, a Migrant Educator's Perspective'.

'*I* should have been asked to do that,' says Donna. She picks up a plastic shopping bag at her feet and holds it up. There is a takeaway food shop logo on the bag.

'There's something rather wonderful in here,' she says to the audience, her tone intimate and teasing. She takes a stack of thirty-centimetre-square cardboard sheets from the bag. She places the stack gently, reverently, on the lectern; the microphone pops loudly.

The audience is getting restless now; it's picking at invisible lint on its clothes, examining the clasps of its school bags, making tiny plaits in the hair of the person sitting in front of it. One of Ari's Thai girls is weaving a thin strip of sky-blue felt into Sharmilla's thick pigtail.

'Now,' Donna clasps her hands together at chest height. 'Every morning, as soon as you get up, I want you to remember this.' She takes a deep breath.

I quickly step forward.

'Excuse me,' I say. 'Before you start on whatever this is, I *have* to do Dangerous Shoes; Stella said so.'

'I think that can wait.'

'No it can't. They're losing concentration.'

'They'll get it back when they hear what I have to say,' says Donna sweetly.

'Right,' I say, and step back, as Donna leans forward again.

'Try to stay awake!' I bark at the audience. The microphone shudders with the force of my voice.

'Thank you, Ms Hamilton,' says Donna, surprised, and not knowing a declaration of war when she hears it. She turns to the audience and rotates her wrists in a winding motion.

'I want us all to remember, every morning, to say to ourselves, "I must start the day with a smile on my lips and a song in my heart".' She waits, leaving room for applause. None comes. Then Owen starts a slow handclap; the audience takes up his cue.

I am standing directly behind Donna now. She cannot see me.

I unroll the poster I'm carrying. It is a picture of a shoe with a fashionably thick sole. There is a blood-red slash across the shoe and the heading: 'A Dangerous Shoe'. I hold the poster up high.

The audience applause increases, and speeds up.

Donna claps too, oblivious to the poster. 'Good! Good!' she cries. 'Now I want twelve people ... that's ten plus two ... *twelve* people to come up here and help me.'

Nobody moves except to crane around to see who is wearing Dangerous Shoes, to compare them to their own and the one on the poster which I'm now rolling up.

Donna looks around at the staff; she fails to catch anyone's eye. She turns to me. 'Ms Hamilton, will you choose twelve volunteers for me?'

'What for, exactly?' I say, softly enough for the microphone not to pick it up.

Donna hesitates, hearing at last the sword sliding from its scabbard, but ignoring the close rumble of thunder behind the curdled clouds above.

She turns back to the audience.

'I know!' she says brightly, over-feigning serendipity. 'The new people can help me, our twelve lovely new students ... Ms Li, help them up here.'

The nine Chinese and three Africans stand in a row on the concrete platform. The Chinese are rigid with the effort of willing themselves invisible; the Africans are grinning nervously and, being brothers, start hitting each other.

'Quit it, you guys,' I growl at them; and they do, even though I am a woman and they're not sure what the words mean.

Lily Li stands at one end of the line murmuring soothingly to the Chinese in Mandarin, but the breeze steals her words away and takes them to the Africans.

At the other end of the line Donna is giving out the cardboard squares.

'Hold them to your hearts,' she says. 'Don't show the writing on them yet. No! Don't turn them around! Keep the blank side towards the audience!'

She turns and barks at Lily Li, 'Tell them Ms Li!'

Lily swears quietly in Mandarin. 'I don't think they're enjoying this,' she says.

'They will when you explain what's happening,' Donna retorts.

'*I* don't know what's happening,' says Ms Lily Li, who was brought up to never answer back.

Donna purses her lips and hands out the last three cardboard squares to the Sudanese boys, who immediately put them on their heads, where they balance perfectly. The audience giggles. The boys do a little jig, the squares stay in place, the audience applauds.

Donna looks around for help. 'Biiiiiff ...' she smiles.

'Nope,' I say, smiling.

'You'll have to wait for the guy from Casual Interpreting if you want to tell them to take the cardboard off their heads,' says Owen.

'I wish people would be there when they're wanted,' Donna whines, and turns back to the audience. 'Today I want us all to admire the excellent posture of the peoples of the African continent.'

The audience applauds; the Sudanese jig in a circle and snap their fingers.

Donna signals to the audience to cut the applause. It trails off. 'Keep a smile on your lips and a song in your heart,' she demands.

The audience stares at her.

'Speak! Say!'

Ari steps forward. He cups his hands around his mouth. 'Copy the lady talk,' he says.

Ah ...

Donna repeats herself.

The audience drones, 'Keeeba smallerernalups unna summa hunnert.'

'Again!'

All at once, the audience looks more alert; I have unrolled the poster again. This time I show them the other side of it. There are two sketches on it. One is of a girl wearing Dangerous Shoes and standing at the top of a flight of stairs. Underneath it is a picture of the same girl, still wearing her Dangerous Shoes, but now lying at the bottom of the stairs with her limbs jutting out at odd angles, a jagged bone protruding from one leg and her head resting in a pool of scarlet blood. The audience shudders deliciously; those wearing Dangerous Shoes blush.

Donna conducts the chanting audience; she seems pleased by their sudden, renewed enthusiasm.

I roll up the poster. Just in time, as Donna reaches the end of the chant and turns to the new students.

'Now, flip your squares!' She claps her hands, once, dramatically.

The new students look at her blankly.

I step closer behind Donna's shoulder.

'Please don't do this to them,' I say quietly.

'Flip their fucking squares?' says Ari to Owen. 'For all they know, she could be telling them to confess their failure to meet this season's production quota and choose their own correct punishment.'

Lily Li says something in rapid Mandarin to the nearest students. They turn over the squares they are holding. A few dark spots start to appear on the cardboard as large isolated raindrops fall across the quadrangle.

Each square has a single word written on it. Those that can be seen read ON. YOUR. AND. LIPS. SONG. AND. IN. A. YOUR. HEART. The Africans turn over their own squares, so that they now read KEEP. SMILE. A. The audience looks at the words, frowns, and moves its lips silently.

Some of the new Chinese are weeping. AND's square tilts sideways as he raises a hand to rub away tears. YOUR is shaking violently. LIPS, the littlest guy, has lowered his square to hip level to hide the spreading wet stain on the front of his trousers.

Lily Li gabbles urgently to them. She is telling them that they are not in trouble, they are not being made examples of; they have not offended the local cadres, they will not be sent back in disgrace to their villages. She says they should take no notice of this woman who crows like the rooster that struts the yard in the morning but that flavours the cooking pot at night.

She does not tell them that the other students will give them hell until they unlearn their provincial fashion sense, though she does advise them to turn their baseball cap peaks to the back.

A squall of wind blows the few drops of rain in horizontal streaks across the cardboard squares before snatching SMILE, A and KEEP from the heads of the Sudanese. KEEP swoops giddily about, then plops to the asphalt. SMILE and A are grabbed back by their owners, but then spun expertly, like frisbees, thrumming over the heads of the audience to the far side of the quadrangle.

The audience squeals with pleasure. The Chinese take heart and throw their own squares. A fleet of cardboard UFOs is brought to earth by a quick mortar round of rain, as the audience scrambles to its feet and rushes indoors.

'I've decided that's all for today,' Donna calls after them. She turns to me.

'I am so sorry, Elizabeth,' she says. 'We didn't seem to have time for the Dangerous Shoes issue, did we?'

A couple of Ari's Korean girls sidle over to him. They seem nervous and are holding hands to share courage.

'Mr Ari, please sir, tell what the song is? We have to learn this heartsong with our lips?' says one of them.

'This a song about how to be good? We not to sing this song when wear the shoes?' the other asks.

'Nah,' says Ari. 'Just keep working on your verbs, sweeties.'

Griffith Review

Another Man

Gerard Windsor

His grief astounded him. Which meant that he was still quite
capable of a detachment. He was able to measure and analyse
this exhausting storm even as it raged up and down and somehow jaggedly across his nerves. In fact he realised early on that
this gave him relief. Once he very deliberately brought his mind
into play, he sensed that he had in a way stepped into the storm's
eye; he and the turmoil around him seemed calmer. Yet if his
concentration wavered, or when the normal sequences of his
daily life forced him to drop this observer in him, the fury accel-
erated again. There was such a fine line between the watcher
and the watched. He might for example be trying to work out
what exactly it was about her bearing and her walk that he found
so endearing and, yes, exciting. Quite suddenly, if predictably,
he found himself locked on an image of her walking away from
him – self-conscious, her arms held out just a little from her
sides, very very slightly tipsy and as if picking her way, but at the
same time almost gliding on her strong legs. And seeing her
there, picturing the shadow of a blush on her face, being sure
she was somehow looking back at him but refusing to turn
around, he lost control over what he was doing. The picture,
summoned up for the purpose of his painstaking analysis, had
come alive, and he was back there in the emotional surge of the
moment, as entranced and in love as he had ever been.

*

When the news came it was someone else who brought it. She was a mutual friend of both Ellen and himself, and Charlie had run into her out walking, and as they followed the curve of the Cooks River towards the rising heights of Undercliffe she said to him, 'Ellen tells me it's all over between you two.'

'Oh yes,' he answered, 'it really is this time.'

'And she's got someone else?'

'Has she?' He struggled to be low-key and conversational.

'Didn't you know? I asked her if she'd told you. She said she hadn't yet, but she was going to.'

He thought he was calm, just a little light-headed. 'It was inevitable.'

The friend, thinking maybe she had spoken out of turn – as she had – said, 'I don't know how serious it is, or whether it's just a fling. He's a musician.'

He probed no further, said nothing more. He waited to hear from Ellen.

It was just over a week before she rang him. She asked if she could drop in to him some books she had borrowed long before, even years before.

She came at eleven in the morning, as carefully groomed as he had ever seen her. Although it was a bright warm autumn day, she came in from her car carrying the blue frock coat that she had had ever since he had first known her and which had always been her one concession to cold weather.

She said no to a drink of any kind. She gave him the books, commented on them. 'I've still got the Alice Munro stories. I haven't finished them all. But I'll give them straight back if you'd like them now.'

He seized on this unbroken tie. 'No, no, keep them as long as you want.' He waited. He'd been preparing his speech for days.

They sat on sofas at right angles to one another, she upright in the middle of hers, he at the far end of his with his legs half-swung up, giving her the distance, showing his detachment. She sat forward and straight, and in another context he could have believed that she wanted to move over and join him.

'Katie told you, I gather, that I've begun a new relationship.'

He didn't take his eyes off her, gave just the slightest nod. He had to steel himself; this was the nightmare moment finally come.

She hovered, not knowing whether that was enough or whether she should go on.

'It's really good of you to come and tell me yourself. You didn't have to.' He wanted to help her, and he wanted to know, at least something. 'Go on, if you like. Tell me about him. I'd like to know – if you're willing to tell me.'

'His name is Michael. He's divorced with two children. I've met his ex-wife; she's very friendly. He works in the television industry.' She gave a tiny shrug, as though to ask, are these the right pellets of information to give you, what more do you want to know, what more do you need to know.

Charlie waited, not quite sure when to make his speech. Her tentativeness, her slightly nervous smile gave her such a humanness in this formal, tense moment that he felt endeared to her even more.

'He's very kind to me,' she said. 'He makes me laugh a lot.'

'Part of me is really glad for you,' Charlie said, 'that you've found love with someone.' Even to himself he sounded artificial and patronising. Getting the speech right seemed beyond him. 'You're the most wonderful person; you so deserve it. It's terrific that you're happy.'

The twitch of a frown passed across her face. 'You pushed me away. You didn't want my love.'

He wasn't going to take this up. Instead he asked, 'What happened to his marriage?'

'His wife left him.'

'Why?'

'She said he took her for granted, and that he was always angry. It was a wake-up call.'

'And how is he now?'

'I've never seen him angry. Not once.' She leaned forward, and for the first time since she had come into the house he saw a vehemence in her. 'It's such a relief, such a relief, Charlie, to have everything out in the open. Not to have to be covert. To be able to meet all his family. After all this time it's such a relief, Charlie.' She looked at him, almost pleadingly.

'I know, I know,' he shook his head; he was so conscious of the truth of what she said, of the way her spirit had risen free.

She eased back on the sofa, her fervour and her pain subsiding.

'Has he met your family?' Charlie queried. 'Your sisters and parents?'

'Not yet. That's a big ask.' She was light-hearted. 'Do you think he could cope with them?'

'They're terrific people. They were always so friendly and tactful to me. Why wouldn't they be with him?'

'I'll see,' she said.

It was the end of her business with him, and she made to leave.

But he couldn't let her go. 'Ah stay a bit longer.' He tried to sound jokey.

She allowed herself to be persuaded, and sat back on the sofa. They were both silent.

Then, as though by way of conversation, she asked him, 'Have you found someone else?'

'No,' he told her. 'I haven't.' He shook his head ruefully. 'I don't seem to have any trouble falling for people. But to make it last … To feel the leisure and the commitment to make it work … Eleven years is a hard one to get round.' That was true, but he was aware that he was saying this to pay tribute to her, and to let her know that she had been, still was, unique. Obliquely he hoped that it wasn't self-pity, and that he wasn't leaning on her at all.

He talked on, unable to stop himself. 'I do hope you're happy. I'll cry, and cry again, but …'

'No you won't. You won't cry,' she said. It was a statement of fact, not an order.

It crossed his mind to see if he could cry then and there. 'Yes, I'll cry all right,' he said, but it wouldn't be there in front of her.

'I must go.' She gathered up her blue coat. 'I'm actually baby-sitting. I can't keep the children waiting.'

He moved from the sofa and knelt in front of her and opened his arms to her. She came into them, gingerly, and he felt the restraining touch of her fingers against his shoulders, and the careful but unhostile tension of her whole body. He sagged back on his haunches and stood up and away from her.

*

Why, he demanded of himself, was sexual jealousy so strong? Or why was his? That was more the question, for he had imagined, and even been told, that there was something anaesthetised, or maybe even necrotic, in the sympathy lobe of his own brain.

If he had had a skerrick of a benevolent nerve in his body, he told himself, he'd be able to scrub away any resentment of another man now in the place where he had been. He had given what he could, maybe not very much, and he had received plenty, of tenderness and solicitude and, yes, grace.

Could what he had known be any less merely because another man had stepped in and made his own attempt to weave some new pattern with her? Yes, he supposed it could, because she, Ellen, might well come to find that what she had was more exciting, more consoling, more full of the pulsing current of everyday life, than anything she had ever had, had ever enjoyed, even, with him. There seemed no getting round that it was a competitive thing – that just as he had hoped, and in fact had believed, he had meant more to her than any other partner, fleeting or enduring, in her life … well it wasn't the end of comparisons and maybe this new man would be valued more highly again. That was to think of it crudely, but if there were as much as one advantage, one blessing this new man might bring to her life that he himself had failed to give her, then of course he would feel he had been bettered.

Oh, in the most altruistic of worlds, even of moods, he would be happy that she had received one extra gift that had not come her way before. And presuming that he still actually loved her, and that love wanted only the welfare of the beloved, he would rejoice that this had been so. And if he couldn't do that, was it simply that his vanity had been wounded? A vanity allowed to thrive because he had never broken free of a child's confidence that in all things that mattered to him, he was at the apex of the world, that whatever he laid his hand to would never be equalled by anyone else, that being in love with him had a refined distinction to it that no one else would ever give? The grossness of the conclusion horrified him.

No, it couldn't be that. The difference was that this was unique. He trawled back through his own past, and the women that had moved on from him to another man. Not surprisingly none of them had called it a day after they had finished with him, or he with them. What had he felt then? Had he been stung, even bloodied, by those moves into another man's arms? He remembered one time, in another country, when for some weeks he hadn't seen or heard from an occasional sleeping partner, and then a friend revealed that this girl had hooked up with a man, Eugene – he always remembered that name – a fellow countryman of hers and the owner of a house, and altogether a better proposition. He had been miffed, his pride pricked, but largely because it took him by surprise, and he couldn't say the hurt went any deeper.

Other movings-on hardly seemed to register with him at all. Except one, nearly thirty years previously. They had blown up, yet again, he and this woman, and gone their separate ways, on the far side of the world, and a few months later she had more or less gone to live with another man, and Charlie had been distraught and had gone home, a man of over thirty, weeping to his mother, and in a few months he had weathered it and detached himself, and then she had turned up at his front gate, saying she had left the other man because it was he, Charlie, that she really loved. So it all began over again.

It shook him that the same emotion could strike him down so much later in his life. Yet equally he was shaken by the similarity of the story – that the woman he had cast off became truly desirable to him only when someone else showed he wanted her. He couldn't bear such predictability, such a pathetic weakness. He was determined that it wouldn't be so. He set himself dead against any pattern. This love, he and Ellen, had been unique, was unique, and he would prove it. But he hardly knew what he meant. He wanted the pain to continue so that he could show, at least to himself, that there was no waning of his love. Never had been. That he had always wanted her. He allowed himself to drift through his sexual history, remembering past slights, ones that he could see were laughable and trivial, so unlike this present anguish. He exercised himself, playing with his powers of resistance and resilience, and he let himself be cornered by the small specifics of jealousy.

He remembered one stab. The cut was unkind, and it hurt, but there was some cheer in the fact that in this instance the woman had come back to him – after some adventure – which almost certainly coincided with an adventure of his own. She was a woman of great spirit – one of those of whom, in retrospect, he actually felt he had not been worthy but whom he doubted he could have kept up with in any case. She had a waggish coarseness about her and this was allied to an almost scientific interest in the workings of the physical human world. He used to present her with his own homemade muesli, and this had in it a number of seeds – sesame and sunflower. She came from the toilet one morning just before she left for work, and she passed by him in the kitchen, and remarked, 'It's a terrible pity I can't retrieve those things. All those seeds just seem to pass through untouched, every bit as good there in the bowl as they were when I put them into my mouth.' He was too thrown by the easy frankness of it to be able to reply at all.

On this other occasion he suspected that he had ventured, at the time of their reunion, into the territory of comparison. Never a good idea, it was positively asking for trouble in this woman's case. He had managed to forget what the foolish probe had been, but her response was carved into his brain.

'Well, Gregory's penis,' she said, 'is nicer than yours, but you do nicer things with yours.'

Whatever did she mean by 'nice', what exactly is a 'nice' penis, and whatever were the 'nicer' things he did with his – after all, he thought, there was a definite limit to the repertoire of the penis itself, and, in his case, and given that he'd been much younger then, he couldn't believe that he'd really had much of a range to offer. At the time though, of course, none of this came out; he'd been thrown by the honest even-handedness of it. At least he presumed it was honest.

Penis comparisons smarted. One other he remembered. A woman he'd been on and off with for five years had the not uncommon habit, when they were in bed together, as part of her love talk, of saying of his penis, 'Oh you're so big.' He wasn't particularly fooled by this, but it served its purpose and was an exciting thing to hear. However there came a time when this woman too broke away, or maybe he from her, but he remembered it as fairly mutual, and she found another man, quite promptly as it happened. Eventually, after about six months, she returned to him, and they went on pretty much as they had before. There was, however, he noticed, one small variation: she never once again referred to his penis being big. He didn't put out any feelers this time.

Ellen however, years later, refined these criteria for scoring a penis. She was blunt, laying it down quite forcefully that a penis could be too long and could cause discomfort against the cervix, but that on the other hand, it could never be too thick. 'After all,' she said, 'the passage is designed for a baby's body.'

Presented with this undeniable fact Charlie felt inadequate. Nor did Ellen ever make remarks of admiration or esteem specifically about his penis. He could live with that given the other compensations she offered. In fact the omission never even occurred to him. But when he was no longer her lover, and he began to squirm under the possibility that she had found something with another man he had never been able to give her, it was this pathetic notion of the penis that clawed most sharply at him. He was ashamed that at his age he could be subject to this adolescent sensitivity. Perhaps, he thought in his vanity, he could not be challenged for his company, for the stimulus of his conversation, for his solicitousness and his various kindnesses – and even as he told himself this he realised he could be too easily challenged on all these – but somehow it was still his body and the way it had been put together that was so obviously not of his doing and beyond his control, and that she could therefore find so decisively second-rate in comparison with some other man.

It wasn't entirely irrational, this otherwise absurd neurosis of his. He was stuck on this genital fixation because their physical intimacy had been so central to them. That sounded to him a stupid thing to say, a truism about any affair. But he stuck by it; he told himself it wasn't just a focused lust that he meant; it was the high dramatic waiting upon one another, and the consolation, and the intimacy, of their love-making that had been at the heart of their great mutual feeling. Their allowing, then inviting one another to do things that they had never, these many years into their lives, done with anyone else. So that their love-making was the emblem for all the other exhilarations and deep contents of their affair. Yet he had never doubted that there were sexual possibilities beyond what he knew or was capable of, and now, he also began to admit to himself, the obvious satisfaction she got from him in her bed had waned over these last years.

For all humans, the monarch, the politician, the aged, being supplanted was one of the great cruel miseries. And the lover perhaps most commonly of all. He knew that it would go on and on eternally, but each man or woman displaced would clutch at the final comfort – that for all their being cast off there would never be another like them, as ruler, as generation, as lover.

Yet what he felt now was the sharp pain of the best being over – even as that best was bettered by someone else while he moved away into the tangible decline towards death.

*

They sat down and looked around them – out across the moorings and the harbour. A layered, three-dimensional pendant of grey cloud hung above the towers of the city. Behind the sharply outlined plunge of it the sky was an unflawed eggshell blue. They were brought up short by it and shook their heads in wonder. A man and a woman having a bowl of soup together in the middle of the day in a discount shopping precinct, and here was this backdrop, too original and subtle in its make-up to be merely theatrical. Instead it had all the apocalyptic overtones of thunder and dense catastrophe, even as the cloud was vaulted, skipped across by the sun-washed blue.

They turned their eyes back to the table and the menus and one another and didn't advert to the sky again.

He wanted, he told her, to discuss their years together, moments, aspects of it, in an affectionate detached way. More mull over them as a couple might page through an old photo album. Get her take on an incident he had never understood, but to which now, he told himself, both of them could give a detached assessment and bring new light. He felt quite calm about it all; there was certainly no matter for recrimination churning toxically inside him. He had neither the case nor the impulse for any bitterness at all. Whereas he thought of himself as the harmer, the inflictor of pain, so that he was aware he should not be presuming on any readiness on Ellen's part to breeze cheerfully through this noting, and maybe untying, of knots. But blithely enough he wanted to try it.

The waiter approached them for the third time. They asked for the cauliflower soup, the piazzetta, two glasses of wine.

'I have seven pieces of correspondence from you,' he said. 'Only one that I could call a love letter.'

She raised her eyebrows. It might have been – he didn't know – in disbelief that there was only one, or that there had been even that one.

'You sent it to me in New York,' he said. 'It was so loving.'

'Oh yes,' she said, and she looked at him and he held her gaze so that he was conscious of the strong sunlight showing up the puckered, very pale islets of skin under her eyes.

'And when you came home, and we met,' she said, 'I so wanted you, so wanted your arms around me. And you held me just briefly, and then pushed me away and said you had decided it was all over.'

He looked away. 'Yes, I know.'

'Is it any wonder you don't have more love letters?'

He saw nowhere to go. He shook his head. 'It's all very well for me,' he deflected. 'I'm a compulsive writer.' For years he had kept up a bobbing string of cards to her. 'Maybe writing was more an indulgence for myself than any brightness to your daily life.'

She said nothing.

'Do you still have the cards?' he asked.

'Do you mean have I thrown them out, have I burned them? No, I haven't.'

'But do you still have them lying around?'

She used to use them as minor decorations, always a few propped against vases or on a mantlepiece or on the kitchen cupboard. He had always interpreted this as a wish to continue the pleasure of the images, to add to the austere decoration of her home these small shining wonders of the world. Yet it made him happy too to find these reminders of himself scattered through the rooms of her daily life, especially the public ones, and to have found them there always, even still in place after a period of estrangement and fierce upset between them.

'Oh yes,' she said, 'some of them.'

He frowned. 'Even with Mike there?'

'They don't seem to bother him. I don't think he notices them.' There was a matter-of-fact shrug in her voice. 'He's not very interested in you, Charlie.'

He couldn't quite gauge the remark, but it hurt him. She was saying he was quite irrelevant to this new daily life she had. Perhaps she was saying that. That he wasn't an issue between them. He couldn't quite believe that having established himself at least as a presence in the atmosphere over those eleven years, he wasn't still hovering there in some way. But it would be graceless, heavy-handed of him to take her comment any further.

Yet he couldn't stop himself letting her know that he was hurting. It was a balance he had to manage in a meeting like this – and for her to agree to a meeting in the first place had been difficult enough. He needed to make the occasion companionable and unthreatening, showing that he rattled along enjoyably in her company and that she could relax into an affable, laughing pleasure in being there. That they had developed into old friends now who could always fall into a bonded ramble round all the common dramas and personalities of their corner of the great world.

At the same time he couldn't bear her to think that he was merely detached and completely cheerful either. There was no point in pleading; there was nothing he was in any position to ask her for. He thought he should just describe his state of mind to her. Quite baldly, almost apologetically, as though he were noting some dental work he had just come from and which made his speech a bit of a mess, a small burr in the smooth roll-out of their meeting, one which he would advert to and apologise for once, and then they would forget, or pretend to forget and not raise again.

'I feel the most terrible sexual jealousy,' he said. 'I can't help it. And I know I'm not telling you anything you don't know all about. I gave you the most terrible cause for it.'

'No,' she said, 'sexual jealousy was not what I felt.'

He almost laughed. She's a great clarifier, he thought. A

conversation with her can be a minefield or a dialectical dance. Good either way for both excitement and clarity of mind. But here, now, she was calm enough, and he had to be the same. He looked at her quizzically, not disbelieving – although he found it impossible to imagine she hadn't felt sexual jealousy – but his expression was controlled, concentrated, asking for enlightenment.

'When you went away,' she said, 'overseas' and she gestured as though this referred to any number of occasions, 'and you asked me to join you, for a time at the beginning or at the end … it was my being offered the scraps of your leftover time that was so hurtful. When you had done with your family or your old lover, that was when you could pay some attention to me. That was how important I felt to you, the picker-up of the crumbs.' She said this dispassionately; the need was to clarify, rather than to show her hurt.

She watched him carefully, determined that he got the message.

He nodded, allowed himself to be set right, and grimaced at his gross cruelty – even as he found it impossible to imagine what else he could have done. But he was determined to make his point and it was not to tell her what her experience had been. 'I'm afraid sexual jealousy is what has got hold of me, and I find it very difficult to cope with. And it is, I have to admit it, such a sexual thing in this case. Making love to you was so unique, I never knew anything like it in my life. It was so utterly special, something that, whatever else, *we had*. So the thought of you with another man … is really hard for me to take. Because also, I am still, more than ever, in love with you.'

She had her head down, slicing another small, precise section of her piazzetta. Some detached part of his mind registered that she had almost finished eating, while his own bowl was still half-full. It was the only time, in all these years, she had ever finished before him.

He slewed away from his *cri de coeur*; he knew he should leave it there. But her sexual presence was so present to him, so whole, so rippling in its subtleties and variations, that the sense of the same edgy talk he had known, the same slightly ambivalent teasing, the same daringly intimate acts they had found that could knit them together in such benevolent longing, the force of the memory of all this, but taken from him and given to another man, left him with a hollow nervous grief. But he made his simple enough statement and shrugged as though in apology, and his gaze had moved away from her out across the water. So that he only became aware of the one thing she said after it had been left floating in the air.

'It *was* unique,' she said.

He was pulled back by the hook of it, wanted her to repeat it, wanted to be looking at her while she was saying it. He did none of that; he just took in the balm of it – even while his ever analytical, dissatisfied self looked for the ambiguities and the outs in her reassurance. Maybe it was always unique, with every individual. But there was something about the conviction in her voice that told him she wasn't making a meaningless statement. It wasn't just his own need to console himself.

Her glass was nearly empty. 'Will you have another glass of wine?' he asked.

She hesitated. 'Yes, I will.'

He craned and concentrated till he caught the waiter's eye.

'Thank you,' she said.

'Are you in love with him?' he asked.

She looked directly at him, her grey-blue eyes quivering, smiling, not evasive. 'I really want him to be happy. I so much want his good. He's very kind to me. I think he's a good person. And he makes me laugh a lot.'

They held one another's gaze and waited just a moment.

'I'm not in love with him the way I was in love with you,' she said.

He stayed slightly hunched forward over the table, but he felt something inside him lean back with a relieved joy. Yet he didn't miss the careful balance of her words. She was no longer in love with him, she was telling him. The hurt of it was somehow outweighed by the admission that she hadn't found herself in love with anyone else.

He saw the sunlight playing on the tips of her light blonde hair. There was a glow and a shimmer in the space between each side of her face and the curtains of hair that draped it. He was aware of all sorts of feelings singing and twisting inside him. An admiration for the equilibrium, the levelling in this assessment of herself. He believed her absolutely, had no sense that she was shaping her response to what he might like to hear, to what would have soothed him, in this wasteland of loss he felt he was in. She was offering him no hope, merely the reassurance that there had been something, that she wasn't going to suggest now that it had ever been illusory and hollow.

Yet he knew too that there was a meanness in him, that he could take comfort, even joy, from the fact that she had not found something with another man that she had found with him. Maybe it wasn't despicable, but he would have liked – or he imagined he would have liked – to have been capable of a generosity that wanted only her utmost happiness. What she had said that she herself wanted for this man, this Mike.

'I was in Adelaide last week,' he said. 'It asked to be remembered to you. It sent you a present. I left it in the car.'

They walked together to the car, not touching, but his spirit was skipping in the silent warmth of her. 'It's only a trivial present I'm afraid.'

They went up towards the roof of the car park through the concrete stairwell, and she said quietly and unexpectedly, 'I've hardly given you any gifts over all these years.'

'Yes, you have.'

She murmured. They went on up. Their cars were on the opposite sides of a causeway linking the two sections of the rooftop. He went to his car, and gave her the small, protectively wrapped box of Haigh's chocolates. For all his awkwardness at his own cliché, the nothingness of it, she was delighted and she kissed him.

'You must have one with me, after the coffee we didn't have.'

'Oh ...' he demurred.

Then it began to rain, a sudden squally shower.

'Come and sit in the car,' he hurried. 'We'll have it there.'

As she unwrapped and moved down through the bow and the box he began a jokey, self-mocking account of how he knew he had had to come back with these, and of having to face blocks and blocks of King William Street, in driving rain, dragging a suitcase, the threat of closing time hanging over him, in his success-or-do-not-return quest for her chocolates.

She was happy to be amused, to enjoy the parodic flattery of it. She took a chocolate herself, and then he did too, and she leaned across and looked at him and then stretched further and kissed him slowly, softly, on the neck.

'Liqueur truffles,' he said. 'I had to plump for something. I really hadn't a clue about your taste.'

She bit into the chocolate, and after a moment she said, 'My girls were asking after you recently. They noticed they hadn't seen you for a long while. It's your pumpkin soup that they've missed of course.'

'Oh of course.'

She went on. 'Would you like to continue a relationship with them?'

He was surprised, and moved, that she would make such an invitation. He had never thought of himself as having any significance to her daughters; they were self-contained girls, with something of Ellen's ironic edge when they did speak, and he imagined that to them he had always seemed a curiosity, maybe even problematic, in the life of their mother. He felt that Ellen's gesture was a way of saying that at this moment she still wanted something of him in her life. But he was even surer that no gesture she made would be doing violence to the feelings of her daughters. 'I'd love to have something to do with them,' he said, 'even as just the caterer.'

'We'll see then,' she said.

They got out of his car and walked across the causeway to hers. She turned and kissed him again, and he felt that there was no limit to the kisses she wanted to give him at this moment, and he put his arms around her lightly and kissed her on the back of the neck, and he felt there was a relaxed helplessness about both of them, neither of them straining against the other's touch, both drawing back from one another in some joint reflex.

When he waved to her as she drove away he was suffused with joy. Even while the low-lying cloud of her choice of another man sat still and aching in him, he felt that the shape of these few hours together had been perfect, that they had been as close as ever they had been, that there had been a consummation, enough to leave his soul replete and singing and more full of love for her than ever. The happiness he felt, as he returned to his own car, was no more the ongoing tingle of sexual readiness than it had been the satiety of sexual release. It had been a communion, simple and pulsing with grace.

*

He had asked to see her. In a surge of feeling, maybe even of decisiveness, he wanted to acknowledge Ellen to his wife. It wasn't, he insisted to himself, a matter of needing to make a clean breast of it, of confessing. It was that he had to acknowledge what she meant to him, and still did, more than ever. This appearance of another man in Ellen's life had thrown him into such turmoil that he was throwing all caution to the winds. To do what, he wasn't sure. But he had to talk, talk to his wife, and there could be no holding back. Whatever the meaning and the consequences of it he could not withhold Ellen from her any longer, could not allow this great tract of his soul to be skirted. It was flailing desperation, he dimly acknowledged, at least as much as honesty.

Ellen was against the idea. He had surged and ebbed on it for weeks, and now he was turning strongly again towards doing it. So he had to see her and put it to her again. It was his need, not hers. But it would affect her if he spoke. Unpredictably but surely.

She emailed him back. It was several days after he had left his own message. But then she never replied to him immediately. Sometimes she didn't reply at all. But this time she said, 'We could talk tomorrow afternoon, after I've had a sleep. Leave me a message if that suits and I'll ring you at four to five-ish.' She was working at the hospital all night.

It suited him and he said so, and he waited for her call. If, in the past, she had ever called him it was always later than she had said it would be. Over the years he had come to read an unwillingness, a shying-away, a lack of enthusiasm into that pattern. This Sunday however she rang him at exactly 4.30. It was unique. Only later did he see an explanation for that.

'Would you like to come round here,' she said, 'or meet somewhere?'

'I'll come round there,' he said, 'if that suits you?'

'Yes, come round here then. It can't be for very long though,' she added.

'No, of course not. I'll come round straightaway.'

'That's fine.'

He was at her door at a quarter to five, in the falling dark. She let him in and leaned across to kiss him on the cheek. Her hair was newly washed and dried, and she was in a black pantsuit with bright red piping down the sharp neckline. She was small-breasted, and there was no revealing ostentation in the way she wore the blouse. The slim grace of her struck him with a new force.

'You look lovely, Ellen,' he said.

She had her back to him. 'Oh, the old slippers. I'll leave them on for Charlie, I thought.'

He hadn't noticed the voluminous warm slippers.

She took him into her living room and she sat in a narrow armchair in a corner, and he on a sofa at an angle to her, and they began to talk.

'She'd be devastated,' Ellen said. Her self-protectiveness seemed slight. Her attitude to her own exposure appeared to be, 'Let there come a time, by preference later rather than sooner, but I'll manage it whenever it comes.' But his wife – she'd be devastated. That was her judgement, and she opened her eyes a little wider and gave a slight upward bob of her head inviting him to have his say.

'I have to acknowledge your place in my life,' he said.

'Why?'

'I just can't go around anymore pretending a person so important to me doesn't exist.'

'Why now?'

He knew the question was the obvious one for her to ask. He was grateful that she didn't turn the screw harder, and bitterly. Instead she was detached, quizzical, almost merely professional.

'I'm not sure,' he said. 'But I can't go on discussing the future of my marriage without admitting this element into it. I'm in love with you still, more than ever. I can't pretend there's some sort of a clean slate of a future. You're there; you're irremovable. Yes, yes, I know it's over; you've got someone else. But that's my state of feeling, I can't see it changing, and I want to own up to it.' He was so aware of all this flailing around inside his own mind. 'I suppose too I'm more strident, more reckless because I've been rejected.'

Her intent expression never changed. She just waited a few seconds. 'I have never rejected you.'

That was true. It had been a silly statement. They had broken away from one another in mutual hurt and frustration, and she had found someone else quickly, perhaps programmatically. It wasn't rejection. He could only use the term wildly as meaning that her choice had put a barrier against his returning to her. In his divided-loyalty way.

At intervals she got up and stood in front of the large, full-blazing gas heater beside her. Then the phone went, in another part of the house, perhaps her bedroom, and he gestured to her to get it if she wished. She waited, distracted by whether a message was being left, and when it was, she said, 'I'd better just check that.' When she came back she resumed, her mind still tight on the threads of their discussion.

Ten minutes later the phone rang again, and Charlie stopped what he was saying and she went away to answer it. He heard no more than her hello and then she walked the phone to a more distant part of the house, and he also heard her laugh, and then, as she returned the phone to its cradle, he heard the rather brisk 'goodbye' that she always gave.

'That was Mike,' she said, and her expression was a shy smile, and even at that moment he thought she quite perfectly balanced honesty and tact and ironic amusement and gentleness. 'He's coming around, but I told him to wait, to do something else for a while. He finished work early,' she added.

Charlie felt the tearing pain across the top of the ever-present ache. But the hurt wasn't of Ellen's doing, and there was no reason to explode or cry out in front of her, and even as the hurt throbbed he was full of admiration for her. Besides he was here to talk about their past, and maybe some sort of future, and in fact they were talking and listening hard to one another.

'You'll tell her; you won't follow my advice. You'll do what you want to do.' She spoke matter-of-factly, but without bitterness, without even wryness.

He sensed the dangers in ignoring her, or at least in not doing what she preferred. 'Whatever I do,' he asked, 'would you still be willing to see me?'

She shrugged. 'You mean if you don't do what I advise. Oh yes, Charlie, I'd probably still be willing to see you. I admire you, I find your company intellectually stimulating ...'

He felt relieved, minimal as the endorsement was, and he relaxed.

She stood up again and moved away close to the heater, her hands by her sides, twitching backwards towards the warmth.

He rocked back on the sofa, his hands clenched around one knee, and then he bounced forward and stood facing her. 'I enjoy your company enormously. I'd love to see you every few weeks – as we've been managing now for these past however many months ... And good, if you admire me and find me intellectually stimulating ...'

She blushed just slightly at that, and gave him a shy, almost covert self-mocking smile.

They stood, no distance apart. And he was quite sure that she had been joking, was invoking some 'if only it were just admiration and a bit of mental buzz ...' He understood quite well – and she knew he did – that her feeling for him was more than a readiness to have her mind teased. It was clear to both of them, and they were laughing in themselves, but there would only be harm in acknowledging it.

Yet it made them easy, almost flirtatious, facing one another, teasing in this way, secure in their affection. At another time, in the past, but not so long ago either, he would have kissed her and she would have responded. He could not do that now, but for him at least there was a long rippling pleasure in this simmering sympathy between them.

She leaned down towards his mug on the table and asked, 'Would you like another cup of tea?'

It seemed an oddly invitatory gesture, so that he found himself responding with the same generosity. 'No,' he said, 'I don't want to keep Mike waiting around out there. Where did you send him?' But then, with hardly a pause, he found himself saying, 'Well yes, I'd love another cup. I'm still only asking for a fraction of Mike's time.'

Perhaps equally confused she looked at her watch and said, 'It's a quarter to six. He's actually coming round in a quarter of an hour.'

'Oh well …' Charlie said, and he picked up his mug.

'No …' She put out her hand.

'Did you tell him I was here?'

'No I didn't. What I mean is you probably can't have another cup. I don't want him to meet you yet.'

'No, no, I'm going. I'm just taking my mug out to the kitchen. You can't leave two drained mugs on the table here. It's a dead giveaway. Don't you know anything about duplicity, Ellen?'

She laughed, they both did.

'You can leave it there,' she said. 'I'll look after it.'

He moved past her, and went to the front door.

'I'm grateful for this,' he said, and he didn't know that there was any limit to what he was referring to.

There was a smile, a warmth about her even as she said goodbye. She stepped towards him and kissed him on the mouth. He barely responded, knowing there was no future, there at that moment, nor in any short term, in holding her kiss. He couldn't tell whether a euphoria and a nervousness about Mike's arrival was fuelling this generous state of mind. Very likely it was, but he also knew that a gesture such as a kiss on the mouth was sacred to her; she would never give it to someone she felt hostile or aggrieved towards; there was affection, even love, towards him in that moment even as there must have been relief to see him going. She stood on the veranda, holding open the flyscreen door as he walked to her gate and down the road to his car.

He drove away immediately, realising he had seen something for the first time, and understanding he was no part of it and had no business loitering or trespassing. The calculation hit him and could not be shaken off that she and this man would have four hours together before she would have to go to work. Four hours in the calm eager generosity of her house. He yanked savagely away from any line of speculation and self-pity there, and tried to work out what it was he had glimpsed. Perhaps it was the ease of her in the house, a domestic world of affection, a man coming into her brightness and her welcome, none of the pressures of assignation and its crimped moments together. A man coming from work to the woman he cared for, and she going off to work herself, but in the meantime a quiet dance between them around the circle of routine, and always the prospect of the next day, and the next week, hardly having to be planned for, but presumed on as the permanent open country for their affection.

Charlie had never known that with her, had never said, 'I'm yours, let me join you, what shall we do together now?' So he had never entered her house and found the great open-endedness of relaxed love. This time, as a visitor, he had sensed it. The house was new, different from any he had ever known with her. And she, relaxed and confident in the warmth of it, could receive him and comfort him and send him away again with an ease that he felt he had never seen in her before.

In the dark, light-pricked machinery of the car he said to himself, You're a selfish and a destructive bastard. Don't wait for anyone else to point out that this is dog-in-the-manger stuff. You wouldn't give yourself to her. For whatever good and bad reasons. But you howl at the prospect of another man who will. What's more you're fighting tooth and nail to undermine this affair, this love, whatever it is. How can you say you love her when you see her happy, as you have never seen her before, and you're doing your level best to destroy it? Because your pride and your so late-found constant need for her are too strong for you. Even when you still cannot offer her a fraction of such a ready, such an always-available affection as this man is giving her.

Even as he thought this he knew that he was making some sort of defence easier for himself by picturing a love that he really knew nothing about. So that he could then say that perhaps this … whatever it was between them … was nowhere as satisfying and joyous as he was painting it. So that he could then justify his hanging around, his shadowy presence, as … what? A fall-back, a reminder of what a real love affair was?

For he knew well enough that she still hadn't eradicated all affection and even desire for him, and she gave no sign that she really wanted to, or was intent on getting the better of it. Of course he was comforted by this extraordinarily durable softness in her, but he knew his comfort was an ignoble thing.

*

'Would you like coffee? Or tea?' she had asked.

'Tea thanks.'

She hesitated, then opened out into a gentle, embarrassed smile. 'I've forgotten how you have it.'

*

Two years previously he had watched at the bedside of a dying friend. The cancer was in the man's brain, his lungs, his bones, but he had always been a very fit man, and the dying was protracted. He lapsed into apparent unconsciousness, but then for days that turned into weeks there seemed to be no further deterioration.

The man's former wife, and his daughters, and a former sister-in-law, and a male friend from long ago who had suddenly reappeared, tended the bedside, and Charlie was occasionally there too. Long after the time when they could speak loudly and slowly close to the dying man's ear and could squeeze his hand, and sometimes feel, or imagine they felt, some tiny pressure of his hand in response, they still looked at him and wondered if he had yet actually gone beyond their reach. They asked one another, there at the bedside, 'Can he hear? Can he take anything in?' In their ignorance they tried to keep sending their messages to him, and his former wife, in particular, offered him her gentle, restrained endearments.

As the days turned over into weeks and there seemed no change in his condition, Charlie noticed a new tack that the watchers seemed to have decided on. They told the dying man, each of them at different times, in their individual voices, that he could let go now, that it was all right, that he didn't have to hang on.

Charlie was bewildered by this. The message was sent so firmly, so unanimously, that he presumed it had the blessing of the palliative care gurus, that it was received wisdom on behaviour towards the dying. But he couldn't bring himself to call out the same words. Was that why the man was still alive? Because, somehow deliberately, even in this state, a man could steel himself against giving up the spirit? That this life behind him could hold such value for him that even in these extremes he would not simply acknowledge that it was all over? Did to die mean a clear-cut decision to shrug the cringing shoulders, give up and drop, and so find peace? But what if he didn't want peace – whatever that meant – what if he was determined to hang on, through all the exhaustion of it, for as long as it was ever in his power, to the memory flashes with their fragments of the exultations and comfort and abiding affections in this one life he had been given? Why, Charlie queried, should someone not yet confronting his own death tell another man to let all that glory go?

Would he hang on himself, the blurred shadows of those he had loved still hovering, his jaws clenched, his eyes shut tight to catch the flickers of his past?

Yet was to let go the final gesture not just of dignity and altruism but also of self-interested efficiency? To leave the living, to extricate yourself from their still honeyed, still bloody lives, to send them happily on without you, so that they could bob away, feeling a new buoyancy in themselves as this weight of a life now past broke free? You let go because it will be best for you – once your mind has moved away from the sharp presence of what you most loved, and eventually comes to rest in oblivion. And because the lives that are readjusting, finding their new entanglements, are better off without the cobwebby clinging of that old. So that the dead are left to bury the dead.

It was a bitter agony, and no one was capable of sharing the grim watches with you. He had no idea what he would do. In the great passion of death, in the great passion of futureless love. But this is what dying is like, he thought, insignificant in its commonness, so unoriginal a suffering, a banality that should be a joke, that didn't merit another word of commentary. Except that it gave every human being a part in a drama that squeezed out each drop of longing and regret and fierce desire and bitter grief that their natures might ever be capable of. Every life tortured out of its pedestrian shape and glorified by this emotional searing.

Twenty Pink Questions

Fabienne Bayet-Charlton

I stand here admiring the bright coral pink of her hot skin while she wallows and frolics in the bath. Her teeth shine so pearly white, in clear clean gums. Her little bottom dimples, legs kicking long into wriggling, pretty, perfect toes. This is my daughter. She hopped into the bath once I had lugged out. The bath's steam evaporates through our ceiling, leaving a damp smell from the cracked tiles freezing on the floor. This is an old house. Stone-cold to the bone during these winter nights so we take advantage of the rationed hot water. Absorb the heat as much as we can before it runs out. This house has been the town's saddlery, tea rooms, general store, deer farm, apple store, cobbler's ... Babies have been born in the lounge room and where Ashlyn's bed now stands. Old folks have died on either side of this whitewashed door and there are those who have tried to spook me with ghostly history. Apart from its inability to retain heat of any kind, the past within the house, settled, I imagine, like powdery perfumed dust, has always been a comfort to me.

I watch my daughter's slippery enjoyment of the warm bubble water while I skip over the ageing folds of my skin, leaving the backs of my knees and inside of my rump damp. I hastily reach for my flannels.

Ashlyn finishes blowing ripples across the soapy surface and asks in her bright voice, 'Mummy, tell me some Aboriginal words.'

'Sorry, possum?'

'Tell me some Aboriginal words,' she repeats flatly, insistent.

'Well ... ' I say, sorting my pyjamas, working out which way is up. 'I don't really know any.'

'But you're Aboriginal ... right?' She wriggles and glides easily within the bathtub.

'Yes ... I am.'

'Teach me some words then.'

'Possum,' I explain, 'I don't know any Aboriginal language.'

Ashlyn puckers her lips and spouts raspberries beneath the water, almost experimentally ... 'Didn't your mum teach you?' she says reproachfully.

'She didn't know the Aboriginal language herself,' I say. I'm pulling on my pyjama top. Where did this all come from?

'Didn't her mummy teach her?' Ashlyn insists.

'Did you talk about Aboriginal languages today at school?' I ask. I'm trying to deflect her by asking questions myself. 'At the excursion?'

'No,' she replies airily, flips over in the bath. Her little pot belly is slicked with soap. The questions continue.

'Your mummy's my nana?' Ashlyn checks.

'Yes. My mum's your nana.'

'And her mum is your nana, right?'

Her voice seems so matter-of-fact for a five-year-old. Only the slight inflection on the end gives it away. I'm looking at her cute little face, her beautiful sea-blue eyes scanning the ceiling. I marvel at her young mind comprehending the connections.

'Why didn't her mum teach her Aboriginal words if she was Aboriginal?' Ashlyn insists, wanting to know. Her lazy floating belies her voice. Quick-fired.

'Because she didn't know.' I sigh. I flick on my knickers, reach for my saggy trackies. Where did all these questions come from? I wonder, but I don't have time to find out.

'Mum, why did the Aboriginals take the children away?'

'Wha–?' A quick intake of breath. I'm stumbling around the bathroom floor hopping into my trousers, trying not to slip.

'The Aboriginals took the children away. The little babies,' she patiently explains.

'Who told you that?'

'No one.' She's still paddling in the luke-warm water.

'Possum, the … Aboriginals didn't take the kids away. You've got that one a bit mixed up there. Aboriginal people had their kids taken away …'

I realise I'm the one using the word 'kids'. My five year old used the word 'children' but she takes on my language.

'Who took the kids away?' she replies. My feet are beginning to freeze on the tiles. I'm frowning. Where's my slippers. I'm trying to think up simple answers.

'The government,' I say. Short. Quick. Flat. I wait for the next question. I'm expecting, 'What's government?' Instead Ashlyn sits up in the bath and accepts this explanation with a sage nod. Does she know who the 'government' is? It seems she does.

'Why did the government take the kids away?'

Oh, where did all this come from? 'Because the kids were a different colour skin from their mums.' I know it's not even the beginning of an explanation. I'm trying to keep things simple, basic, for her to understand.

'Really?' she says, looks at me with her perfect face, ginger-coloured eyebrows, sweet rose lips.

The steam from the bath brings out the V on her forehead. A wide red arrow that points down and peaks between her eyes. It's from when her head was wedged into my pelvis preventing her birth. She had to be pushed back up, then cut out. Her skin blotches red now only when she's hot or upset. I'm watching …

'Like how I'm different from you?' she says.

'Yes, like how you're pink and I'm – more brown. Like how my hair is brown and yours is blonde.'

'Yes?' Her eyes are wide now. With understanding? 'And Nana's *quite* brown, isn't she?' Ashlyn asks.

'Well, yes, compared to you or me. I suppose.'

I'm not really comfortable with all these skin-colour grada-tions. Why can't you keep on being colour-blind? my heart is ask-ing. Just for a little while longer …

'Did they take you away from your mummy?' she asks.

'No.' I find my arms folded across my chest.

'Even though you're Aboriginal?'

'Well, by the time I was a little girl the government had stopped.'

'Stopped taking the babies and kids away?'

'More or less, yes,' I reply lamely. I can't help looking at her little pink nipples while she sits there in our bath. Wondering if they will mature into big brown pennies like mine. Maybe if she has children. In time.

'Did they take my nana away from her mummy?' Ashlyn's taken a step forward.

'Time for you to get out,' I say. 'I'll warm up a towel.'

'Did they?' my girl insists.

'No.'

'Why?' she asks.

Why do I want to cry?

'Because she was darker than her.'

'Darker than your nana? Why?'

You are too young to understand that yet, I want to say but I won't, so I ask again, 'Where did all these questions come from, my Possum-Blossom, hmmm?'

I won't look at her beautiful face now. Possum-Blossom is my nickname for her because she is like a beautiful exotic flower in my life and practically nocturnal. Since the day of her birth I have suffered from permanent sleep deprivation.

'They won't take me away from you. Would they, Mum?'

'No,' I reply. My voice sharper than I wanted.

'I would kick them as hard as I could if they tried,' Ashlyn proclaims. I look at her stick-like arms, her pink chicken legs. The skin on her toes has wrinkled like puckered tissue paper.

'Yes,' I say, 'so would I.'

I grab the fluffiest towel I can find. 'I'll warm this up for you, Poss. I'll just pop it near the fire. Back in one minute,' I say. I grasp the handle and flap the door behind. Ashlyn dives back into the water.

In the space of five minutes my girl has unpicked my heart and left my guts to unravel behind me. I blunder my way to my husband, pass him the towel. How do I begin to find the right answers to her questions? I feel as though I failed something imperceptible. An impossible task. I want to wrap my shell-pink girl in the towel, cuddle her forever, but I can't brave the bathroom again and I can't explain away the past with logic or reason and I can't explain why.

I can hear her singing a little song. It's her own composition: 'Twinkle, twinkle little star, rock-a-bye baby. Up! – above in the sky-y!'

Her high tinkerbell voice floats from the bathroom through the house, mingling with the powder dust of the past, wedged between the cracks of the stonework and the damp rising beneath the floorboards from the tired earth below.

I just wonder at the precious gift I've been given and witness the terrors of history's idiosyncrasies. It doesn't take much to remain vulnerable to fits of government policy. What seems acceptable now may be unforgivable in another decade. It's only luck we are now on the outside of the barbed wire. That's the only logic to this world's chaos. I wonder what scared me most about my daughter's acceptance of my explanation. But then, she said she'd kick at it with all her might. This, above all, is what connects us with the past, the mothers suffering in our present and what makes me cry.

Meanjin

The Good Howard

Tony Birch

A pattern soon set in. For several weeks I had been waking in
the middle of the night. The first time it happened I was sure
for a moment that I had wet the bed – a man of fifty. I looked
over to my wife edged on the other side of the bed, before sitting up and palming the bedsheet and mattress. It was only
when I felt my pyjama top clinging to my back that I realised it
was sweat.

I was aware that I had been dreaming, although I could recall
none of the details. My concern over the dream only increased
my already heightened anxiety. Too embarrassed to confide in
my wife I decided to talk to one of the other managers at the
office. I soon realised this was a mistake. He told me that I should
keep a pen and pad near the bedside, so that when I wake in the
night I will be able to document the details of the dream before
it vanishes.

I tried explaining my predicament. 'But I can't write it down.
As soon as I know that I am awake, the dream, well, it has already
slipped away. There is nothing left to write down. It is gone, all
of it.'

He looked at me suspiciously. 'Well, if it's gone, how do you
know you've been dreaming? You must be worried about something.' He put his feet up on the desk and began to laugh.
'Midlife crisis. That's what it will be. I'd put money on it.' He
stood up and patted me roughly on the shoulder while winking

at me. 'Don't let it get to you. Chat up one of the office girls. A night out on the town, that's what you need. You'll soon get over your worries then.'

I was stuck on one of his comments as I drove home from work that night – worried about something? I would not have thought so, not until he posed the question. But, yes, maybe I am. I must be. I am aware that in the minutes after I have woken from the dream I have an overwhelming sense that something is very wrong, that something catastrophic is about to visit me. I just do not know what it is. And by the next morning, after I have finally drifted back to sleep, only to be shaken by my wife telling me that I will be late for work if I don't get up, I attempt to reassure myself that everything will be fine. It is only a dream, I tell myself.

But things are not fine. They do not get better. They become worse. The sweating and the nightmares, or what I think may be nightmares, continue until I am unable to sleep at all. I become exhausted. But then, strangely, just when I have resigned myself that I need professional help and will need to visit my doctor I sleep right through the night, like a baby, as they say.

When I wake in the morning after a full night's sleep I feel fresh and relaxed. It feels like a good day. Today will be my day, I attempt to convince myself in the shower that morning. The first day of my new habit, of sleeping through the night undisturbed, I tell myself. I have a quick breakfast, grab the car keys, and leave the house, deciding on an early start to the working day.

But the car refuses to turn over. I have a quick look under the bonnet before realising that I had left the lights on the night before. I go back into the house and tell my wife that I am catching the bus. She wants to call the RACV there and then, but I tell her not to worry. There is no hurry. She can ring them during the afternoon. I am taking the bus, I tell her. She looks at me as if I am crazy. She repeats that she can call them for me. But I tell her no. Today it will be the bus.

Rather than walk to the end of the street and along the main road to the bus stop, a ten-minute walk, I cut through the lane behind the house to the nature reserve that follows a creek cutting through the middle of the suburb. I begin my walk along a bicycle path that meanders beneath a line of trees alongside the creek. The occasional jogger and cyclist pass me. It is a beautiful autumn morning, crisp and clear. I feel so happy that I begin to swing my briefcase through the air. I even consider whistling.

When I come to I am lying on my back. I can feel the familiar dampness of my shirt against my skin. I look up, not at the ceiling of my bedroom, but at a dappled blanket of sky. I try sitting up. I can see my briefcase between my legs. I feel dizzy and a little nauseous so I rest my head back on the wet ground and turn on my side as I vomit bile onto the grass.

A fluoro-suited cyclist passes me just as I am clumsily getting to my feet. She brakes, turns an arc off the side of the bike path and comes back to me.

'You OK? Can I help you?'

I look up at her. The woman is young, and pretty. She has straw pigtails protruding from each side of her helmet. She looks like a Viking. Viking Woman. I feel as if I am a little drunk. I want to laugh at her and tell her she looks silly. But I don't, because I realise that I am the one who must look silly as I have spit and vomit dribbling down my chin, the knees of my pants are covered in mud, and although I have not noticed it yet, I have damp autumn leaves stuck to the back of my suit jacket.

'Thank you, but I'm fine. I just tripped over on that tree branch, there.'

I search around on the ground, attempting to locate something, anything that may have been the cause of my fall. Her eyes follow mine, combing the ground with me.

She asks me again if I am all right before remounting the saddle, locking her plastic slippers into the pedals and taking off. I brush myself down as best I can, retrieve my briefcase and decide that although I am still a little unsteady on my feet I will continue to the bus stop. I have not taken more than a couple of steps before I feel a second spell of giddiness and then lucidly recall my mysterious dream for the first time.

In the dream I am in my house, which, although eerily familiar, is not my house. I am running from room to room, becoming increasingly frantic as I open and shut each door. I get to the end of a long hallway, where I find an open doorway. I am welcomed into the room by a soft yellow light.

As I step through the doorway I see my mother standing in front of me. She is looking just as she did in the weeks before her death. She is wearing that floral housecoat that became her uniform: the one we teased her about because she was never out of it in the last months of her life.

The room she is standing in is not a room as such, but a long corridor vanishing into the distance. The walls of the corridor are lined with shelving from floor to ceiling. And cluttered along the shelves are the hundreds, if not thousands, of cheap ornaments my mother collected during her lifetime.

I look at my mother with fear, certain that I have seen a ghost. I then see myself, or my reflection at least, in an etched glass mirror on a shelf behind her left shoulder. But it is not the image of a fifty-year-old man I see. In the mirror I am a boy of ten again, with the head of blond hair and the soft unmarked face I wore back then.

I look away from the mirror and back to my mother. She has transformed herself. She is no longer a hunched 85-year-old housebound pensioner, but a vivacious thirty-something woman. I look down and see that she is wearing a pair of red dancing shoes that she had favoured as a younger woman.

As I continue to the bus stop I replay the dream again and again, desperately wanting to make sense of it. I make a mental note that I will write down the details of the dream as soon as I am on the bus. While standing on the bus stop, looking down at my watch and then up at the timetable attached to the bus shelter, I hear a voice behind me.

'The 8.05. The 8.05. He is two minutes late. He always is. He will he here in … in around ninety seconds.'

I turn around. I see a man, maybe a little younger than myself, sitting on the red-brick front fence of a house. He has one of those old-fashioned haircuts that seem to have come out of the Great Depression; a razor-sharp part down the centre of his head, a fringe flopping onto his forehead, with a shaved square back and sides. His clothing looks as if it comes from a similar age, although it is not aged or worn. He is wearing a checked shirt, buttoned to the neck, under a brown hand-knitted cardigan with wooden buttons, grey pants and a pair of brown leather shoes, freshly polished.

He points to the timetable. 'The 8.05, it will be here in,' he looks down at his own watch, 'in sixty seconds.'

I do not answer him and walk to the other end of the bus shelter.

He is correct about the delayed bus. Before a minute has passed it turns into the street and pulls into the kerb.

My travelling companion motions me onto the bus in front of him. I look for an empty seat, at a safe distance from both the elderly passengers huddled together at the front of the bus and a group of raucous schoolkids bouncing across the back seat.

As I search for a seat I can sense his presence. As he walks down the aisle behind me several passengers greet him.

'Good morning, Howard.'

'How are you today, Howard?'

'Lovely morning, isn't it, Howard?'

I take my seat. Although there are several empty seats on the bus he sits down next to me. He looks around and waves to people on the bus before turning to me, smiling and offering his hand.

'Good morning, I am Howard.'

I look down at his open hand before tentatively offering my own, although I do not give my name away. Howard looks closely at my face. 'You don't catch the bus, this bus. The 8.05. You don't catch the 8.05. What bus do you catch?'

I look ahead and answer without turning to him. 'No, I do not catch the bus. Never.'

He leans across the seat and picks something from the shoulder of my jacket. I move away with a slight jump. He shows me the leaf of a liquid amber. As he swirls the leaf between his fingertips the light picks up its bruised colours.

I ignore Howard and turn away. I do not want to talk to him, or anyone else on the bus. I open my briefcase, take out a client file, close the case and put the file on top. I take my fountain pen from my suit coat pocket and try concentrating on the paperwork. It is pointless, as I continue to worry over the dream, quizzing myself as to what it may mean. I put the file away and take my notepad from the briefcase and begin writing.

Howard leaves me to myself for several bus stops. We pull in alongside the railway station. The noisy schoolkids from the back seat and a few other passengers get off the bus. I pray that Howard will be leaving also. But he doesn't. He appears to have settled in next to me. Some of the remaining passengers begin pointing to Howard and calling out to him.

'That's not you, Howard. You're the good Howard. That's not you, over there.'

I look up. They are all smiling at Howard, even the bus driver. He smiles back at them. He then nudges my arm and points to something outside the window of the bus. 'That's not me. I am the good Howard.'

I look out of the window but have no idea what he is talking about.

He points again. 'Look, that's not me. I'm the good Howard.'

I finally realise what he is referring to. It is a piece of graffiti scrawled on the side wall of the railway station – HOWARD LIED – AND SOLD OUT ON REFUGEES.

I don't get it. Not at first, at least. But when I do I laugh, to myself mostly, but just loud enough so that 'the good Howard' hears me. He leans across and smiles.

As we are about to take off the railway gates come down so that the train can pass. Several minutes after the train has left the station the gates have not lifted. The bells continue to ring. The gates are stuck. I rest my chin on my hand, place my forehead against the window and drift off for a moment. I feel myself falling back into the dream again, so I sit upright, wanting desperately to keep myself awake.

Howard leans across from his seat. 'Are you tired? You look tired.'

I try ignoring him but he won't be put off.

'You have to get your eight hours, your eight hours. Do you get your eight hours? You look tired.'

I look across at Howard, finally realising that I am stuck with him.

'No … Howard … I don't usually get my eight hours. I did last

night, funnily enough, but most of the time, no, I don't get a
great night's sleep.'

He rocks back and forward in his seat a couple of times. 'I do.
Eight hours. Nine hours. Ten hours. Why don't you get yours?'

I look down at the notes that I have been scribbling on my
pad. I look at Howard. He is patiently waiting for an answer from
me. 'It's nothing. Just these dreams. I have dreams. They wake
me sometimes.'

He becomes inquisitive. 'Dreams? You have dreams? What are
your dreams? Tell me about them.'

I look at him, this total stranger, who is probably a little strange
as well. I peer out of the bus to the graffiti, and then back at
Howard. The traffic is not moving. The driver gets on the microphone and suggests that the passengers may like to get off and
take a detour via the next train. A few more passengers leave the
bus. I cannot follow them, as I have to go across town. So I stay.
And so does Howard, who continues to look at me, waiting for
my response.

As I recount the details of the dream Howard appears to
hang on every word. When I have finished telling him about
the dream I feel that my story is unfinished, that I need to say
something more, although I am not sure what it is. I shrug my
shoulders. 'I don't know what it means. One of my work col-
leagues, he tells me that dreams need to be interpreted. If we
learn to understand our dreams, we come to understand ourselves. But I cannot understand much of my dream. Not just yet,
anyway.'

Howard looks straight ahead without saying a word. I look
down at the notepad on top of my briefcase while thinking about
my mother. I feel reasonably certain that the dream must have
something to do with her death. On the day of her funeral I
could not stop crying. I was surprised by my reaction, although
I should not have been. After all, this was my mother's death. But
in the weeks before it was all over, when she had been quite ill
and in pain, I had rationalised that she had lived a relatively
good and long life, as they say. And that her death would bring
her peace, as they also say.

As I had stood at the graveside my crying had become more
audible. I looked around at the other mourners, a little embar-

rassed, and covered my mouth with the back of my hand. My wife put an arm around my waist, attempting to console me. 'It's OK, it's OK.'

A few days later she commented again that it was all right to cry, before reminding me, 'You used to cry all the time when we were younger: at the movies, when Elsie had her paw caught in that rat trap down the back. You even cried when your football team lost that final by a point. Remember that? You were like a big kid.'

But I could not remember.

Howard pulls at my sleeve to get my attention.

'Tell me about the end again, the end of the dream.'

'The end?'

'About your mother, and the red shoes.'

I tell him again, about seeing myself in the mirror as a child, and then looking at my mother, suddenly much younger, all dressed up for a night on the boards.

Howard screws his face up while listening again to the end of my story. He looks down at his watch before replying to me. 'Your dream, I think it is about dancing. Your mum, she liked dancing?'

My mother loved dancing, when she was younger, at least. She and my father would go to the '50/50' dance every Sunday night at the Brunswick Town Hall. As I sat on the bus I could suddenly see them in the front room of my childhood home, ready to go out for the night. Him in black suit with his hair slicked back, my mother wearing those shoes.

Howard interrupts me. 'It's the dancing. I think you need to go dancing.'

I look across to Howard in bemusement, about to tell him that I have never been dancing, that I can't dance, when he suddenly jumps up from his seat and walks to the front of the bus. The driver opens the door and Howard moves to the lower step. He turns around and waves to the other passengers and then at me.

As he leaves the bus the few remaining passengers call out to him, 'Goodbye, Howard, see you tomorrow morning.'

Howard walks to the other side of the road and stands alongside the graffiti wall. The boom gates lift, which causes the elderly passengers at the front of the bus to cheer in childlike unison. As we take off I look over at Good Howard. He waves.

The following weekend I am down in the back garden turning over the compost. My wife is up in the kitchen going through the papers. I can hear music drifting onto the patio but cannot recognise what is playing. When I have finished my work I put the shovel and pick in the shed and walk up to the house, thinking about a cup of tea. I leave my boots and socks at the backdoor before opening it and walking into the kitchen. My wife is at the sink rinsing a wineglass.

I am also greeted by the voice of Ella Fitzgerald belting out her version of 'Mack the Knife'. As I walk through the kitchen, on my way to the bathroom to wash my hands, my wife looks over her shoulder and smiles at me. I stop for a moment and look down at her hips as they sway with Ella. In the bathroom I stare at my unshaven and wrinkled face as the warm water and soap caress my hands. As I look down into the ivory sink and inspect my hand I realise that my bare feet have been shuffling an awkward rhythm across the floor tiles.

Heat

Jet Lag

Catherine Ford

Martha Solburn, an American woman, plump and unaccustomed to vacations, eased herself out of a taxi into the late-August morning. Her companion, Stewart Winter, adjusted the seat of his jeans and followed, wheeling a new Samsonite suitcase.

'I'd forgotten about all this,' she said, eyeing the crowds on the way to the airline counters.

'The security measures?'

'No, the *thrill* of leaving New York.'

'*Frisson*,' he corrected, creaking open their passports. 'Like it or not, I think we ought to get practising.'

They had holidayed in Europe, separately, throughout their youth. Martha had spent entire childhood summers holed up in Parisian hotels with sybaritic parents, but this was their first visit as a couple. The prospect of travel now generated in her the same kind of dry-mouthed alarm as the news from her dentist six months ago that she needed major bridge work, but she rallied, planting her sunglasses, tiara-style, on her head. 'It's great, isn't it,' she said, 'that we're still capable of impetuousness.'

Martha managed a small gardening business, conducted from a set of suites in a Manhattan office tower, and her busiest time was spring. She schlepped around the boroughs all year long investigating possibilities for green spaces wherever she was asked – dingy rear courtyards of cramped schools, the immaculate balconies of starchy widows on the East Side, sidewalk cafés needing buffers from traffic. By late summer, though, business usually fell off. People returning from vacations had neither the money nor the inclination to spend on *trompe l'oeil* or water features and it was during the height of the summer of 2004, while flicking through her tomes on foreign landscapes, that she was seized by the desire to buy a ticket to France, take Stewart, hire a car and meander through the hazy and salubrious countryside of Burgundy.

'Why France?' Stewart argued. 'What about Ireland?'

Martha frowned. 'What about it?'

A lean, twitchy man, Stewart was an out-of-towner who had lived the whole of his adult life in lower Manhattan. He was expert in the construction of complex models for large architectural practices but his hobby was food. He considered himself something of a gourmand, scouring Manhattan on weekends for exotic supermarkets selling outlandish foodstuffs and small out-of-the-way cafés serving authentic artisanal cuisine.

'OK,' he conceded, 'France, then.'

'France will be free of patriotism,' Martha said, 'at least this kind, with flags stuck on every damn thing and people going on and on with their moronic convictions.'

Recently her own bouts of hysteria, produced in the main she thought by unhealthy levels of exposure to George Bush Jnr and friends, were beginning to feel like a chronic incurable illness and she feared them. She yearned for France's charms, its dense breads and jangly wines, its contrary people talking over each other in shops. She wanted to flee the streets of mid-town Manhattan, which she knew no amount of greening could ever cure of heartlessness.

So, after arranging for their work to be looked after for the first week of September, they found themselves at Newark, cooling their heels before a dawn flight to Paris, eating a breakfast snack of pancakes and syrup with side orders of papaya salad and abominable coffee. 'Ireland would have depressed us,' she told Stewart as their plane angled into a cheerful sky and droned eastwards, 'I'm certain of it.' But he didn't hear her. He gazed, enthralled, at a miniature Throgs Neck Bridge in the distance – he had once built one exactly that size for a client – and he was anticipating a glimpse of Ground Zero.

He twisted in his seat searching for Manhattan's tip, wanting a new view of it, another perspective, a perspective he had found immensely difficult to conjure in his imagination. It came into sight and he pulled Martha towards the window and they stared in silence. The island slipped away beneath them and she closed her eyes and waited for the impressions to fade. Ever since the attacks she had practised an amateurish meditation – a sequence of loving declarations to herself – to escape from anguish as it loomed. It took some discipline to be blind, she discovered, to shield oneself from horror.

She wondered if it wasn't the general depressive climate since the planes hit the towers that had brought about so much fresh perturbation in her, or whether it wasn't something more personal, the onset of menopause perhaps, a too-small living space, thinning hair. At times it was impossible to know what the causes of anguish were now that there was so much of it around.

After they arrived at Roissy and found the hire-car depot, where a charming man who spoke good English gave them their keys and papers, they drove towards the city and along the *périphérique* in their new Citroën hatch-back Picasso, glimpsing the sugar-coated spires of Sacré Coeur and the Eiffel Tower.

'A crazy Meccano prop,' Martha suggested, and then, down-playing just how deeply the tower moved her, added, 'the kind of thing your spoilt little nephew might try to screw together in his bedroom.'

'The little guy has class, you have to admit.'

'The whole place,' she continued, staring absently over the city's rooftops, 'looks kind of *pellucid*.'

The view made her heart beat fast, but she shook herself down. No more cities, she told herself, not even this little baby. They needed peace and pinot noir. Onward.

Their first night was spent in a small *chambre d'hôte* hidden well away from the autoroute among acres of vineyards. They were shown a room on the second floor by a Madame Bernier who wore a calico apron around her large middle and her hair cropped close. Martha pondered her appearance, wondering if she was undergoing treatment for cancer or merely keeping things nice and simple, *à la* Gertrude Stein.

She practised saying '*merci*' two or three times for the benefit of the *châtelaine* as she left them, and then she hugged and kissed Stewart with a weariness shot through with the charge of novelty. It wasn't every day she kissed someone under a chandelier the size of a mature pear tree.

When she said she was '*totally crevée*' and was climbing into bed for a nap, Stewart hesitated, thinking he should join her, but he crossed instead to the room's high green shutters and opened them, sending obscene clanking and shrieking noises out into the yard. 'For the love of God,' he muttered, 'would a little oil be asking too much?'

He checked on the furniture in the room. A heavy brocade cloth draped over a table in a corner, three innocuous little Corot prints hanging crooked on a wall. He ran his fingers through the tasselled fringe of a lampshade. 'I'm stepping out for a look around,' he told her. 'Sleep it off, baby doll. I'll be back in a while.'

It was nearly seven in the evening. Madame Bernier had told them they would need to drive into the nearest village for dinner, but before that he wanted to wander and he went down the stairs two at a time, crossed the gravel car park and headed into the cool woods.

He followed a path which led him towards a stream that gurgled sweetly. There were birds high up in the trees singing ecstatic melodies, looping phrases with complex time signatures, he noted, part Chopin nocturne, part Neil Diamond show tune, and amid the tree trunks he saw liquid shafts of evening light shining pinkly on their pristine bark. He stopped in his tracks. The garden took his breath away.

The scene inexplicably brought to mind his and Martha's fish tank at home, the way it looked so other-worldly and seductive in the hour of his return from work and which often prompted in him a longing to shrink, a loose anti-Darwinian fantasy, so that he too could practise floppy tumble-turns against the mush-green walls of a tank.

How like New York State's wooded pastures, he thought, and yet different. He turned to look at the farmhouse, partially hidden by foliage now, and saw a light come on in a window on the upper floor. He was moved by the building's pale stone and green shutters, the dreamy salutation it extended. He saw the yellow lamp-light drip its mournful wax down the farmhouse walls and mused that if there had been a painter who might have understood the luxuriant paranoia of jet lag it surely would have been Magritte.

Such a profound moment, the first evening in another country when the reality of change sank in. One minute he'd weighed a ton in New York, the next he was buoyant in Burgundy. He continued along the path sniffing the air, ripe with the unfamiliar mustiness of grapevines, he supposed, and dust.

And as he walked over the uneven ground, stumbling here and there, a struggle started up in his thoughts. His mind's voice jabbered away as it often did when he was unsettled, it picked up on the details of his day and worried them, transforming them. *Your apartment is now dark and empty*, the peremptory voice said. *You won't really understand what French people say to you. You and Martha are all alone here. Martha is looking for someone to love.*

A shiver ran down his arms. He kept on the path until he came to the property's high iron gates that guarded the farmhouse entrance. He peered through their elegant grey grillework at the deep and even rows of the grapevines on the other side of the road.

He felt self-conscious standing there, as if someone, perhaps Madame Bernier and her family or perhaps Martha, was watching him from behind the curtains of her room. With an effort he composed himself as an actor might on returning to a stage after a break in the wings.

Perhaps becoming a tourist, looking at things anew, peering at this and that, exaggerated a suspicion of someone spying on him from a distance. He tilted his head to one side, let a quizzical smile elasticise his lips.

As he turned to go back to their room he looked up at what he believed was their window and saw a figure pull away from it, as if the person inside had been caught spying. Was it Martha?

It dawned on him while crunching heavily over the gravel towards the building's impressive oak doors that he didn't understand, with any clarity, what was bothering Martha. She seemed to be the only one of their social circle who argued, at every opportunity, that she had little to lose by breaking free of New York, now more insular and ghetto-ised, she said, now even less relevant, than what she perceived to be the 'real world' she read about in newspapers. Martha had taken to telling Stewart and anyone else who would listen that 'if she could leave permanently she would' – it seemed to be her theme, post 9/11 – and Stewart was only just beginning to sense that she might be serious.

Was she, when she threatened with so much passion to leave, speaking metaphorically? Did she intend to walk away from something about an American identity, or from the place they lived in, or from *him*?

He parked the Picasso on the village edge and locked it with the magician's gesture – pointing the key, casting a spell – that he loved, and, holding Martha's hand, walked with her down the tiny town's main street.

None of the shops – a newsagency, a bakery, a down-at-heel chemist – was open. The shops' interiors were dimly lit and they peered in at each window anticipating something authentically French displayed there. Madame Bernier had instructed them to walk towards the main square in the town of St Gengoux-le-National and there, she told them, they would find a small café serving pizzas. In due course, they stumbled on a square that housed a bar which was still open and a building, outside which was a raised wooden platform where two couples sat rather stiffly at tables.

The village was still and calm except for the sound of men talking inside the bar. Martha and Stewart took a table, ordered a local wine and two pizzas.

'I was hoping for snails,' she told him, 'or bourguignon.' She shrugged. 'I guess this way we get Naples thrown in for free.'

'Were you asleep when I was out earlier?' Stewart asked.

'I think I dozed,' she said, 'although I'm very excited.'

They sipped their wine, Martha gazing around her with rapturous respect.

'Isn't it deliciously strange,' she said, 'to feel that drag on the mind? We could be down on Mulberry Street, at Chez George or some place, but we're actually in Europe, baby. We're really here.'

'Maybe we should have caught the subway down town and pretended,' he joked, settling the strands of his errant fringe. 'Would have saved ourselves a couple of thou'.'

She leaned in to him. 'We can try and lose ourselves here. I need to, don't you? I need to wash the last few years off me.'

'Better *fermez la bouche* then,' he said.

'My French is OK.' He wasn't going to poke holes in that.

'We look American. They get us even before we open up.'

She frowned, pensive. 'Is it the extra pounds?'

'I believe it's the slob factor.'

'Speak for yourself, buster.'

'Well, let's be real. We want people to love us no matter what the hell we do or look like. Usually they oblige.'

'How come they do look so good?' She sized up the other couples waiting for food, but they were Scandinavian campers, she felt, close relations in their synthetic subfusc jackets and wilderness sandals. 'We look eccentric, which has its own charm, but we're definitely amateurs at that come-hither-and-fuck-off mode the French do.' She considered this for a moment and felt desultory resentment stir.

'I like the French style,' he said. 'Who doesn't? But to attempt it ourselves?'

He knew these were trite sentiments and yet they sounded perfectly fresh and original waiting for pizza at dusk in a darkening square in France. It was also true that conversing with his beloved without the crutch of TV and newspapers at hand, without the easy escape to the kitchen for a drink or the toilet for complete solitude, produced tension in him. A holiday, minus gadgets, would force a whole new level of sociability, one he feared was beyond him now.

Martha leant forward with a thought. 'Hey, OK, here's an idea. Do I have your total and undivided attention?' She saw his eyes flicker and tighten. 'Why don't we attempt it while we're here?'

'Attempt what?'

'To sex things up a little.'

'But I thought this was a holiday.'

'So? It couldn't hurt us, could it?'

'What?' He lowered his voice, looked around to see if the other couples were comprehending. 'We impress each other, or we go looking elsewhere?'

'You put your mind to pleasing *me*, and I, you.' She scowled at him.

'Oh, I see where this is headed. This involves boutique shopping, right?'

'Maybe we could shop around for a new lease on life.'

'That wasn't on the itinerary.'

'True, but so?'

He was unsure whether they were still in a jokey discourse or not.

'What will you do for me then? Short dresses?' He folded his arms. 'High heels?'

She let out an ironic laugh. 'Stilettos? Are you kidding? Have you seen the amounts of gravel they have in this country?' Her eyes swept the periphery of the square. 'Anyway, we have a lot of châteaux to get through.'

'The French handle gravel.'

'I didn't bring heels.'

'We'll get you some in the next town we come to. *Touché*, as they say in Marseille,' he said.

She shook her head, sniggering. 'OK, sucker.' She lifted her wineglass with a pitying smirk. 'You're on.'

After tiptoeing, slightly drunk, up the stairs to their room, Martha and Stewart lay under the velvet canopy of their enormous bed and touched each other as they hadn't done in months. Martha grasped Stewart's cock and tugged on it lightly until it swelled and then, in a shuddering spasm of erotic tension, seized it as if she'd mistaken it for an arm in the dark.

'For Christ's sake, you'll break it in two,' he yelped. 'Then you'll really be sorry.'

She felt utterly discombobulated with wine and jet lag. 'You mean they don't grow back?' Her voice sounded younger and less fretful in a room heavy with velvet.

'Shh, turn around.' He brushed her breasts as she did. 'Lie back,' he murmured. 'Think of England.'

'That's almost funny,' she said, 'but, really, tell me ...' She had lost her bearings. She had drunk too much. 'Where in hell are we again?'

After breakfast at Madame Bernier's table, they packed their car and drove towards Cormatin through a landscape that made Martha's eyes strain with wonder and envy. Did the locals she spied hopping in and out of their lord-of-the-manor SUVs appreciate their dumb luck? Did they look up every day and give thanks for the inexplicable randomness of fortune and fate?

'I'm sorry you have to drive,' she said, 'that you can't be a passenger through this heavenly countryside.'

Stewart checked for pushy drivers in his side mirror. 'Make it up to me later. You'll have to wear three-inch heels for a week to break even!'

'Oh, that whole thing.' She'd hoped it had slipped his mind. Waking up in the *douceur* of the morning she knew she had left America to cleanse her soul, to ease an amorphous grief that threatened to break from its hiding place in her heart. The idea of trumped-up bedroom athletics wearied her in the extreme.

'I think ...' she started, but he interrupted.

'I agree with you,' he said. 'I was thinking about it in the shower this morning. You are so right. We're taking each other for granted. Let's go all out while we're here, draw on the French *savoir-vivre*, re-energise things a little.'

He threw the car down a gear and swung out to overtake a tractor trailing hay. 'Let's liberate ourselves. You be that gorgeous *femme fatale*, Jeanne Moreau, I'll be that guy ... you know, swathed in cashmere, dark brow, libidinous. What's his name? In all the Truffaut films.'

'Depardieu?' It was the only name that came to her.

'No! My God. Better looking than that.'

For years she had wanted Stewart to take a mature approach to their relationship, put aside the jocularity he used on the subject of their *related-ness*, but the stresses and strains of their relationship had passed through him as though his core were a filter of lightly packed sand. Dissuading him from this new earnestness would be foolish, counterproductive.

'I thought you would have forgotten.'

'No way. It stayed with me all night.' His profile, when she

looked over, seemed newly etched. 'I dreamt we were the hap-
piest pair, radiant! And we flew along, wearing these sensa-
tional outfits, delirious, barely touching the ground beneath
our winged feet.'

'Oh.' She sighed. 'Really?'

'Speaking of feet,' he said. 'Let's call in to the next town and
look for clothes and shoes.' She stared non-committally out the
window at a distant château.

'Winged feet?' she said. 'I'm going to be a fucking cripple by
the time we get home.'

'Hell, we're cripples already,' he said. 'The worst has already
happened. It's all up from here.' He lowered his foot on the
pedal and made the car roar. He grinned through the windscreen, seized by a freakish optimism. 'Let's just hope they stock
American sizes.'

They parked in the centre of Mâcon and wandered until they
came to the clothing boutiques clumped together on a busy
street. With an anxiety she couldn't quite name, Martha hesitated. 'I guess if we're going to do this,' she told Stewart, 'we
should do it properly.'

They slowed down outside Christian Dior, Martha peering in
at the candy-cane opulence of the place. She shook her head.
'*Désolée*. No can do.'

They wandered on and fronted the Prada boutique, the
lonely province, it seemed, of just one person, a beautiful young
woman behind the counter who was so absorbed in a heated
phone conversation, a series of spiky exclamations curtailed
into whispers, that she seemed not to notice them when they
entered.

Martha pricked her ears and listened in as she walked along
the racks of clothing with Stewart, who parted the pieces here
and there.

'*Lui? Mais non!*' the girl hissed, her tone seriously aggrieved.
'*Tu es folle, ou quoi?*'

'You know, twenty years ago I might have handled this garb,'
Martha mumbled to Stewart, 'but I'm too earnest, not to mention too fat, for this, this … iconoclasm or whatever it is these
taupe shifts are meant to mean.'

Stewart looked around bewildered. 'My God, is this stuff

couture? Since when have women been dressing like adjutants for the Third Reich?'

'Shh. She probably speaks English.'

They wandered about making to leave, yet Martha, curious about the girl's phone call, hesitated, pretending to be interested in a coat.

'To be totally frank?' Stewart announced loudly. 'I don't think I'm excited by this. And have you seen the prices? Who buys this stuff now that the Japanese are out of the picture?'

Martha hushed him. 'I'm trying to listen in. Someone's pressuring that girl on the phone, trying to make her commit to something she wants nothing of.'

Stewart looked over at the tiny woman with the creamy brow. They watched her turn to a mirror behind her and stare hard at her reflection.

'*Bon, OK, on s'est bien amusé à Ibiza, mais ça ne suffit pas.*' She bent towards the mirror and ruffled her fringe. '*Peut-être bien qu'il m'aime mais je ne vais pas me marier à quelqu'un qui ne me comprend pas.*'

'What's she saying?' he asked.

Martha began to translate and as she did the girl's words stirred something in her.

'The man she's seeing loves her. They had a nice little holiday together in Spain over the summer, and she likes him, maybe even fancies him. He'll do anything for her. But the problem is she doesn't really give a damn. She's unhappy, generally and perhaps even very, very specifically, because the man really doesn't understand her.'

Stewart's stomach rumbled loudly. He cast a look at the young woman. 'What's to understand?' he said. 'She doesn't look so complicated.'

Martha went on in an absent tone, but she was involved and provoked. 'Maybe he's just too simple for her. Maybe he's just right and a great guy. But she's deluding herself if she thinks a man's going to get her, deep down. Maybe he'll love her in his own sweet uncomplicated way. Sex, sex, sex. A comfortable home. Shared nights of televised sport. But what she's asking for is intimacy with him. She doesn't know it now, of course, but she's never going to get that with a man.'

'Fuck you,' he said, casually.

'Well, yeah, but isn't that the truth?'

'I think I understand you,' he said. 'Christ, the time I've spent listening I should've got you by now.'

'Well, then, why are we so lonely? *All of us?*' she asked, her tongue lobbing safely on the collective pronoun.

'We. You and me?' He turned to face her. 'Or women in general?' But he didn't wait for an answer, he sped on. 'Because you cultivate your "loneliness", that's why, like some precious goddamn house-plant that needs bouts of misery and deprivation to sprout. You thrive on being lonely and disappointed. It's your staple. A way of existing,' he said, finding, to his surprise, that he *had* theories on the subject. 'You may be lonely, Martha, but not necessarily because of me.'

They stared at each other for a moment and then with the friction generated between them they propelled themselves quickly from the boutique onto the pavement where they stood about awkwardly, facing into a breeze which blew fragrant with warm brioches and coffee.

'I do not think we're going to find what we need here,' Martha said, and she briskly moved on.

Stewart walked after her, hotly contemplating how open-ended amounts of time spent with Martha always complicated rather than crystallised his feelings for her.

He caught up with her under a plane tree and announced he was hungry. Unnerved by what had passed between them, they glanced around, hoping a restaurant might materialise in their sights. Instead an oversized photograph of Uma Thurman, immaculate in a white fur, eyes the shade of summer icebergs, challenged them from the windows of a Louis Vuitton boutique.

'You think I'm chronically self-involved and disaffected?' Martha shot at Stewart. 'Take a look at *that.*'

He looked at Thurman. 'Uma?' He suddenly found something very funny. 'Good ol' Uma, bristling with her weapons of mass seduction. If only we'd had the brains to hit old Saddam with that!'

Martha turned her back on Stewart. 'I need to eat,' she said, huffily. 'I need a three-course meal and a glass of burgundy as a matter of urgency.'

'We were asking for trouble back there.' Stewart settled himself across from Martha on an old leather banquette in the Brasserie Saint Pierre. They peered at menus. 'All we needed was a nice pair of heels.'

'Heels aren't going to fix a thing!' She glared at him with a glittering contempt. Her beautiful plans for their peaceful little sojourn were unravelling, and all over some *psycho-politico-sexual* crisis she herself had triggered.

'But,' he said, 'I thought we were just having some fun, tweaking at things between us, playing some games.' He stared down at the tabletop.

'You think a pair of shoes is going to solve this? Our great grief, our sorrow?'

'Well, no, I was just thinking you were right when you implied we should be having more fun with each other.'

'That girl in the shop,' she said. 'Daring to say what every woman fears and never mentions.'

'You think I don't understand you?'

'How can you understand when you never listen?'

'But I listen!' he objected. 'How I listen.'

'Well, you listen perhaps, but you don't hear me.'

'What is it I must hear?'

'Deep interior *things*,' she started hesitantly.

'Things.'

'Fear. A well of sorrow.'

'But we live a good life, in a decent rent-controlled apartment, in a prosperous city. We want for nothing. OK, we've taken a hit, and we live in a confused and fucked-up country. Our president is a retard. But it's not all bad.'

'It's all these things, and more. Don't you see?'

He smiled. 'You're a nut-case,' he said with affection.

'No,' she said. 'I just need to be as candid with you and with the world as that courageous young woman in the boutique.'

He ignored this. 'Let's have some late-summer fun,' he pleaded. He bent forward over the table, his eyes moist and entreating. 'Mart, *je t'aime*, baby. I'd do anything for you. Isn't this something?'

She reddened. 'I don't know,' she confessed. How he turned it on when the crunch came. She didn't want episodic backflips, she wanted, well, *what, what, what*? 'The truth is,' she confessed to him, 'I'm not sure what I want from you.'

He was lost with her moods, her pitches and slides into melancholia and something else, something hysterical.

He ordered a bottle of Pommard without even looking at the wine list. '*Nous avons besoin de manger, aussi,*' he told the waiter.

'I thought we were just having some fun together,' he said to her quietly. He wondered if she wasn't working around to a confession. He wondered if she wasn't going to tell him their life together was over and that he would have to move out.

They watched the waiter uncork the bottle and pour. Stewart knew this much for certain: they would not be drinking a wine as good as this every day of their lives. They would not even be drinking one every day of their vacation.

They ordered food and Stewart raised his glass. 'Well, here goes,' he said. 'I propose, with this magnificent glass of wine, we drink to mutual understanding,' he ventured, 'that overlooked yet critical little matter. What do you say? Let's drink to tolerance and wisdom, to *fun.*'

Martha's mouth quivered.

'You're tired,' he told her. 'What you're feeling is jet lag. I feel a little crazy with it myself. The shoes, the dressing up, let's forget it until we can get a handle on the time difference.'

'I confess I am feeling a little unhinged. I didn't expect to feel so alien here.'

'It's all new,' he admitted. 'We are aliens here.'

A holiday, once you actually left home, was a significantly different experience to the one planned for – another reason he usually avoided taking them. In light of all they'd recently witnessed, he thought it a wonder they'd left home at all.

They drank some wine. He watched Martha's tongue run over her empurpled lips.

'Here's to our goldfish,' Stewart said, 'waiting patiently in the dark for our triumphal return! We'll eat and drink,' he told her, as though recalling an itinerary for an excursion, 'and then we'll visit the château at Cormatin. What do you say?'

His voice sounded a little over-emphatic, but their equilibrium as a couple depended, he felt, on the execution of the afternoon's plan. 'We'll drive slowly back to Cormatin and buy tickets for the tour. We'll gape at the faded elaborateness of the place, and contemplate how depleted life has become.' He gazed outside at the lunchtime traffic.

He would try to keep apace with her when she needed him, keep her company.

'They make a good cheese at Cormatin,' she offered quietly. 'I read about it in the guide. They sell it to tourists wrapped up in vine leaves.' She began to brighten.

'Apparently they've set up this neat little *crèmerie* in the grounds of the château. Hey, let's buy some. I adore a good goat's cheese, don't you? We'll take it on a picnic tomorrow.'

Goats. Cheese. Château merchandise. A picnic. She was back again, returned from the brink, and so was the waiter with their food.

'*Alors* ...' he said, looking down at them with impatience, Stewart thought, and a humorous thought forming in his head. He placed the plates of food before them. 'I hope you enjoy your lunch,' he said, his English pronunciation so good they were startled. He poured a little more wine into their glasses and stepped back from their table with a small bow and a smile.

'Have a nice day!'

Monthly

Mattress Sale

David J. Kramer

I took up dog sitting because it seemed an easy way to make money while I looked for a proper job. My first client brought over a small, black Jack Russell terrier in heat. It darted into the apartment, zipping around my rug in a white pair of underpants. I discovered they were special dog underpants, designed to hold an ordinary Tampax pad. I had no idea female dogs menstruated just like women, but I acted professionally and didn't ask questions.

I stopped changing the pad when the splotches grew fainter, but I had quit too early. I woke up in the morning, the dog curled at my feet, a smattering of small brown shapes on my pillow. I lifted my head and surveyed the bed. They were all over the sheets: some big, some small, like countries in an atlas. The dog watched me, its ears pricked up. When I pulled the sheets off I saw the blood had permeated its way to the mattress. I scrubbed at the stains with a bar of soap and tea towel and then flipped the mattress and tried to forget about them.

Now I was leaving Sydney and selling the bed, my most expensive possession. A woman named Margaret had responded to my Internet classifieds posting and told me she'd be over to see the bed in an hour. I was having a second shot at the stains with the rough side of a dish-cleaning sponge. I managed to fade them but Margaret rang the doorbell early.

Standing in the hallway's fluorescent light was a skinny middle-aged woman with deep wrinkles in the corners of her eyes. She wore red lipstick that looked odd with her crushed-pink tank-top, and tights that didn't cling to her twiggy legs. We introduced ourselves and I shook her hand, which was soft and bony as a cat's paw, but with a surprisingly firm grip. Sweating from the scrubbing, I took her through the living room.

'That's the bed,' I said, pointing at it.

She took her handbag off her shoulder, placed it on my desk, then sat on the mattress and bounced a couple of times. She slid her jogging shoes off with her feet and swung her legs over, spreading her arms and legs, closing her eyes. My room was small, not much bigger than the bed, and I was standing right over her. She lay still for a good minute. I thought she might want some privacy so I stood outside my doorway and looked out the window for a while. When I poked my head in she was still lying down, now on her stomach, her head to the side. She'd been given enough time with the bed. I walked in and cleared my throat and she rolled over and propped herself up on an elbow. I looked back at her, trying to gauge whether she was interested in buying the bed.

'Can I try it with a pillow?' she asked.

The pillow was on top of my blankets, heaped in the corner, and I handed it to her. She put it under her head and lay down again, straight this time, with her hands by her sides, staring at the ceiling.

'What do you think?' I asked.

She took her time before answering me. 'I can give you cash right now,' she said, 'but I'll need a favour. I have rope to tie it to my station wagon's roof and I'll need a hand piling it on.'

I told her that was no problem.

She continued, 'Then I'll need help taking it down at my home.'

I had a lot to do and thought I could easily find another buyer at the low price of ninety-nine dollars I had advertised. 'Um,' I mumbled. 'I don't know.'

'You're going to have a hard time selling this thing with that blood on it,' Margaret added.

She was right. The stains were faint but unmistakable.

'That's not human blood,' I said. 'It's from a small dog I was looking after. It was in heat.'

Margaret stood up off the bed. 'I just moved out on my own,' she said, 'and I really can't ask anyone else for help.' She looked me in the eyes. 'Please.'

'How far away do you live?' I asked.

'Not far.'

I agreed and Margaret immediately began lifting the mattress onto its side. She got it up before I could help her. We lifted the box spring together, taking sides and moving it towards the door. I had trouble negotiating the angle and she guided me out. She went so fast I struggled not to lose the thing down the stairs. We raised it on top of the car and went back up for the mattress.

'You can wait in the car while I tie it up,' she said.

I offered to help but she insisted. As she tugged on the rope the car rocked back and forth. She did a thorough job of securing that bed. It was a hot night and I wound down the window, hoping she would hurry so the airconditioning would start flowing. When she finally sat down she took a make-up kit out of her bag and checked herself in its mirror, applying more lipstick and examining her teeth.

We travelled for a while in silence. It was nine o'clock. At this rate I wouldn't be home until late and I had a lot to organise before I left Sydney. We kept on speeding further down the Princes Highway. Margaret drove fast and I understood why she tied the mattress down so tight.

'I'm sure the stains will come out,' I said, breaking the silence. 'Try bleach.'

We turned off the highway, way beyond what could be considered close to my house, rolling into a quiet street, pulling up beside a row of adjoined terraces with a chicken-wire fence. We untied the ropes and pulled the mattress off the roof racks, resting it against the car.

'Where are we?' I asked.

'Marrickville South,' she said. 'It's a little different to Dubbo, where I'm from. It makes me homesick actually, but I work at the airport, so it's convenient.'

'You're an air hostess?'

'No, I'm in security.' Margaret smiled proudly. 'Does that surprise you?'

'I suppose it does.'

'Look at my muscles.' She flexed her arm for me. Her bicep was small, but round and defined.

'You must lift weights.'

'Feel them.'

I gave the bicep a quick squeeze. 'Wow.'

'Feel them properly,' she said, grabbing my hand and placing it back on her bicep, wrapping her hand over mine. She flexed back and forth, making it bulge. 'My shoulder too.' She moved my hand up and curled her arm into her chest, flexing. Her skin was loose and soft over the muscle. 'Are you impressed?'

'Yes. You're stronger than me.'

'Probably.'

We picked up the mattress and she led us up to her front door. Inside, there was a plastic card table in the middle of the room with some wooden folding chairs around it. The rest of the room was scattered with cardboard boxes.

'I've just moved in so the furniture is only temporary,' Margaret explained. 'My boyfriend kept the bed, but he'd stunk it up anyway.'

She laughed and I laughed and we moved into her bedroom. There was a single blow-up mattress on the floor that she shoved to the side with her foot. We went back out for the mattress on the car and slid it on top of the box spring with the stains facing up. As soon as it was in place she fell on top, face down. I wiped my forehead with the bottom of my T-shirt. I waited for her to get up, but she stayed there.

'Aren't you tired?' she asked into the mattress.

'I'm exhausted,' I said. 'And there's still so much I have to do when I get home.'

'Why don't you relax? I think we deserve a break, don't you?' She wriggled over on the mattress to make room for me. 'At least sit for a minute.'

I sat on the edge of the mattress beside her. She was still, and let out a quiet sigh. 'I'm drenched,' she said. 'I'm going to have to have a shower before I take you home. Would you like a shower?'

'No, thanks.'

There was a box on the floor and she lay across her bed and reached into it.

'I'll wait in the living room,' I said.

I pulled out a folding chair. Margaret came out of her room a minute later, a pink towel covering her middle, her skinny legs showing from the tops of her thighs. I heard the shower begin. It was late. There was no TV, no magazines lying around, no pictures to look at on the walls. The shower went on and on. I could hear her humming, taking her time.

When she came out her hair was wet and slicked back and with her make-up washed off she looked different, older. She smiled. 'Thanks for waiting,' she said. 'I'll just throw something on.'

'Sure, fine.'

She went into her room and closed the door. 'Are you hungry?' she called out.

'Not really.'

'Well, I'm starving.'

I heard Margaret shuffling about inside, boxes sliding across the floor, the bed creaking. It was otherwise totally silent. There were some sharp, clunky footsteps and then the door opened. Margaret stepped out in a sleeveless red summer dress that reached her knees, and short red stilettos. She stood still in front of me, her arms stiffly by her sides, smiling shyly with fresh red lipstick.

'What do you think?' she asked, holding the corners out and turning around for me. 'I just unpacked it so it's a little crushed.'

'It's a very glamorous dress,' I said.

'Thank you.' She sashayed past me to the kitchen. 'Now I'm going to make us dinner.'

'I'm really OK,' I insisted.

'You've come all the way out here for me; it's the least I can do.' She opened the fridge. 'I don't have anything to cook with so I hope sandwiches are OK. Oh, and I'm afraid there's only peanut butter. Do you mind peanut butter?'

'No.'

Margaret tore open a packet of plastic knives and another one of paper plates. I watched her prepare the sandwiches.

'How would you like me to cut yours?' she asked. 'In the middle or diagonally?'

'Diagonally.'

She brought the sandwiches and a bottle of Sprite over and

went back for some plastic cups. 'You know, I've barely spoken to anyone since I moved here,' she said, sitting down on the chair beside me and pouring a drink. 'I thought I'd meet all sorts of people out here, you know, the Big Smoke and everything. But this is the most time I've spent with anyone.'

'Well, you haven't been here very long. I'm sure you'll meet a lot of interesting people.'

She patted my knee. I finished the first half of my sandwich and absently checked my watch, then felt guilty and hoped she hadn't noticed. She nibbled at her sandwich, putting it back on the plate between bites.

'How is it?' she asked.

'Just the right amount of peanut butter – not too thick, but not too thin. Thank you.'

'I'm so relieved,' she said. 'You should come back another night and I'll make you a steak. My boyfriend used to say I make the best steak in New South Wales. The trick is to tenderise the cutlet completely with a mallet and let it marinate for at least an hour. I do it in cognac. People think you can just throw a steak in a pan with some onions and maybe some soy sauce, but if you really want it to taste special you have to put in the time and the love. Do you like steak?'

'Sure, but I'm afraid I'll miss out. I'm leaving for Melbourne tomorrow.'

'Oh no,' she put her hand on my wrist on the table. 'Why?'

'Sydney's an expensive city and I haven't found any work.'

'What field are you looking in?'

'I studied journalism.'

'How romantic!' she said. 'I read a lot, mostly health magazines. I love an informative article. It would be so wonderful to have that talent, but I'm such a terrible speller.'

I took a few big bites of my sandwich. I wasn't hungry – it was too hot – but I wanted to finish the sandwich.

'Look at you!' she laughed, standing up and fixing her dress. 'I'll make you another one.'

'No,' I blurted and tugged her arm to sit back down. She dropped into her chair. 'I'm really OK, thanks,' I added quickly.

Margaret watched me finish my sandwich, which I did with one last big mouthful. She maintained her stare as I wiped my mouth with my hand. I leaned back in the chair trying to look satisfied, drumming my fingers on the table, trying to gesture a readiness to head home. I looked at Margaret, hoping she could sense my readiness. She looked back at me closely, as if there were something on my face, like a loose eyelash. I could smell her perfume, a pleasant, vaguely familiar smell that I associated with old people. With a sudden jerk, Margaret put her mouth on mine. The kiss could have lasted three seconds or it could have been fifteen, I'm not sure. I don't know why I didn't stop her right away. I didn't feel like myself. I let her put her hand on my shoulder, and felt her teeth against my lip. When I finally pulled back I said, 'Whoops.'

When Margaret leaned in again, I turned my face before she made contact. Her mouth opened, as if she were about to speak, but then she closed it. She stood up and careered to the bathroom, a wobble in her heels. I tapped on the bathroom door and called her name, but she ignored me. I was embarrassed by my tactlessness. I tried to think of something nice to say, but couldn't come up with anything. 'Would you like me to go?' I asked.

She said, 'Yes, I would, please.'

'All right,' I said. Again, I couldn't think of anything nice to say. I said, 'Thanks for dinner.'

The problem was she owed me ninety-nine dollars. As much as I wanted to, I thought it too callous to ask through the bathroom door. I slipped as quietly as I could into her bedroom, spotting the bag on the floor at the foot of the bed. I sat on the mattress, rummaging among her make-up and Freddo Frogs and Aspirin, finding her purse. There was only a twenty note and a five inside. I put them in my pocket and poured the change into my hand. Her tights lay over one of the boxes beside her T-shirt. I felt them through, but they didn't have pockets, of course.

I gave up, treading lightly back through the house, slamming the front door so she'd know I was gone. It had cooled down outside and the lights were off in every house on the street. A plane landing interrupted the quiet. I hurried along, looking for a bus stop or station – I didn't even have enough money on me to cover a taxi fare. Everything I had to do before I left was back on my mind, and it was so much.

The Legacy of Rita Marquand

Carmel Bird

The first Rita Marquand oil painting I ever saw was at a garage sale on the sloping lawn of a huge old house in Launceston a couple of years ago. Ever since I was a girl at art school I have been collecting the works of lesser known and unknown Australian women painters. The collection is now quite extensive. Rita's picture was on a smallish piece of plywood, framed in an elaborate chipped gilt frame – two young girls in filmy white dresses playing among yellow grass. The grass is alive with subtle colours, the girls caught in a moment of intimate laughter. It was titled and signed on the back in red pen – *The Deedees*, Rita Marquand, Fatima, 1927. I bought the painting in 2000 for two dollars from a man who said it had been done by a distant relative of his late wife. This is a typical story from my files – the discovery of a new 'unknown' woman painter who sets me off on a journey into the poignant past. There was so much talent, passion, beauty locked away in the lives of women before the liberation of the '70s came along and gave girls the chance to show what they are made of.

This journey led me from Launceston to Devonport, to Blackwood Creek, to Hobart, and finally to the Huon Valley, where I found at last the house called 'Fatima' in which Rita Marquand had lived and painted. Along the way, I was able to collect five other pictures that had somehow been preserved – one was a glowing image of a blindfolded angel standing sorrowfully beside a burned-out gum tree. There was a strangeness to Rita's work that fascinated me, a strangeness that I do not often encounter in the paintings of my unknown women, most of whom paint fairly simple landscapes, gardens, houses. I get pictures from op shops and skips and cellars and attics – and sometimes from kitchen shelves where they have been for two or three generations.

By the time I tracked Rita down to 'Fatima' I was very interested not only in her paintings but also in the story of the lives of the two girls in *The Deedees*. With her large family and a small farm to manage, it is a miracle Rita ever put brush to canvas. But this is something I have discovered about my women painters: they kept their sanity by snatching moments of creative passion from the hours of duty and family responsibility.

I discovered that Dymphna and Dolores were sisters, born at 'Fatima' in a small rural town in the Huon Valley. I have pieced together as best I can the story of what happened to them. I have taken the liberties of a storyteller at times, trying to imagine how people must have felt, how they must have thought about things. Some of the material I found in small diaries that Dymphna kept over the years. These were often illustrated, showing that Dymphna had inherited her mother's talent. However, I never saw a finished work by Dymphna. Between the pages of the diaries I found old letters and cards from Dolores to Dymphna, and one pale blue love letter to Dolores from a man called Geoffrey (*My Sweetest Angel, Dolly* ...). The girls had two older brothers, a baby sister and baby brother, Sissy and Jo-Jo. The place was described as a dairy farm but, in fact, it was a small property where the Marquands kept some cows, grew some apples and kept their heads above water. Everyone on the farm – Rita, her husband, Paul, and all the children – worked really hard: up before daybreak, finishing long after dark. I sat in Rita's old kitchen, at the table where she had made the bread for the family, and I listened to Margaret, the young wife of another Jo-Jo, Rita's grandson. Her baby crawled around on the wooden floor where Dymphna and Dolores must have crawled. Born in 2005, he is the only descendant so far of Rita and Paul in this generation. The older brothers died in the Second World War and Sissy never had children. Margaret and Jo-Jo were amazed that anybody would be interested in Rita's paintings.

Dymphna was named for an aunt who was named for the patron saint of the mentally ill (or, as they said in the '30s, the insane). Dolores was named for the very sad aspect of the Virgin Mary. The names turned out to be, I am sorry to say, prophetic. The two girls were known as the Deedees. They were inseparable. Dolores (Dolly) was eighteen months older than Dymphna. Dolly was very bright and pretty, with softly curling brown hair, and Dymphna (Dimples) had, as it happened, a dinky little dimpled smile, and hair 'as straight as a packet of candles'. When in the bath, with her stringy hair wet and stuck across her forehead in strands and down her back in damp ribbons, her mother said she was a dying duck in a thunderstorm.

Apart from their connection with the painting, the lives of Dymphna and Dolores are now of a certain historical interest as they illuminate a past that exercises a fascination in the present. Television is larded with programs where innocent people are forced to relive the lives and times of girls like the Deedees, struggling with the lack of conditioner for their hair, eating bread and dripping (which is the fat that is saved in the baking dish after meat has been roasted). These programs generally emphasise the terrible difficulties of past lives. What I will tell you about the early lives of the Deedees will probably seem impossibly romantic, with a hint of paradise, in spite of what I have said about their being up before dawn.

So, on the Marquands' dairy farm they blossomed. In the spring, apple trees, plums and almonds, too, turned the hillside into a frothy springtime snow leading down to the river. Note what I said about paradise. Snow, they always called it snow, as they ran, children on legs like elves' legs, across the long grass where the red sorrel grew, wild and rough underfoot, knee-high, and they rolled over and over down the hill. Over and over and over. And then, in the summer, they picked the plums for jam and bottling and harvested the almonds to stir into the dark damp Christmas cakes and the pobbly puddings that hung for months in their calico cloths in the dairy. The girls pelted like the wind, the wind in their hair and in their eyes, danced down the hillside, falling and rolling, tumbling under the almond trees, pastel cotton dresses made by their mother at midnight, skirts flying up, pink pants rude and visible, bare feet hot and lovely, and they lay there, the dappled shadows of the leaves flittering across their faces, faces flushed and glowing. Laughter twittering up into the blossom trees, coin spots of sunlight glimmering across them. Well, was it paradise or wasn't it? This is what Rita captured in *The Deedees*.

The future was wonderful then. The Deedees were living and laughing – with potatoes and sausages to eat and milk to drink – and fruit – while around them was the Depression. They were in the Depression but they did not know it. They knew a copper full of boiling sheets seething in soap, sheets rinsed in blue from the bluebag, flapping on the clothesline in the sun. Running in and out diving through the flapping sheets, that were sewn down the middle with a heavy seam because they had been split and 'turned' to make them last longer. Their beds were high – tall maple ends with curved edges and a raised wreath of leaves like a medallion in the centre. These were grand old beds from their mother's old home. They called them the American beds, I am not sure why, but maybe they associated them with faraway luxury. They gleamed golden by candlelight. When I came to 'Fatima' and saw the beds they were still beautiful, although the surface of the varnish was now dulled. A child had written her name on one of the bedheads – 'Sissy Marquand slept here' – and somebody had tried to clean it off. But the room, now a guest room, was, Margaret said, much as it had been when the Deedees lived there in the '30s.

Above Dymphna's bed was the traditional picture of the Immaculate Heart. If you are looking for sentimental horror, this is it – the sweetly peachy smiling woman (sad) with her greenish-blue cloak and her crown of rosebuds. But then, in her hands, surrounded by a wreath of thorny roses is her heart, which radiates pink and gold light and is surmounted by a hot red flickering flame. This picture would not have been seen as strange by the children. It was the normal image to hang above a bed, but if you think about it, it is really most peculiar.

Then, on the wall over Dolores's bed hung what I thought was a print of a work of art – *Madonna of the Goldfinch* by Tiepolo. But, lucky for me, Margaret drew my attention to it, saying, 'Rita did that. She used to copy things, apparently. I think it's so ugly, but we keep it because Rita did it. It's not original – we haven't got any originals – but I suppose it has sentimental value, you know, because she did it.' This is not the only masterpiece I have found reproduced by one of my women – Georgia James used to do excellent copies of Goya – but it added an exciting new dimension to Rita, in my opinion.

Now, I would rather like to rush ahead and tell you what eventually happened to Dymphna and Dolores but, in fact, the pictures over their childhood beds are relevant to the outcome in a strange way, and so I must pause here to think about them. Life, I find, can sometimes be infused with prophecies or at least shadows and foreshadows. And I need to dwell for a moment on the *Madonna of the Goldfinch* by Rita Marquand, which hangs on the wall of memory above Dolores Marquand's old American bed. The child Jesus holds the goldfinch firmly in his left hand, tight, a bundle of taffeta bluish feathers with a bobbing scarlet head. The Holy Child is naked – a striking feature of the picture being the deep red bloody highlights on the mouth of the mother, her collar and sleeve, the head of the bird. The mother gazes downwards, the child looks straight at the world, at the viewer, his deep blue eyes still, knowing, sad. Startling and sickening is the bruised red luscious cherry of the baby's lips, as if he had sucked on berries or fresh game. The flesh of the mother and child appears to be not so much alive as on the point of corruption. These observations are mine. Similar thoughts just might have crossed the minds of the Deedees, although I doubt it. Yet it is my understanding that the effects of the images above the beds entered the girls' deep imaginations.

Rita told them that long long ago, at the time of the Crucifixion, a goldfinch took a thorn from the crown-borne-crown of Jesus, and the blood from the holy brow went splashing out and landed on the head of the bird. Hence the little bird's scarlet head. Privately, the Deedees liked to puzzle over that story – if the goldfinch didn't get its red head until it pulled the thorn out of the crown on the dark day of the Crucifixion, how was it the baby Jesus was holding a goldfinch with a bright red head? Ours not to reason why, Rita counselled.

Apparently, there are about 600 known paintings of Madonna and child with goldfinch. I don't wish to burden you with a lot of academic detail, but I think it is worth knowing that in 1952, a writer named Jacques Schnier published an essay entitled 'The Symbolic Bird in Medieval and Renaissance Art' and in that essay he says that the goldfinch signifies the mother herself, the mother is the lost object over which the child desires control. The goldfinch also signifies fertility and is associated with Lucina, ancient goddess of childbirth.

These somewhat heavy little messages hanging above the American beds at 'Fatima' can be seen to cast an ironic shadow over the lives of the Deedees. I need here to draw attention to the matters of sex before marriage, unplanned pregnancy and abortion – matters that naturally give rise in the modern mind to the question of contraception. Safe contraception was not dreamt of until the '60s and would not even then have been possible for the Catholic Deedees. You can see that to get pregnant before marriage in this family at that time was to go to hell in a handbasket, and you feel the problem looming, dangling like the pictures over the American beds. Who is going to get pregnant, and what is she going to do next?

Well, it was Dolores, the cheerful one with the very sad name. To the delight of the proud family, Dolores went off to Hobart to study at the Teachers' College. She was to live at the Sacred Heart Hostel, safe and sound with the nuns, the curfew and the Catholic faith. Her mother made her skirts, coats, blouses, dresses. All afternoon and well into the night the sewing machine would be going k-chick-k-chick-k-chick. Dolores would flit about and try things on and her mother, with pins in her mouth, would say, 'Stand still' and 'Hold up your arm' and 'Stop wriggling'. Auntie Bee knitted jumpers and cardigans for Dolly. Sitting by the fire or under the holly hedge her needles singing away tik-woo-tik-woo-tik. Hot-water-bottle covers. Two brown suitcases filled and folded and fluffed up with everything including a new silver compact with face powder. She took a small framed picture of Our Lady of Perpetual Succour and also the painting her mother did in the orchard, *The Deedees*.

When she was in Hobart, Dolores went to dances on Friday nights. She started smoking and drinking and dancing with all kinds of young men. And some not so young. To start with, she was back at the hostel by ten, but then she discovered how to climb in the laundry window after midnight, having bribed another girl to sign her in at ten. She got up on a stage and sang in the After-Dinner Conservatory. She was incredibly pretty and popular.

She was on the downward slide. Lying in bed during the holidays, she would tell Dymphna about some of the things she did, and Dymphna was amazed and fascinated and frightened for her sister's immortal soul. She would wonder how safe it was to ride in cars with men you hardly knew. Dymphna had heard of at least two girls who had been killed when a car ran into a tree and, of course, there lurked, just below the surface, the terror of pregnancy. Girls would sometimes disappear for a few months, gone to stay with relatives on the mainland, and then they would come back and stay at home with their families and never marry, scarred for life.

Dolores was kissing and hugging and driving fast into the countryside. At night, she would cuddle in dark cars beside the river. 'But you have to be a virgin dressed in white and pure when you get married,' Dymphna said, and Dolores said, 'Maybe you do.' She looked at her sister sideways from under her hair and she smiled her little winking crooked pink cherry-cherub smile. It was a naughty smile, a smile that Dymphna somehow linked with the smile in a story the nuns had told them – a girl smiles at a man who beckons her to a doorway, and in the doorway he takes her hand, and he rings the bell and the door opens and they go in and are never seen again because it was the doorway to hell.

Then, one day, Dolores told Dymphna she had a real sweetheart, Geoffrey.

'Why don't you tell Mum and bring him home then?'

'He's a Baptist.'

'Have you been to confession?'

'No.'

The answer came swift and defiant, and Dymphna knew there and then that the writing was on the wall and that the whole thing was out of control. To be involved with a Protestant was worse than having sex and getting pregnant. Geoffrey was going to be a lawyer and he was not a very good Baptist, smoking and drinking and dancing as he did. Dolores planned to get him to convert. Surely he would see reason. If his own family's religion mattered so little to him, why couldn't he become a Catholic? But when she lay in his arms on the grass by the river, none of this mattered, and her wicked heart sang for joy and her blood simmered with a hot excitement that sent her conscience off to sleep.

In the window of a smart Hobart shop one day, Dolores saw something so amazing, so desirable, so drenched in beauty that she did not pay for textbooks but bought the thing instead. It was a dress. I think this was maybe the real beginning of the end, spending the textbook money on the dress to go to the Winter Garden Dance with Geoffrey. When Dolores told Dymphna about the dress Dymphna knew in her heart of hearts that the bell of the doorway to hell was ringing.

Dymphna's head was spinning and her heart was beating fast with excitement and desire at the thought of the dress and the dance and the money and the man and the non-existent textbooks. This was the true beginning of the locked-up things that Dymphna could never tell anybody, the source of the guilt that was going to poison her life. Catholic girl meets Baptist boy – Juliet and Romeo – until something fatal and inevitable and blindingly terrible occurs, like when a plane flies into a mountain and explodes, killing all on board. Dymphna held the black box, held it in her shadowed and sorrowful heart, and it stilled her blood, stopped her thoughts, right there in the bedroom of the dairy farm in the lovely valley of the Huon.

It was Dymphna who gave up on life at that point, Dymphna who stopped eating, stopped talking. Not altogether, but she did what they called 'going into herself' and she became a joyless wraith out of the reach of her family and friends. People naturally thought she was considering entering the convent and, in fact, she did feel drawn to that life but (and this is so sad and deeply ironic) she knew that she could not, simply because she would have to confess to all she knew, in due course, about her sister, and that was impossible. Somehow she could hold her knowledge back from everyday confession, but if she entered the convent, everything would have to come spilling out. She would have to spew toads of truth in the dark box of the confessional, and Dolores would never forgive her. Nobody would forgive her. Would God forgive her? God was supposed to do that, but who can divine the depths of reasoning of the mind of God? So what it amounts to is that while Dolores was going to hell, Dymphna was beginning to go, quite simply, mad. The poor Marquands and their two lovely daughters who both ended up so tragically. Margaret was very up-front about this – she had no problem telling a perfect stranger that Dymphna had gone mad.

Dolores would tell her sister about the things she did with Geoffrey, sometimes in letters, and Dymphna loved getting the cards and letters, the photographs of picnics and warm days at the beach. The secret thrilling wicked sinful parts of the letters were in secret little envelopes inside the leaves of the main letter. Here is a letter from Dolly – and she would read out the main letter at the family dinner table, driving the evil deeper and deeper into her own heart as she read, knowing she was lying. Dolores went to lectures and wrote essays and played the piano in concerts at the hostel. She described in the secret letters the marvellous miraculous dress she had bought with the textbook money. Dymphna wondered if she would ever see this dress.

She did see it. When her mother went to Hobart and brought all Dolly's things back home. It was lying in the suitcase, on top of everything, the last thing Rita had put in. It was wrapped in white tissue paper and Dymphna saw it slide out of its parcel. It slithered onto the white counterpane, underneath Rita's picture of Jesus and his mother and the goldfinch. For some reason, Rita had left the picture of the Deedees at the hostel in Hobart.

They were accustomed enough to deaths in the family – two dead babies, grandparents, an uncle in Egypt in the war, a simple aunt who drifted away from this world, a fish disappearing in an ancient Mongolian stream. But they were not prepared for Dolores, the lovely wild sister. Dolores had come home on the train from town and had died in a fevered pool of blood in the bedroom. There had never been a death like this one in this family. Dymphna was in a trance of shock, all the details of the sin and the crime flooding into her brain and heart, blocking reason, dashing reality into shards of broken clay.

In the 1930s, sex before marriage, unplanned pregnancy and abortion were highly risky enterprises. Pregnancy was OK in marriage, indeed required, but the other pregnancies were sins, and abortion was, of course, also a crime. If you saw the movie *Vera Drake* you would know all about that.

The bedroom curtains, white linen backed with sunlight and flittered with shadows, were drawn against the day, and Dolores lay there dead in the half-dark.

'Dymphna,' Rita said, in a firm, cold, steady voice, 'get your father, then call the priest and the doctor.'

'Call the priest and the doctor,' she said, in that firm, cold, steady voice. That was the order in which she placed them – first the priest and then the doctor. And that was the way she designated them. Not Father Gayle and Doctor Rush, but the priest and the doctor. First of all, Dymphna got her father from the deep shadows in the pungent darkness of the milking shed.

Between the telephone calls to the priest and the doctor and the inky arrival of those specialists in mortality, Rita sent her living daughter to the linen press for clean sheets, to the laundry for water and soap and towels. It was a secret now between the mother and daughter, a secret spelling the death of Dolores and its meaning. It was already a dark bond and a smudge of dirty ice between them. What would the doctor make of it? He would know what had happened for sure. But Dr Rush was a Catholic doctor. Would he describe the matter as being the result of a 'miscarriage'? Death the result of excessive loss of blood. Is that what he would do? To save the Catholic honour of the family. Well, in fact, he could only half save it, since Dolores was not married. Wasn't he bound by law to report the truth? Truth. To discover the name of the person in town who had done this to Dolores, who had opened her up (ripped her open?) and let the baby out and sent her home to die? Wasn't it his duty to see that a judge would send those people, that person, that woman, that witch – to prison? To save other girls from the fate of this glittering fanciful unmarried Dolores who could not believe that this was happening? Dymphna wondered what her mother was thinking of saying to Father Gayle. Perhaps, she thought, my lies have killed my sister, lies that hid the truth she shared with me. The truth that Dolly shared with me like secrets in the white and yellow bedroom long ago, so long ago in the giggling twilight of summer childhood. Perhaps the lies have killed her after all.

'Just lend me ten pounds,' Dolores said, 'and when I come home it will be all over and nobody will know any different.' But Dymphna knew it wasn't going to work like that – they would never get away with it. Ten pounds from her bankbook was a great big sum of money. Dolores sold a coral necklace left to her by Auntie Caroline. Somewhere or other. She had a life of mysteries beyond her sister's understanding. How did a girl sell a necklace of darling little antique coral bead strung out in family prayers and unforgotten laughter? And what if their mother got to wondering where it had gone? 'Oh, then I'll say I lost it,' Dolores said, quite solemn, like an actress, she said that. 'I lost it. The clasp was weak. I should have had it attended to, mended. I was saving up to have it mended. Just think – for a little three and sixpence I could have saved Auntie Caroline's coral necklace.' She smiled. She had a cute pink pixie slightly crooked smile.

Paul came to the bedroom door and Rita went to him. They stood together in a tight embrace, silent, and then they went out to the backdoor and stood again together, talking, underneath the cherry plum trees. She was explaining; he was listening. He was a silent man, always. He followed his wife's lead in most things, and gynecology was her province. The blood and the pain and the sometime joy of babies in and out of the womb. Morality was also her area. She had taken on the particular role of wisdom, also practicality. You could see them, a couple, through the open door, framed in the green doorway, as Dymphna dialled the number for the exchange and asked for the presbytery. Vilma Jones at the exchange would wonder, in her wide-eyed, wide-mouthed, frizzy-haired, blue-dressed way – or perhaps she would know – why Dymphna Marquand was calling the presbytery. Why was she calling? For a blank moment of idiot shock Dymphna suddenly could not remember what this was all about. Then she remembered. When next asked for the doctor's number Vilma knew. The priest and the doctor meant a death. For certain sure. Death or promise of death.

All the time, Dolores was lying on her bed beneath the gold-finch, and the blood was drying, caking, ruby-brown and brilliant, and her father had gone back to the milking shed and Dymphna was arriving in the bedroom with the water and the towels and the clean linen from the sweet lemon linen press. And all the time Rita was firm and cool and clear-headed and cold-hearted and hating Dymphna and blaming her. She was guilty, with the black box of truth buried deep inside her heart.

The mother became the priestess at the temple of her dead child and the other child her servant, silent, obedient, afraid, doing everything required except tell the story.

You will have noticed that Geoffrey disappeared a while back. He just went on with his life, occasionally giving a bit of a thought to Dolores Marquand, wondering sometimes what brought on the hush-hush fever that caused the sudden death of this bright and promising young woman. It occurred to me to go on another little treasure hunt, looking for the traces of Geoffrey, but that would be another story altogether.

The priest and the doctor smoothed the way for the sin and the crime to be concealed beneath a convenient felting of lies and half-truths. There was a quiet funeral to which some of the girls from the hostel (their knowing eyes lowered in respect) and two of the nuns (sad faces open as they swallowed the fictions of the fever and the death) came.

And the sequined dress lay forever after in the wooden trunk of fabrics beside the sewing machine. Buried in its coffin, waiting to be cut up into sections, divided into bits, drawn and quartered and reduced to a heap of purple scales. Why was it not destroyed at once? Things old and unwanted or wicked were always being burned. Was the dress perhaps too strange, too exotic, too desirable, too lovely, too wicked, too powerful? Too mysterious in origin and design, too poisonous? It also obviously held the answer to the question of the death of Dolores. The family could not confront the question, let alone the answer. They prayed every night for the soul of Dolores. Dymphna went slowly spinning into what they called melancholia, as thin as a rake, as mad as a hatter, locked up inside herself, never coming out.

One day, long years after the death of Dolores, Dymphna, who talked and sang a little to herself, opened the camphorwood trunk. She found two small pink dresses her mother made for them one Christmas Eve, tiny rosebuds printed on the artificial silk, the machine going k-chick-k-chick far into the night, tickling their ears as they wondered what treasures were created, what glamour was being prepared for Christmas day, hot games under the fruit trees, roly-poly who can roll the fastest to the bottom of the hill. Hair ribbons for church, new and pale pink and silky. Straw hats. A new enormous silky flower on their mother's elegant little navy spotted dress. A handsome family walking with some dignity to church on Christmas day with new pink dresses k-chick-k-chick. Long, long before the tragedy. Dymphna turned the dresses over in her hands, reverently, and remembered the old cherry plum trees at the backdoor, how they smelt when they were covered in fruit to be collected, picked and plopped and heaped into large white enamel buckets. They would take the cherries around and dish them out to everybody, the priest and the doctor included, and when they came home they would go to bed, and the sewing machine would start up, singing them to sleep. Cream, too, they took gifts of cream from their happy cows to their sometimes happy neighbours. In the milking shed they sang to the cows. 'Bluebird of Happiness', 'Faith of our Fathers', and a song made up by Dolores all about how cows are silly, cows are funny. Dymphna sang the old song over to herself as she rifled through the trunk until she came to Dolores's glittering dress.

It was what was called a cocktail frock, completely covered in purple sequins, all attached by hand to a black net background, arranged in tight little scales of glitter, in the pattern of the wings of a giant butterfly – shimmering glimmering, with the back so empty and low it dipped right down to the tailbone, and no sleeves, and the front scooping in a swallow dive right down between the breasts. Like a snake it took your breath away, like a quietly singing snake, humming and murmuring and bursting into flames. Royal purple and just a wisp of the wing of a delicate evil insect, so very very beautiful. It lay in the trunk, wounded, defiant, shining, shining through its tears.

'So what do you know about this dress?' Rita had asked.

'I don't know anything about the dress,' Dymphna lied.

Mostly, Dymphna had been guessing anyway. But in her clear imagination she had a picture of Dolores in the purple dress, a picture of handsome Baptist Geoffrey smoking, drinking, dancing under the palms in the Winter Garden and going – going where – somewhere the dress took her and she stood quite still while Geoffrey lifted it up-up-up over her head, brushing her fingers, tangling and catching in her hair, and then Geoffrey lifted her up and placed her on – on a bed, perhaps it was his bed and she was going to get into trouble back at the hostel because she was late-late-late. Like a late lament.

And his kisses and caresses were so sweet and so chocolate dark and she was dizzy with desire.

Then, one day, Dolores borrowed the ten pounds from her sister and told her she had sold the coral necklace, and she said everything would be all right and she started singing 'cows are funny, cows are silly' and then, quite suddenly, her bottom lip unsmiling quivered and she began to sob.

The next thing she arrives at the railway station, white as a sheet and comes home and goes into the bathroom and starts to bleed and bleed. And that is all. Father Gayle blessed her and forgave her sins, firm in the belief that she had made a final Act of Perfect Contrition. Dymphna prayed and prayed about that. Dolores was at least wearing her Miraculous Medal at the time of her death and so, chances are she went to heaven. Doctor Rush did nothing special. He signed the Certificate of Death. But Dymphna was holding the centre of a whole beaded shiny slippery spider web of lies, and could only keep saying she knew nothing at all. Rita did not believe her. When Dymphna went to confession she confessed to telling lies, to withholding the truth. Father Gayle must surely have known the nature of some of the lies. The penance he gave her was an insult, so light and routine it did not touch her seething bubbling guilt – he gave her the Sorrowful Mysteries, and that was all. Dolores was buried in white.

Three years passed and one day poor weird Dymphna Marquand dressed herself up in a sequinned gown that had belonged to her long-dead sister. She stood by the window as the afternoon sun came slanting through the glass, the rays hitting the sequins and throwing a strange pink cloud of liquid flickering light onto the white walls of the room. Then she ran, a glittering purple scarecrow down through the orchard and down to the river, the cocktail sequins of the mermaid marvel of the dress flittering and glittering and flapping. She must have tripped and fallen into the water. The family and the police and the neighbours searched the district. Nobody found her for three full days.

You could talk about madness and accidents and drowning – but not really about suicide. No, you could not speak of suicide. After Dymphna died, it seems Rita never painted again. They buried Dymphna next to her sister in the churchyard, and twenty years later her sad father joined her, and only one year after that, her mother. Their older brothers were buried in blood-soaked foreign soil.

So, as you can see, the picture of the Deedees has a very special significance for me, as does the copy of *Madonna of the Goldfinch*. I felt it was improper for me to ask Margaret and Jo-Jo if I could buy the goldfinch painting and so it still hangs, as far as I know, above the American bed in the old bedroom at 'Fatima'. A few months after my visit, I received from Margaret an envelope containing fresh copies of two small cracked black-and-white photographs. One was a picture of the Deedees playing under the blossoms in the orchard and the other was the Deedees again, with Rita. The girls are standing beside their mother, who is seated at her easel. None of them is looking into the camera – Dolly is staring at the painting, Dymphna is staring at Dolly and Rita is intent on her work, the paintbrush poised a few centimetres from the piece of plywood. She is painting *The Deedees*.

Griffith Review

Nhill

Patrick West

As I had hoped, when we arrived at the lake we were the only people there. Neither of us had seen any other cars at the place where the road ended and the desert began. Yet perhaps there was another way in we didn't know about; or somebody had decided to camp overnight on the shore of the lake. Somebody who didn't have a car, perhaps. But there was no one.

The evening before, over a shared ice-cream dessert at the motel restaurant, my wife had told me that she would be going to bed as soon as we were finished, to be rested for our early start the next morning. Though worn out myself by the half-day drive from Melbourne, I had stayed up for some time after her: getting together the things we would need for our trip into the desert; estimating distances and times.

Our room was next door to the reception area. The manager had his TV turned up loud and kept switching irritatingly between the channels. There had been a movie on, and the local news, and it wasn't until after the movie that I had turned off the main light. Getting into bed myself, next to my wife, I lay on my back and thought of the pair of empty fish tanks on the manager's desk. And then I think I took a long time falling asleep, because when our alarm clock went off it seemed as if the movie were still going on inside my head.

There had been no lights shining in the motel complex when I eased the room door closed behind us, and unlocked the

passenger side of the car for my wife. The only artificial illumi-
nation came from the frosted lamps around one side of the
swimming pool, which made the water bright green. Although
I had remembered thinking, upon our daylight arrival, that I
had never seen water so blue. There had been clothes-pegs on
the bottom that afternoon. Children were diving for them.

Some of the fainter stars had been dimming out as we drove
along the road that would soon veer right and become the main
street of the town of Nhill, Victoria. Our motel was about at the
point towards the end of a long stretch of highway where the
speed limit begins to be lowered on white-and-black signs. We
both saw a rabbit in the headlights.

A few minutes after we had departed the silently sleeping
motel, my wife spotted the turn-off to the Little Desert before
I did. Her vision was much keener in the pre-dawn light. The
road to our destination ran alongside the railway tracks on the
edge of Nhill. Our tourist map showed us that halfway to the
desert the road and the tracks would diverge, meet again,
then finally part for good. I slowed down to take the left-hand
turn.

While the light continued to increase and alter, she had been
the one to say the morning had broken. A sliver of sun flashed
across my rear-vision mirror as we parked on a slope of dew-
dusted earth. I turned off the engine. For the first time that
morning it was perfectly quiet.

For a while we hadn't even been sure if we were really in the
desert or not. Then we came to a turnstile in a short run of wire
fencing, and we knew. We had arrived. The turnstile had a counter attached to it; as we went through the white numbers noise-
lessly turned over. It was probably part of someone's job to note
how many people went into the desert. Perhaps this information
was important. I couldn't help thinking about those people who
deliberately went around the fence or used the turnstile more
than once. My wife must have read my mind. She had said quietly, perhaps it all evens out in the end.

That had also been when we first noticed the real sand mixed
with the soil beneath our feet, and that the Little Desert mainly
consisted – the vegetation falling away – of a serried formation
of low rises and shallow dips. We were now into a new landscape,

walking across the first of its modest plateaus, incongruously headed for water.

Tucked into my shirt pocket was a map of the desert produced for walkers, and we weren't long in our progress towards the lake before the cartographic marks like the diminuendos and crescendos on a page of music became signs we could interpret. The map gave the lake a neat edge, filled in with a colour that by convention indicated deep water. But my wife and I had speculated that at that season, and at the very centre of the desert, the lake would be a salt lake. Its water would be shallow and its shore uneven, we had guessed. And we were right.

The whole morning, from the surface of the path and from the rest of the ground, the air had been rising in warm waves. What little there was of copper-coloured, needle-like grass had been the first to respond. An hour later, the same waves had brushed around our faces, slowly continuing to ascend, moving through black and blonde hair like fingers of gentleness. This was a sensation we hadn't felt before, out there in the relative flatness of the Little Desert. And then, when our watches showed that it was almost noon – hour and minute hands about to touch the twelves on our wrists – we noticed again how peculiar nature is.

Although there wasn't a breath of wind, the few trees at first appeared to be straining against their confinement in the earth, all of themselves rejecting the land from within.

The next moment, however, this had curiously seemed not to be happening. Precisely the absence of even the weakest breeze now manifested itself as decisive, as if the trees that we could see here and there on the landscape, not needing for their equilibrium to be rooted and heavy and thus not being so, were no longer rebelling against their connection with the lowest part of the visible desert, but were touching it with only the smallest possible touch, nothing of themselves actually buried into the loose soil. As if roots had withdrawn completely into trunks, as if something had turned completely and utterly around, as if the few trees were held up sheerly by the rising air – a delicate balancing act – and into its cloud-headed warm waves.

I had walked with my binoculars around my neck, seeing two eagles. Or perhaps the same eagle twice.

At times, the silence was extreme.

There had been low signs by the side of the path at irregular intervals, sometimes three or four clustered together. They had on them descriptions of the interesting aspects of the desert and its life. Here were indicated two trees that had grown into each other in a cleft of rock, and become one; there, the same thing had happened, but with one of the trees having died. A few of the signs had referred to rainfall or temperature change in the Little Desert's unique microclimate. Others said that at this spot one could often see a particular bird or furtive animal. My wife had told me that the signs looked like church lecterns springing from the ground, or tombstones made to resemble open books. (A rare parrot we read about had last been seen in 1961, by N. Green.)

Our route to the lake had taken us through a part of the desert supporting very little in the way of scrub or other plant growth. The ground had to it what my wife called an angry tone. In places the sand gathered in drifts deep enough for our legs to disappear up to the bare flesh of our calves.

At the point where our walkers' map told us that we would arrive at our lunch spot by the salt lake in just under an hour, we had found ourselves on a slightly higher plateau, where the fine sand gave only a few grains of cover to the shale beneath. In view before us was an expanse of clumpy bushes of a bleached-green colour: a prospect of palest olive. Obviously we were on the edge of fertile soil. It had almost looked as if we might walk, from where we were, right across the top of the scrub, to the next low rise; although by careful observation, if nothing else, we knew we couldn't. The surface of the scrub was even and uninterrupted, but the smallest bird to alight on it sank beneath the feathery leaves and tips. Sank to fly out of the scrub's surface bafflingly elsewhere (the same bird? or another?).

I had related to my wife what I knew about a certain type of mixed bush-growth in western Tasmania, described in forestry literature, which was often able to sustain – for considerable distances – the weight of people who simply wanted to walk above the land for a while. My wife had only grimaced in response. She was becoming tired; the comparison, furthermore, was a vague one. The scrub we were faced with then was not only unable to support us, but allowed no sort of passage through its web of lower branches either. We were therefore forced to make a long detour, by the fainter trail around its stunted-grass perimeter, in order to regain our path to the lake on the further side.

For no known reason, we had each taken a different way from the other. Tiny desert mice and prodigious desert rats were in shadowy motion within the scrub, chittering among themselves without regard to size or species. Under blazing sun, it had felt nevertheless as if I were looking into darkest night.

There was orange peel on the ground where the main path took up again: the first sign of recent intrusion that either of us had seen.

We caught sight of the salt lake just a little later than my planning had allowed for.

As I had hoped, when we arrived at the lake we were the only people there. Neither of us had seen any other cars at the place where the road ended and the desert began. Yet perhaps there was another way in we didn't know about; or somebody had decided to camp overnight on the shore of the lake. Somebody who didn't have a car, perhaps. But there was no one.

Across the lake we could see three waterbirds still as statues, a little way in from the opposite shore. They did not disturb at all the few centimetres of water they were at rest in. It gave out almost nothing, that salt water: without movement and shallow at every point. Reflections from the surface of the lake were mixed with the appearance of its bottom. It was difficult even to be sure about what sort of a body of water we were looking at. An oversized puddle? Ridges of land that began well back in the desert around us continued out into the lake as thin fingers of earth, which dropped beneath the surface only when almost to the middle. They were the ribs of the Little Desert, I had thought to myself, and this was its watery heart.

The ducks' heads were nestled comfortably into the plumage of their napes. Nothing stirred. All between our words was without noise. For a moment, I almost believed that I could watch the silence that surrounded us. It had been as if the visible landscape – the few trees; the copper-coloured, needle-like grass – were listening to what we said, finding it eventually acceptable, and allowing our utterances to pass back into the quietness unhindered.

We had arrived. The two of us. At a heart of salt.

It was difficult to have to quit the lake's irregular and pock-marked shore so quickly, now that we were finally where we wanted to be. But it was past the time to have our lunch, we were both tired, and the path to the nearest shady place to eat and rest was going to take us a short distance away from the lake. My wife and I had removed our hiking boots and socks to test the temperature of the water; now we needed to sprint across the burning ground to the spot we had decided upon almost imme-diately after our arrival. Even several long steps from the edge of the salt lake, however, the sand was cool and moist.

Water usually darkens whatever it touches and I have read somewhere that this proves it is not really crystalline but pure black, which is to say that it makes things black by an invariable law of change and resemblance. Nowhere in even the immediate vicinity of the lake, however, did the colour of the sand vary from the salty whiteness presented by other parts of the Little Desert. Even the thin fingers of land like the spokes of a gigantic wheel had a pale and glazed hue. More than likely the same went for the bottom of the lake, although through the shallow depths of the water we couldn't tell for sure.

As we opened our backpacks, ate our sandwiches, splashed our cold drinks into our mouths, we talked about such things. A million days of evaporation, my wife said through a mouthful of bread and mortadella, had done something to the Little Desert to make its surface impervious to the effects of water. An ele-ment in the rain was not taking on the sand, I had thought with-out saying it.

When we had finished our lunch and felt rested again, we went back to the shore of the lake. The ducks were exactly as they had been upon our arrival. We stood on the damp sand and watched over them.

There was nothing mystical about the scene in the end. No unworldly presence suggested itself in the shallow water. There was only the salt lake precisely as it was, and a sky that all day had not been disturbed by an aeroplane. All the same, it was a place (the lake, the sky, the whole sense of it all) that you didn't want to treat like more familiar places.

When we made up our minds to go it was in sadness. A single

duck's cry carried to our ears with almost no volume at all, the smallest increment imaginable before deafness begins.

*

Our return hike through the desert took much less time than the journey we had begun just as the sun was rising. We walked quickly, shut out distractions, only parted company once, each of us taking the grassy route around the pale olive expanse of scrub that the other one had taken when we were still making our way towards the unknown salt lake. Our voices sang out across the even surface of the bushes so each other might hear, and perhaps be comforted.

The sign requesting visitors to leave the Little Desert around either end of the short run of wire fencing is easy to miss, as we had been guilty of, when proceeding in the direction of the water. We couldn't pretend we hadn't seen it now coming back. Climbing over the turnstile, however, would save us any further time today in the desert. It looked easy enough. Together we took hold of one of the metal arms.

Perhaps it was some chemistry of our four hands simultaneously gripping this object (palms of a man and of a woman) that made it suddenly turn the wrong way, shift backwards without warning from the salt-lake side. Whatever the reason, in an instant we were ejected from the desert and needing to pick ourselves up. My wife's pants required dusting and I was happy to oblige. Checking the white numbers – the dry bodies of insects caught between the discs of the meter – I realised, by some fluke of memory, that they were exactly as they had been after our entrance at dawn.

This seemed to mean two things: our inelegant departure had not registered on the counter; and, no one else had come through. We had always felt ourselves alone that day. Yet perhaps the white numbers had, in fact, surreptitiously registered our exit, had clicked back (once? twice?) while we tumbled out of the Little Desert, and either a single person or a couple, whom we had never seen, had entered after us. Perhaps they were still in there.

Starting the car, I suddenly thought that our trip to the salt lake was somehow never to stop happening. And then I had the impression that I was having the same thought distinctly and clearly again.

*

The next morning, we ate breakfast sitting on the double bed in our room. A stray leaflet advertising the house-museum reputedly the Nhill home of the nineteenth-century romanticist poet John Shaw Neilson slipped between the sheets. Afterwards I swam several slow laps of the nauseatingly chlorinated pool – one clothes-peg still winked from the bottom.

Melbourne half a day away. In her reclined seat, my wife recited the back of our tourist map. The Little Desert and the Big Desert are two unique geographical and climatic regions; each is different from the adjoining countryside, and each is different from the other. She pointed to the north, without turning her head my way, and said that the Big Desert was less than 100 kilometres – pointing vaguely northwards, with splayed fingers – over there …

That afternoon, turning into our street in the suburb of St Kilda, I glimpsed again the brilliant green waters of Port Phillip Bay. How could such intensity ever seem so deep to us again? My wife started telling me that everything was going to be fine in a little while and I needed to listen to her with great care. Every word she used sounded as though travelling to me through both water and sand, and from much further away than she really was.

'I love you.'

The Jesus of Ants

Amanda le Bas de Plumetot

Glenda had never begrudged the time she'd spent caring for her mother or working at a job that neither interested nor fulfilled her, she simply did as was required. She'd watched her mother fade from a bird to a stick insect to a thread, her life passing from one breath to the next, hovering in between until there was no next. After the shock of it, after the grief and loss and yearning and probate and insurance were all over, Glenda found that she had enough money to quit her job. She sold the old house and bought herself a nice little unit.

'Mine,' she said, slightly surprised by how good it felt to be living alone, surrounded by furniture she had chosen, colours she'd decided on. Oatmeal instead of beige. Camel, not tan; ceilings of Arctic Snow, not white. She would not live her mother's life: sad and alone, trapped in a house, in a room, in a body. She bought a big TV and she began to read those magazines she'd always just walked past at the supermarket checkout. These, she thought, would help her to understand what it was she'd been missing out on for all those years. With these magic portals she would be drawn out of her mother's time-twisted existence that lurked somewhere between the 1970s and the Victorian Era, and into the twenty-first century.

It started with the supermarket. Did she go with the food that was *lite* or the food that was regular? Lite meant low fat, which was supposed to be good. Except that there were some fats that were essential, and she wasn't sure which. Then there was the question of fats and carbohydrates. What was the point of going with low fat if the food was loaded with carbos? She was supposed to look for food that was low GI. The thing was, apparently the actual flavour of any given food was somehow locked on to all those bad fat, high GI, sugary carbohydrate molecules so that when she sat down to a meal of perfect, sanitised food, it didn't taste like anything.

Glenda was not bored. She had always believed that boredom was the realm of people who lacked imagination. She had a lot more time, that was all, now that there was no more job to go to or Mum to look after. Shopping had become an important part of her life. The thing is, she liked doing a bit of window shopping and a bit of sitting in the coffee shop people-watching, or just having lunch and a magazine before she did the groceries. Only now she couldn't do all that because her bladder just didn't have the capacity and there was this problem with public toilets. Toilets had only become an issue after she read the article about which toilet people choose. Why did anybody do that study? Who cared which toilet people chose? Why did some bored and stupid editor see fit to use that particular article to fill in five centimetres of column space? She was sure they could have chosen an equally riveting snippet on UFO sightings or what colour cars people chose. Why toilets?

In public convenience situations, Glenda had always confidently gone to the cubicle second-furthest from the door. There was something about the toilet second-furthest from the door, it seemed more private, more secure and brighter than any of the others. Then Glenda read the article. Apparently everyone preferred the cubicle that was second-furthest from the door and that was the problem. Did Glenda want to go with her instinct, and risk contact with bottom germs from all the other people who felt the way she did? At first the answer seemed obvious: use some other toilet. She suspected that the cubicles closest to the door and furthest from the door probably saw less actual traffic, so she started using them. Until she realised that it was the ordinary, average people like herself who were using that cubicle second-furthest from the door. Sure, she was risking bottom germs, but they were germs from bottoms similar to hers. Little kids and weirdos used the other toilets and their bottoms were undoubtedly worse than the normal sort.

She had always had a reputation for being a flexible, lateral thinker at work. She solved the toilet problem by shopping at the market. Apparently the local council had given up trying to explain to people from certain cultures that it was unacceptable and even dangerous to perch on toilet seats. Instead they'd installed a whole row of cubicles with squat toilets in them. There was a footprint etched either side of an inground porcelain trough. It was a bit of a balancing act but worth it. Her bottom didn't touch anything, Glenda was safe.

There weren't any labels on market foods but it didn't matter. All the magazines and TV shows agreed that you had to eat a lot of fresh green things, so she bought broccoli and leeks and bok choy. She picked the shiniest apples and the thinnest-skinned oranges and golden bananas in bunches that looked like hands. She chose tomatoes that weren't quite ripe and kept them in a bowl on the sideboard at home because she'd read that you don't keep tomatoes in the fridge, and that they burn if you put them on the windowsill in the sun, the way her mother used to.

Glenda bought a little trolley of her own and lost herself in the market smells of earth and fruit and damp concrete. She learned to swing her hips out in order to make a space for herself between the packed bodies of men who strutted like royalty, blowing cigarette smoke into the crowd, and small, rotund women who shone like olives. She recognised the shouts of the stallholders:

'Dollar kilo, dollar kilo, dollardollardollar kilo.'

'*Nice* bananas, dollar fifty. *Nice* bananas.'

'Two for one. All go now. You buy, two for one.'

Past the squalling, dark-eyed children she would go, visiting her favourite stalls. The man at the far end always smiled at her. She decided that he had the best fruit. She never bought her vegetables there, though. She wove through the crowd, avoiding sharp-faced grannies and children swarming like monkeys, to get to the vegetable stall run by a thin, birdlike woman with shining black eyes. There was something about the way she ran the stall that seemed honest and earthy. Glenda loaded her trolley with wholesome vegetables that were going to fill her system with antioxidants and protect her from cancer. She was sure that going to the market was exercising her immune system as well. Mingling with all those people had to be good for her. She was no longer eating sanitised food packed by machines into plastic bags. This was real food. This was what her body needed, a connection with the earth, the birdlike woman and the smiling man.

Once the shopping was done, Glenda loaded it into the boot of her car and then she was able to treat herself to something to eat and a browse through the other parts of the market: clothes, handcrafts, plants, junk.

She always had either lunch or a snack, depending on how good she was feeling. Cappuccino from a cardboard cup and sugar-covered jam donuts, still hot from the oil, was her choice on a bad day. On a good day she might opt for a cheese croissant from the deli and an apple from one of the stalls. On a really good day she bought herself a small bag of nuts and a bunch of flowers as a reward. It all just went with the flow and she accepted that sometimes she needed sugar donuts and sometimes she didn't. It was life.

She met Strachan on a good day. She was sitting on a low concrete wall in the sun, drinking cappuccino made with skim milk and admiring the scent and colour of the bunch of freesias she'd just bought. He walked by and she admired him, too. Glenda had always liked the look of men with long, slender legs and she had a weakness, years out of date, for shoulder-length hair and a full but well-trimmed beard. He wore a cheesecloth shirt and battered, paint-stained jeans and sandals. He walked back again, carrying a drink in a cup, and he smiled at her.

'Are you saving this spot for anyone?' he asked.

She liked that. It always annoyed her when people said 'Is this seat taken?' when the seat was clearly empty.

'No,' she said, and flicked the spot beside her clean of a line of ants.

'You shouldn't have done that,' he said as he sat down beside her. She wasn't sure what he meant. He looked at her, his gaze holding hers for a long time.

'Done what?'

'The ants,' he said. 'If you're very careful and use a leaf or something you can move them without hurting them.'

She didn't think she'd done any harm to those ants but she was willing to listen. His dark brown eyes got caught up in that smile and he was solemn and joyful all at once.

'It was only a few ants,' she said. 'There'll be thousands more back in the nest, they won't even be missed.'

'But what,' he said, 'if one of those was the Jesus of ants?'

She said: 'The what?'

'What if God sends His son to every creature, in its own form? What if it isn't just humans, but every species on earth that gets a saviour, a redeemer?'

Although the day wasn't particularly warm, the top two buttons of his shirt were open and she could see the sleek line of his neck leading down to the smooth, hairless bulge of his taut pectorals.

She sipped her coffee. 'Why would God do that?'

'Well, think about it. Do you think there's life on other planets?'

It wasn't actually something she spent a lot of time considering. 'Yes, I suppose there is.'

His cup wasn't cardboard like hers; it was pottery and looked handmade. He was carrying vegetables in a hessian bag with a faded image of a leaf on it. 'Well, surely as part of His creation, God would want them to be absolved of sin. He would send Jesus to them, I mean, we're just being egocentric otherwise, aren't we?'

'Of course.'

'So why would He just stop there? Dogs, pigs, dolphins, apes … they're all intelligent, self-aware animals. So if God's sending a redeemer to all those aliens, surely He'd want all the species on earth to be saved.'

'A Jesus of everything,' she said, so caught up she nearly spilled her coffee. She could smell his peppermint tea above the freesias. His hair shone in the sun and the warmth released the scent of patchouli.

'Of everything!' he agreed. 'When God made the earth He saw that it was good. It's right there in Genesis. All good, no exceptions, and if it's all good then it's all worth saving.'

When she sat down to her chicken fillet and vegetables that night, Glenda wondered if she was eating the Jesus of chooks. She managed one or two bites, but it didn't sit right inside her. She considered throwing it into the bin, but that would have been irreverent, blasphemous. If this really was the breast of the Jesus of chickens on her plate, she needed at least to bury it.

She only had the courtyard with a couple of small pots in it. The next day she visited a nursery and bought large pots and bags of potting mix and suitably spiritual plants. She hadn't been sure why, but potted palm trees seemed good. She buried her frozen chops, mincemeat and sausages as well as the piece of chicken. She waited for days, fearful of a resurrection. It came as a bit of a surprise to realise she had just become a vegetarian. She was hungry at first but the fear of eating some species' Jesus drove her to experiment with lentil curries and tofu.

Glenda lay in bed and wondered how the animals would betray their own Christs. Would the Jesus of chickens wear a crown of thorns on her stumpy comb?

She tried to picture the crucifixion of the Jesus of cows but its front legs wouldn't spread properly to the arms of the cross and the thought of that udder just hanging there was neither aesthetic nor dignified.

She met Strachan at the market the following week. They sat under the tin roof, listening to the rain and watching puddles form. He had the pottery cup again, he always brought his own. 'Landfill,' he said, and shook his head. He was an artist, he told her, stroking the tight clip of his beard with one paint-stained hand, and he'd made the cup himself. He had a herbal teabag floating in the hot water and when he finished drinking he put the cup and the teabag away in his cloth bag. It was made of hemp, not hessian. He would put the used teabag into his compost heap when he got home.

Glenda thought he probably had the Jesus of worms living in his compost heap.

Her courtyard was beginning to smell.

'It's the fertiliser I put on my new plants,' she told a neighbour.

Glenda probably had the Jesus of blowflies.

She learned to like the texture of tofu. It was as satisfying as cheese, in a spiritual sort of way.

If the Jesuses of other species were not crucified in the literal sense of the word, she wondered how they were represented. Perhaps sardines made the sign of the can when they went to worship. Was Colonel Sanders the Antichrist of chickens? Did cattle turn in fear when they saw the sign of the golden arches?

'Plant herbs in your pots,' Strachan told her. 'Thyme, rosemary, sage, basil. You can use them in your cooking and they'll put the flies off.'

'I need something,' Glenda said.

He'd met her early at the market and walked with her through the crowd. He carried the hemp sack over his shoulder and smiled and chatted with the stallholders as if he knew them all. She felt the warmth of him beside her and matched her stride to his confident gait. The crowd parted around him, never pushing him, never treading on his sandalled feet. She led him towards the corner stall, her birdlike woman with the vegetables.

'You don't get your veggies from there?' he said.

'She's really nice. The veggies are good quality and she's cheap.'

Strachan shook his head. 'Those things are loaded with pesticides and fertilisers. The plants take it up and then you go and eat it.' He shook his head in dismay. 'This is what you want.'

He led her to the organic stall and she bought all of her fruit and vegetables there. The organic vegetables cost nearly a third more than her regular shop and they had a raw, earthy taste. The broccoli was lank and slightly yellow, the carrots were lumpy and a strange, pale colour. Her hands got red and itchy when she cut up the celery and one of the potatoes had a grub in it. Glenda deposited the grub and bits of potato reverently in her bin. She hoped there was enough potato peel to keep it happy at the tip: she didn't want to be thought of as the Pontius Pilate of potato grubs.

The organic vegetables were gritty and vital. She could feel their iron entering her bloodstream, their wholesome auras brightening her own colours. She bought a vegan cookbook and practised recipes and decided to ask Strachan what he was doing on Christmas Day. She would invite him to dinner with her: marinated tofu, roast potatoes, home-grown rosemary.

The crowds at the market were heavier than they had been, full of schoolchildren. Strachan didn't meet her early and she shopped alone and then waited. She sipped dandelion coffee while she sat under the shade of the black-and-white awning. When he came there was a child with him, a girl of about eight with amber eyes and a wistful smile.

'This is Koninderie,' he said.

Glenda tried to smile. 'That's a lovely name.'

'It's Koori for rainbow.'

'Oh.' Glenda wanted so desperately to ask more about this child, wanted the resemblance to be imagined. She had to be a neighbour, a niece, even the child of his ex-wife. 'So you've come to help Strachan with the shopping.' She felt as if she was holding her heart out to him, stripped of her dignity like a crucified cow.

'Well Mum works in the office,' Koninderie shrugged. 'She's going to retire when Dad's art gets famous.'

Strachan smiled up from his daughter. 'We all have dreams,' he said.

Sometimes dreams, sometimes delusions.

Things had begun getting a little easier for Glenda. She stopped going to the market and shopped at the supermarket. She bought a frozen turkey breast, solid as a brick and encased in plastic. Nobody shoved her or grabbed at the fruit she wanted. It was neither rainy nor hot and she hummed along with the Muzak Christmas carols as she took things off shelves and loaded her slightly errant trolley.

She picked a sprig of rosemary from the pot in her courtyard. It went well with lamb chops. The meat was tender and fragrant and Glenda served it with frozen minted peas and eggplant. It didn't bother her that she might have been eating the Jesus of lambs: what was the point, after all, if he didn't die?

Page Seventeen

Rockpools

Girija Tropp

Soon after he breaks up with Nat for the second time, Sam's parents get back together for his sake. They tell him so in the interests of honesty. HONESTY is a big deal. He feels sick when he tries to hold anything back. His dad has resigned from the police force; he and his friend, after the gay-bashing incident and just before the Royal Commission got going. There is good reason to go away. The Indian doctor two houses down has been in a bad car accident, and the Vietnamese woman, the nurse, has gone a little crazy – she comes out into the front garden and talks loudly to herself. His father considers himself the kind of guy who could get along with just about anybody which is why he became a police officer. Now that he has had to leave the service, he plans to be a businessman and has bought a pub.

On the way down to their seaside holiday, Nat blurts out that he's got a large bottle of vodka and a tobacco pouch-full of reef, plus some other stuff.

He is quick to emphasise that he personally does not indulge since he's been picked for the Eastern Region football team and in full training. His explanation that his friends' parents are very hardline about those sorts of things, and would kill their children for doing drugs, does not cut him any slack.

In the car, where he is squeezed between packed bags, they read him the riot act for the next three hours, waking him even when he nods off, with some new reasoning they think up. His mum tells him horror stories of when she was sixteen and house-breaking on a dare with friends. 'Bet your friends won't be around if you were caught with the stuff.'

'Of course they will,' he replies.

His parents laugh uncontrollably in the front seat like they've gone spasticated. 'Fair dinkum?' his dad sneers.

At least it's better than hostile silence. Sam's parents don't argue since they patched up. He wonders if they talk about what really happened on the night those guys were battered to death, if they turn it over in their minds when they are alone in bed. The day before they were due to go down to the beach house, his mother was in the corridor talking in a sweet voice, the one she uses when she is trying to make everything work out. She was saying, 'There is a leak in the bathroom.'

Something is wrong with his dad's face, and it happened after his mum spent 400 dollars on the coat with rabbit skin on the collar. Life's all about shit.

*

At the beach house, Sam shaves the sides of his head, dyes his hair blue, tips it orange, and mohawk-spikes it with his mother's gel. He bandages a razor cut near his ear, next to a pimple that wants to explode. 'You can't play football like that,' his mother says but he tells her that he's got the summer vacation to play around, and takes off with his surfboard to catch himself a wave or two and to have private thoughts about Nat.

'Be careful,' she calls out from the porch.

'Bloody pooftah,' he thinks his father says.

The coastline belongs to experienced surfers and he is amazed that his mother thinks he needs warning. Down at the beach, there are too many tourists staring at the waves and while he's trying to decide on the lie of the rip, some guys he met the week before ask if he wants to sand surf. He falls in as they go up single file through the coastal grass to get a decent run down the other side. On the grassy knoll, the tourist girl is organising her hair into a pink bandeau. On seeing him, she steps into his path. His friends keep on going.

He made the mistake of speaking to the girl out of embarrassment. She caught him staring at her boobs at the Pizza Hut and deflected attempts to sever the connection by attaching herself to his new friends. His inability to make small talk does not deter her. At the end of three weeks, he is alarmed yet thrilled to have attained a status in the eyes of others that he cannot quite define.

She's got barbed wire for a mouth, jeans baggy and worn low on her hips, rolls of fat around her waist like they are the latest fashion; she's staring at a sky pierced with light filaments too bright (sunglasses worn around her neck like a necklace).

'I didn't ask for you to go out wiz me,' she says. 'Just talk, like friends do.'

'I have plans with friends,' he replies.

'How can you have friends? We hav not been here long.'

He's been told that she's been asking about him, and his mates are having fun obtaining his life history and relaying it back to her.

'The boys and I, we are going sand surfing.'

'I can com too … and I shall play in rock pool.'

'We don't hang around with girls when we're surfing. How 'bout right now for talking?'

'In my country, men are not childish.'

He is taken aback at being classed as a man. 'When in Rome,' he says virtuously.

'Would you like to fuck with me?'

'I am not trying to fuck with you.'

'Why not? Am I too fat?'

He rears back, shocked.

'At ze moment, there is no one in ze house.' She extends her hand. 'I will let you do whatever you wish and then we'll talk.'

Following her, he is in shock. When he takes her hand, he is still shocked. Her hand tickles as if he's scooped a sand crab. When he walks back to the holiday house, he is thinking about what he needs to do so he can start working out what to do and this creates bright shards of light that he cannot examine. What he knows for sure is that this is not what he wants and he needs to think if he's to stop what's going to happen from happening but his mind has taken a vacation.

*

The next day, he gets to the beach where the guys have organised a tournament, and she's there. 'Fate, it is unavoidable,' she says. 'That's just slack, saying something like that.'

'You do not agree wiz me?'

'Some things are true and some aren't.'

They are standing with his mates, all four of them, on rocks that had been occupied earlier by a fisherman. The tide is coming in. They are drinking beer out of cans, but she's brought along a champagne glass and the stuff to fill it with. He expects that it is from her dad's cellar.

Her face is amazing, she's done something to her mouth which reminds him of a swelling wave and her long hair is tied back in a pony tail with black velvet. He's seen his friends look at her breasts with the same respect given to football stars. She doesn't look fat anymore in her black halter dress.

She holds out her champagne glass and drops it off the side. They hear a tinkle as her arms spread wide to match her pronouncement. 'My heart is broken, that's a fact.'

He thinks this is when he loses track of her. After that particular strangeness, he goes walkabout and sits in a cove and stares at the waves. The blue heeler belonging to one of the locals, a working dog, comes and sits with him for a bit and then goes and chases breakers. That's cool to watch and after a while he feels as if it's him in the dog's body, jumping and chasing and nipping foam between sharp teeth.

When he goes back for another beer, one of the guys has an arm around Claudette's waist and he wonders if he should say anything but he does not know what she wants. If it is what she wants, then peace to her, is what he would say. Then he thinks this is the kind of thing his father would say and how pukey was that? He must be drunk – shakes his head when someone tilts some scotch in his direction. Of course, at some point, he takes over the bottle. Then he thinks he'd better get off the rock. Then he moseys on around the corner to get rid of the thing that's moving violently in his belly and then he lies on the sand to get his bearings but that does not work so he goes hunting for a good propping spot. When he finds one, a concave of rock and a stony pillow, he sees how gloriously violent the sea is and imagines his life if he were a singer. How powerful is fate and how small is man and nothing's for sure, and what about the fisherman who got swept away on a rock similar to what they were standing on earlier; these beaches have freak waves and unstable cliffs and he thinks she's right about fate and perhaps he should check that his mates did get off the rock and sand surf but he really is too comfortable and getting up is too much and he sleeps and wakes with his head gripped by pincers and the horizon has a pale pink blush rising from indigo-black and the wind is biting and he gets up like he's a robot and says *fuck man* and makes his way, unsteadily at first, and then more surely over the rocky outcrops and then along the beach where the sand massages his feet, and he says to himself that this is a *grouse* experience, and maybe it's nearly morning, and his parents will worry and *where the fuck is his mobile?*

His mates are up on the rock and the sun is making its way up the sky, and they say where the hell was he and they've been surfing all night. Claudette's mouth is mashed into a blur of unhealthy pink and her skin is blotchy and her mascara has run and she looks pretty gross. There is a short moment when everything is fine; there's her and there's him without anything in common and in a few days she'll be back in Melbourne and sometime after that she'll leave and go back to where she belongs and won't be his problem. Then she looks at him and he totally freaks and he's not sure why, until she raises the bottle and smashes it on the rock and lets fly on her wrists and it takes all of them to hold her down and get the glass off her and haul her kicking and struggling down to the scrub, and screaming and abusive down the steep sand slope to the beach, where they keep her under control and Julien, the owner of the heeler whose father manages the holiday homes, says, *This is some depressed chick.*

He finds out that she's been crying and sobbing intermittently through the night and that she's dropped e and speed and has been outdrinking even John H., the son of the tavern keeper. 'She's like sick in the head,' says John looking at him as if he's done something to cause all this injury. In fact, they are all looking at him to fix her up.

*

When the holidays are over, he meets Claudette again, this time her family as well. Unfortunately, it takes place at his ex-girl-friend Nat's house – he has yet to reply to her hand-delivered letter saying she's sorry for everything. He still can't forgive her for using him to get an introduction to his cousin who plays front pocket for the Richmond Tigers. It was a wise political move, but still.

Claudette's mother is wearing DaNang pants and a tight black singlet with Prada written across the bust and chunky silver jewellery and a navy beanie with Armani across the rim.

'Hi,' he says politely to Claudette's amazing boobs.

'Do you want a bundy and coke?' he asks without raising his eyes. Please no holiday repeats, his mind says from a distance as if it were a movie running quietly in the background with sea and waves and classical music and a killer whale and only him to save the tourists.

The main house is for looking at, for relaxing at the end of a hard day's work, not for fooling around in so the oldies mosey on down to the renovated shed, and he follows Nat from a dis-tance – she's heading for the pool tables set up specially in out-buildings nearby. Her stereo is there as well and when everyone is settled, drinking and rolling joints, perched on beanbags, makeshift cushions, handrails or upside-down plastic crates, Sam looks through her CD rack and is gratified to see mostly what they've collected together. He fiddles with the controls try-ing to get the sound right.

When Claudette finds him, she holds on to his hand as he squirms away through the crush. Her pool skills are extra-ordinary – strong swimmer's muscles he thinks, and she offers unwanted advice, even leaning over to correct his arm position. He tries introducing her to everyone but she is sticky.

He is aware of Nat's stare. He's been with Nat ever since he was two. She snickers *French pussy?* in his ear when he moves back, and points out to Claudette the large framed photograph on the wall: two toddlers.

'I love swimming,' Claudette says.

'I play football,' Nat says.

'Girls play football?'

'Her case is before the Supreme Court,' he tells Claudette. He tries giving Nat's baby sister to Claudette, expecting her to go goo goo gah gah, but it doesn't work.

He resigns himself to entertaining her. On the way back from the bar with two bottles of beer, Nat prowls over and says in a low voice, *She needs a good fuck … the bathroom's free.*

When Claudette stops finally, a glazed look in her eyes from a fat joint that's been making the rounds, Sam goes to Nat's bedroom to get a jacket he left behind months before and strolls back to the main house.

Sam has an opinion about women who run their tongue over their lips but it suits Claudette's mother to act like she's in a movie about herself. He wonders about her age again.

Claudette's father comes and stands next to his wife. A short guy talking about working out and passing around advice about personal training. The man owns the latest model Alfa Romeo and talks in a disparaging voice about women spending his money, but his hand is always on his wife, hooked in her waistband or around her shoulders. Sam thinks about them making out and looks at his dad who, come to think about it, looks macho. From what Sam can hear, another of his father's friends had to leave the force. Everyone is calling for a speech. They want to know about his dad's new business venture.

When toasting the decision to leave the CIB, Sam's dad goes on and on about the good fight and how crime is being beaten down into submission.

In the corner of the room, he sees Nat and talks to her about his love for pork pies as if shielding her. No one said anything about the charges being dropped against the two police officers. Sam has heard his teacher say 'Remember gay bashing as the team sport of the '80s?' Anyway, here is his dad, trapped into speaking in public, wanting to do the right thing; reaching for truth in the one breath – what will future generations think of us? And the taint of AIDs in the other, saying jovially, 'A great cop can make a good publican … showing his dedication to society.' This last bit intended as a joke that falls flat but everyone is well and truly toasted, so there is no one to care. His mum is stripping chicken off the bone with her teeth and joining the cheese conversation and adding her own – how wonderful was it that so-and-so's kid had a computer job? Sam takes Nat away by promising to take her to the movies the next day and they sit in the garden with a case of his father's Carlton Light. They can hear people *cacking* themselves over nothing. 'So how did your dad get the money together to buy The Knights Arms?' Nat asks. But he doesn't really want to talk. There is an expectant pause and nothing else to do. He opens his mouth like an airplane going for an emergency landing.

On a garden bench next to the tack room, he finds the first sprinkling of autumn leaves and takes his shoes off, tucks his feet under and closes his eyes. A light rain drizzles through the overhanging ash gum and onto his cheek. Nat perches on a low branch, smoking a cigarette. 'Your girlfriend is fucking some bloke in the toilet,' she says and leaps down.

He sees that she is holding a horse bridle. Swivelling her hips, she saunters, twirling the reins like a cancan dancer. 'Tell me something,' he says in a drowsy voice.

'Yeah what?'

'If I was caught with your stash of dope and was in big trouble, would you own up?'

She hooks a leg over him and settles down and rocks about while staring off into the distance. 'No, I don't think so,' she says finally. 'My dad would crack the shits. Besides, wouldn't you want to make sure that I didn't get into trouble?' She leans down and her long hair cascades around his face like storm clouds.

He has a waking dream where he is married to Claudette and she is making him a quiche with fine herbs, and it has the most brilliant taste. She is pouring him a wine from her father's cellar, saying these kinds of foods are only available in France. His head fills with a subdued evening sun blaze like the golden crust of the quiche and his tongue is touched with a memory of sea spray.

Southword

The Pact

Laurie Clancy

Going through his wife's belongings some two weeks after she had been killed in a car accident, throwing out some of her clothes, packing up others that looked in good shape, trying to distract himself, John Stanton came across a small cache of letters in the bottom of a drawer of a filing cabinet. The cabinet had been locked but there had been no real attempt to keep the letters hidden. Stanton had found the key without difficulty, on her desk next to the paperweights, and had unlocked the drawer, ready to throw her papers out. He stared at the small bundle, neatly wrapped in an unsealed manila envelope, and thought how insignificant they looked compared to the fifteen boxes of letters, manuscripts and papers down in the cellar that he was saving for posterity.

Jack was the writer in the family. Julia had been an educational psychologist and counsellor, freelancing in theory but in practice employed mostly by the Education Department as a kind of troubleshooter for troubled kids.

Just a few weeks before she had run off the road and hit a tree she had asked him, half-seriously, half-satirically, what he wanted her to do with his papers. 'After all, you promised to predecease me,' she laughed.

Vanity and mortification had prevented him from replying. He was not too old still to write a best-selling masterpiece that would have scholars and critics beating down his door, begging for possession of his papers. He felt like saying this to Julia (though he was sure she already knew it) but the thought of the expression on her face – loyal, tender, wonderfully affectionate and utterly disbelieving – deterred him from doing so.

Reality bit in at last. The papers were worthless. He would destroy them completely, but to make the process less painful for himself he would take one document per day, read it and, in secret, kill it. He did not try to calculate how many years this would take; if he were slipping behind he could always increase the tempo of destruction – unless, like Julia's, his life was suddenly truncated.

In just five weeks, the ritual had come to completely absorb him. His miniscule auto-da-fé had become the highlight of his day. Bills, contracts, letters from his agent were of little interest to him but the personal notes he read avidly. He exempted from the bonfire letters to him from writers more famous than himself but he was astonished to find how many of the identities of the senders he had completely forgotten, especially if there was no date or address or surname on them. Correspondents wrote and declared their admiration for his work. There were highly laudatory reviews of his books which he had forgotten about – and also the others, which burned in his memory and re-opened wounds he had thought long healed.

He looked at this pitiful hoard of letters his wife had saved and decided they should go in one fell swoop, before they reawakened what would no doubt be painful memories. No death of a million cuts like his niggardly efforts on his own collection. He thought they were probably letters from Julia to her mother when she was unsuccessfully battling cancer two years ago and he had no desire to relive those agonies as well as his own.

He picked up the top letter and glanced at the address. Strong, bold handwriting that looked familiar. It was addressed to Julia at one of the schools she habitually visited. Why not to her home address? A tiny spasm of dread seized him. Hands trembling, he looked immediately at the signature of the writer, groaned loudly and sat down on the nearest chair. It was signed 'Gary'. Gary Webster had been more or less his closest friend, the longest lasting at any rate, at least until about two years ago when, without any actual sundering, their relationship had seemed to cool and they saw less and less of one another.

John Stanton looked at the date on the letter – about two years ago, just about when Julia's mother was beginning her chemotherapy treatment and when Stanton, battling with the novel that he thought might finally give him his breakthrough, had perhaps not been paying as much attention to Julia as he should have. And Gary Webster had gone out of his life about that time too.

He turned the letter over. 'Jewel dear,' it began. He groaned again. He had not thought anyone else would have known, let alone used, his private term of endearment for his wife, but he would have let it slip out in public once or twice and who more likely than Gary to have heard it? He looked at the signature at the end again. 'With all my love. Gary.' He rifled through the dates on the letters. They seemed to be arranged in reverse chronological order, the letter on top being the most recent and the others going back in time so that the collection read like a history of the relationship in reverse. He could not face them. He knew what to expect. He closed the filing cabinet, went out into the kitchen and poured himself a glass of whisky. Then he walked back inside and opened the file again.

When John Stanton awoke the next morning it was to the usual familiar blanket of misery that his wife's sudden death had flung over him but after a few seconds a newer, sharper pain stabbed at him as he remembered the discovery of last night. He glanced at the illuminated clock by his bed and saw it was 7.45. He had slept better than he had expected, eventually. Then he remembered that he had not changed it for the end of daylight saving and it was actually only 6.45. He could lie in bed for another quarter of an hour and still get up at his usual time. Except that now he could lie in bed all day if he wanted to, though he knew he wouldn't. He was a creature of habit.

He lay in bed for a few minutes, thinking about what he should do. He had no desire to get up. It was warm under the blankets and even though it was only April it was nippy in Melbourne in the early hours. The best thing surely would be to destroy the letters, read no more of them, and try to forget they had ever existed. Do nothing to despoil the memory of Julia. But he would not be able to do that. He lacked the self-discipline. Besides, he might still be jumping to the wrong conclusion; they might be perfectly innocent. 'Dear Jewel.' 'With all my love.'

He crawled out of bed and made his way to the bathroom, where he stood under the shower for a long time, trying to get some warmth into his body. When he had dressed and shaved he made his way to the kitchen and prepared a breakfast of chipolata sausages, eggs and toast, and drank several glasses of orange juice. He felt dehydrated from all the whisky he had drunk the night before, though strangely he had no headache. Then he went upstairs to his study, sat down at the desk and stared at his laptop.

Since the accident he had been deluged with emails expressing sympathy and grief, as well as letters and telephone calls. Julia had been loved and had a wide range of friends. He knew most of the messages were really for her, rather than himself. He had replied to none of them.

He switched on the computer and waited. Julia had always hated the slowness of the machine, which she called Macwait. She had never been a patient person even at the best of times. Sure enough, there were three more messages from yesterday, as well as a piece of junk mail offering to enlarge his penis by four inches. He scrolled down the screen. There must have been fifty of them altogether, including four from Gary Webster. He looked at these. The first three were quite long. The fourth, which had been sent only a few days ago, was short and exasperated. It said simply, 'Jack, come on mate, I know how you must be feeling but you can't stay locked up forever. Julia wouldn't have wanted it.' Well, he should know.

John Stanton switched off the computer and sat there, thinking of the bundle of letters downstairs. He knew he was going to read them all but he wanted to put it off for as long as possible. Stanton used to think to himself that he had done only one strong thing in his life – and maybe that was a wrong one.

When he and Julia had first become engaged he had told her he didn't want children. She had looked surprised but not upset and had immediately agreed – perhaps, he had begun to think from time to time in later years, a little too quickly, too willingly. Writing was a hazardous business and anyway children took up a lot of time. He had already seen what they had done to the lives of some of his older writer friends.

'We have our careers,' he said.

She had smiled at him lovingly. 'And we have each other,' she said.

He blushed. It was the nearest she would ever come to a rebuke.

As the years passed, and the success Stanton craved failed to come, and he found himself living to a considerable extent off his wife's income, he wondered increasingly whether he had made the right choice.

In the early days, before Julia had begun to earn a salary, they had been poor but very happy, living in a run-down, cockroach-infested flat in West Brunswick. Stanton had never laughed so much in his life as in those days. The two of them made jokes about the cockroaches, how they would eat them if they were ever starving, and Julia would print out a variety of elaborate recipes with detailed instructions: 'First, catch your cockroaches.'

But all the time she had been serious about her 'career', though she never called it that. She hated the word so much she refused to use it. Perhaps, Stanton began to wonder, she had been more serious about her work than he had been. She had completed her master's in educational psychology and then had written a Ph.D while working full-time. As for himself, he had some minor successes – a novel that was well reviewed and made a couple of short lists for prizes and that earned him a small twelve-month grant from the Literature Board – but in his heart of hearts he knew he wasn't doing what he should be doing.

All of his friends, especially the non-writers who were easier to fool, were impressed by his work ethic – all except Julia who, though she would never have said a word, he knew saw through him. All the energies that should have gone into the laborious, solitary task of inventing a world, peopling it with characters, trying to understand them and making them believable to read-ers, had instead been diverted to peripheral activities – book reviewing, giving talks to schoolkids, judging suburban literary competitions. All worthy things in themselves, no doubt, and carried out under the guise of making urgently needed money, but all carrying him away from what he used to call, only half-ironically, his vocation. They lived frugally and both of them knew that they could have survived off her salary.

Julia could well have wondered if this was what they had given up the idea of kids for, but if she had she would have suppressed the thought immediately. Her most abiding quality, and the one that Stanton loved most in her, was unconditional loyalty. Besides, unlike himself, she was by nature and temperament an optimist. She would accept any situation and then begin to look for the positives in it, and act upon them, as she had with the idea of her 'career'.

As they moved into their thirties the stability of their marriage was a constant source of wonder and discussion among their friends, most of whom were into their second or even third liaison. Some friends with children even envied their childless state.

One afternoon John Stanton was drinking in a pub after work with an old friend, Steve Bowers, when Steve told him that he had spent the whole afternoon calculating how much money he had spent over the years on his kids.

'It's not just the obvious things, Jack,' he said, showing him a piece of paper with long lists of figures on it that must have taken him hours to prepare. 'Food, clothing, medical expenses, education fees, amusement. Think about that little terrace cottage of yours. I could never have raised four kids in a house that size. So I had to take out a huge mortgage that I'm still paying off.'

Stanton could have mentioned that Steve received many tax breaks through the kids, that the house now represented a huge capital asset which one day, after his kids had fled the nest, he could cash in. He could have mentioned that even in his strait-ened circumstances Steve still spent, on Jack's conservative calcu-lation, at least five thousand dollars a year on alcohol. But he said nothing except, 'Your shout.' It was the husbands, oddly enough, he thought, who usually complained, even though most of the hard work of rearing the children fell on the wives.

One Friday, on the tenth anniversary of their wedding, Jack took Julia out to dinner at Matteo's, courtesy of a modest Public

Lending Rights cheque that had arrived earlier in the week. Under cover of the din and the subdued lighting they held hands and whispered in a way they hadn't for years. They both loved Matteo's though they reserved it for special occasions. The food was excellent and the clutter of the scurrying waiters as well as the loud hum of the diners' conversation gave them a paradoxical sense of privacy.

But Jack had other things to talk about. 'Jewel, I've been thinking about the ban on children and how selfish I've been. It's not too late to change it, you know. I could be a house father when you go back to work. I've read books on it. Don't laugh. Despite what you think, books *can* teach you things sometimes.'

'I wasn't laughing at that,' said Julia. 'It's your sudden enthusiasm for a child – for me – after all these years. But Jack, it *is* too late. No, stop,' she said, as he began to speak. 'I know women have babies in their thirties all the time these days, I know it's not too late biologically. But it's too late psychologically. I … we've constructed a life for ourselves that's workable, in many ways satisfying.' Their life was assessed as a 2A, Jack thought with a touch of bitterness. 'I couldn't start all over and do it again.' She held his hand. 'Let's just go on as we are and try to love each other as much as we can.'

So she had wanted a child after all, and yet there was not a word of reproach. He had never loved her so much, had never felt such a pain of remorse.

'In that case I have an idea but I don't want you to misunderstand me. Let's call it a pact.'

'A pact?'

'Look,' he said. He was speaking with an earnestness that was unusual for him. 'I don't want you to misunderstand me. If you're bored with the marriage, if you feel I'm not paying you enough attention, I don't mind if you … take a lover. As long as you're honest about it, of course. And as long as you don't fall in love with him,' he added foolishly.

He watched as a frown of incomprehension came over her features. She rarely frowned, he realised suddenly. More often she smiled. She had a generous mouth, its corners turned down slightly from all that smiling.

She spoke slowly, choosing her words with a kind of fastidiousness, as if she were speaking a foreign language. 'And you,' she asked, 'where do you fit into this ... pact?'

Jack hadn't thought of that, he suddenly realised. He considered it for a few seconds. 'I suppose it would have to apply to me too, in all honesty. But I wouldn't have any intention of using it.'

Julia looked puzzled. 'Jack, what's the point of conferring a freedom on someone who has no intention of exercising it?'

It was a fair question. Eventually he said, 'I suppose that's the point of it. The very fact of its being there, even if it's never used, is a kind of safety valve, a release of pressure.'

Julia sighed. 'Existentialist to the last.' Then unexpectedly she burst into laughter. He watched as the corners of her mouth came down again. 'Jack,' she said, 'it's lucky I know you so well. Do you realise what most wives would have thought? That all this is an excuse for you to see other women, under the guise of equality, fairness. But I know it isn't.' She tweaked his nose comically. 'You're quite sincere. But I don't think I'll be taking you up on your offer.'

Jewel dear,

I suppose I wasn't entirely surprised to receive the letter calling our whole relationship off but that didn't make it any less shattering. Is it possible that you could still change your mind?

I'm prepared to grovel, to have you on any terms, to marry you if you would let me – and no, I know what you've always said about never leaving Jack. I also know that he's a decent enough person in his own way. I know how angry you become when you think I'm not giving him his due. I know how badly you feel about deceiving him. I don't feel so hot about it myself, though I know I can stay out of his way, which I try my best to do, whereas you have to go home to him every night. But if I sound begrudging it's because my blood boils when I see the indifference and condescension with which he treats you.

One other thing. I don't know how that bastard Steve Bowers found out about us but I swear I didn't tell him or anyone else anything. I've tried all the time to play completely by your rules, bizarre as they seem to me at times. Maybe he saw us hold hands briefly once, maybe it was just a glance – one can't keep what one feels entirely under lock and key – but

I'll tell you one thing: if it weren't for the fact that it would cause you further embarrassment I'd go round and smash his face in.

John Stanton put the letter down. So it was as he had expected. He felt like a tennis ball that had been struck back and forth to either end of the court, as if he had no agency at all, as if he only existed in the minds of other people. That was what hurt him even more than the revelation – that, plus the fact that Julia had not felt that she could tell him, even after they had agreed that honesty was far more important than sexual possessiveness. He stared at the letter. Webster was not much of a lover, he thought contemptuously, the literary man in him beginning to take over. If he were a woman, would a letter like this catch him up in a tide of passion? It was querulous, rather than ardent.

Why had she kept the letters? Surely she must have intended to destroy them one day. But people never anticipate sudden, violent death. No, the distinguished visitor usually came creeping up on one, invading the liver or the colon or the prostate, gradually stiffening limbs, slowing the working of organs to the point where they stopped functioning completely.

He picked up the next letter.

I don't understand the crazy deal, the so-called pact, you made with Jack, but from what you've let slip it had a lot to do with honesty. Are you being honest now? You seem more worried that Steve might know about your affair than that Jack might. Is public opinion more important to you than your husband? And where do I come into it? If you wanted to, you could leave Jack, come and live with me and have our kids. You know I'm a good father, whatever mess I made of my marriage. Even Nicole said that. I've tried not to say anything about Jack but the truth is that his writing is like himself – completely self-absorbed. His only subject is himself. Proust might have been able to get away with that but Jack isn't an interesting enough person, to put it brutally. I'm no literary critic, as you know, but that's my view.

Jack put the letter down. He could read no more for a while. Pain was like food; in times of emergency it had to be rationed. Logically, he knew, he should have gone to the bottom of the pile and read the letters in chronological order but there was something mysteriously attractive in this slow, retrospective revelation of deceit. It was like reading a novel that eventually returns the reader to the original point of departure. Unravelling, was the word he thought of at once. It was an unravelling. The question was, what to do now?

That night Jack sat by the fireside, a bottle of liqueur muscat by his side, and stared into the flames. Now, however, he was thinking about Gary Webster rather than Julia. What he was slowly piecing together was a long-term pattern of manipulation, of which the affair with Julia was maybe even the final stage. Was it paranoia? Or was it that he had simply been too naive to see it before?

The friendship between the two men went back a long way – back to school days – although they had always been keen competitors and rivals, first on the football field, then with academic studies and finally with women. There had always, Jack felt even then, been something compulsive, almost obsessive about Gary's competitiveness, especially when it came to women.

Girls liked Jack when he was young. They thought he was 'sweet'. It took him some years to discover that sweetness was inimical to sexual attractiveness, that it had a fraternal, platonic quality. It took him even longer to realise that as women grew older, sweetness could make a comeback, was reinstalled but with a higher place in their lexicon of virtues. Sexual excitement wore off. Warmth, companionship, loyalty didn't.

Gary wasn't sweet. He was sharp, astringent – and extremely accomplished in attracting women. Often Jack was the one who invited a girl from their year out first. Gary's technique was subtle. He would always begin by praising Jack's taste in women and assuring him how obvious it was the girl liked him. Then after two or three dates he would, still under the pretence of praising the girlfriend, begin to put the knife into her. 'Boy, she can sure sock it away,' he might say, knowing that Jack didn't like heavy drinking. Or, 'What I like about her is she has such a vivacious personality. She always has guys hanging off her.'

Jack's confidence with women had never been very great – he had none of Gary's film-star good looks – and it did not take long for self-doubt to begin to seep in. The relationship would peter out – sometimes to the puzzlement of the girl – and then a few weeks later he would discover that Gary was taking her out and not only that but had managed to do what he himself hadn't and got her into bed with him.

Why did he not protest?

There would have been no point in accusing Gary of disloyalty. He would merely have looked surprised and said, 'But I thought you'd lost interest in her.' Sometimes Jack felt that he had been reduced to the status of procurer. His fragile self-esteem became even more fragile. Until Julia.

Julia Norton was the most intelligent woman in the class of that year. She was also far and away the most beautiful. She was what the fashion magazines call 'willowy' – tall (like Jack), long-legged, dark-haired with intense blue eyes, that irresistible Irish combination. She reminded Jack of the woman Theodore Roethke wrote about in his wonderful poem 'I knew a woman lovely in her bones'. All the males in the literature class pursued her – all except Jack, that is, because he thought he never would stand a chance.

Maybe that was what did it. She began talking to him after class sometimes and because he didn't make a pass at her but merely responded amicably she started to relax and fall into an easy, bantering intimacy. Sweetness. 'Those boys,' she would tell him ruefully, and recount another self-mocking account of her last-ditch stands to protect her virtue. He discovered that he could make her laugh too and spent hours every night planning the spontaneous remarks that he'd make the next day so that he would have the pleasure of hearing that throaty laugh of hers. He called her Penelope because she had so many suitors. He made a big show of assessing each one, his merits and demerits, and giving him a point score out of 100, as if he were assessing wines. 'Rather tart on the palate.' 'Lacks length and structure.'

After a while she started going out with him, as if by mutual consent, and not long after that they went to bed as naturally and easily as one could imagine. A few weeks later Jack startled her by telling her he wanted to marry her.

'Do you think you can hang on to her?' Gary said to him one night after he had come across them drifting obliviously along the street, hand in hand. For the first time, Jack caught a glimpse of malice in his eyes, a flash of envy and frustration at the one that had got away. But Julia, the most beautiful woman he had ever been out with, was also the first one he completely trusted. She was always polite to Gary, who hung around a fair bit in their company, but Jack often saw her look at him with a wry, ironic expression on her face, an expression he had never seen on her before then which she had certainly never turned on him. And Gary must have sensed it because he never assumed the teasing, flirtatious tone which he normally adopted with attractive young women.

Gary was Jack's best man at the wedding, of course. It was not exactly that he was his closest friend, though he was certainly the longest lasting, but rather that they were bound by old ties of ... complicity. After the wedding he congratulated Jack warmly, gave Julia an uncharacteristically decorous kiss – Gary usually treated any excuse to kiss a woman as a kind of smorgasbord – and in general behaved in exemplary fashion. Jack was only beginning to wonder, as he stared at the half-empty bottle of muscat, whether this was the beginning of a long and carefully planned campaign.

About a year after their marriage Jack was able to return the favour and act as Gary's best man. He had become engaged to Julia's closest friend. Nicole was a wonderful woman whom Jack liked very much. She was not exceptionally good-looking but, like Julia, had a kind of animation that gave her a look almost of radiance at times.

Once again, everything went off as planned except for a strange thing that Gary said in passing, that jarred Jack more and more the longer he thought about it. 'Well,' he said, as they clinked glasses of champagne together, 'at least I got the second prettiest girl in the class.' He hadn't realised they were rating the women like fillies and as the implications of the remark sank slowly in he was rather shocked.

A few months after they were married Gary picked up a job in Bangkok, teaching English as a second language. A year later the couple moved to London and in the space of less than three years Nicole gave birth to three sons. Right through this period Gary remained, rather surprisingly, an assiduous correspondent, writing quite funny and informative, if very brief, letters. He knew Jack always passed them on to Julia.

When the boys were born, he became the proudest of fathers, constantly extolling the virtues of his sons and the delights of parenthood. It was re-reading the old letters in which he had raved about his sons that Jack began to suspect what he had been doing – pouring his poisoned honey into Julia's ear, playing on what he sensed were her ambivalent feelings about not having children.

Jack staggered to his feet, went to the desk and pulled out one of the letters that he especially remembered.

The boys are very well and I think if possible we grow to love them even more each day. Josh is a fine, handsome chap with the most delightful grin. Bernard is his characteristic taciturn, introspective self. One of the most moving things I have ever seen is his affection for Josh – quite unself-conscious, untaught, and which can only grow as Josh responds to it, though even now he watches Bernard with fascinated concentration.

Nicole told me about an incident that occurred in the shopping centre the other day. She had taken the boys to Sainsbury's and was hauling them through the supermarket on a shopping trolley. For no apparent reason, Josh began to scream and yell at the top of his voice and Bernard moved across and put his arms around his younger brother. There were murmurs of approval from various onlookers, who seemed inclined to burst into applause.

Wonderful stuff. Full of sincerity, and with a … sobriety that Gary rarely displayed in his conversation. There was hardly a letter that did not make some reference, however slight or oblique, to the boys, to how well they were doing at school, to how good-looking they were ('They take after their mother,' he wrote modestly – or disingenuously), to how proud of them he was. His only complaint was that they spoke in English accents! What did he expect when they were born and reared in England?

And then, after a few years the letters abruptly stopped. Until six months later when he wrote to say that he and Nicole were getting a divorce. He was coming home to Australia while she was staying on with the boys in London, where she had an excellent job with the BBC. He said nothing of why they had separated. Perhaps English women found his inscrutable charms as irresistible as Australian women had. Or were there tensions because Nicole's career as a TV producer had taken off and she now made far more money than he did?

Jack was surprised he was returning to Melbourne, given the way he had raved about his kids. Surely he would have stayed in London to be with them, at least until they had grown up? Still, he said to himself, I am hardly in a position to judge ... Gary asked if he could stay with the two of them on a short-term basis until he got himself settled and of course they said of course.

When Jack met him at the airport he was surprised to see how little he had changed. The faint wrinkles, the slightly leathery skin only added to his charm and he could see the covert glances of appraisal women gave him as they walked past.

'G'day, mate.' Gary held out his hand, casual, amused. 'How're they hangin'?' He was putting on his Australian act again. Jack took his bag and suitcase from him and began to walk towards the car.

'That's all the luggage you have?'

'Travellin' light, mate.'

His accent had become, if anything, more rather than less pronounced, as if he had suddenly developed some kind of protective mechanism against the Poms, drawn a linguistic shell around himself. Or perhaps he had simply learned to exploit its novelty value. On the way back to Jack's place he deftly deflected the one or two questions put to him about the divorce and seemed almost to have forgotten that his sons existed, so that John Stanton finally fell silent.

Gary, predictably, was the perfect house guest and he and Julia, who had said nothing for or against Jack's decision to allow him to stay with them while he looked for a flat, treated each other with what seemed almost exaggerated courtesy. And Gary was as good as his word. It took him a few weeks but he searched diligently for a flat and a job and eventually found both. In the meantime he helped out with the housework and buying food. He seemed to have plenty of money. When Jack hinted delicately at this he said, 'Savings, Jack. There's nothing to spend it on in

London.' Jack could not judge from his tone whether he was being ironic or not.

Jack helped him shift his few possessions into a flat in Northcote and even went shopping with him for the basic items of furniture he needed – a bed, a desk and chair and a television set. After that life returned to normal for Jack and Julia. He never talked about his kids anymore or about Nicole and seemed quite cheerfully resigned to resuming the life of a bachelor.

This he did in a big way. From time to time Jack invited him to dinner and he always brought a companion, though usually a different one. They soon learned they had to be careful with names. It was obvious that he was not going to be 'tricked' into marriage again (that was how he put it, though they had never seen any signs of scheming on Nicole's part). The women he brought over seemed younger and younger, as if he were regressing to a decade before and was reliving it.

The sun was beginning to ascend over the horizon. It was time to go to bed. Jack had been sipping liqueur muscat for many hours now and his head was feeling clouded. The question remained: what to do about Gary? He had no idea. All he knew was that he had to see him again before he decided anything and for the moment at least he wasn't going to tell him he knew about his affair with Julia. A slow anger was beginning to rise in him, the longer he thought about the calculations, the exhaustive strategy of his deception. He held his cards face down. He wanted to see how Gary would react under pressure. At the same time he knew he had to get hold of himself. He was not used to drinking heavily and he felt it was unmanning him.

John Stanton awoke sometime in the afternoon with his head pounding and a tongue that felt as thick as cardboard. He missed Julia dreadfully; it was as if she had been taken from him twice. He grabbed at every cure he could find – two Panadols, a Berocca and several glasses of orange juice – and stood under the shower, trying to decide what he should do. Wouldn't it be best to leave the whole thing, to forget he had ever seen the letters, to leave the memory of Julia in peace? But he knew he couldn't do that. The curiosity, the need to understand, were too intense, far stronger now than jealousy or bitterness or anger. With what he knew he could play Webster like a fish.

He rang Gary the next day, when he felt he had recovered his senses, and suggested they have lunch together soon. His reaction was that of a man who had just encountered Lazarus returned from the dead.

'Fantastic, mate. It's just great you're coming out of your cocoon. Where'll it be and when?'

Amid the surprise in his voice there seemed to be a genuine note of warmth as well – unless he was very good at faking it. They arranged to meet at a Carlton pub on Friday. It was a mellow afternoon and they sat in the garden of the pub drinking pots of beer before progressing to white wine. They exchanged banalities about football, the treachery of the government, the ineffectuality of the Opposition, the situation in Iraq. It was as if neither of them wanted to make the first move. Their silences seemed to be in a strange rhythmic harmony with the sudden, periodic eruptions of the airconditioning plant nearby.

Finally, Gary said, 'I know it's going to go on for a long time yet but are you beginning to get over the pain?'

It seemed terribly strange to him – nightmarish even – to be talking about his wife who was dead. There was something quite unreal about it and he didn't know how to answer. At that moment a mutual acquaintance approached. Denis Mahony was a plumber but his real existence was as a Carlton Character, one of those inveterate fringe pub dwellers who construct an identity for themselves out of hanging around pubs and telling yarns and lies.

When he saw them together, he roared enthusiastically, 'Hey, Gazza, who was that gorgeous-looking bird in the yellow dress I saw you with at lunch a few weeks ago?'

Gary shrugged his shoulders. 'Can't remember, there's been so many lately. Yellow is the in colour for women this year.'

Jack tried to think back to how many women wearing yellow dresses he had seen in the last week but could not remember one. About six months ago Julia had arrived home one night looking unusually flushed and carrying a large box which she opened in front of him. It contained a sleeveless yellow dress, very short, low cut, which she spread out on the table. Jack's first thought was how small it was and how small women's clothes were in general. Julia spent a fair bit of money on clothes but they were usually work-related – skirts, smart business tops, stylish and expensive leather boots – which she insisted were all necessary for her job. But even Jack could tell this was not her normal line.

'I just felt like being … frivolous,' she said, half-apologetically.

'Good for you,' he said, and didn't think about it again.

After a slight nervous movement Jack retained his composure. But so, he had to admit, did Gary.

'Julia bought a yellow dress not very long before she died,' Jack said.

'There you are.' Gary gave the impression of having just proved his point.

'Still laying them in the aisles, eh Gazza?' Jack enquired, after Denis the Menace had departed. Gary looked at him sharply. Jack had never called him Gazza before.

'To tell you the truth, Jack, I've rather lost my interest in women since the departure of the girl in the yellow dress.' He put up his hand like a traffic policeman, to forestall what he thought Jack was about to say. 'No, I think I've suddenly become too old for this caper.'

An appalling thought crossed Jack's mind. Was it possible that he had really loved Julia? That would be too awful to imagine. Worse, even, than if she had loved him.

He played his trump card. 'I feel as if she's died twice, Gary. I think she was having an affair.'

Gary looked shocked, and Jack thought he genuinely was – but at what? Not, of course, the revelation of the affair but perhaps the fact that he had suspected it.

'That's impossible,' he said quickly. When Jack looked at him he said, 'She wasn't the type.'

'Is there a "type" for adulterers?' He relished the sound of the old-fashioned word on his lips. And yet in a strange way, until the discovery of the letters Jack would have agreed with him.

'And in any case,' Gary said, contradicting himself completely, 'she would have told you. Oh yes,' he added, as Jack raised his eyebrows. 'She told me about your "pact". Who else could have thought of such a bizarre idea?' They stared at each other in mutual hostility. I have made a start at least, Jack thought to himself. There is a chink in his armour. Though there is in mine as well.

A week later, Gary rang and suggested they go out for dinner. Jack drove to his flat about six in the evening and found him not ready to leave yet. 'I'm just going to have a shower. I'm stuffed from school. Fix yourself a drink.' He gestured vaguely in the direction of the cabinet.

While Gary was in the shower Jack quietly went through his study. He had thought about the letters all week. The damn things had to be somewhere. Desk, drawers, filing cabinets. He had managed to acquire quite a bit of furniture since he had moved into the flat. Jack's mind was racing even as he listened to the sound of the shower. Where would her letters be? He was sure Gary would have kept them, they must be here somewhere. He opened the drawer of the desk and rifled through it frantically, his fingers trembling.

'I thought so.' He looked behind him and saw Gary standing in the doorway, dressed in that sumptuous white dressing gown he had bought at David Jones. The shower was still running. He had been tricked.

'I think this might be what you're looking for.' Gary crossed to the filing cabinet and pulled out a manila folder. As he flung it down on the desk Jack noticed it was marked 'Gourmet Recipes'. Was this another example of his satanic sense of humour or simply a bad filing system?

'You are a dishonourable man,' Gary said.

I? Dishonourable?

'Your shower is still going,' Jack said with foolish irrelevance.

Gary stared at him coldly, turned and went into the bathroom. When he came back he said abruptly, 'I knew it. All those questions. The yellow dress. I wouldn't be surprised if you'd hired that idiot Denis. You played me like a fish.'

'*I?* Dishonourable?'

With a rapid movement he stripped off his dressing gown and reached for his clothes. He had never had any inhibitions about appearing naked. Jack remembered him wandering around the locker rooms naked when they played football together. He had tried to repress the physical images of his wife and her lover, the two of them in bed in one another's arms, but now it was impossible. He almost swooned. Fortunately, Gary didn't seem to notice. Having changed into his shirt and slacks he walked over to the sideboard and poured them both a shot of whisky.

'I loved Julia. With real love. Pacts!' He drained his glass and poured them both another shot. 'Your love is just like your writing. All it's ever designed to do is put circles around people, box them in.'

'You've always been jealous of my creativity,' Jack said.

'Creativity? Ha!' He didn't seem to feel he had to answer that accusation. Instead he waved his whisky glass aggressively. 'And I'll tell you one more thing. She loved me.' He gestured at the folder sitting on the desk. 'It's all there. If you read those, you'll find out I'm right.'

Jack stared at the letters. He suddenly knew he could never read them. That way madness lay.

'I didn't know you had become a literary critic.' It was a feeble response which Gary completely ignored.

They were both drinking as quickly as they could, not in competition but in a mad, mutual search for self-immolation. Jack was beginning to feel weak from the sudden rush of alcohol.

'And I'll tell you something else. I don't believe her death was an accident. I think she killed herself because she couldn't bear to hurt either of us. She loved me but she felt loyal to you. She knew you couldn't take it if she left you.'

Jack stared at him in horror. The wilful destruction of those lovely bones. Was it possible? He staggered slightly, and reached for the chair.

As if he had all at once become aware of the effect his revelations were having on Jack, Gary softened his tone, became more conciliatory, almost matey.

'You can't help being what you are. I can't help being what I am. She did what she felt she had to do.'

This universal absolution of responsibility did not impress Jack.

For one thing, he didn't believe it. She would have destroyed the letters if she had intended to kill herself. And why would she have asked him not long ago what he wanted done with his papers if she had planned to die first? Trees were unreliable exe-cutioners. And it was not the first time that in her haste she had forgotten to fasten her seatbelt.

It was Gary's last act of spite. He had won, got everything he wanted but even beyond her grave he was not satisfied. Neverthe-less, the faint possibility haunted him, terrified him. It would be as if she had died a third time.

She had been a poor driver even at her best, something she freely admitted. They had often laughed about it. She was far more interested in talking to whoever was sitting next to her than she was in looking at the road. He had implored her not to buy one of those rotten 4WDs with their phoney macho names – Territory, Explorer, Voyager, Escape – that slid off the road like ice-cream. He didn't believe it.

He looked at Gary. 'I don't believe it,' he said desperately.

Rabbit

Leanne Hall

I'm out sailing with my little friend. I say 'little' only because he's a good deal shorter than me, not because of his age, which remains a mystery to me despite relentless interrogation on my part. Sometimes I think he might even be my father, but he's the one who calls me Dad. Which is strange, not least because I'm a woman.

We've been on the water for several days at least, but, honestly, we haven't been counting.

The only thing to look at really is our rowboat, after you've got sick of looking at the water and the sky, neither of which ever ends.

'What are we doing?' I ask. 'Are we sailing around the perimeter, or what?'

I'm thinking that would be pointless. We don't even know if there are edges to this thing.

'I thought we would sail in a straight line, towards the horizon.'

'Which one?' I say. 'There's more than a few.'

'We talked about this yesterday.'

'I don't remember.'

We fall into silence, or, rather, the boat rocks us there. I keep paddling, but by this stage I'm just pretending. I look over to my right and finally see something different. It's a wave – a huge swell that's growing bigger as it races towards our boat. Waves are

like nightmares, with frothy manes and gaping jaws. I'm thinking we're finished for sure.

'Look at that …' I breathe, and then the wave is on us. Our
boat is lifted up high, like a newborn in a doctor's hands, and
then unceremoniously dumped into a cauldron of saltwater and
spray and bubbles. I hold my breath and hang on to the sides of
the boat, while gravity and the other physical laws sort themselves out.

When it's calm enough I turn to my little friend. 'What was
that all about?' I ask, because he looks guilty.

'I was angry because you're not rowing hard enough,' he says.
'I've been meaning to say something for days.'

I'm silent while I decide if this is too stupid for a response.
There's water in the bottom of the boat now and a few strands of
seaweed too. I wonder if I could eat it.

Finally my little friend says, 'But I'm not angry anymore.' He
rests the oar across his lap and trails his left hand in the water.
The water is smooth and thick like the top layer of cream in a
milk bottle. There are no obvious landmarks. The sun pummels
the top of my head; my clothes are beginning to dry already. The
sky is a gigantic magnifying glass.

'Isn't it funny how, when you're cold, you can't possibly begin
to imagine what it's like to be hot?'

'Dad, do you still love me?' asks my little friend.

Nobody likes being asked that question, especially when they
haven't had their last question answered.

'Not today,' I admit, 'but I'm pretty sure I did a few days ago.'

I'm hot. Our situation is becoming increasingly hopeless. It's
not only that we're lost, but that we never even knew what we
were doing in the first place. I try not to, but …

'You're crying,' he says accusingly, 'but I'm the one who nobody
loves.'

'I'm crying because we don't know where we're going or what
we're doing.'

'You're crying because you're a woman.'

But I notice he's got his oar and he's flipping sea water up into
his face like he's trying to hide something. I decide not to press
the issue.

'You've changed,' says my little friend.

'I've got a tan, that's all. So have you.'

He draws an imaginary line across the middle of the boat with his index finger. 'This is my side. I want you to know that this is my side and you'd better not try to cross that line.'

I'm silent while I decide if this is too stupid for a response. My little friend holds his oar with both fists so that it is standing up straight in front of him. The gesture looks vaguely tribal. But he looks small behind the paddle and he's breathing with small huffs through his nose and, more than anything, he looks like a rabbit.

'Don't look at me,' he quivers.

'I'm a vegetarian,' I reply.

Sleepers Almanac

Running from Right to Left

Margaret Barbalet

I am learning Arabic. D is made like a C back to front. Lessons take me back to kindergarten and 1956, my first year at school, in a town where it was always raining. The letters had to face the right way, the only way. Now they face the other way, and run from right to left.

Sounding out. I am sounding out Arabic words from my childish wobbling letters, going backwards across the page. Opening my mouth while the teacher watches unsmiling, listens to my mistakes with tolerance. B-aa-b. I look up. I have done a simple word, B'b. *Baab.* That sound means door. But there are no capitals in Arabic. There, you see, already I have forgotten a cardinal rule. Words fail. What is it about opening your mouth?

Sharia means straight road. I had thought it meant the law, but now I see that it can mean both. The right way, the truth, the straight right path. Sharia Hamdan bin Mohammed. Down on Hamdean Street there is always life. The soukh was bulldozed the day I arrived in this city but lives on in the Indian textile shops and the Lebanese eateries, the bread shops and barber's shops, shops where women might glance in, not meeting anyone's eyes, but never go through the doors, where men sit till late at night to be shaved and pampered.

Sounding out is humiliation. I stare at the letters and try to remember which sounds they make and why. What is it about opening your mouth and trying out words that is so humiliating?

Not really humiliating, I persuade myself as I sit doing home-work: humbling. It's humbling, I decide, but somehow calming. I realise that I love to sit with a clean white sheet of paper and a fountain pen and start the wonderful letters on the paper. I try another word: B-n – *Bin* – son of. You see it everywhere. All the streets are named after men who were the sons of other men. No one escapes family. Everyone is daughter of someone, *binte*. I am *binte* Adam, daughter of Adam: but also *umm* Sarah, the mother of Sarah. I can recognise *bin*. B is like a back-to-front L with a dot underneath. N is called 'nune' and I like its feminine appear-ance, like a cup or a breast with a dot in the centre. I can't say this. I cannot remark out loud, chattily, this is the way I remem-ber 'nune', but I think it. My teacher is rather severe, and young. She would be horrified. How I long for her rare words of praise.

At the traffic lights two women walk arm in arm across the street in front of me. Both wear shalmar kameez, freshly ironed, but worn. The older one is supported, helped along by the other. The older woman's limp is terrible, the slow-legged, gap-bent swing of a congenital hip condition never repaired, a burden for life. In the West you'd never see that now in people under fifty. So easy to repair if caught before six months. Her face shows she's mustered the energy, just, to walk for the past sixty years; every lifted step now lines her face.

My apartment here in this city on the Gulf is brand new, in a new city built on sand the colour of the nearby desert. One side looks out on the Straits of Hormuz, the other side looks out to an asphalted alley where I could throw a book at the apartment opposite, and attract attention. It's April, spring. Sometimes at night I drift to the window and look out at the anonymous lives in other apartments. People watching TV: I recognise the BBC announcer even from here. Couples having dinner, talking, but I can't hear their words. They seem motionless. One lunchtime on Thursday, the first day of the weekend, I watch a young Fili-pino woman bring out a plate to a crumpled middle-aged man. She waves her hands angrily in his face as she disappears back inside. He laughs and eats looking out at the square.

I have never lived so high up. I was unprepared for how detached I would feel. I rarely go out. On the fifteenth floor I slowly furnish all the bedrooms, and bring in everything, shower curtains, cushions, beds, tables, chairs, my computer that sings along under the endless pulse of the building's airconditioning. A building is like a city in itself, with four lifts so swift your ears pulse. I can't distinguish the features of people below.

One night, late, turning out the lights so I am not visible, I watch floors above me in the adjoining tower, a woman dancing at the window. The room, like most, is dimly lit. It must be the twentieth floor, perhaps the penthouse. I gaze up into blackness: cold, slanted light from the other bedrooms like sleet, the light around her like a thin ice in her desolate room. She dances at the window, always alone for many of the nights. She's young, thin, always dressed, but like a cutout, reaching up her arms, a black figure against silver light. There's no one watching, and no one to clap or laugh or join in. You can't hear the music she dances to, but you can see she's a real dancer. Night after night, and then suddenly, never again. Where did she go? Did she move out? Why?

There is nothing left but light. Outside, it is fifty degrees. July, and I understand summer. On the pavement walking back from Modern National Laundry, at noon threading my way from shade to shade, dark squares flooding from the side of skyscrapers, I walk past Pakistani labourers asleep on the pavement, their heads neatly placed on their shoes. They sleep the sleep of the lost, oblivious to the car horns, the wind, the sun. The city must be an infernal place to them, somewhere to endure, to make small change and send it back to a hundred high valleys of Pakistan. Seven out of ten people here are from Pakistan or India. This year, for the first time, a new rule is introduced: no working in the sun between twelve and four p.m. That's why they sleep in the shade on pavements, under awnings, on the grass under trees in the neat divisions between one side of the highway and the other, their turbans untressed and curled over their faces, their exhausted bodies on the grass, any grass, any shade.

There are no narrow roads. The roads are only narrowed where parked cars crowd them. Every *sharia* – every straight road – is four lanes wide and as neat as a pin. This is a tidy city with traffic lights, an absolutely modern city with new buildings, almost every one is a skyscraper, and no rain. I have lived here through all the seasons and in a whole year it has never rained. There are cloudy days and windy days, infernal days and ordinary days, but never rain.

On the fifteenth floor there is silence but for the hum of air-conditioners and plumbing. Ceiling tiles expand and creak, wall timbers bang, oddly, now and then. Nothing happens. Others tell me it is like this in their apartments, far away on other streets on the other side of the city, and that it is a sound that signifies nothing, the wood in new walls expanding, the cracks appearing in old walls. Out there in tiny hamlets away from this city barefoot children at play fall down old wells, or down sewerage outlets carelessly left uncovered. Here they scribble graffiti in Arabic on the walls. At night they play soccer in the square, ragged games unevenly matched with boys on the outer appearing and disappearing into the alleys, less well lit. They play right up next to the mosque, and I dodge between them on my way to Modern National Laundry in the windy dark.

The first time I hear her I think it is a mouse. A tiny tapping winds its way past above my ceiling, waking me. Sleep is so precious that I am affronted. The tap-tapping continues, and then vanishes out and down to another bedroom. Suddenly in this brand new building someone has moved in above me on the sixteenth floor.

At the traffic lights, I pick out words one letter at a time between red and green. I don't say them out loud. I can't talk. I can't speak. I can't read. Words are unknown to me.

Every night it's the same now. Someone in high heels walks around from room to room, stopping, pausing and then walking on. Sometimes it starts at one o'clock sometimes two. In bed, eyes shut, I imagine those shoes. Only in the Middle East, in the Gulf: high heels, open toes, beads and sequins. Sandals and slides seem all of a sudden down to earth and sensible. They don't have high narrow heels that echo on marble floors like morse code. Silly shoes. You couldn't run or work in such shoes. I imagine her in a cloud of perfume, her black shaylah over her head, moving from room to room tidying up. Tap, tap, tap. One night she cries and shouts. Later I am something between relieved and annoyed when she puts on strange wailing music, then I hear laughter and then silence, some tapping and sleep. For both of us.

A stillness falls after evening prayers. It's late summer, August. The light is fading fast. Down on the Corniche someone is taking a photo of a friend and I can see a flash even at this distance. Learning Arabic makes me conscious of the pen in my hand, the shape of the letters, as I write, even like this, in English. Ten minutes ago the sun was a pale apricot on a bed of indistinguishable smog, clouds out in the Gulf. Now everything is grey and the sea between here and the island is pewter. Then the sun becomes a disc and disappears in the smog before it reaches the horizon.

Two Indian men are fitting bed bits together in bedroom four. That room is going to have too much furniture, I predict already, and after walking round the apartment I decide on a tallboy in the study and another in the corner of the family room. The old white children's chest of drawers can go in the maid's room since I am not going to have a live-in maid. It can squash in with my second fridge, a cheerful garrulous monster given to clearing its throat as fridges do in the middle of the night. I will have as many beds as a motel, and enough fridge space to survive a siege.

I learn a new H looking at a shop front as I wait at the traffic lights in my car. H for Harley Davidson, an H like a surfboard sitting flat on top of a wave.

Human frailty is nowhere more carefully detailed than in the latecomers to Friday prayers. Some men at least must be early, for the little mosque is always full. But outside dozens, then hundreds of others arrive long after the sermon has begun. They line up, side by side, neatly, each one self-contained, parallel to the rows behind, and square with the man at the left or right. Each one usually has a small rug to sit on. Sometimes a man arrives, or a man and his son, with a large rug or even a square of clean plastic, and carefully spreads it out so others can share it. The other latecomers silently take their place behind them, line by line, square by square. By the end there are hundreds lined up outside the mosque usually seeking the shade, ruled into squares by its shadows. From my vantage point on the fifteenth floor, they form a patchwork of every colour, red, white, green, black, repeating random checks.

Three more nights of being woken at two a.m. and I am becoming angry enough to reach for a metal pole. Standing on my bed

I reach up and bang on the ceiling. The music is so loud I doubt she hears.

August. Yesterday morning, I stopped at the lights and there was a young Indian newspaper boy collecting dates. The palm was very low and thick with fruit. He was picking them after careful consideration, looking at each one before putting it carefully in a pocket. He wasn't eating any, not there in public at the side of the road. His bicycle was propped against the curb in the slip lane. After he had a couple of handfuls I suppose, he put them carefully in his pocket and climbed back on his bike. As I drove off, he pedalled away. His face was young, delicate. He was all of sixteen or seventeen, not fully grown, a solemn, intelligent, nervous gaze. So far from home. Indians are everywhere in this city, so essential, and so disliked. It would grind to a halt without their patient care, their long hours, their silence. All that dependence. And yet when I consider their precarious hold on comfort, on their place, the endless hours of hard work and the lack of rewards, I see underneath, less clear but still witnessed like a reflection in water, what they come all this way for: who they send money back to, in villages at the end of dusty roads. They complain, quietly when you listen, and who wouldn't, about rents, food prices, the way they're treated. Such a balance. I wonder if he's a young tailor.

That night I decide the dancer woman upstairs must be Sudanese or Eritrean, and comes home late and dances to the strange wailing African music because she's been out smoking shisha with friends. There can be no other explanation for the noise and the heels. I abandon her black clothes, and regarb her in bright African Muslim dress. Yesterday in Carrefour I saw such a dress, orange and yellow striped, hip-hugging, chic from head to toe, an amazing angular patterned cotton, thin gauze, a cross between a sari and a burqa but meant any which way to cling. There will be a name for such wonderful bright African Muslim dresses but I don't know it. I don't want to know it. Women from Eritrea and Ethiopia wear such clothes, and dance in such shoes. Flaunt comes to mind. Always decorated high-heeled shoes, henna on the ankles and the soles. And they are dancing above my head, tiny steps, the back heel lifted always off the floor.

I learn a proud high C like a Z, really a K. C for Carrefour.

Every Friday I shop at Carrefour. I drive my shiny new car along the new Corniche past the little picnic tables set up by the blue, blue sea, and along the edge of the giant hotel, which is fenced off with high railings, and park in the blazing sun, arranging my car so that the young palm tree's knife-hung branches won't scratch the bonnet. I descend into Carrefour and buy food enough for a famine, for a week, for a month. I wheel it to my car in a shopping trolley. On the way home I look at the dashboard: forty-five, it says. That's the outside temperature. Inside the car the temperature's descending already, but still so hot I can barely touch anything that hasn't been protected by a cover.

Walking across the square to the second-floor supermarket in the evening dark, I come across three little children flying kites, two boys and a girl. The wind is worrying everything, kite strings and gutters full of papers. The kites are pitiful things, pieces of cardboard on white strings. But they fly. The little girl has wiry pigtails standing straight up on the top of her black head. A kite string has tangled with a pigtail. Her brothers' kites are setting off for the lit-up square of night sky. Before I can think, I unlace the white string from that black wiry plait. She throws me a look: not quite a smile, not quite a scowl and runs away after the kite.

The tapping and dancing upstairs doesn't go away, but I buy earplugs.

A man can adopt a swagger when he tucks a shirt into trousers. At the lights three men move off as I wait. One is in Pakistani traditional dress, even a turban and full erratic bushy beard. The one in the middle, I notice, has trimmed his beard back to a moustache and is wearing a shirt over Western trousers. But he still walks with the wide-armed walk of someone in traditional dress. The Pakistani trouser with the long frockcoat over the top means a different walk. A man's body is hidden and he occupies a bigger space, claims a bigger space around him. With that traditional dress, a man extends his arms more away from the body. With the shirt tucked into trousers, I think, watching a Pakistani man cross the other way, it is all about the hips. The waist and hips are exposed. So the space shrinks, the pace changes, and the walk is all about the hips.

I look down from bedroom three at noon through the back alley, between the tall buildings where there's a vertical view to the smaller mosque. It's 12.45. An old man is coming down the steps with a walking stick, step by slow step. Ahead of him by a step jumps a grandson. They are both white-robed, on their way home. I think of the Arabic word for shaky, *teftefer*.

In the foyer of the ministry, where I am waiting for the VIP to arrive in the line of cars, a man unloads boxes of paper, two at a time, two at a time, over and over again from a van, sweating as he brings them inside, and lines them up neatly against a wall. His face is contorted with the effort. He doesn't have a trolley, I realise. *Darma*, to endure. Where is the goods entrance, I wonder. Outside cars jostle and chauffeurs exchange glances. It's next to the stock exchange and no one can find a park. I see a Lamborghini, red, new, worth half a million. It finds a park.

There are two words in Arabic for baby. One, *radir*, means a baby still breast-feeding. The other, *tefil*, means a toddler, a child who can walk.

Sometimes I sleep through the call to prayer at 5.30 a.m. There's no explaining it. Snoring wakes me. Girlfriends across the room, a boyfriend, rather closer: if they snore, they wake me. This call is amplified a hundred times, from the tower only metres from the fifteenth-floor window. And there are two mosques only ten metres apart. Sound bounces off the tall buildings in the back alley, and it's so amplified you can hear the reverberation and then the intake of breath as the next phrase begins. Sometimes the singer holds the note for forty seconds or more. And yet willing myself not to hear, I sleep right through it. Sometimes I use earplugs and still wake. Other times I wake at seven to the light and haven't heard it at all. I try everything: airconditioning turned up to make white noise, blankets over my head. If it will, that call still wakes me.

I can sing the call to prayer. I appreciate the singer in the older white-walled mosque at the end of the back alley. He's a tenor and his voice shudders through quarter tones in the falling phrases, and I wind down my window just a little to catch it as I drive home from work.

Then one night, when I am not even asleep, screams and shouts erupt from upstairs. The woman's voice, high and desperate, crying and shouting, screaming defiance, falls through the ceiling in a storm. There's a thud, the sound of running bare feet, a slammed door. More screaming, straight through the ceiling. I follow the chase from room to room. I feel sick. I wonder should I call the police. Something is happening and I am witness to it. Then I hear a door being locked. There is the sound of sobbing, and later music, muted, low. Over the next month I hear several other fights, always late in the day. Always she sounds desperate, affronted, angry, defiant. Does he object to her hours, her dancing, her clothes?

I never hear her dancing feet again.

There's no missing *Asr*, the 3.30 call to prayer at weekends. It's the most melancholy and hopeless. When I hear it I never fail to hear the silence, a full ten seconds, in between the beginning and the middle phrase, that single call: *All-la'ah*, as if perhaps He isn't after all listening to man speaking, to a man addressing his God. Full of despair as the heat and afternoon yawn on. That's the hour when *djinns* can confound and blacken hopes, the hour between *Asr* and night, the hour when you have to be careful.

Now there's lawn down in front of this brand-new building. Boys play soccer there after school. I watch from the fifteenth floor. They are a raggle-taggle lot, young and old, and they fight fiercely for the ball. Older boys tuck their kandoras into the undergarment to run better. Guttra tails get tied into turbans. Later in the week, walking past, I see there are two white rocks placed neatly at each end of the field: goal posts.

On the Corniche a woman is holding her baby boy. I cannot tell if he's a *tefil*, but he looks more than a *radir*. They are watching a jet-ski, with a young brash Emirati on it. Showing off, shooting water out of the rear jet, bare-chested and muscled, he whirls and turns, roaring past, going from one end of the blue water to the other, spraying the weekend workers, out on their Friday stroll. She holds her baby tighter.

I am learning the colours. *Aswad* is black. *Asfar* is yellow. The evil-sounding *grehmik* is dark. *Azrak* is blue. I cling to English and think of azure. Here you never have to think of anything else. The sky is blue or grey. For the months of summer, June, July, August, the sky is always blue, a tired used blue that fades to white. It's too hot to look at the sky. Dark glasses might become permanent.

At night from bedroom one, looking up across the back alley I see the moon refracted a dozen times through the glass by the light from the towers on the other side of the street, an overlapping line of coins descending to the glass.

I am tired from last night's boozy dancing, men in wigs and the other women in rather little. I'm in a dress that's ten years old but with flattering colours for my skin. I have bought a pair of dancing shoes, Middle Eastern feminine dancing shoes, pale blue thonged slippers, which started out in life as thongs and grew up to be mistress shoes, covered in braid and sequins, high heels, no toes, no backs, and amazingly good, I find out, hours later, to dance in.

Coming out of the office I have to button my coat. It's January, winter, and the pavement is damp. As I drive home I look through the windscreen, finely misted with what could be, but isn't, rain.

Meanjin

I So Do Not Want To Be Having This Conversation

Frank Moorhouse

While in New York last month, I went on a date with a young American woman I'd met at a book event for Edmund White; I suppose it was a date.

After we had settled at our table in the restaurant, I opened the conversation by asking her what her present marital-cum-relationship status was.

'I'd rather not go *there*,' she said, laughing. '*Don't even think of going there.*'

I wondered why not, and I wondered if we would ever 'go there'. Which I was hoping we would.

To loosen her shyness, I gently introduced a tone of candour by offering a small revelation about myself. 'I'm still seeing a man whom I first seduced when I was seventeen and although married he keeps dropping in to, well, visit me, so to speak.'

'Whoa,' she said, 'whoa – *too much information.*'

It seemed precious little information about a rather amazing tale from the very heart of my life. However, I rushed to disembarrass her, 'I wanted just to let you know I was bisexual – it's not as if he's *in my life*, so to speak. It's a rather amazing tale from the very heart of my life. But I know that being bisexual is always a rather unbefriended state of being. You might've heard of him, even in New York, he's a big deal.'

It's my policy to get small life details such as this out of the way.

I mentioned his name.

'I'll pretend that I haven't *heard this*,' she said, smiling.

I ploughed on, 'But it's not as if it would ever get in the way of what might happen between us ...'

To my amazement she'd now put a finger in each of her ears and was making a buzzing sound – *bzzzzzz* – to block anything I might say and then said, laughing, 'Hell-low? Hell-low? I think you dropped out.'

'"She thrust a dimpled finger/in each ear, shut eyes and ran ... we must not listen to goblin men ... who knows upon what soil they fed ..."'

She laughed, 'Rossetti, I know that poem.' She reached across and touched my hand, 'I'm not like that. Don't worry.'

Not like what? I changed tack. 'I take it you don't have any trouble with our age difference or you wouldn't be here,' I said. 'I don't myself have any problem with age difference; in fact, I think cross-generational affairs are enriching. To both parties.'

'*Whoa* – let's keep our boundaries.'

'Boundaries? I have no boundaries,' I said, smiling, and continued. 'In the 1970s we had no boundaries. We thought boundaries put people into emotional prison cells. Back then, we "let it all hang out", we put everything "up front". I am a member of People Without Borders,' I said, with a big laugh.

'Oh, it's just that it raises privacy issues for me,' she said, with a smile, reaching across and patting my hand and then withdrawing her hand.

I said, with a smile, 'That's another prison of fear, of separation of people from people. Why should we hide away from each other in quaint nineteenth-century notions of privacy? Why should we worry what people know about our income or our health or our orgasms?' I then rushed to add, laughing, reaching over and touching her hand, 'Except the "state and its instruments",' quoting from my old anarchist days.

She laughed, 'Definitely *no comment* on that. I'm rather big on confidentiality.'

'The plague of those so-called "confidentiality agreements",' I said, laughing. 'They're pushed in front of us and we are supposed to roll over and sign,' I said, with a laugh. 'They're all unconstitutional. You can't sign away your freedom of speech, you can't sell your freedom of speech. Those agreements won't stand up in court. They're all intimidation and bluff.'

'I hope they do stand up in court,' she said, laughing. 'I surely hope they do.'

'Returning to cross-generational sex ...'

'*Do I want to hear this?!*' she said, with a laugh.

I did not know if she was talking to me or herself. I decided she was asking the question to herself. I went on, 'To me it's like having sex with a very fat person – or a very thin person if you're a fat person – or with a disabled person – or if you're a disabled person with an undisabled person – it creates a tantalisingly new carnal dynamic,' I said, with a smile.

'*Excuuuuse, me!*' she said, with a laugh. '*I'm really not in the mood for this right now,*' she said, with a smile, and then she made a sound like a smoke alarm – *beeeeee* – and said, 'Change of Subject Alert! Change of Subject Alert!'

I sat silently for a few seconds and then I guessed that we could talk safely about the event where we'd met. 'What did you feel about Edmund White's speech?' I said, with a smile. 'Didn't you love the story about the man who was driving along with his partner who suddenly announced that the relationship was finished and that he had a new lover and then the jilted lover simply drove the car off the road and over a cliff? They spent six months in hospital in the same room.'

'Oh, I found his speech was way over the top,' she said, without a smile. '*What was he thinking!* There was a whole bunch of stuff in the talk with which I was distinctly uncomfortable,' she said, with a smile. 'To be honest I could've so done without the details of his sex romps. And he used a few not-out-loud words. *So unnecessary!*'

'But that "bunch of stuff" was his *life* – he was talking about his memoirs and candour,' I said, with a laugh. 'He was talking about his life as candidly as he could, that's what the talk was all about.' And then I added, with a smile, 'I suppose he could've talked about his pets.'

'*Hell-low!*' she said, waving a hand in front of my face, 'if that's what he got up to with people I don't think I want to know what he gets up to with his pets. *Pur-leese, so-do-not-want-to-know.*'

She studied the menu.

I took the menu up too.

'What's *mouclade*?' she asked.

'Too little information,' I said, chuckling.

'Pardon?' she said, smiling.

'The menu – too little information,' I said, tapping the menu, smiling.

'Sorry? I don't follow?' she said, smiling.

'Doesn't matter.' I told her what *mouclade* was. 'The moule – mussel – with cream,' I said. 'French,' I mumbled. 'From Charente.' Embarrassed that I knew.

I was then compelled to forge on with self-revelation in an effort to connect, or perhaps to challenge, or perhaps, for Christsakes, just because it was what I wanted to say. 'I found the White talk interesting, having been into that scene myself – I'm a bottom in male-to-male relationships.'

'Whoa – *I so don't want to hear this*,' she said, smiling, and made the smoke-alarm sound again – *beeeeee* – 'Change of Subject Alert. I think maybe you're a tiny bit on the outrageous side tonight, yes?'

I treated her question as rhetorical. We ordered the oysters. My conversation didn't seem to me to be *that* outrageous. I didn't find sex outrageous. I guess.

Changing the subject somewhat as I think I'd been instructed, I volunteered the information that oysters switched their sex every year or so. 'Perhaps humans should try that,' I said, lightly, with a laugh, pleased with its thematic coherence with our earlier 'conversation'.

'Heavy, *heav-ee*,' she said, with a laugh.

'No, hold on – I wasn't talking about *sex* as such,' I said, smiling. 'I was simply observing the creature.'

'*Yeah, right!*' she said, with a smile.

We lapsed into silence.

I began again, lightly, with a smile. I said, 'I heard that Matt and Dee-dee are in some sort of trouble,' naming acquaintances we had in common.

'*Into the vault*,' she said, with a laugh, making a gesture with her hand and mouth as if turning a key on a lip-lock – a lock on her vault, I guess, I suppose, perhaps. 'I hate people tattling on other people's lives,' she said, laughing.

'But isn't that how we find out about the world?' I said, with a grin. 'Through other people's lives being reported to us? It's called community.'

'It's called gossip,' she said, with a smile.

'Gossip is fun,' I said, with a laugh. 'Gossip is good. I find that nothing brings you face-to-face with the treacherous nature of the human condition and its frailties more vividly than gossip – including the very act of telling, the betrayal in the telling. It's the most creative part of communal storytelling.'

'I never reveal the contents of any conversation I've had with anyone without their permission, never,' she said, with a smile. 'And I would hope you would respect our conversational privacy.' She placed a finger vertically over her mouth, the *don't-tell* sign.

I wondered if she had conversational release forms in her handbag. 'I thought that we said "keep this to yourself",' I said, with a smile. 'And then afterwards we never honour the promise,' I laughed.

'No – *sor-reeey,*' she said, without a smile, 'it's the other way around now – all conversation is confidential unless it is specifically released by the other person. Sorry, mister-writer,' she said, with a laugh.

She had a law degree, although she said she didn't practise law. I knew that much, but perhaps I shouldn't be revealing that. 'Do you mind if I ask you where you did your degree?' I asked, moving to neutral ground.

'Yes,' she said, smiling, 'actually, I *do* mind. There's a lot of snobbery about colleges – I don't want to buy into that. Just because I was privileged enough to go to an Ivy League university – and to have passed very well by the way – is none of anyone's damned business. N-O-Y-B.'

'I heard that you worked for Clinton for a while after graduating.'

'Don't ask; don't tell,' she laughed.

'Why not?' I said, with a laugh.

'Go figure,' she said, smiling. 'I just don't think it's appropriate to talk about former employers,' she said, with a smile. 'Especially *that* former employer.'

'Public figure; public property. I've even met Clinton, although he may not remember me.' In all likelihood.

'Whoa – *I so do not want to be having this conversation*,' she said, with a laugh, covering her ears with her hands.

'I think former work relationships are rich experience – to be shared,' I said, smiling. 'Especially *that* former employer, a controversial, elected official on the public payroll, who had the destiny of the world in his hands. It informs the polity. And "appropriate" is one of those words.'

'How do you mean, "appropriate is one of those words"?' she said, with a laugh.

'One of those superior words we use to put other people in their place – and to stop a line of enquiry,' I said, with a smile. 'It's a shut-up word.'

'How *very male*. I won't comment on that – too hypothetical for me,' she said.

I tried to figure the *very male* part of what I'd said. My mind threw up something about females preferring a narrative approach to life rather than a rule-based approach, but that didn't seem to apply here; in fact, it seemed to be going the opposite way; so instead, I wondered out aloud, with a smile, 'Why is it that politicians won't comment on hypothetical questions? When was that rule introduced in the Westminster system? I think hypothetical questions are a non-committal way of exploring matters of public concern. Politicians should always enjoy hypothetical questions. A chance to show how their minds work.'

She smiled at me and winked. She didn't answer.

I didn't have a clue what the wink meant.

The oysters arrived.

I segued into some more of my oyster knowledge, wondering why it was that I couldn't use the word 'segue' without embarrassment. Why is that?

'Men in every country seem to believe their oysters are the best in the world. I think it has to do with oysters and the male folklore of virility which surrounds the eating of oysters. Now *that's* very male.'

'*Whoa* – time to call the waiter,' she said, with a laugh.

'Waiter?' I queried.

'Oh, it's just another way of saying *I'm out of here*. That does sound very *men's business* to me. Not for my ears. N-F-M-E. Delete, delete.' She made a computer-like noise – *deek, deek* – laughing.

To lighten things up, I introduced a literary reference. 'In connection with our …' I hesitated … 'our, well, our "conversation", so to speak, about Edmund White – I think,' I said, 'that I'm on the side of Lytton Strachey when he remarked that good biography should pass lightly over those performances and incidents which simply illustrate vulgar greatness in someone's life and instead the writer should lead our thoughts into domestic privacies.'

'I've never warmed to Strachey,' she said, with a laugh. 'Sackville-West described him as "that drooping Strachey".'

But I thought my American friend was right: she would not have been at ease with the Bloomsbury crowd. 'I take it that you don't care for domestic privacies?'

'It's a girl thing,' she said, with a smile, patting my hand. 'Don't-you-worry-your-pretty-little-head-about-it.'

I excused myself, and went to the toilet, discreetly paid for the meal, and did not return to the table.

I still had 'a whole bunch of stuff' I wanted to share but I could see that I was perhaps a Lost Soul of the '70s floundering in the Sea of the New Inhibition.

Was it for this that Kinsey was hounded to death?

And as I left, I said to myself:

I am done here.

You are done here.

We are done here.

Flame Bugs on the Sixth Island

Patrick Holland

Go down to the rock pools when the evening tide is out and
there is a chance you will see them. Sometimes one will swim in
among the mangroves in the tidal flats but the rock pools are
best. Flame bugs are what we call them. I do not know if they
have other names. I do not know where else they are found but
our island. I have never heard them spoken of by anyone who
doesn't live here. The north-east wind comes in spring and blows
the flame bugs to our shores. One October in boyhood, I took
to going down to the rocks alone to look for them.

I never asked the boys to come with me. If I had asked one,
the others would have been jealous, not for any particular fond-
ness of me but only at being left out. Also, I was worried they
would try to catch and torment the creatures, though they are
rarely caught by hand. I thought about how those boys dragged
mud crabs out from under rocks with hooks and tried to crack
their shells.

The most precious time I went looking for the flame bugs was
with the girl we called Shell. We called her Shell as before anyone knew her she was seen collecting shells on the south beach,
and because she wore a necklace with a by-the-wind sailor pendant. She belonged to that tribe of children whose European
blood naturalises here; whose blonde hair the sun and saltwater
turn white and the white skin olive.

One afternoon I saw Shell sitting bored in her front yard and, though I had planned to go alone, I asked her if she wanted to come look for flame bugs and she said that she did.

We left Ooncooncoo Street at twelve years old and six o'clock.

Shell had only recently moved to Moreton Bay, which is so close yet so far apart from the big city. She was lonely and a little intimidated at school. Most of us had grown up together and there were more boys than girls and we boys were very rough unless isolated. First I pitied her. Then I wondered at her: at her way of sitting with her knees beside her; at her speech and her interests that were cultivated and strange to me. I made a habit of noticing her. But I did not know how to introduce myself. This night looking for flame bugs was the first time we had truly spoken. Walking off her street I got the feeling she was excited at the prospect of making a friend, even of me, and that she would have followed me anywhere: far further than the rock pools.

She told me how at her old school she had played the violin but here there was no teacher. Her mother was doing her best in a proper teacher's stead. She told me she liked the island but for that. I told her I knew a girl who played piano, which was true. I told her my mother, being a schoolteacher, could let us into the community dance hall any time we liked, where there was an assortment of old instruments and the opportunity to nurture a band, which was not true at all. Between fact and fantasy we decided her musical ambitions did not have to end. We arranged public concerts that would never take place.

We walked off the bitumen streets, through a paddock of cattle on saltwater couch, to the Esplanade lined with wooden buildings and drooping streetlights not yet lit. We came to the sand where more than a dozen tidal pools reflected the twilight arch. The sun sets quickly here and amid the pools we stood in true twilight.

I wonder if I had hoped we would be left alone, or if that jealousy is mine – the man's rather than the boy's.

No one came onto the beach to disturb our isolation. The ocean was uninhabited but for a lonely mast-light far away.

I gave her my torch. I told her to shine it into the pools and look for the reflective eyes that would indicate the animals. You almost never found them in the tidal pools on the sand and mud and I did not hold any serious hope, only I was hoping to stretch time by putting more movements into it. A thing I knew was possible. She checked every pool on our way toward the headland where my true hope was.

We left our shoes on the sand. Our children's feet found all the footholds in the rock, and a girl of twelve gives up nothing in agility to a boy. Soon we were kneeling by a captured pool, a deep one the sea had only recently left. We did not need the torch now. Its light would not penetrate that depth of water. And anyway, all that was needed was to swirl your hand in it and if the pool held a flame bug it would light like an underwater candle.

She told me she had never seen one. If there was a flame bug there tonight I wanted it to be her find.

'You try.'

She put her arm in past her elbow and stirred the water.

Two came alight. She cried with delight.

'It's a good pool,' I said. 'We're lucky.'

'Yes. We're lucky, all right.'

Though she did not know how lucky we were. It was possible to come for days on end and not see one.

'Should we look in the other pools?'

'Stay here,' I said.

'Yes,' she agreed. 'We should stay here where we've been lucky, as long as we can.'

I want to say she was beautiful then, when she spoke those transcendent words. It is impossible for a girl of so few years to be truly beautiful, yet I think she must have been as normally I would have gone checking the other pools and left this one that was certain. Instead I wanted to stay where she was pleased.

I told her how flame bugs were rarely seen together like this. How their eggs float on the foam, through the air. At first she did not believe me. I assured her it was true. This was what my father had told me. Perhaps he had been speculating or restating a myth, but nothing I have learned since has falsified it. Our shores are protected, still the flame bugs seem to have no device for coping with even small waves – no muscular foot like a limpet, nor the ability or inclination to bind themselves into crevices like urchins. They are only ever seen at night. I do not know if they are resistant to high rock temperatures and drying out or if they die when low tide coincides with the heat of day or if instinct tells them when it is safe to come close to shore.

The existence of flame bugs seems to have no practical point. Nothing in the pools ever rises to snap at them. Though if they are prey to some furtive thing, their glowing when disturbed can only aid it. They cannot be eaten by humans or used for bait and they die when put in tanks. Flame bugs seem to exist only to carry light.

'Try to catch one,' I said.

'I don't want to hurt it.'

I laughed, happy in my better knowledge; happier I had the opportunity to share it.

She stirred up their lights then made a grab at one that was at the far side of the pool by the time she closed her fingers. She tried again and we laughed together.

'It's nearly impossible,' I said.

She sighed agreement. They could not be caught.

We sat contentedly watching them for I do not know how long. Their unpredictable movements and light meant there was no possibility of boredom. Children do not possess the accumulated pasts and anticipated futures that dwarf the present – happiness in the moment is complete happiness. Since time no longer pained us it was suspended.

There must have been a point that night when we decided it was late and we should return. I do not remember the decision. My parents were native islanders and did not care how late I came home, but her family was new to the island's customs and would be worried.

I did not wish it, but I found myself delivering her to her front gate later that night. I stayed, hidden behind a fig tree, to see her father come out and pretend to be angry when he heard her footsteps on the path. He hugged her and took her in.

I was jealous. The night might have lasted forever had we not given up on it.

I never spent another evening with the girl we called Shell. Two years passed and circumstance and my shyness meant we never became the companions we might have. Though, if at any time during those two years I had been asked to choose one of my classmates as a favourite, it would have been her. This would have surprised everyone, though not, I suspect, the girl herself. Childhood relationships may be complex and not require explanation.

Our relationship was locked in that night away from the island's inhabitants, when we found ourselves at a perfect distance from both juvenile dependency and adult sexuality, where love was unthought of, unplanned, immediate and inevitable.

She moved back to the city for tenth grade. The day before she left she came unexpectedly to my house. She told me she did not want to leave the island. She had not told anyone else. She took my hand. It was the second time we had been alone together. Then she left.

Three years later I heard she had been accepted into the city conservatorium for violin. It was two years after that, having rowed back from my launch, my mother asked me if I remembered a girl who used to live on our island and pointed to a photograph in the already-old city newspaper, to a face that was hers, though I had to look twice to be certain. My mother told me she had been killed by a man in a nightclub who had baited her drink. She possessed a beautiful future, the paper said, that had been meaninglessly cut short. Did I remember her? I cannot explain why I lied and said I did not.

I went to the beach after my mother had left me. I looked out at the ocean, at the riding light of a distant boat. I was heartbroken, though I had little right to be. I had not seen the girl in more than five years. I wondered if my love should stop now, as the pessimists would have it, since it became futile with the death of its object.

I have heard it said our souls only live after death if God remembers us. I am frightened of forgetting. This clumsy attempt to write the night of her and the flame bugs is an attempt to redeem a night in time that meant something to me, in this world where not all, and ever less, of our time has meaning. Why do I remember the feeling of that night better than its forms? I cannot be sure all I have written here is factual, though it is – in some inexplicable way – true.

I am still here on the island. I will never leave. Men still fish these waters, but they do not live on the island or build their own boats and they say there is no future in living as I do. I am not concerned with the future. I am a man who most say has done little. But I have already seen more than I understand, and lost much more than I have kept.

The flame bugs are few now. Like all beautiful things, they grow fewer as the world moves degraded through time towards its end.

I walked down the beach to the headland and climbed onto the rocks. I stirred the pool, the same pool ... An unlikely flame bug rose and lit.

I spoke to the creature, to the stars, to eternity, to whatever would hear me. I asked it to remember the lost and inimitable movements of that night that time had passed by.

Should we look in the other pools?

Stay here.

Yes. We should stay here where we've been lucky, as long as we can.

Why can't I keep you?

Deep in the pool a second bug lit and rose up beside the first like a fallen tear of light.

Griffith Review

Ashes

Alex Miller

A Cricket Story for My Daughter Kate

It is raining again and a little while ago I put *The Gondoliers* on the gramophone, but I have not really been listening to it. Mum and Dad have gone out and Janet is on duty. I have been listening to the rain instead and trying to imagine him in Wellington. That is not Wellington the capital of New Zealand but Wellington the country town in New South Wales. There must be so many Wellingtons in the world if only one knew about them. I could go down to Dad's study and look in his gazetteer and count them. Then I would find myself trying to imagine Wellingtons in Canada and America and Africa and other countries whose names don't immediately occur to me, but which I know would be countries that were naming their towns at about the time the Duke of Wellington became famous for defeating Napoleon at the Battle of Waterloo. If that is what he really did and all history is not a lie as Mr Stanford says it is. And none of those Wellingtons, of course, would be countries in the Old World. Which is a phrase that has always intrigued me. As if the Old World was brand new at the time, say, of the cave men, who are the first people we learn about, and was worn out by the time Columbus discovered America in 1492, and we needed a New World like Dad needing a new car when the old Pontiac finally refused to start and no amount of tinkering and cranking would fix it, or whatever they did to it to make it go. Which makes me think that eventually we are going to need another new world, which the people of the New World will have to call something like the Third World. But of course the people who are in the Third World won't know they are in it any more than the people who were originally in the New World knew they were in something called the New World but just thought of themselves as being at home. I have never, until this moment of thinking about it, really thought of myself either as being in the New World. Partly because I have not been sure that Australia qualified as the New World. But I am definitely not in the Old World. Which is slightly embarrassing for a reason that is not immediately clear to me. But perhaps I am not the only one to feel like this. I don't know where all these thoughts would get me in the end if I were to persist with them but I do know that if I went down into Dad's study and looked up Wellington in the gazetteer it would be rather like getting on a train that would never reach its destination or get back to where it started from. And although the connections between one point and the next along the track would not be obvious if you weren't on the train with me, if you were on the train with me there would be quite interesting and even logical connections between one thing and the next. And if, by a miracle of persistence and imagination, I did actually manage to finally reach the end of the line of associations of one thing with another, I feel confident I would by then have managed to link up everything with everything else, including the Old World with the New World. And by that time I would have forgotten to think about him for a whole morning.

So it's lucky for him I'm so comfortable here in my bed, and that I'm sliding further down the bed and getting more and more comfortable the more deeply I sink into thinking. Which means I shan't be bothered getting up and going downstairs to Dad's study and looking up Wellington in the gazetteer. Anyway, if I did, I know that the emptiness of the house would seem eerie and even a little threatening, as it always does from downstairs when I am alone in this house. Though it never felt like that in our house in Ballarat. As if I am being reminded by some force or presence here that all the years of the past of this house do not belong to me or to my family. As if Dad is not really the

freehold title owner but we have just moved in casually for a
short stay and will soon be gone again. As if there is something
furtive in our presence here. It is a disturbing feeling and makes
me want to hurry back up here to my bedroom where I can look
at my own world through the branches of Mum's beloved elm
tree and feel reassured that I really am at home. I'm never sure
whether to grace the names of trees with a capital letter or not.
In Edmund Spenser's or William Shakespeare's day I would have
taken the liberty and put capitals wherever I felt they were
deserved, just as I did with the Old World and the New World,
even though there is some uncertainty in my mind whether
these are strictly speaking proper nouns or not. But I don't possess Spenser's or Shakespeare's liberty with our language. Now-
adays we must all obey Mrs Jackson and the rules of grammar.
And even if, just for argument's sake, I imagine myself to be in
possession of Spenser's or Shakespeare's liberty with our language, I'm still not sure I would give the names of trees capitals.
So perhaps it is me after all. I suppose I really do believe that
things ought to be classified into strict orders and that there
have to be general rules for all these things that we must all
obey. The truth is, I am not at liberty to be whimsical about
these things without being made to think of the consequences
of incurring the censure of people I love and respect. I respect
Mrs Jackson. I respect her knowledge of the rules of English
grammar and her intentions in teaching these rules to us. But
I don't love her. I love Dad. I love him more than anything.
Achingly sometimes. I could weep for him whenever he places
his trust in someone who it is obvious to the rest of us is going
to let him down. But still he persists in trusting people and finding excuses for their failings. Which is one reason I love him.
And is a reason Mum married him I'm sure. But I know Dad
would agree with Mrs Jackson on this question of the rules of
grammar and would find himself unable to discuss the grace of
capitals for trees, or even to see the question as a serious one.
If, despite these misgivings, I were to write elm with an initial
capital I know I should feel as if I were transgressing something
quite fundamental in my sense of what it is that holds us all
together. So I don't do it. Not even in play. Which is a proof,
I suppose, that the liberty to do it is not mine.

The Gondoliers just finished and I hardly heard any of it and now the house is very still and quiet and empty. The window is up and the rain is making a soft insistent sound as it falls into the garden. The rain is putting life back into Mum's poor old plants. The smallest amount of rain has more effect on the plants than all Mum's nightly waterings. What is it that is in the rain that does this? I have never been to Wellington and am not even sure where it is, so I am having difficulty imagining him there. But I suppose he must be enjoying himself having Saturday afternoons as well as Sundays off. Wellington is a bit of a blank I'm afraid. If I looked up Waterloo, on the other hand, I suppose there would be hundreds of them too. All blanks for me. Except that I have heard Dad mention Waterloo Station and I have an image of it that is probably nothing like the real thing. There is the battlefield itself, of course, which has the original name, strewn with dead soldiers in red and blue uniforms. It is quite possible to imagine that. In the middle of the Old World. Where exactly? Mum and Dad will be home soon and hoping I've done something about setting lunch, so I'd better get up and have a bath. I wonder if they got tickets to *Gigi*?

I am writing a letter to him and the doors to the garden are open and I can hear the traffic going along Burke Road. It is lovely and sunny but not too hot. I can see Mum's back. She is on her knees weeding and looks as if she is digging in the earth for something she has lost, or perhaps buried there years ago, when she was young, and wants to recover it now. She's a sight. If only she could see herself. Janet was on night duty and is sleeping. The house is ours on days like this and forgives us our furtive presence. Dad has a book open but is really listening to the cricket on the wireless. I'm not sure whether he barracks for Australia or England. I think he sits on the fence and I wonder if he sometimes still thinks of himself as English. I would like to ask him except I feel it is a question he asks himself and has no answer to. You can love someone and still not be free to ask them questions that may trouble them. That is one of the things that gives our lives the feeling of irresolution and melancholy sometimes, even when we are happy. Like a shadow cast on the ground in front of us where we must walk. So we hesitate. As if we possess a sixth sense that knows something of the infinite. Which may be the inspiration of music. A medium against which we measure our private mortality. Except *The Gondoliers* is not music of that sort and avoids noticing the infinite. When I am writing to him I don't actually think about him but think about myself. The truth is I can only feel really interested in a letter that is about myself. I don't know that I would want to admit this to anyone. When I am not writing to him I struggle to imagine him, to see in my mind what he is doing. But mostly I am unsuccessful at this and am reminded of the difficulty of really knowing someone. I remember when Janet and I were little. We were sitting out after a tennis lesson and I asked her, What is it really like to be you? She hugged her knees and looked at the other girls hitting the ball back and forth to each other and she thought about my question for a long time. Then she looked at me and said gravely, as if she had just discovered this, I don't know. We were both astonished. Even though we must have been no more than eight or nine years old at the time our discovery that we could never really know someone else or even ourselves was like the sudden beginning of the mystery of grown-up life. That was our first experience of irresolution and melancholy. We hugged each other. I don't think we have ever spoken about it with each other since. Dad makes a sudden exclamation and I look across at him. Gilchrist, he explains. Caught behind. I ask, Is that good? He makes a face at me, so I'm not sure. Is Gilchrist English or Australian? I ask him. He says, *Ros*! His gaze lingers on my writing pad. Writing to Bill? he says. Give him our best won't you. When are you two going to tie the knot? He laughs and puts his finger to his lips to shush me, in case I am going to answer him. The commentator is confiding in hushed tones that the new batsman has taken up his guard at the crease. Dad leans closer to the set. If only he had a son with whom he could share his enthusiasm. They would look at each other with such understanding at this moment. I know Don Bradman is Australian. But the others I'm never sure about. The duel between the English and the Australians for the Ashes is a parallel in Dad's heart to the duel between his Australian and his English identities. The Ashes is such a portentous idea. The ashes of a dead man. Are they? The ashes of a hero. The Duke of Wellington. All that is left of him. It is so poetic and insubstantial, this sacred trophy of their game. Whose idea was it to duel for ashes? An Australian's or an Englishman's? Someone said to someone else one summer day on a village green somewhere, Let us play a game of cricket and the trophy will be the Duke of Wellington's ashes. And it was agreed. And so they played. And after several years the ashes began to be graced with an initial capital and became the Ashes to distinguish them from the ashes of the commonplace dead. The Ashes standing for all of us and for our endeavours. The Ashes as the Platonic form of ashes. The sportman's melancholy music, to remind him of the infinite and of his mortality. To be a hero one day and ashes the next. To sober the hero in his moment of triumph and save him from the fault of hubris. Which the gods hate. The idea is Greek in its measure, surely, not Australian? The Spartan youth would not have turned up his nose at a contest for the ashes of a great general. The Ashes displayed in the sanctuary of Artemis Orthia, where the Spartan youths were flogged in the contest of the whips. Made to play cricket instead. But being Spartan youths they may have preferred to be flogged than to go in to bat. It's the over, so I ask Dad, Whose ashes are they, Dad? He looks at me. He has been miles away. A stump, he says. The burned remains of a cricket stump, my darling.

Bean Paddock Blues

Barry Cooper

The work day might have begun in darkness and quietness, with the dew on the grass and the early hour damping bickering and banter, but it sure as sugar finished with coarse cursing, jokes and laughter as the tired pickers waited to be paid for their day's work.

Martha sat among them while her husband wandered between the long rows yarning up to the men. They had picked fifteen bags during the day but Martha wasn't satisfied. If Jeff hadn't gone off squawking half the time they might have stood twenty up – or at least eighteen. She was awake to his scheming too. The old coot had tried all day to pick a fight with her so he would have an excuse to get on the grog. He was the only man she knew who performed this fortnightly fault-finding ritual in order to take a drink. And even though it was pension day tomorrow, it looked like he was trooping off with the boys that afternoon to get on it a day early. Wanting him to at least bathe, shave and spruce up a bit before beginning his three-day binge, she tried to think of a way to keep him home for the night.

'Come on, old fella, come on. You gotta get home and finish the billycart for the boy. So come on.'

Jeff threw his smoke into the bushes. 'I got all weekend to do that, woman. We ain't got the wheels for it anyway. Can't ya see I'm giving lessons here? Trying to teach 'em how to box.' All skin and bones, he jabbed at the air in front of him like a giant praying mantis wearing an Akubra. Feinted a left hook at a dark figure seated below him.

Budda, tall with skin the colour of treacle, made his vertebrae crack like walnuts when he lifted himself off his drum and stretched about. He couldn't kneel on the ground to pick like everyone else. The dirt clods hurt his knees too much. Sent him home with bruising that lasted all winter. Preferred stooping over, arching his back like a boomerang, which he prayed would return upright once the day was over. Smiling, he straightened up some more and launched a question across the rows to Martha.

'Hey, Aunt. You want me to take this tormenting man with me and give you a coupla days' rest or what?'

'If he don't wanna help his only grandson build a billycart then take him, sonboy. He's been itching to get inta town all day. Might even have another woman waiting for him in there for all I know.'

'*Must* have another woman waiting for him in there I reckon, Aunt. Real good-lookin' sort too, I bet – with gapped teeth, ten kids and a *big* pension ta spend on him.'

'All the pretty miggaes want me,' Jeff weighed in, rolling himself another smoke. 'Got one in every town. You over there,' he winked and nodded towards Martha, 'is lucky she caught me.'

And while everyone in earshot cracked up laughing, Martha slowly rose to her feet and ground her smoke into the dirt. She produced a hanky from beneath her shirt, worked three knots out of it, twisted a twenty-dollar bill free from other notes, slipped the twenty into her cardigan pocket, knotted the hanky back up and returned it to her bosom with the same lightning speed she used to pull stubborn beans from tangled bushes.

Twenty dollars was Jeff's allowance for the next three days. The price of a flagon of McWilliams wouldn't have changed since last fortnight. As for food, let the simple soul find his nourish wherever he woke up. If he played up, let the gunjies throw him in jail for the night. And if he came home and started in on her, let the big boondi from beneath the bed knock some sense into him. She had hit him with the stick so many times over the years, swinging it became her second-favourite form of therapy: just behind betting at the TAB.

She wished the whacker was at hand right now. Pictured the lumber sailing through the burnt sienna sky until it struck Jeff smack-bang on his hardwood head. Saw him hit the dirt as limp as a cooked strand of noodle. Watched as Budda and Cream picked him up and carted him off to the gum tree at the end of the paddock. Ding! Ding! All over, red rover. Championship to Martha.

'That'd be right. Only place I can shut him up is in my ...'

'What's that, Aunt?'

Martha looked up. 'Hey, my nephew, hey. Didn't see ya come up there.' She pulled the twenty from her pocket. 'Here, give this to motor-mouth over there. Tell him ta cadge a lift inta town with Big Merv. I want you ta take me home as soon as Doug gets here to pay us. Is that OK?'

'Of course it is, Aunt, you're right. I'm just gonna duck off for a quick jillawaa first: been bustin' to go all afternoon. If Doug gets here before I get back can you grab me pay for me? Got eight bags up. Not too bad for a uni student, I reckon.'

'Not bad at all, my son. Not bad at all. All ya need now is a good woman ta spend it on.'

'Wouldn't know where to find one,' Budda fired back, handing the twenty over to Jeff. 'Wouldn't even know where ta look!'

'Oh, I'm sure your uncle could help you out there,' Martha replied, addressing the smiling face of her husband. 'After all, *he's* got one in every town.'

Jeff took the jibes and the good-natured ribbing of the men with him as he walked towards Big Merv's car. Shortly after that Doug pulled up at the paddock gate and everyone moved towards him to get paid. Martha stayed behind to give everyone else a go first. She stood as still as a charcoal drawing in the deepening dusk and breathed in and out real slow. Eventually the glow of her cigarette followed the pattern of her breathing and the gentle blinking of that soft point of light enabled Budda to locate her when he returned from the river. Everyone else had shot through when he walked up to her at the main gate. The paddock was as quiet and dark as a confessional and they swapped yarns for a spell into the evening. Budda told her about his dislike of shopping malls and how they made him feel insecure and envious.

'You know what me mate Choompy calls them don't ya, Aunt?'

'What's that?'

'The white man's temple of misplaced faith!'

'Mmm.'

'I said, "If that's right, Choompy, then what's the black man's temple of misplaced faith?" And you know what his answer was?'

'What?'

'"The white woman"!'

'Oh lawd!'

'Yep.'

'God help us!'

'He's mad that Choompy, Aunt. Mad but smart.'

'Sure sounds like it. But it's hard to keep the centre of a person untouched by the world, my son.'

Budda turned towards her.

'What I mean ta say is that if a person gets knocked around by the way someone looks at them or the way people talks to them or shuns them and if it happens long enough they start ta get hard in the heart. Look at me. I been with your uncle for years and tonight I gotta go home and take the axe in from the woodheap and lock it away just in case he comes home drunk. Years of doin' that have made me hard, son. Harder than him, I can tell ya. So take care of yourself. Don't be around people who put ya down too much. And if ya can't help being around them then come on home more. Spend summers pickin' with your mob. Laugh and act the goat a bit. You know your father said that laughter was more important to the bean paddock than rain. That's why everyone loves ya simple uncle. He takes their mind off things with his antics. They don't have ta live with him, mind you, but he has his purpose.'

They stood and smoked together in silence for a while longer before trudging off towards Budda's old two-door Valiant Regal. It took just ten minutes to get to Martha's front gate and the dust cloud that followed them coated the house, trees and dogs upon their arrival. When Martha had pulled her swag from the back of the car Budda watched her shuffle over to the woodheap and work the axe free from the chopping block. He was tempted to get out and help her but he knew she wouldn't like that. She had let him in close enough already. He had never heard her talk that way to anyone before. And as the car headlights cast her shadow obliquely across the empty house, Budda prayed it would be the only figure to appear that night. His uncle might have some purpose in life, but it had nothing to do with frightening his aunt half to death. Not if he could help it, that's for sure.

Meanjin

Barcelona Honours the Prostitute Maria Llopis

John Bryson

Protected through the night by the severed arm of the embalmed Saint Teresa on his bedside table and by the mantle of the Virgin of Pilar on the bedhead wall, so the nuns taught us at school, General Francisco Franco slept with arms crossed over his chest as if already laid out in a crypt, and woke while Carmen Polo y Martínez Valdés, his wife now of fifteen years, moistened his lips with a rosewater sponge. He had dreamt of a rampart through a monastery in Castile where he walked with all the kings of the Spanish Reconquest and of the Golden Age, who told him he was to rule Spain from this night onwards accountable only to God and to History, as they themselves had, so Carmen Polo sat him on the side of the mattress to dress him over his sodden night-shirt in the medalled jacket of his finest uniform while his bare feet swung scarcely brushing the floor. 'I now decree death as the penalty for treasonous crimes,' he said still in reverie, 'and let a Crucifix of Jesu be displayed in all Courts of Justice.' Carmen Polo made the sign of the cross over her breast, as did the nuns when they reached this part of the story, and she knelt to kiss his hand.

Protected in daytime by soldiery, by secret police and the Guardia Civil, which was more the way we heard our parents speak of him, Francisco Franco held court with the forty-eight bishops who delivered to him the blessing of the Holy Father in

Rome, and raised the red and gold standard of the deposed monarchy over his own palace. He appointed his brother Nicolas Franco and his brother-in-law Ramón Serrano Suñer as his trusted advisers, dissolved all political organisations other than his own, revoked the autonomy the Basque Country, prohibited Catalán language and culture, held state receptions for himself in the capital cities of all provinces, and decreed that 1 October be celebrated by the people as National Day for the Leader of All Spain.

The day chosen in secret for his reception here in Barcelona was no surprise to anyone, even to us in the school pews, since the garrisons on the waterfront at Atarazañas and in the castle atop Montjuic were now crowded with the regiments of Navarre and with African Moors; the Guardia Civil enforced the night-time curfew with companies on horseback, and factories were closed for three days so smoke would not entice rain. For the banquet, so the rumours flowed, fishes and crustaceans were flown in from Cádiz and roasting meats from the southern slopes of the Sierra, since no Catalán foods could be warranted free from stealthy poisoning; water was drawn from the catchments of the Llobregat River upstream from the aqueducts that supplied the city, poured into hogsheads and sealed for the journey with the Escutcheon of State burned into crimson wax. Riflemen cordoned the square while sappers dressed as gardeners dug the flowerbeds with shovels sharpened to sever hidden lines of gunpowder, and the School of Our Lady of Concepción was granted an afternoon holiday so the children could play skipping games through the cloisters and the courtyards in case of hidden mines beneath the flagstones. Rooms overlooking the square were emptied, and the Guardia requisitioned tailors' dummies and mannequins from the boutiques, arranged as a crowd at the windows and on the balconies, dressing the female heads with silken scarves so the breeze might give an illusion of human movement.

Seats of honour were taken by dignitaries in fascist blue shirts and by their ladies who fluttered fans in recognition of one another, and the standing room behind was packed tight with flustered strollers from the boulevards, shoppers from the fish-market and hawkers from the alleyways, amassed by soldiers at gunpoint. School classes, including mine, were herded in by our fussing nuns to stand at the back, although we could see little between the crush of dutiful adults.

Came time for the speeches, loudspeakers carried to us, also to the silent streets behind, the Mayor's booming welcome; they carried to us the proclamation of Freedom of the City for the regiments of Navarre and of Africa, as if they did not have it already, the bastards, and it was here my classmate caught a hot clip over the ear from a soldier for not hiding his schoolboy snigger. I remember the squeak of the microphone lowered to an altitude no higher than my own, to suit the smallest general in our history, they carried to us the tin-whistle voice of the Great Leader, which even the quick increase in bass-volume could not make imposing, they carried applause from the near seats and, in the pauses for the shuffling of his notes, they carried to us the cheering of thousands of zealots and cries of Arriba! Arriba! which we knew to be a fake like everything else, wild applause in fact recorded when the striker Horacio Alfaro kicked the winning goal for Real Madrid against Zaragoza a month before.

The Guardia had searched rooftops all around, and Francisco Franco on his podium was not in line of sight from any unguarded pediment, but Jacinta Llano Moya, markswoman of the anarchist cell named for the radical and prostitute Maria Llopis, had climbed the parapet days ago and loosened the stone bust of another immortalised tyrant that sat high above so that now, sighting her carbine from the eaves of the Institute of Useful Mechanics, her one bullet toppled the head of Peter the Cruel to dash out its brains on the cobbles at the feet of the Saviour of All Spain, causing the sound engineer to set the recording again to broadcast Arriba! Arriba! so as to cover El Caudill's sudden loss of words, but we knew, out here, we all knew, Jacinta had pulled it off; a classmate caught my eye, I saw Joàn the Sweeper shaking his broom, and others in the pressed crowd lowered their heads or turned away to hide smiles from the furious Guardia who were pacing up and down behind.

And we all shouted Arriba! Arriba!

Meanjin

Cold Snap

Cate Kennedy

When I go down to check my traps, I see the porch lights at that lady's place are still on, even though it's the morning now. *That's an atrocious waste of power,* my dad says when I tell him. His breath huffs in the air like he's smoking a cigar. The rabbit carcasses steam when we rip the skin off and it comes away like a glove.

Skin the rabbit – that's what my mum used to say when she pulled off my shirt and singlet for a bath. Mr Bailey gives me $3 for every rabbit to feed his dogs. I take them down in the wooden box with a picture of an apple on it. In the butcher's, rabbits are $2.50 but Mr Bailey says he likes mine better. I've got $58 saved. I want to get a bike.

Dad reckons it's good to save up your money. The tourists who stand around the real-estate agent's window looking serious, pointing, touching each other on the arm, he reckons they're loonies. When the lady up the road bought that house, my dad went over after the sold sign got stuck on and everybody had gone, and he took one of the palings off the side of the house and looked under at the stumps, and made a noise like he was holding back a sneeze. *That lady's a bloody wacker,* my dad said. *Those stumps are bloody atrocious.*

He stood there looking at the house and rolled a cigarette. *Throwing good money after bad,* he said, and kicked the paling. I kicked it, too.

After she moved in I didn't set no more snares up there on the hill. I walked on the tracks round the lake, the tracks the rabbits make. I made myself small as a rabbit and moved through them on my soft scrabbly claws. I saw everything different then. Saw the places they sat and rested, the spots they reached up with their soft noses and ate tiny strips of bark from the bottoms of the river willows. You've got to set a trap so that it kills the rabbit straight off. On the leg is no good. All night the rabbit will cry and twist, then you have to kill them in the morning when their eyes are looking at you, wondering why you did it. Mr Bailey, he tells me he can't believe I can catch them so near the town. I say you just have to watch things and work out where to put the trap, that's all. He nods so small you can only just see his chin moving up and down. *You've got it there, Billy*, he says.

After he gives me the money we look at the dogs and have a cup of tea. His dogs know me and why I come. Their eyes get different when they see me.

In the morning, everything is frozen. All up the hill are the trees, and every time I look at them I think of the time in school when I was right and Mr Fry was wrong. He showed us a picture and said trees lose their leaves in autumn and the other kids started writing it down but I felt the words come up, and I said they didn't, they lost their bark.

Mr Fry said how typical that the one time I'd opened my mouth in class I'd come up with a wrong answer. I looked at the trees standing bare in the mist and thought about how I'd kept shaking my head when he told me to say I was wrong, and the other kids sitting smiling staring down at their hands, waiting for after school like the dogs wait for the rabbits.

When you smell the leaves, they're like cough lollies, and the bark goes all colours when it's wet. One day I was looking up at them and my eyes went funny and I flew up high and looked down at the tops of the trees all bunched together and they looked like the bumpy green material on the armchairs at my Aunty Lorna's place. I never told no one about that, not even my dad. The trees talk loud when it's windy and soft when it's quiet. I don't know what they talk about, probably about rain. When they get new gum tips, they're so full of sap they shiver in the air. Maybe they're excited. Or frightened.

But now that it's winter, the trees just look dark and sunken in, as if they're just hanging on by shutting off their minds, like my grandpop when he had the stroke and Dad said his body was just closing down slowly like something in the winter. And on the track, there's ice crystals on the clay, and when you look real close you can see the crystals are long, growing into lines, and the more mushy the clay the tighter the crystals pack in. They do it in the night, in the cold snap. You can put your foot at the edge of a puddle and just press real gently, and all these little cracks come into it, rushing outwards like tiny creeks.

Sometimes there's frost on the rabbits' fur. I brush it off with my hand. Rabbit fur smells nice, like lichen or dry moss. My mum left behind some leather gloves with rabbit fur inside and when I put them on once I pulled my hot hands out and smelled her smell. *What are you bawling for,* my dad said. I hid the gloves just under my mattress. When I touch them they feel like a green leaf, just soft and dry and bendy and not knowing autumn's coming.

I looked up at the lady's porch lights the morning I got my new hat for my chilblains. Dad made it for me with rabbit skins. He rubbed my ears hard with his jumper and my mouth ached with holding it shut then he pulled the rabbit fur flaps down and tied them.

See you back here with the bunnies, he said, squeezing his hands under his arms before he stoked up the chip heater. One day a boy at my school who works at the feed supply told the other kids we were so backward we didn't even have hot and cold running water at our place. He said, *It's like deliverance down there with you-know-who.* I asked Dad what deliverance was and he rolled a cigarette and said why. The next time he wanted chook pellets he asked for them to be delivered that day and then he stoked up the chip heater so high that a spray of boiling water gushed up and hit the roof like rain and it sounded like the fancy coffee machine at the milk bar. When this boy came around with the pellets, Dad told him to empty them into the bin and then said would he like to wash the dust off his hands in the kitchen. The boy went in. I stood looking at the chooks and made myself small like them and felt the straw under my claws as I scratched

around, and felt how the wheat powdered as I cracked it in my
beak, and then there was a scream and the boy came running
out holding his hands out in front of him. And they were bright
pink like plastic. As the boy ran past, my dad called, *Don't forget
to tell your friends.*

I pushed the rabbits into a hessian bag and heard music coming
out of the house with the lights on. It was violin stuff. I saw the
lady who'd bought the house come out onto her porch as I cut
across the ridge. She was wearing King Gees and you could see
the new fold marks in them. She had hair the colour of a fox.
When she saw me her face went all bright and excited even
though she didn't know me, like the lady doctor who did all
those stupid tests on me at school just saying stupid words and
expecting me to make up more words and say them straight away
and not giving me any time to think it over.

She said, *Well hello there, has the cat got your tongue?* She had lipstick on. I thought maybe she was on her way to church.

I said I didn't have a cat and her eyebrows went up.

*You're up very early on this wintry morning. What's that you've got in
your bag?* she said, like we were going to play a joke on someone.
I showed her the top rabbit's head and her mouth went funny
and she said, *Oh dear, oh the poor little things. What did you want to
kill them for?*

I said for Mr Bailey. I said they died very quickly and always
got the traps right around their necks. She hugged herself with
her arms and shook her head and said goodness me, looking at
my rabbit-skin hat. I turned my head slowly round so she could
see better.

She asked me suddenly if I lived in the house down the hill
and I said yes. Then she said what a marvellous location and
what a shame the power would cost an arm and a leg to put
through, otherwise she would have made an offer, and that this
little place she'd picked up was such fun and a goldmine. She
said all her friends from the city thought she was quite mad but
she'd be the one laughing when property values went up and
she'd done all the extensions. I was waiting for her to finish so
I could go. I could feel the rabbits stiffening up inside their bag,
I could smell them.

What's your name? she asked me finally and I said Billy.

And do you go to school, Billy?

I looked at her and said you have to. Her eyes went all crinkly and happy again.

And is it a special school, just for special children?

I couldn't work her out. Maybe she didn't understand about school. I said not really then my mouth blurted out: *You got hair like a fox.*

She laughed like someone in a movie. *Good heavens*, she said. *You are a character, aren't you?*

A man in a red dressing-gown came out onto the veranda and the lady said, *Look darling, some local colour.*

Love the hat, said the man to me. I waited for them to tell me their names, but the man just complained that it was bloody freezing, and thank Christ they'd got the central heating in. The lady said yes, the whole place was shaping up well, then she looked out down the track and said, *The only problem is there's no bloody view of the lake.* Then she said, *Billy, show Roger your bunnies, darling*, and I pulled one out and Roger said, *Good god.*

They both laughed and laughed and Roger said, *Well it looks like the light's on but there's no one home.* Which was wrong. They were both there and they'd turned the light off by now.

When I walked down the track past the sharp turn and through the cutting my boots cracked on the black ice. You can easy go for a sixer on that. People say it's invisible but it's not really, but you have to get down real close to see where the water's froze then melted a bit then froze again, all through the night, till it's like a piece of glass from an old bottle.

Dad had had his shower by the time I got home. The rabbits were harder to skin because more time had passed. They ripped off with the sound of a bandaid like they put on your knees in the school sickroom. *Get them off*, my dad said when I came home one time with the bandaids on. He was watching me so I pulled both of them off fast and they bled again. *Call that first aid? That's bloody atrocious*, said my dad. *Get some air onto them.* I looked at my knees. They felt like the hinges inside had got stiff and rusty, like the oil in them had leaked out.

Every day for the next few weeks, people drove up the hill to fix things in the house. You could hear banging and machines and then a pointy bit of new roof pushed up over the trees. The lady's friends, the ones who thought she was quite mad, came up a lot at first but then it got colder and they stopped. The lake froze over at the edges and the ducks had frost on their feathers. One day I crept up and saw the lady standing with her arms folded on the new veranda, which was covered in pink paint, just staring out at the trees. All around her garden were piles of rocks and I saw a duck standing still as anything under the tree. I went closer and she saw me.

Well, Billy! she called, and I went over and saw the duck was a pretend one.

Look at all these bloody trees, she said, sighing. *I'm sick of the sight of them.*

She had on the overalls again but they didn't look so new now. The digger had left big piles of dirt everywhere.

What are *those trees anyway, Billy?* she said suddenly and I said they were gum trees and she laughed and said she might have guessed that would be my answer, even though I hadn't finished and was only sorting out what I was going to say next.

I said it was going to be another cold snap that night and more hard weather. And she said how did I know and I started explaining but she wasn't really listening, she was still looking down the gully towards the lake, turning her head like the ladies in the shop when they're buying dresses and looking at themselves in the mirror, deciding.

Three weeks after that time I was up in the trees, just listening to them and looking for good spots for snares, when I found the first sick one. When I touched its leaves I knew it was dying, like when I touched my grandpop's hand. It was a big old tree and used to have a big voice but now it was just breathing out. And it was bleeding. All around the trunk there was a circle somebody had cut and sap dripped out which is the tree's blood, my dad says. It was a rough chopping job and the person had used a little saw then a hatchet and I could see how they didn't know how to use the saw properly and had scratched all up and down around the cut. There was nothing I could do for that tree. I wanted to kill it properly so it wouldn't just stand there looking at me trying its hardest to stay alive.

The week after that one I found another tree that was the same and then it just kept on happening, seven of the biggest trees got cut. When I looked real hard I flew up again and saw them from the top and the dying ones made a kind of line down to the lake all the way from the lady's house on the hill to the shore. Then I came back down onto the ground, and I saw how it was.

You've done it again, Billy, said Mr Bailey when I came past. *I don't know what I'd do without you, two big fat ones today.*

I got my money and walked up the hill towards the lady's house and I saw her through the trees planting something in the garden. Dad said she kept the whole nursery in business.

Now I got quite close to her and the pretend duck before she saw me and she jumped backwards.

Jesus, kid, just give it a break, will you? she said in an angry voice. I stood there holding the empty box from the rabbits.

Just don't creep around so much, Billy, OK? she said, getting up. I saw she had a special little cushion for kneeling on and I was looking at that cushion when she said something else.

Where did you get that box, Billy?

I said out of the shed. She laughed and looked up at the sky. I looked down at the box with the picture of the apple on it.

Out of your shed? That's a finger-joint colonial box, Billy. Do you know how much some of them are worth?

Her voice was all excited, like that lady at the school who pretended boring things were interesting on that test.

What about selling it to me, she said.

I said it was my rabbit box and she said did I have any others in the shed. I said I would have a look. She was a loony. My dad sometimes split up old boxes for the chip heater. He kept nails and bolts in them.

I know where there'll be a lot, I said. *At the Franklin's garage sale.*

Her eyes looked a little bit like Mr Bailey's dogs' eyes inside the netting.

When is it? she asked.

On Sunday. They got lots of stuff.

Like what? she said, and then said a whole list of things like *fire pokers? ironwork? cupboards?* and I just kept nodding.

Lots of that kind of thing, I said. *Lots of these little boxes with writing and maps of Australia and animals like emus.*

She folded her arms and looked at me harder. *Boxes with emus and kangaroos on them? With joints like this one?*

Yep, I said, *but you got to get there real early in the morning. Like 6.30 or something. 'Cos other people come up from the city.*

She asked me where Franklin's was, and I told her.

I can get there earlier than the dealers, she said, looking down the hill at the trees all secretly dying in a row to the lake.

On Saturday I set a snare just inside a little tunnel of grass by the lake. Dad says it's bad to kill something without a good reason but I knew the rabbit wouldn't mind. The trees were very quiet now. It was going to be a black frost. When the moon came up there was a yellow ring around it like around a Tilley lamp when you take it out on a frosty night.

I couldn't hardly get to sleep with thinking. I thought of her going out there with her new saw from the hardware shop and cutting open their skin. In the night, while the rabbits nosed around with their soft whiskery mouths and Mr Bailey's dogs cried and choked on their chains over and over all through the night.

When I got up it was still dark, as dark as the steel on the monkey bars, cold metal that hurts your chest. I felt a still, stiff rabbit in the trap and I felt sorry for it. I knew she would, too. Because in the lady's head you can feel sorry and worried for rabbits but not for trees.

It looked like it was sitting up there by itself on the track, alive. All the crystals had grown in the night and now the black ice was smooth as glass all round that turn.

I got back into bed when I was finished. I felt my mum's gloves.

My dad knew I'd got up early when he came to wake me up again. I don't know how.

You'd better go out and check your traps, he said as he split the kindling.

Up the road Farrelly's tractor was pulling her car out of the ditch. It had crumpled into one of the big gums and leaves and sticks had been shaken all over it. Mr Farrelly said the ambulance blokes had nearly skidded over themselves on the bloody ice, trying to get in to help. *What's a sheila like her doing getting up in the bloody dark on a Sunday morning anyway,* Mr Farrelly said as he put the hooks on. *Bloody loonies.*

Under the front wheel I saw white fur, turned inside out like a glove, like my hat. I went down through the trees, touching the sick ones. On the way I stepped in a big patch of nettles. No use crying if you weren't looking out for yourself, my dad says. I looked around and found some dock and rubbed it on and it stopped hurting like magic. That's what nature's like, for everything poisonous there's something nearby to cure it if you just look around. That's what my dad says.

I made a little fire and smoked my traps. Five more weeks and I can get a mountain bike.

from *Dark Roots*

There Are Not Many Good People Left in the World

Mandy Sayer

I was on my way to meet a man who was taking me to lunch, my first date since my divorce, when I saw an elderly woman ahead of me, almost doubled over, clutching the iron bars of a garden fence. At first, I thought she'd vomited or had dropped something precious, but as I drew closer I could see she was hyperventilating.

Are you all right? I asked. I put my hand on her shoulder and could feel her convulsing as she struggled for air. She smelled of musk and stale wine. Her mascara was beginning to run.

She looked up, raised one gloved hand and pointed down the street. *Down there,* she said, gazing through the corridor of plane trees that ended where the road met the harbour. It seemed as if she were concentrating on some invisible man or a mirage that only appeared for her. Her eyes were grey and rheumy and I wondered if she'd been crying. *You will help me, won't you?* She took my wrist and squeezed it hard. *My legs have gone today.*

She passed me her walking stick and wrapped her arm around my waist and before I could say anything I was helping her down the block. She took tiny steps, like a toddler who'd recently learned to walk. As I supported her, my hand was lost in the soft dough of her belly. Every now and then her breath faltered and we'd have to stop for a while until she recovered. She reminded me of my grandmother in the last months of her illness, before the cancer riddled her brain. I felt impossibly sorry for this woman, and wondered if she had any family or at least a friendly neighbour. By now I was running late for my date and wasn't able to call him because he didn't believe in mobile phones. I'd invested a fair amount of money and time grooming myself for this lunch: a new haircut (cropped short, blonde highlights); a facial (one-hour, including skin scrub); and a new summer dress (white cheesecloth, very '70s).

You're so good to help me, chimed the woman, after another of her resting spells. *There are not many good people left in the world.* Her breathing was becoming more regular and I wondered if she could now walk on her own, but before I could suggest it, she grasped my waist even more firmly and said, *It's only another block.*

By this time, the girls from St Vincent's were pouring out of the school gate in a tidal wave of blue-and-white gingham. There were hundreds of them rushing towards us, weighed down by backpacks, chattering, texting, flicking back their hair. Once they were upon us, the old woman stopped in the middle of the footpath – and of course I stopped, too – forcing the girls to part like a river and stream past us on either side. The old woman stood with her eyes closed, as if better to hear the bravura of their voices and inhale the scents of their cheap perfumes.

After they'd passed, she tossed her head and remarked, to no one in particular, *I used to dance on the stage. These legs have taken me around the world eleven times.* Then she looked down at her stockinged feet, swollen inside orthopaedic shoes, as if she didn't recognise them. It was hard to imagine her once leaping and pirouetting from country to country, across oceans and continents, but the slight crack in her voice and her doleful gaze persuaded me it was at least partially true. I ran a dance school myself out of a church hall in Surry Hills, because my former husband didn't like the idea of my touring with a company. He also didn't like the idea of having children, which is why we broke up. But six months after we separated he began living with a woman with twin five-year-old girls.

The sun was coming out from behind the clouds. I guided her towards the end of the block and across the lane, where the surface of the harbour was studded with silver stars and the air was laced with salt. Suddenly, she stopped in front of a single-storey white cottage thronged with flowering vines. In the front garden pansies and buttercups nodded in the breeze. A black cat was curled up on the doormat, asleep in a triangle of sunlight.

She turned to me with her watery grey eyes. *Just till I get inside,* she said. *You've really been too kind.* I was surprised she lived in such a well-kept house and wondered how she managed the garden on her own. As I helped her up the path I had a momentary fear that she didn't own this cottage at all, that she was suffering from dementia and probably lived in a cramped bedsit in Woolloomooloo that stank of incontinence and mothballs.

But once we were on the veranda she greeted the cat, whom she called Chaplin, and fumbled in her bag for her keys. I finally found them in an outside pocket, hooked to a silver bangle, and opened the door for her. Walking her into a living room, I was further surprised by its antique cosiness. The hardwood floors were polished, partially covered with a Persian rug; a pink, art-deco lamp glowed on a sideboard; the walls were decorated with bevelled mirrors and gilt-framed oils from another century. A marble hearth stood against one wall. The ashes and a half-burned log made it obvious that she'd recently lit a fire, in spite of the summer's soaring heat. The mantelpiece held only two objects: what looked like some sort of photographic album and an empty, cut-glass vase.

I guided her into one of the overstuffed chairs. *Oh,* she said. *Would you mind putting the kettle on? I'm dying for a cuppa.*

I glanced at the wall clock. I was now over twenty minutes late, but when I looked at her swollen legs and pale face mottled with running make-up, I couldn't find the words to tell her I had to go.

OK, I replied. *Can I use your telephone first?* Even though Ellis didn't use a mobile, it occurred to me I might be able to catch him at the restaurant.

She smiled and waved me over to a small table near the adjoining kitchen. On it sat an ancient black telephone. I rang Directory Assistance and was put through to Fratelli's on Challis Avenue. I described Ellis to the Italian waiter – six and a half feet; cropped blond hair; he usually wore a baseball cap. The waiter let out a sigh of recognition. *Yes,* he said. *Corner table. He drank a sparkling mineral water.*

I was about to ask him if he could deliver a message to Ellis, when the waiter cleared his throat, and added, *He left a five-dollar tip.*

I hung up, dejected. I'd missed him by three minutes. He was probably back at work now, but I didn't have that number.

The old woman was stroking the cat and humming a song to herself. I slipped into the kitchen and put the kettle on the stove. Through a glass-paned cabinet I could see a cache of medications: plastic prescription bottles, boxes, tubes of lotions, all printed with the name *Miss Millicent Darling* and the address of a local pharmacy.

Miss Millicent Darling, I said through the doorway. *That's a pretty name.*

She'd taken off her shoes and had put her feet up on a leather ottoman. *Stage name, Sweetheart. When I retired I decided to keep it.*

I remembered that Cary Grant's original name had been Archibald, and Marilyn Monroe had once been called Norma Jean. *What's your real name?* I asked.

A professional, she replied, *neither reveals her age, nor her original moniker.* She announced this loudly, as if she were still on stage, playing a role. *I –* she added, smoothing back her hair – *was always a professional. Still am.*

I had the feeling she'd said these lines many times – perhaps they were even part of a play she'd once starred in.

My name's Jane, I said, though she didn't seem to hear me. The kettle began to sing and I made her the tea – *white, one sugar!* – and a cup of instant coffee for myself.

I sat beside her, in a floral tapestry chair, and she told me that one day recently she'd felt so lonely she'd invited two Jehovah's Witnesses into her home. For two decades, she'd had a pen pal in Vienna, but he'd died of an aneurism a few years before. Her sense of isolation nearly made me weepy: I'd been divorced seven months and knew what loneliness was.

It's so hard, she said, staring into the hearth, *when you outlive all your friends. No shared memories.* I asked her if she'd ever been married but she just sipped her tea and gazed into the hearth again. After a minute or so, she suddenly brightened up and declared, with great theatricality, *Get thee to a winery!* and waved at the decanter of amber liquid glowing on the mantlepiece.

I usually didn't drink during the day but, since nothing was going according to plan that afternoon, I poured us two glasses of what smelled like plum wine. Millicent raised her glass and declared, *To Jane, my new special friend!* I was surprised by the toast, and not a little uncomfortable with it, but I managed a smile, clinked her glass, and swallowed a mouthful.

Jane, dear – she raised her hand and gestured at the album on the mantlepiece – *could you fetch me the scrapbook?*

I stood up. *Of course, Millicent.*

She flashed me a smile. *Call me Millie.*

I picked up the album and placed it on the table. It had hard, rectangular covers, tattered and fraying at the corners. The original colour looked as if it had been pink or even fuchsia but time and probably hundreds of handlings had bleached it to a musky grey.

Millicent gathered herself and leaned forward. *I never kept up this scrapbook, of course. Too busy! It was my older sister, Edith. She died at eighty-seven.*

Natural causes? I asked, trying to make conversation.

Millicent shook her head. *She was walking to church one morning and an airconditioner from a high-rise fell on her head.*

I gulped my drink and studied her face, wondering if she were joking. Unfortunately, she was gazing at the hearth with such a sad, nostalgic expression that I had to conclude she was telling the truth.

Suddenly, she brightened up again and opened the scrapbook, as if it would provide an antidote to her growing melancholia. I edged my chair closer and saw, on the first page, a yellow newspaper clipping of a young girl in a sailor suit, proudly saluting to the camera. Someone had written, *Wangaratta, 1934,* in blue ink at the bottom.

My first panto, she said, smiling to herself. She began turning the leaves of the album with great care, taking each upper corner between her thumb and forefinger, as if they were pages of a rare and ancient Bible. And as she did so, I saw Millicent grow from a gawky urchin to a shy, flat-chested teenager, to a poised ballerina in a frothy tutu dancing the lead of *Giselle* at London's Royal Philharmonic. It was hard to believe the muscular legs catapulting above the stage in the photo were the same ones next to me now, swollen and pulsing with varicose veins.

In one photo she was curtsying, her lips and high cheek bones hand-tinted pink, her head crowned by a halo of yellow flowers. *So beautiful*, I said, touching the sepia border.

Yes, replied Millicent, her eyes narrowing as she looked me up and down. *You know, you could do yourself a few favours.*

I sipped my drink nervously. Perhaps she didn't like my new spiky hairdo. Even the hairdresser had thought she'd cut too much off.

A bit more make-up would do wonders, dear. Foundation and mascara would highlight your eyes.

I willed myself not to glance at my own reflection in the mirror. I'd never been a great fan of cosmetics, but after Millicent's observation I suddenly had the impulse to rush out and splurge on powders, lipsticks, rouge. All I had on was some liner and strawberry lip balm – so plain and dull when I compared myself to the sanguine beauty of the younger Millicent.

The clippings were faded – the edges crumbling so much the album looked as if it were speckled with dandruff. There were also playbills and original programs and the occasional airline ticket. No pictures of her family, not even a boyfriend.

So Millie, I said, *do you have any children?*

She frowned and pursed her lips, as if I'd just asked a ridiculous question or had made a whopping faux pas. *Do you think I'd be entertaining Jehovah's Witnesses if I could enjoy the company of my own offspring?*

I gulped at my drink again; I was beginning to feel hot and a little dizzy.

Millicent began running her finger around the rim of her glass. *Of course, I wanted them. I wanted three to be exact. But my husband didn't. We danced together in New York.* Swan Lake. The Red Shoes. Scheherezade. *When I was forty-four and too old to fall pregnant, he left me for a younger woman, a chorus girl from* My Fair Lady, *who pumped out three boys in three consecutive years.* She paused and drained her wine.

I refilled her drink and topped up my own glass. Again, I felt a stab of sympathy for her, for the kids she'd never had, and for what little happiness she would experience between this day and her death. I'd only had three lovers in my life and didn't know how many more I would attract. I was thirty-five and running out of time. My body was still lithe and strong but I was so depressed during certain periods that I'd lost the will to be charming and flirtatious. Only a few weeks before I'd met Ellis, I'd visited a psychic who'd told me I'd had an abortion when I was very young, that I was an extremely neat person, and that I loved my dead father. She also mentioned that I have a tendency to put the needs of other people before my own and that I needed to be more assertive. But when it came to my future she was vague and general, as if there was nothing ahead of me that warranted her attention. At the time I suspected that perhaps I'd die quite soon, that the psychic knew this and was merely being diplomatic, but sitting in Millicent Darling's living room that afternoon convinced me that the best years of my life were probably already behind me and that one day I too would stop a stranger in the street and ask her to help me home.

I suddenly felt drowsy and short of breath. Perhaps it was the wine, but it was as if the old woman's loneliness was now in the air itself and was beginning to infect me. In a wave of panic, I decided I would hurry home and leave a message on Ellis's machine, to apologise and explain why I'd missed him at the restaurant, to set up another date. *I have to go*, I said, putting down my drink, though she didn't seem to hear me.

Do you know what I miss most? said Millicent.

I shook my head, even though she wasn't looking at me.

Flowers, she said. *Roses, to be exact. Every opening night my husband would give me a dozen red roses. Every opening night for twenty-one years.*

I stood up and smoothed down the wrinkles in my dress. I glanced at the empty vase on the mantlepiece and felt a wave of vertigo, as if I were standing on the edge of a very tall building.

I have to go now, I said, *but I'll visit you again.*

She looked up at me with those watery grey eyes. *People always say that.*

I will, I said. *I'll visit you tomorrow.*

Millicent sniffed and clasped her hands together. *Even the Jehovah's Witnesses didn't come back.*

I'll bring some sandwiches for lunch, I assured her. *We can look through the rest of the album.*

Millicent smiled and put out her hand, touching me on the sleeve. *Dear Jane*, she said, *my new special friend. There are not many good people left in the world.*

I leaned over and kissed her on the cheek. Its crepey softness felt like a pillow against my lips.

I'm so glad we met today, she added.

Me too, I said, even though I didn't entirely mean it.

I let myself out and made a beeline back to my apartment. Hands shaking, I dialled Ellis's home number, rehearsing what I would say when the machine clicked on. I waited and waited – five rings, ten, twenty – the muscles in my neck tightening – but no cheerful message, urging me to leave the time and date of my call, announced itself through my handset. Finally, it rang out and I reluctantly hung up. I knew even then I would never hear from him again.

I had a sleepless night. When I managed to doze off I had nightmares about Millicent's bad legs being attached to my body and having to teach a *pointe* class to seven-year-old girls. Another one in which my ex-husband fathered eleven kids, all to the same woman. I awakened in a cold sweat and an outbreak of eczema on my arms.

Later, I showered and dressed. Even though I was exhausted, I was determined to keep my promise to Millicent. Back then I believed in karma and honouring commitments. I cheered myself up by going out and buying Greek olives, gourmet sandwiches and a bottle of expensive red. I usually didn't treat myself to such delicacies – no mother sends her daughter to a fat dance teacher – but since we were on break for six weeks, I thought one day of indulgence would do me and Millicent Darling a whole lot of good.

It was another hot afternoon and, as I walked to her house, the sun angled through the plane trees on Darlinghurst Road. I passed the florist and glimpsed scores of blossoms and ferns standing on long stems in the window. I couldn't help myself – I wanted desperately to make her happy – so I spent the rest of my cash on twelve red roses and had them wrapped in a bright green ribbon. Passing a chemist shop, I decided to slip in and try on some cosmetic samples: translucent powder on my cheeks, burgundy lipstick; the cashier helped me with the mascara.

By the time I arrived at her cottage it was the middle of the day and sweat patches were spreading under my arms. The gate was already open and I rushed up the path and onto the veranda. Chaplin was nowhere to be seen. I was excited by the fact that I'd kept my word, by how surprised Millicent would be that I'd returned so soon. I couldn't wait to see the expression on her face when I presented her with the bouquet.

I rang the doorbell and waited. A breeze blew up from the harbour and I heard the honking of a ship. I thought I saw the living-room curtain flutter and pushed the bell again. After what seemed like a long time, I heard the slow, monotonous rhythm of approaching footsteps.

Who is it? Millicent's voice was imperious and flutey as ever.

It's me, I said. *Jane.*

She coughed three times. *Who?*

Jane, I repeated. *From yesterday.*

There was a lengthy pause and then I heard a low murmur, as if she were talking to herself.

I helped you home. Remember? Your new special friend.

There was more murmuring and a jangle of keys. Finally I heard the lock click. The door opened only slightly, and suddenly the confused, wary face of Millicent Darling was peering back at me. She was still wearing the same black dress and stockings from the day before.

What do you want? she asked, her hand clutching the frame of the door.

I came back, I announced brightly. *I brought us some lunch. And these are for you!* I proffered the roses, but she merely looked through them, as if they weren't there.

Who is it, Millie? someone called from inside the house. As Millicent turned to answer, the door swung further open, and I saw a woman about my age perched in the same chair that I had sat in the day before. On the coffee table stood the decanter of wine and two filled glasses. Millicent's scrapbook was open and the woman glanced away from it and looked me up and down, as if she were offended by my make-up and yellow dress.

No one, cried back Millicent. She then turned and frowned. *Now please go away*, she said, closing the door, *and stop bothering me.*

Today on *Dr Phil*

Tom Cho

Today my Auntie Lien and I are appearing on the television show
of the famed psychologist Dr Phil. The *Dr Phil* episode we are
appearing in is titled 'What Are You Really Mad At?' and Dr Phil
is asking Auntie Lien and me about how we deal with anger.
Auntie Lien is right in the middle of talking about her propen-
sity to explode in anger when Dr Phil asks her why she gets angry
so easily. Auntie Lien hesitates. Dr Phil advises her, 'You've got
to face it to replace it.' Hearing Dr Phil say this prompts Auntie
Lien to confess that her anger stems from the many difficulties
she has experienced with relationships. She says that she has
been unlucky in love. Furthermore, she says that the sadder she
gets, the angrier she gets. I feel that I can relate to this statement
and so I join the studio audience in enthusiastically applauding
my auntie's comment. Auntie Lien suddenly says something in
ancient Greek. Dr Phil looks at her blankly, and she explains that
she was quoting from *Medea*, the classic play by Euripides. She
confesses that she likes to study the work of the great Athenian
dramatists. She translates the lines for Dr Phil: 'The fiercest
anger of all, the most incurable / Is that which rages in the place
of dearest love.' As Auntie Lien goes on to discuss in minute
detail the structural imperfections in Euripidean drama that
have puzzled scholars for centuries, I can tell that Dr Phil and
the studio audience are struck by the fact that they are sharing
a room with one of the finest scholars of ancient Greek drama

that the world has seen. Me, I have always found it interesting that Auntie Lien has such a great mind for scholarly pursuits as well as such a great capacity for flying into fits of anger. This makes me think about my own experiences with intellectualism and anger. Sometimes I have a tendency to 'intellectualise first and get angry later'. Interestingly, like many people, when I get really angry I can transform into what seems like a completely different person. This makes me turn to Dr Phil to ask him: if anger can transform me, in what other ways might anger be transformative? I suggest to him that perhaps I could use my anger creatively, even proactively. For example, surely some of the most significant political revolutions in history have been in part driven by a sense of rage? This then leads me to consider my attraction to anger. Could it be that I associate anger with power? This would be ironic, given that anger can occur as a consequence of not feeling powerful enough. But Dr Phil is too absorbed in Auntie Lien's discussion of the function of the chorus in ancient Greek drama to listen to me properly. However, eventually the topic turns back to anger when Dr Phil begins reflecting upon the murderous actions of the character of Medea following her betrayal by her husband. In fact, Dr Phil declares that Medea ably demonstrates his belief that people who experience uncontrollable rage actually have unfulfilled needs that must be addressed. Hearing this makes me think of my own life, and so I confess to Dr Phil a fantasy that I have recently had. In this fantasy, I become extremely angry. The fantasy begins with me starting to sweat from my anger. My heart starts beating faster. I clench my fists and the anger makes my face heat up. In this fantasy, I am like the Incredible Hulk in that the angrier I get, the stronger I get. So my muscles start to grow. My muscles become so big that they start to outgrow my clothes. The seams of my shirt and pants begin to split. My neck becomes thicker, and my thighs and calves swell and become harder. I am growing and growing, putting on height as well as bulk, and soon I am around eight feet tall and full of strength and fury. First I go rampaging through the streets, smashing things out of sheer anger. No one is stronger than me. I can bend lamp posts and break walls and throw cars. It does not take long for the police and the military to be sent after me. But they cannot stop me.

Their guns and explosives only make me angrier and stronger. I rip apart their trucks and tanks. Then I move on to the sheer satisfaction of destroying whole buildings. After a good hour of smashing and destroying, I stomp all the way to my girlfriend's house. She opens the door and looks a little surprised to see me. I am standing before her, breathing hard and still very angry. She says to me, 'I was just watching you on the news. You were destroying all these buildings. You should have more respect for the property of others.' I pause for a moment before replying, 'Don't make me angry. You wouldn't like me when I'm angry.' I enjoy saying this line to her – it is what Dr Banner used to say before he turned into the Hulk. But, as it turns out, my girl-friend does like me when I'm angry. She begins looking at my muscles in admiration. I glare at her but that only makes her sigh happily. This just makes me glare at her all the more. I am so angry. The angrier I get, the stronger I get. And the stronger I get, the more aroused she gets. She looks at me and her face begins to flush. Her breath starts to quicken. And the more aroused she gets, the younger she gets. She used to be thirty-three but now she is getting younger. She smiles and winks at me as she goes back into her twenties. Fascinated, I watch as she gets younger and younger, and she doesn't stop until she is in her teens and blushing and cuter than ever. And the younger she gets, the fewer people she has had sex with. She slips her hand into mine and tells me that she is sixteen years old and a virgin and that she is eager for me to teach her all about sex. So I scoop her up in my arms and take her to her bedroom and we spend all night having the hottest sex you can imagine. After I have finished telling Dr Phil my anger fantasy, there is complete silence in the studio. I had been hoping that the audience would enthusiastically applaud my fantasy but they just stare at me. It is then that I wonder if I have said too much. Finally, Dr Phil breaks the silence to tell me, 'You have to name it before you can claim it,' and he encourages me to look inside myself to work out what I really want in life. He then says that we have run out of time and so he faces the camera to deliver a final address about the issues we have spoken about today. He begins to deliver a very moving address about how life is managed, not cured. As Dr Phil speaks, I think about the pain that anger can cause and

I start to feel sad. I look at Auntie Lien's face and I can tell that she is feeling sad about this too. In fact, the more poignantly Dr Phil speaks, the sadder Auntie Lien gets. But then I remember that the sadder Auntie Lien gets, the angrier she gets. I soon notice that she is clenching and unclenching her fists. Her eyes dart around the room in agitation. As Dr Phil continues to speak, she begins to mutter angrily under her breath. Finally, it is too much for her. She explodes in anger, jumping out of her seat and attacking Dr Phil. Security guards run up to the stage and try to pull Dr Phil and Auntie Lien apart. The studio audience is hollering and chanting and Auntie Lien is swearing so colourfully that her words will have to be bleeped out before the episode goes to air. Auntie Lien calls out to encourage me to join in the fisticuffs. I am unsure about this but she reminds me that releasing anger can be very satisfying. The thing is, Auntie Lien has a point – quite a valid point that not even Dr Phil has raised. But first, I take the time to intellectualise about Dollard et al's 'Frustration-Aggression Hypothesis' and its subsequent behaviourist / neo-associationist reformulation by Berkowitz. Having considered this and its implications for research on factors affecting aggression, I become angry and join Auntie Lien in releasing my rage. As Auntie Lien and I engage in a dramatic punch-up with Dr Phil and his security guards, the show's end credits start to roll. A few people in the studio audience begin to applaud. Auntie Lien and I still have plenty of rage left but, soon, the show will be over.

Heat

The Coral Cay

Sandra Hall

There were a few moments of unarticulated anxiety while they got the newly repaired engine going, then they were away – away from the sandflies and the mangroves and across the sandbar into the blue.

'Not far to the reef,' Jay, who was at the wheel, shouted to her above the din of the engine, grinning into the wind like a dog let off the lead.

She put on her sunglasses and started rubbing sun-block into her arms. The whole world was shining: an explosion of blue and silver streaked with gold and flecked with the white of the boat's wake.

Above to the left was the crooked mountain shaped like an upraised thumb and ahead was the cay – a small, yellow mound rising out of the glassy water.

Jay throttled down the engine. As they went in carefully over the shadowy patches of coral, he readjusted his cap over his eyes and surveyed the oval expanse of sand.

'Nobody here.'

She gazed out over the blue and silver emptiness. 'Should there be?'

'Usually is.'

'Pull the other one.'

'This is Queensland, the tourists' paradise. There's always somebody.'

'Not here surely.'

'Yes. We're on the main track. People stop off here all the time on their way out. Look.'

On cue a boat appeared on the horizon. Jay's attention returned to the cay. If it was any comfort, he said, it never got any smaller. 'This is full tide.'

'You're an authority, are you?' This was Hal. Hal and Jay were her brothers. In childhood, her brawls with them had pushed her mother to the edge of hysteria. Now they were closer to her than anyone else she knew. She even liked their wives. They were the only family she was ever likely to have. Jay gazed at the sun, made a silent calculation and unrolled the blue sheet of plastic he had been carrying under his arm.

Marking a spot in the sand with his toe, he started digging a hole to plant the boathook.

Hal winked at her.

Without looking up, Jay said, 'Come on. Help. This is a bloody altruistic act on my part. Some do. Some just stand and watch.'

After he had fastened the plastic sheeting to the hook, she took one end and Hal another and they spread the plastic to make a tent providing a patch of shade large enough to accommodate a human body.

After they had piled enough sand on the sheet to hold it down, she obediently sat in this patch while Hal took a commemorative photograph.

'You don't know what you're missing, you know.' Jay was standing by the tent, scrutinising it in a proprietary way.

'I know exactly,' she said. 'Seasickness and the sight of you two swilling Foster's and playing yobbos.'

'All right. If that's the way you feel, we'll be off.'

At the water's edge, she looked out to sea. The other boat had gone.

'We'll just be at the other end of the reef,' said Hal.

If she needed them, she'd whistle, she said.

They both smiled, pleased with her. It was their kind of joke. A showing-what-you-were-made-of kind of joke. It helped to compensate for the fact that watching fish die made her sick.

Jay said they would be back in an hour, which was also a joke. She already knew that the blue tent, flapping a bit now against its weighting of dry sand, would be her home for the rest of the day.

She waved them off and they laughed back at her.

'You had it coming!' Hal yelled then the boat started to move away and the laughter was lost in the noise of its engine.

Wearing a T-shirt against the sun, she sat on the wet sand with her snorkelling gear, letting the tiny waves lap over her legs.

She tried to imagine what it would be like if Rod were here, a strictly hypothetical exercise as he would never be caught so far from a racecourse or a stock exchange. But if he were with her, he would be pacing the sandy oval while staring across the water, expecting the worst. Rod believed that the world was organised along conspiratorial lines and when she had been with him, she had, too. They had spent their marriage discussing tactics – a conspiracy of two against the rest.

Here on the cay, they would both have been pacing: trying to cover their backs while Nature decided what it was going to spring on them. A cyclone? A shark attack? Like a child excited at being alone in an empty house, she teased herself with these perils before her mind wandered off to consider again the blue-green water, the fineness of the sand and other things so slight and evanescent that she couldn't put words to them.

It was a fair swim to the first stands of coral, but the water was very warm – no sudden cold shocks here, as there were near the beach, where the estuary currents mingled with the seawater. Here the temperature was just the way she liked it. She felt cushioned by the water.

The first patch of reef turned out to have a deep drop-off, harbouring schools of sweetlip, and putting her head up to fill her lungs, she dived down the coral cliff, surprising two coral trout and an angelfish which darted away from her in a flash of silver.

On the way back in, she had to work hard against the current, feeling ridiculous because the cay, seen through her mask, seemed so near and finally, after she'd reached it and hauled herself out of the water and up the slope, she lay back on the sand, still breathing hard, but happy with herself. She was new to snorkelling. Hal had talked her into it early in the holiday and at first she had behaved as if finding herself on another planet, twisting back at every second stroke to look for horrors beyond the rim of her mask. Then, magically, she had relaxed, gliding through the water, safe, weightless, delighted with everything.

The swim had made her hungry, so she wandered back up the beach, ate her sandwiches and dozed in the shade of the blue tent, her unread book open beside her.

The boat was the first thing she saw when she woke up – a motor boat a little smaller than Jay's, bobbing at anchor beyond the reef. Then she saw the figure stepping gingerly across the coral, floating a square plastic box and carrying a speargun.

He waited until he was on the dry sand before he waved – a gesture so fleeting that she thought he was going to turn towards the other end of the cay and try to forget that she was there.

She actually held her breath, hoping for this, but he hesitated only for a moment before starting towards her with a bow-legged stride that seemed vaguely familiar. When he was halfway across the sand she recognised him.

Recognised him but refused to believe it. As he got closer, she sat staring hard at him, waiting for his next step to prove her wrong.

'Well, well, looks as though you've set up lighthousekeeping.' He sat down and gave her a smile as perfunctory as his wave.

'Sort of – although I wasn't expecting company.'

'Well, you're not Robinson Crusoe.' He laughed at his own joke, clearly expecting her to do the same, and when she failed to respond, he leaned back on one elbow and gazed up at her, eyes narrowed against the glare. She glanced quickly at the Irish face, ruddy in the sun.

'I come here quite a bit,' he said, 'when I'm not wanted ... elsewhere.'

She kept her head down, postponing the moment.

'Hey! ... Don't I know you?'

She still didn't look at him, concentrating on the sand as it slipped dryly through her fingers. Finally, she said, 'You're Michael Ford.'

'I know who I am. Who are you?'

Rubbing her hands together, she tried to shake off the powdery touch of the sand. 'We worked together once. I'm a publicist.'

'Go on.'

'I worked on one of your films.'

'Well, bugger me.' He sat back, shaking his head at the returning memory. 'I remember all right. Not that I want to.'

He let out a bellow of a laugh, took another long look and said with satisfaction, 'You look a lot older.'

The smug schoolboy smirk was almost reassuring. The monster she remembered was bigger and scarier than this one. If this is all, she thought, it'll be all right.

He was still staring at her. 'Gerry ...' He clicked his fingers.

'Gerry Bartlett.'

'That's right. I knew there was a "b" in there somewhere.' Then mouthing the words under his breath: 'Bartlett, the bitch.'

She gave him a bland look as if she hadn't heard. 'I'd read that you were shooting somewhere around here.' She waved her arm, taking in sea and sky.

'But you didn't expect me to come walking across the water.' Again he produced the laugh and this time she studied the mechanics of it, a child at the zoo.

When he stopped, she was still gazing at him gravely. His smile faded. 'You know why I come out here? To get away from the crap. How about I pitch camp over there and we have a demarcation zone. Strictly half and half. I swim over there, you have from here to here.' He sketched an arc in the air. 'And at half-time, we switch. I assume there is a half-time. Someone is coming for you eventually, are they? Or are you a member of some fancy amphibian species I haven't caught up with yet?' He glanced inside the tent. 'With a detachable pouch fitted out with Aquasun 30+ and a Dan Brown book. Scientific name: *femina bloody romantica*.'

'It's Margaret Atwood.'

'Oh, excuse me.'

Before she could stop herself, she burst out laughing. For a moment, he looked almost friendly. 'Tell you what ...' He burrowed in his plastic box. 'I've got something here you might like.'

'A few coloured beads for the native, is it?'

'Something like that.'

He produced a mini-disc player. 'Mozart and Bach.'

She didn't need the music. The sounds of the waves and the seabirds were enough, but she put on the headphones and watched him walk down the beach. He strutted and there were creases below the shoulderblades of the broad back.

It wasn't long before he was back. 'Come on, it's terrific.'

'I know. I've been in.'

'The tide's going out now. It's different.'

They swam together, pointing out the sights to one another – a giant clam, some coral trout and, just as they were about to turn round and come in, a reef shark, swimming quite close to them. She knew it was harmless. Even so, the broad white throat and the spade-shaped snout unnerved her and she recoiled. Ford grasped her hand and steered her away from it.

Back on the beach, she was embarrassed, which astounded him. 'For Christ's sake, they don't look like your average household pet. Most women would have been scared.'

She raised her eyebrow and he went into a Yiddish comic routine. 'Sorr-y. What was I thinking? Most persons.'

They were lying side by side with their heads in the shadow of the tent.

'Know what my part is in this epic we're shooting up here?'

She hesitated but only for a moment. Then she said she could guess.

'Go on then.'

What the hell, she thought, and said it. 'The hero's best friend. Heart of gold, fists of iron and not much going on upstairs.'

He lifted his sunglasses and peered into her face. 'Well, your teeth are just as sharp as ever. You shouldn't be worried about Mr Reef Shark. Other way around.'

He flopped back on the sand and after a moment, she reached for her book.

'You think it's funny,' he said.

She opened her book, shook it free of sand and propped it on her belly, going carefully this time. 'Not funny, no.'

'Bloody ironic then. Is that better?'

She tried to make a joke of it. 'Look, the camera likes you. That would make most actors very happy.'

He sat up, repeated the routine with the sunglasses and stared into her face again. 'Oh, we've developed a few *theories* along with the wrinkles.' He stood up. 'I'm going in again.'

Relieved, she went back to her book, telling herself to take it easy, and was dozing when he came back. She was awoken by the tingle of cold water on her skin and looked up to see him standing over her, towelling himself so thoroughly that getting dry might have been all in the world that mattered.

He took up their conversation as if he had never left it. 'I must be good at it – at being liked.' He bit down on the word, spitting it at her. 'Because my present director, Wonderboy, thought I was actually going to *be* one of those good ole boys I've been serving up all these years. Thought all that was for real. What you see is what you get. That's what he thought.' He dropped the towel and gazed at the horizon. 'I'm actually having quite a lot of fun with him. You've got to stop yourself being bored to death on a bloody shoot. It's not as if any of the women are worth …' He had begun talking to himself. When he remembered she was there, he was amused. 'Oh, excuse me. I almost said something that might have offended you – your feminist sensibility. Anyway, enough of me. Let's talk about you. I seem to remember a husband. That's right. He came out to the shoot one weekend.'

He paused and she waited, getting her smile ready. Her armour.

'PR, wasn't he? That's it. You worked together. He liked the horses and a drink if I remember rightly. I had a feeling he might go for the chicks, as well.'

She cut it short, giving him the smile. It had a touch of complicity in it that she didn't like but couldn't help. It said, we've both been around. We know how things are. Then she told him that she was divorced.

'Oh, really. Interesting state, isn't it?'

'I'm still making up my mind.'

'Christ. Not nursing a broken heart, are we?'

'Did I say that?'

'You didn't have to. Anyway, divorced is the way to be, let me tell you.'

'And how long did it take you to find out?'

'A year. After that I didn't look back. It takes a special kind of woman to be married to an actor.'

She couldn't help her smile and hoped he hadn't seen it. But he had. He turned his head and the sun flashed off his glasses. She couldn't see his eyes – just her own reflection in the lenses.

'You think I mean a doormat,' he said. 'Well, I don't. I mean a special kind of woman – the kind that doesn't care about all the crap. Genuinely doesn't care.'

'There can't be too many of those around.'

He sat down close to her. 'You don't understand a bloody thing, do you?'

'Then don't tell me.' She was angry at last, desperate to escape the glare. 'I didn't ask.'

He put his hand on her arm. She shook it off and he raised both hands, resorting to the Yiddish comic routine again. 'Sorry, sorry.'

She was still, head down, smoothing the pages of her book.

'Lovely woman, my wife.' He kept up the accent. 'But you want to know her trouble? Well, you're going to know anyway. Her trouble was that she let it all get to her. She was weak.'

When she didn't look up he nudged her leg with his foot. 'Come on, lighten up. You look to me like the type who keeps it all in. Do that for long enough and it all goes rotten on you. Actors can't afford to be like that. We get faced with it every day of our lives.'

'Look, I want to read for a while.'

Again the explosive laugh. 'Of course you do. It's a lot prettier in books. I'm a bit raw for you, aren't I?'

She had been about to stand up. He grabbed her arm. 'I think we should talk a lot more about being divorced. It's a good sub-ject. I want to know what you don't like about it. My ex-wife likes it. She's always telling me how much. But you know that, don't you? She started crying on your shoulder as soon as she met you on that bloody shoot. Probably still doing it.'

She smiled sweetly. 'Not anymore.'

'Yeah, not anymore. The sisterhood cured her. What I want to know is why it hasn't done the same for you.'

She remembered Rod and Ford playing poker together on the weekend they had met. Rod had taken to him – his kind of man. No doubt someone had told Rod exactly what had happened after he'd left but she never had.

She kept her smile going. 'I'm getting there. You know what I like best about divorce? Being on my own.' She gently loosened his grip on her arm.

He leaned back on his elbows and said evenly, 'So where's old … Rod? That was his name, wasn't it? Where's old Rod run off to? No, don't tell me. I bet he's living with some sweet-faced young blonde who actually talks to him and makes him feel good – somebody who doesn't sit around trying to work out how she feels and how she should feel and how he doesn't quite measure up to her bloody standards for living.'

'Something like that.'

'Come on. Let something out for once in your life. Or do you have to be boozed before you do that?'

'All right. She's younger, blonder and sweeter but she's also a lot tougher.'

He laughed. 'I find that hard to believe.'

He had already lost interest. He was gazing out to sea, thinking of something else.

He broke his silence with a laugh. 'Know where Wonderboy thinks I am today? Up the coast smoking dope with some friends who grow the stuff. He got paranoid this morning when I told him that's where I was going. I like to keep him on his toes. The creative tension's good for him.' The laugh was deeper in his throat this time. A real laugh.

He fished in the plastic box and came up with a hip flask which he offered to her. She shook her head but he persisted, pressing the flask against her forearm.

'You hate to lose control, don't you? Just the thought of it throws you. I saw it out there with the reef shark. You hated yourself for that.' He took a long pull on the whisky. The breeze was getting stronger, making her shiver as it cooled her sunburn. She put on a sweater.

'That's what acting's like, you know,' he said.

'I must have missed something. What's it like?' She met his glare this time, putting all her dislike into her eyes. But the heat seemed to go out of him and when he spoke, it was in the damped-down monotone of their first conversation. 'Like being scared of something harmless. Except that it's not really harmless. It keeps chipping away at you, keeps showing you things you don't want to see. Things like age, for instance.'

He swallowed more whisky and offered it to her again.

Again she shook her head.

'Come on. God, that's what I remember about you. All the booze you put away.'

'I don't want it.'

He looked at her, realisation dawning. 'Ah, ha. So it got that bad, did it? AA. The whole deal?'

She nodded, not wanting to tell him anything. She could imagine it all burlesqued later in off-camera performances sharp enough to help him live with the blandness of his work.

He stood up, complacently surveying the greying sea. Then he started towards the water's edge, swaying and tipping back the flask as he went.

'I want you to have a drink with me.' The whisky was working now, the words sliding around in his mouth. He crouched beside her, holding the flask in front of her face.

'I don't drink anymore.' She said it evenly, spacing out the words.

'Since when?'

'Since that shoot as it happens.'

He was delighted. 'Don't tell me I changed your life?'

'No. I did.'

The sad thing was that she had lost all memory of the only part of that night worth hanging on to. At some stage she must have felt pleased with herself. For a few triumphant moments she had experienced the sensation of saying exactly what she meant and would not have dared to say without the drink. Yet all she remembered were the preliminaries – the silent frustration of sitting with the others at dinner watching Ford perform. His wife had been the first victim of the evening, then he had moved on to the assistant director and finally, it was Gerry's turn. She had drunk plenty by then – so much that she had wondered afterwards how she had got the words out. Even now she had no idea what they were and knew their effect only because others had told her, unable to believe that anything – even the amount of booze she'd consumed – could blot out anything so satisfying. But all she had next morning was the remorse – the familiar realisation that she'd lost control. Whatever the drink gave, it also took away. That morning at last she'd learned the lesson. That was why she now pushed the flask away.

She took him by surprise. The flask fell from his grip, the whisky trickling thickly across the sand. Suddenly he was shouting: 'You bitch! You bloody bitch!'

And his anger inflamed hers, making her stubbornly mute. She grasped her knees, digging her toes into the sand. Battening down.

The blow sent her sprawling across the sand, eyes watering, ears ringing, and for a moment she couldn't move. She lay clutching her cheek bone until his voice came through to her, his tone nastily quiet, his mouth close to her ear. 'Come on. Get your things. We're going in again. I'll take the speargun this time and get one of those coral trout. Come on.'

'I don't fish.'

'I'm not asking you to damn well fish. You're going to watch me fish.'

'No.'

He hit her again. After a moment, she slowly got to her feet, took off her sweater and fetched her mask and snorkel from the tent. He watched her, amused, and nodded towards the water. 'You go first.'

At the water's edge, she sat down, taking her time, fingers fumbling with the strap on her mask, hoping he would give in and leave her. But he waited, standing over her, speargun propped against his leg.

As they waded across the first patch of the coral towards the deeper water, he gripped her hand, letting go only when she had floated off and started to swim. Then he caught up and stayed close beside her, repeatedly glancing at her as they swam.

He left her near the coral cliff. She had to raise her head above water to see where he'd gone and very gradually she increased the distance between them, not daring to trust completely her swelling sense of relief.

As the moments passed and he made no move towards her, she ceased to look at him and concentrated only on the cay, now growing larger with each stroke.

She felt the spear as a rush of water near her thigh. Then she saw it, caught in a cluster of staghorn coral beneath her.

She couldn't remember reaching shallow water – just her frantic, stumbling progress across the coral with him close behind her.

He caught her up where the coral ended and the sand began, grabbing her by the ankle and bringing her down so hard that she had to fight to keep her mouth above water. Then suddenly he let her go. For a moment she couldn't believe it and stayed down, getting her breath, expecting at any moment the hand on the back of her neck. When it didn't come, she raised her head.

There were two of them – in shorts and matching sunhats. A man and a woman, perhaps in their sixties, manoeuvring an Esky out of their dinghy. Now they were pausing to wave. Their boat was on the blind side of the tent, sitting at anchor on the grey and white water.

She glanced at Ford, who was half-turned away from her, as if she no longer existed. He was looking at the couple. And as she watched, he smiled. The authentic on-screen version. A real Mick Ford grin.

Emily

Daniel Wynne

In order to get my novel published, I told book publishers Allen & Unwin that I was the reincarnation of Emily Brontë.

I know it sounds ridiculous, but I really wanted to get their attention. I didn't want to be another unpublished nobody with a failed novel rotting away at the bottom of the slush pile. I didn't want to write another letter that said 'Dear Allen & Unwin, I have written a novel that you may think worthy of consideration … blah blah blah.' I wanted something that would make an impression. So I told them I was Emily Brontë, the young English woman who wrote the tragic Gothic romance *Wuthering Heights*. I told them I created every character: the passionate Catherine, the dangerous and bad-tempered Heathcliff, the pompous rich snob Edgar Linton. I told them that literature fans everywhere would celebrate the news of my resurrection.

And in return, they sent me a letter that said:

Dear Emily,
If this is the best you can do after Wuthering Heights, *we're in serious trouble.*
Yours sincerely, Allen & Unwin

My girlfriend, Patricia, was mad. She was always mad. She spent most of her waking hours looking for a reason to yell at me. I had just given her another opportunity.

'You are such an idiot, Tom!' she yelled. 'How can you honestly expect them to take you seriously with such a stupid made-up story? Your novel isn't even a damn thing like *Wuthering Heights*. It's a fantasy epic about dragons and knights, and it's a pretty bad one.'

I was hurt. She didn't have to be such a bitch.

'At least I'm trying to do something with my life,' I said. 'Do you want me to work at *the supermarket* forever?'

'Nobody cares about Emily Brontë anymore,' she shouted. 'You could at least tell them you're somebody popular and hip, like Hunter S. Thompson.'

'That's so unoriginal,' I said. 'Every young writer thinks they're Hunter S. Thompson.'

She started yelling about something else. I didn't want to hear it. I closed my eyes, stuck my fingers in my ears and fantasised about bonking a more attractive girl.

I had to prove her wrong. I was going to put my novel into every unpublished manuscript competition and send it to every publisher in Australia. Sooner or later, somebody would publish it. And then I'd get major publicity for my crazy made-up story. The media would love it. News polls would ask viewers: 'Is he really Emily Brontë? Ring this number to vote.' It was genius.

A couple of days later, I sent my book to Penguin, who were equally unenthusiastic. They sent my manuscript back unread, accompanied by a letter that said:

Dear Ms Brontë,
Please do not send us unsolicited manuscripts. We only consider submissions sent by a reputable literary agent or manuscript assessment agency. And if you seriously wish to write for a living, please consider adopting a pseudonym.
Yours, Penguin

I was depressed. Rejected by two publishers! This really wasn't working out the way I had planned. I felt sad. And angry. I wondered how to convince them. Maybe I could find an actor to pose as a past life regression therapist and publicly verify that I was indeed Miss Brontë? Maybe I could burst into the publisher's office wearing a Victorian-era corset? Hang on a moment, where could I get a corset?

I became tense and anxious that day. At night, I paced until dawn. While Patricia was in bed, I walked back and forth across the carpet in the eerie darkness of the lounge room. I dwelled on the burden of being undiscovered and unappreciated and the gloom of my existence.

After a few nights of little sleep and much pacing, Patricia lost it with me.

'Stop walking all night!' she yelled at me over breakfast. 'It's very, very annoying.'

When I told her what my problem was, she recommended I take sleeping pills. I told her I didn't want to be a druggie. I reminded her that her brother started off smoking a little marijuana and now he was in jail for breaking into cars. That was all she could take. She took her things and left. She wouldn't tell me where she was going to stay. She told me not to ring her. I was alone.

Insomnia quickly became dead boring. I decided to spend my restless night hours surfing the Internet. I discovered that I quite enjoyed chat rooms. I was drawn to the anonymity of them. They were secret meeting spots in cyberspace where I could be anyone I wanted to be and nobody could see who I really was. One night, I decided to make it interesting. I logged in to one under the name Emily B. and told the other users I was a young English girl who liked to write poetry in her spare time. I had a lot of interesting conversations, and I kind of liked the attention when SexyGuy81 asked me to email him.

As I was lying about myself so much, I didn't know whether or not to believe anything SexyGuy81 told me. He described himself as 'a little on the wild side' and said he loved good whisky and fine cigars and rocky mountain climbing.

When I was feeling particularly frisky, I logged in as Bronte-Babe666. I told SexyGuy81 how I liked to wear Victorian-era corsets. Extra tight, to show off my hips. I found that I was really enjoying our flirting. Sure, I was a little ashamed of it. What would Patricia think if she were still with me? But I reassured myself that it was just a little innocent fun. I wasn't gay, I had no interest in being a woman and I had no desire to be seduced by a dangerous bad boy from the Yorkshire moors.

It wasn't long until I mailed my manuscript to another publisher. This time it was University of Queensland Press. History had shown me that I shouldn't expect any success, so it was no surprise when they delivered me another cold hard rejection.

Dear Sir,

Please refrain from sending us photographs of yourself wearing corsets. In fact, we don't want to see you in any kind of women's clothing, no matter what century it's from. What you do in the privacy of your own bedroom is your business, but it's not something we wish to be confronted with during our busy working schedule.

Yours, University of Queensland Press

I gave up. Disillusioned and miserable, I left my manuscript on a bus and hoped that some day somebody may find it and even appreciate it. I burned my copy of *Wuthering Heights* and every possession I had that related to the Brontë sisters, including my Jane Eyre cookie jar. I kept the corsets though. I just thought … well, I may need them. You know?

A year later, I kicked myself for my own stupidity. The driver of the bus found my manuscript and sold it to Penguin by claiming he was the reincarnation of J.R.R. Tolkien. It turns out there was nothing wrong with my novel. I just didn't know the art of the sell.

Griffith Review

Dust

Patrick Cullen

The rain broke early. The sun pitched into the narrow courtyard behind the terrace and Pam went out, put the basket down beneath the clothesline and ran her hand along the length of each of the dripping wires. A fine black dust gathered on her fingers. She rubbed her hands together and the dust worked its way into the creases of her palm.

The dust came from the steelworks across the harbour, drifting across the water, day and night, to settle over the city. Pam had been living with it from the day she and Ray had moved in from the suburbs but it still got to her and, though she wouldn't admit it to Ray, she'd even started to hope that there was some truth in the talk of closure. It was years since Ray first told her that there'd been talk of closing the steelworks, that there was no kind of certainty to their jobs, and back then Pam asked Ray if he should think about moving on, if he would consider picking up something on the waterfront or in the shipyards, if he'd ever head out into the mines if he had to. But Ray had just said that he was going to stay at the steelworks and stick it out for as long as he could. She'd only once complained to Ray about the dust and he'd told her that it would always be there and that she'd just have to put up with it. 'That's what we do over there,' he'd said. 'We make steel and we make dust.'

Pam went to the tap beside the steps, found the end of the hose and held it between her knees while she washed her hands.

Water pooled at her feet and a plane passed through the reflected sky. Pam turned off the tap, looked up and searched for the plane but it was already gone. She went back to the clothesline and the water seeped away between the pavers.

She spent the rest of the morning cleaning – vacuuming, and wiping dust from the sills and architraves – and she was back out in the courtyard folding the clothes down into the basket when she heard the water pipes hammering away under the house. She glanced at her watch and looked up towards the kitchen window. 'Ray,' she called out. 'Is that you already?' The hammering stopped. She called out again but there was no answer. She dropped the last of the clothes into the basket, pulled it up onto her hip and headed into the house.

Pam stopped in the doorway to the kitchen. Ray was sitting at the table. His hands were flat on the table and there was an empty water glass in front of him. He looked up at her. His face was smeared with black dust. There were patches of clean skin under his eyes.

'Have you been crying?'

Ray shrugged and then nodded like he couldn't make up his mind.

'What is it?' Pam said, dropping the basket. It turned onto its side and clothes spilled out onto the floor between them.

Ray kneaded a thumb into his palm.

'Is it the kids?'

He shook his head. Pam pulled a chair out from the table and sat across from him. 'Then what?' she said. 'What is it, Ray? Please tell me. What's wrong?'

'It's Geoff.' Ray worked his thumb harder into his palm.

Pam leaned forward in her chair. 'Did something happen in the mill? What happened? I had the radio on,' she said. 'Why didn't I hear anything, Ray?'

He got up from the table and went and leaned over the sink. 'No,' he said. 'He's done it himself.'

'What, Ray? What's he done?'

Ray turned around and leaned back against the bench. 'Geoff didn't make it in to work today,' he said. 'Judy called looking for him. She said she had something she needed to tell him. I said he wasn't in – that I thought he must have been home sick but she said she was sure he'd gone to work.' Ray put his hand to his face. 'Then she asked me to wait because she could see his car in the driveway. I heard her call out to him and then a moment later – it was only a couple of seconds at most – I heard her,' Ray said, biting down on the corner of his thumbnail. 'I've never heard anything like it before,' he said, looking across at Pam. 'She was all the way out in the garage and I could still hear her. She just made this awful sound and I knew it, I did. I knew that he'd done it.'

'What's he done, Ray?'

Ray came back to the table. 'He's killed himself,' he said. 'Out in his garage. He hung himself. He got up and dressed for work, backed his car out into the driveway and then went back into the garage and hung himself. As soon as I heard her,' he said, shaking his head. 'It was awful, it was, the sound she made. It was like some kind of wild animal all hurt and angry at the same time – and I knew it, I knew what he'd done.'

Pam pushed the glass aside and reached for Ray's hand but he pulled it away and started chewing on his nail again. 'I drove straight over,' he said. 'There was an ambulance in the driveway and Judy was in the garage with Chris and they had Geoff down on the ground between them and Judy was there in her dressing gown kneeling down beside him with his head in her hands and Chris was just standing beside her. He was dressed for school – it was awful, it was. No kid should have to see something like that.'

Pam went around the table and leaned down over his shoulder. She pulled his hand away from his mouth and held his arm against his chest. 'I'm sorry,' she said, holding him. 'I'm sorry. I'm so sorry.'

They stayed at the table until Ray got up and looked at Pam as though he was about to say something. She held out her hands to him and waited for him to say whatever it was that he needed to say but he just looked down at the floor and said that he was going to bed. Pam mentioned dinner and Ray, saying that he couldn't stomach it, headed upstairs. Pam looked out into the courtyard. It was still light out.

*

It was almost twenty years since Ray and Pam had lived out in the suburbs a couple of streets away from Geoff and Judy. Ray and Geoff had started in the steelworks on the same day and soon worked out where each other lived and settled into sharing a ride to and from work.

Geoff would sometimes drop by to borrow a tool or something for the yard and there were other times when he would come round for no good reason at all and he and Ray would sit out in the backyard, drinking and talking about what they'd do different if they had their time over again.

'You should hear yourselves,' Pam said one afternoon when Ray came back in to the kitchen.

'What do you mean?'

'You're like two old men out there. Counting down the days.'

Ray just laughed and took more beer from the refrigerator and went back out into the yard. Pam went through to the lounge room and called Judy. They talked for a while and Judy asked Pam over. Pam went out and told Ray where she was headed and Geoff sipped his drink and said, 'Tell her that I'm not sure when I'll be home. She might be on her own tonight.'

'Maybe she'd like that,' Pam said and started walking. Ray and Geoff laughed behind her.

Judy made tea and she and Pam went through to the sunroom at the back of the house where a low window stretched across the width of the room. They sat in low cane chairs and looked out over the freshly mown lawn. 'Guess what?' Pam said as Judy started pouring the tea.

'What?' Judy said, then looked up at Pam smiling. 'You're not?'

Pam nodded. 'I am,' she said. 'I'm pregnant.'

Judy put the teapot down. Tea ran down the underside of the spout and pooled on the table. 'That's great,' Judy said, leaning over and grabbing Pam's hand. 'That's so great for you two.'

'But please don't say anything,' Pam said. 'I haven't even told Ray yet.'

'I won't,' Judy said. 'I won't say anything. That's great,' she said again.

They sat and sipped their tea, and smiled and laughed without speaking.

'We've been trying,' Judy said, crossing her legs.

Pam sat up in her chair. 'Any luck yet?'

'Not yet. But it's got to happen sooner or later, doesn't it? If you keep trying?' Pam just smiled and Judy grabbed her hand again. 'That's so great.'

The day before Ray and Pam moved into the city, when all of their things were packed into boxes, they went for dinner at Geoff and Judy's. Ray and Geoff took over the barbeque, and Pam and Judy – who were by then both heavily pregnant – worked together to set the table. They carried the white plastic table sideways over the lawn, laughing, and Ray and Geoff turned and shook their heads at them. Pam and Judy both shrugged as if to ask, 'What?' and laughed again and disappeared into the house. They came back out nursing bowls of salad and coleslaw on their hips.

When it came time to eat, Ray and Pam sat on opposite sides of the table and Judy eased in beside Ray. 'Looks like it's you and me tonight,' Geoff said, as he brought the meat to the table and pulled out the chair beside Pam. Pam passed her plate across to him and told him what she wanted. The others passed their plates in turn and then they all got down to eating. They soon started talking about what they thought life would be like – if it would be much different – when the babies arrived and their voices trailed off as they reached the edge of the things they knew for certain.

By the time they'd finished eating, Ray and Geoff had decided between themselves that they shouldn't be any busier than usual but that Pam and Judy probably would have their hands full. Pam and Judy both shook their heads and gathered up the plates and took them into the house. Pam found the bin beneath the sink, scraped off the plates and then, standing side-on to the sink to accommodate her abdomen, set about washing up.

'Don't worry about that,' Judy said. 'Geoff can do that for me.'

'No,' Pam said. 'I've already made a start. I may as well finish it now.'

Judy pulled a stool out from under the bench and sat and kicked off her shoes. She started cutting up the cake. She ran her finger along the blade of the knife and licked the icing from her finger. 'Do you think Ray will make a good father?'

'Too late now,' Pam said, patting her belly. 'The damage is already done.'

Judy nodded and looked down at her bare feet, ran her instep over her other foot and said, 'I had an affair.'

'What?' Pam turned away from the sink.

Judy looked back over her shoulder towards the yard. 'I had an affair,' she said.

'Does Geoff know?'

'No,' Judy said, shaking her head. 'Nobody knows.'

'Why would you tell me such a thing?'

Judy shrugged. 'I just wanted to tell someone. I needed to tell someone.'

'But you didn't need to tell me this. I didn't need to know,' Pam said. 'I don't want to know.'

Ray and Geoff started up a chorus for cake and Pam and Judy both glanced towards the door.

'It wasn't much of an affair, anyway. Hardly worth it. He asked me to leave Geoff and I almost did,' she said. 'But Geoff will be a good father, I know he will. I want my child to have a good father. I could have left him, though,' Judy said. 'I could have. The only reason I'm still here is because I want to be. I want you to know that.'

Pam looked past Judy. Geoff was walking up behind her. When he saw Pam watching him he put a finger to his lips. He leaned over and kissed the back of Judy's neck and put his arms around her belly. 'You're not going to have your cake and eat it too, are you?'

'I was just saying how much I love you, wasn't I, Pam?' Judy laughed and got up off the stool. She slipped her shoes back on and headed out with the cake. 'Bring the plates,' she called behind her.

Geoff picked the plates up off the bench and winked at Pam as he followed Judy out into the yard. Pam put her hands back into the water. The water was cold and she pulled the plug and felt the weight of the water drain away.

As they ate the cake Pam watched Judy laugh and lean back in her seat. She saw how Judy put her hand on Ray's arm when she laughed. Pam looked across at Ray and Judy. She tried not to imagine them together.

'You know what?' Pam said. 'After all this time that we've known you I don't think you've ever told us how you two met.'

'It's a long story,' Geoff said, picking up his drink. 'We don't have all night.'

'Give us the *Digest* version, then,' Ray said.

Geoff stalled and sipped his beer. 'Well –' he said and looked across at Judy.

'It's simple enough,' Judy said. 'I won him over.'

'Just like that?' Pam said.

'Well,' Judy said slowly. 'He was seeing a friend of mine at the time.'

'So where's your friend now?' Ray said and laughed. Judy laughed too and put her hand on his arm and left it there.

*

The morning after Geoff's suicide, Ray and Pam drove out to see Judy. Ray pulled up opposite Geoff and Judy's house and left the motor running. They both looked across at the house. It sat low, stretching most of the way across the front of the yard. Two narrow strips of concrete cut across the lawn and ran down the side of the yard. Geoff's car sat in the driveway and beyond the car was the garage. Pam could remember the last time they were there, all of them together, and Judy telling her things that she did not want to know. 'It's been a long time,' Pam said.

'Too long,' Ray said under his breath and cut the engine.

They went to the front door and knocked and waited. Judy came to the door. 'Sorry,' she said, waving them inside. 'I was just packing up some things. Trying to get this place cleaned up before the funeral.'

'When is the funeral?' Pam asked.

'Friday morning. Can you come? Both of you?'

Ray nodded. 'Of course,' Pam said.

'Good,' she said. 'Come through.' And they followed her down the hallway into the lounge room. There was a pile of boxes inside the doorway. 'I've got somebody picking those up this afternoon,' Judy said, gesturing at the boxes as she passed.

'There'll be more to go tomorrow,' she said and turned and stopped in front of Ray. 'I've got some things for you, too.'

Ray hesitated. 'I'm sorry,' he said. 'I really am sorry.'

'It's OK,' Judy said, going through to the kitchen. 'Life goes on – isn't that what they say?'

Ray nodded and Pam just looked at her.

'Sorry,' Judy said and went to the sink and filled the kettle. 'I've always thought that that was such an odd thing to say and now here I am saying the same damn thing.'

'It's OK,' Pam said. 'There's probably not much else to say.'

Judy put the kettle onto the stove and lit the burner and took some cups down out of a cupboard beside the stove. 'Do you know what I realised this morning? I realised that I didn't really know my own husband. Geoff just went out each day and came back again and hardly said a word about his work. All I knew was that he used to come home covered in dust and I was forever washing out his clothes trying to get rid of it. It was everywhere,' she said, then looked at Pam as though she was seeing her for the first time. 'Sorry,' she said. 'Listen to me complaining.'

'I know what it's like,' Pam said. 'The dust, I mean. I have to live with it too and we're right in the thick of it where we are in town.'

The kettle began to whistle and Judy switched it off and made a pot of tea. They went out to the sunroom and sat in cane chairs. 'Are they really going to shut it down, Ray?'

Ray shrugged. 'There's always been talk of it but I don't think it'll happen for a while yet.'

'Geoff never said much about it,' Judy said, pouring the tea. 'He did say once that it could happen but he said he couldn't see it happening in his lifetime.'

They fell silent and Ray and Judy picked up their cups and sipped at the tea. 'How's Chris?' Pam asked.

'As well as you might expect. He stayed at his girlfriend's place last night but I'll have him back here this afternoon.'

'Will he still sit his exams?' Pam asked.

Judy nodded. 'It's probably the last thing he needs at a time like this. But – as they say – life goes on,' she said, then laughed and asked, 'Who the hell are *they*? What the hell would *they* know about life, anyway?'

'Sorry we didn't bring flowers,' Pam said, finishing her tea. 'But we figured you'd probably end up with more than enough of those. We would like to do something for you, though. Something to help you out.'

'Thank you,' Judy said. 'I'm OK for now.'

'But do let us know if you need anything, though,' Ray said.

Pam and Ray said that they had to go and they got up from the table. Judy got up too and put her hand on Ray's arm. 'I have some things for you,' she said. 'It's not much – Geoff's shirts – but you might get some use out of them.'

Ray followed Judy back through the kitchen. Pam sat back down and looked out over the empty backyard. She crossed and uncrossed her legs, then got up and took their cups through to the kitchen and left them on the sink. She went into the lounge room to wait for Ray. She heard Ray and Judy talking in the next room, and she went down the hallway and stopped in the bedroom doorway. Ray was sitting on the bed beside Judy and she was running her finger over the collar of one of the shirts on her lap. Ray and Judy looked up at Pam and nobody said anything. Pam left them alone and waited across the street in the car.

*

Months after the boys were born, Ray came home in the afternoon and took Luke for a walk so that Pam could sleep for a while. He pushed the pram as far as the beach and looked out at the bank of dark cloud that sat off the coast. The breeze picked up, unsettling Luke, and he began to cry so Ray turned back. Within a couple of blocks Luke was asleep again.

'Thanks,' Pam said when she came back down from the bedroom and saw Ray peeling vegetables into the sink. 'I'm ready to go again now. I'll give you a hand.' Pam got a saucepan out of a cupboard and put it on the bench beside Ray. 'How was work?'

'Same old, same old.'

'Has Geoff said anything about how he and Judy are getting on?'

'Chris isn't giving them much sleep.'

'Still?'

Ray nodded. 'Geoff said it's wearing them down, most days they've been at each other's throats.'

'Well I'm glad we've got such a good little sleeper,' Pam said, looking at Luke in his pram. 'I don't know how people survive without a decent night's sleep. I think I'd die.'

'You'd get by,' Ray said, putting the vegetables into the saucepan. 'We'd cope.'

The telephone rang and Pam went through to the lounge room to answer it. It was Judy. 'You haven't told him have you?' she said.

'Told who?'

'Ray,' Judy said. 'You haven't told Ray have you?'

'Told him what?'

'The affair,' she said. 'You haven't told Ray about my affair, have you?'

Pam looked towards the kitchen and lowered her voice. 'No,' she said. 'And I'd almost forgotten that you'd ever told me about it. Why are you calling, Judy? I haven't seen you for ... for I don't know how long and now you're calling me to ask me about this.'

Judy was silent.

'We should catch up again,' Pam said. 'We could talk.'

'I don't believe you,' Judy said and hung up.

'Who was that?' Ray asked when Pam went back in to the kitchen.

Pam looked out at the clothes on the line in the courtyard. 'Just somebody trying to sell me something I don't want,' she said. 'We should have them over, don't you think? It's been a long time since we were all together.'

Ray shrugged. 'I don't know,' he said. 'I already talked to Geoff about it but he said that he and Judy aren't doing so well and probably wouldn't make great company.'

*

On the morning of the funeral Pam went out into the courtyard and sat on the bench against the fence to drink her coffee in the sun. Ray came to the top of the steps and said that he was going for a walk.

'Wait,' Pam said. 'I'll come with you.'

'No, it's OK,' Ray said. 'I wouldn't mind a little time to myself this morning.'

Pam stretched her feet out in front of her. 'I won't go far, then,' she said, leaning back against the fence. She closed her eyes and listened to Ray go back through the house. She heard him shut the front door behind him. The sun was on her face and she was thinking about Judy when she felt something moving over her foot. She looked down and saw a procession of small black ants moving between a dead cicada and the small funnel of sand that marked the entrance to their nest between the pavers. She watched the ants dismantle the cicada and ferry its limbs across the pavers, over her foot and to the mouth of their nest, where they fed the broken pieces down into the ground. Pam watched the cicada gradually disappear. She was still out on the bench when Ray came home.

He came down the steps and sat on the bench beside her. He'd had his hair cut and he pulled his collar away from his neck and tugged at it. He leaned forward onto his elbows and brushed his fingers through his hair, dislodging clipped lengths of hair. Pam ran her hand over Ray's back and onto the back of his neck. She felt the muscles tense. She worked her fingers into the back of his neck, felt the soft prickle where the hair had been shaved and she ran her fingers up into the hairline. She felt something smooth between her fingertips and saw that it was dust. Pam held her hand up to her face and looked closely at the dust and she saw that the black particles reflected the sunlight, they shimmered, and when she looked at the dust a certain way the particles were more light than dark.

After the funeral, Ray and Pam went and parked above the beach and watched the swell roll in. Surfers drifted about and rode what waves they could.

Ray started tapping his fingers on the dashboard. 'She had an affair,' he said, looking across at Pam. 'Did you know?'

Pam looked down at her hands in her lap and nodded.

'Chris is his son, though,' Ray said. 'But I guess you know that, too? That Chris is Geoff's son?'

'No, I didn't.'

'Geoff said that he'd forgiven her for the affair but a couple of months ago he started saying something about not being able to forgive himself.'

'What for?'

'For asking her to stay.'

'Did you know that he was going to do this? Did he say anything?'

Ray shook his head. They sat without speaking. The sky was cloudless and, behind Ray and Pam, the sun was sinking over the city and the suburbs beyond.

'Would you forgive me if I had an affair?' Pam asked.

Ray shifted in his seat to face her.

'I'm not saying I did –'

'I know, I know,' he said. 'I was just thinking that we can never really know everything about each other.'

'Do you think you'd ever really want to? What if you found out something that you didn't want to know? What would you do then?'

'I don't know,' Ray shrugged. 'That would be the hardest thing, working out if it was something you could live with.'

Drop

Shady Cosgrove

Sun-washed sky faded. Almost white in the glare.

Stubborn cars chase each other along the concrete corridor below.

The overpass meek in comparison.

Beside me, Carl is a kid with a round head and mean pockets.

His fingers are stubby; his nails dirty. But he's got strength in them.

'Come on,' he says.

Takes two of us to lift the granite. It's jagged with rock sparkles that catch the light. It balances gently on the railing. Carl starts counting backwards, waiting for a red one. They score highest. I wait. When he reaches 'one', we let the rock go and start running. My sweaty hands, over my mouth, catch what breath I have left as we dart off the bridge. A horn blares from below and then braking, swerving.

But no crash.

Carl's legs are pumping madly in front of me and he's laughing. I'm laughing too, but shrill, my voice echoes back from the asphalt valley beneath us. I push him along when he wants to stop and look out over the road.

Overland

Train

Shady Cosgrove

Mitch was filling in that week; he wasn't used to the late morning shifts. Trash littered the floor of the driver car – unapologetic. The stations seemed further apart in the daytime. He squinted against the light refracting off the rails.

She first appeared like a mirage, moving in slow motion. A girl. Arms outstretched, walking along the track, the nape of her neck glinting in the sun.

He'd seen her two days before: at the station two stops back. A fake leather mini-skirt. Her thin hair pulled back in a plastic clip. The bright pink Mardi Gras beads around her neck offset by her stained lips, a few shades too dark. She'd stared at the train that morning, daring it to leave without her.

She still had a defiance to her posture as she balanced on the ties. Mitch yanked the emergency brake. Steel clashed against steel. Shrill grating echoed in his ears. He watched in horror as she turned towards him, smiling.

He shut his eyes and visualised her jumping. He imagined her standing safely beside the tracks while the train came to a belated halt beside her. But when he opened his eyes, she was still facing him. Smiling. Too close.

She threw her arms in the air, laughing, and strings of Mardi Gras beads came raining down as the train connected with her body.

Overland

Woman Weeping

Anson Cameron

I stood behind my mother listening to the story she was telling to the marble head in her lap. The bust of her famous dead lover, the only man she spoke to in such a loving tone, stroking his head as if he were the senile one in need of understanding. He already knew the story. He was one of the players in it. So he didn't need to hear it. But she cradled his stone features and told him anyway.

Told him that Laszlo was a bohemian. He had long black hair slicked back with lavender pomade and muttonchop sideboards and smoked a long-stemmed pipe. He wore loose flannel trousers up around his belly and a tight vest of mohair, topped always with a black leather coat to his knees. He hung around, leaning on walls with a foot up behind him on the brickwork, watching the passing river of Parisians, wanting to be watched in return. Hoping to be reviled, I suppose, and feared, by the working people whirling past headlong in their endeavour.

He had been known to paint, but he didn't paint by 1937. He had been known to sculpt. But no longer. He wrote some poems, the best refrains of which he had stolen, and were stolen again from him so wantonly by poets of his acquaintance that he no longer wrote or stole poems. The one was so hard and the other so easy, that it was clear there was no money in poems.

In truth, by the mid-'30s he was a courtier of successful artists. He found more artful ways to praise their art than anyone else could, and for his groundbreaking sycophancy he was called a connoisseur and taken under the wing of the beau monde and fed scraps off their table. He ran errands and procured opium and delivered smarm of such naked virginity that famous artists felt discovered afresh, they felt young again, on the verge of success.

This is how he found his way to Picasso's studio. It was almost impossible, by 1937, to throw Picasso a compliment he hadn't heard. But Laszlo famously said to him, 'I'd rather spill my seed before *Woman In An Armchair* than fuck Claudet Colbert.' *Woman In An Armchair* is a painting. Mademoiselle Colbert was a famous beauty of the day, and everyone, but everyone, wanted to fuck her. Picasso was tickled pink to have created a woman more erotically desirable than Claudet Colbert. It was as though God and Pablo had each entered their girl in a beauty pageant and Pablo's girl had won. Laszlo became his cheerleader of choice at once. And soon enough Picasso became to depend upon him, for compliments, for opium, for hashish, to buy his groceries, to walk his poodle. He became Picasso's – how would you say … squire … yes, his Sancho Panza. Picasso admired Quixote and always kept a squire.

But Laszlo became addicted to opium. Picasso was an occasional user himself and carved Laszlo an opium pipe from jade and amber, the constant refilling of which pipe placed Laszlo deeply in debt to his supplier, a nightclub and opium den owner by the name of Django Meinheer, who was a Jew and a homosexual, which twin abominations must have frustrated the Nazis terribly when they could kill him only once in Buchenwald some years later. As an addict Laszlo's compliments lost their edge and he often brought home a ficelle instead of a baguette as instructed, and had begun to tie up Lisle, Picasso's poodle, outside Django's opium den in the mid-afternoon and stagger home at midnight without her, whereupon Picasso and Dora Maar would flee luminous in their nightwear through the dark streets of Montmartre to rescue her.

Picasso, needless to say, was unused to such a wayward squire and one midnight, having sent Laszlo back to the opium den to retrieve Lisle, he then snatched her from Laszlo's arms and consigned him to outer darkness, telling him never to enter his

milieu or venture an opinion about his work again. In anger
Laszlo snatched the dog back from Picasso and told the great
man he was going to sell her as recompense for the many favours
he had done him. Picasso's dog would not fetch a stick, but it
would fetch a pretty penny, Laszlo sneered. Maybe a collector
would buy her. Maybe a collector with an oversexed boxer.

But Picasso's dog was only worth what any dog is worth. That
is: all the world to its owner and naught to all the world. Laszlo
paraded Lisle in and out of the cafés and opium dens, telling the
beau monde he had le chien de Genius for sale. He blew opium
smoke in Lisle's face until her lips drooped and she leaned up
against a wall and stood yipping at the cats of her dreams while
he strutted in front of her playing the auctioneer, 'Le lapdog de
Picasso. For sale to the highest bidder. Dwelt seven years in the
great man's lap and privy to his innermost secrets. Le lapdog de
Picasso.'

Needless to say, there were no buyers. Neither would Django
Meinheer take a drug-addled dog as payment of Laszlo's debts,
no matter in whose lap it had sat and secrets it knew. Meinheer
didn't give much credence to the notion it might have become
wise in the great man's lap, having seen many sweet young things
dwell there for a time and end up as simple-minded as they had
begun. He started making threats. He knew bad people. And
the only thing of value Laszlo still owned was a key to Picasso's
studio.

So a month after being exiled Laszlo sneaks into Picasso's
studio and steals a painting that will, in years to come, become
known as the *Weeping Woman*. The painting of Dora Maar feigning the grief of war, the horror of Guernica. He must feel he has
claim to the *Weeping Woman* because he steals only this painting.
He passes up the opportunity to steal many others.

Picasso has canvases leaning against walls up against one
another like pages in books. Laszlo steps around benches laden
with unfired pots covered with centaurs and fish, tiptoes across
the star-patterned paintdrip-spattered oak parquetry. Skirts
huge unfinished canvases aloft on easels and bullskulls grimac-
ing at the ceiling. 'Papa?' he calls. 'Papa?' to verify Picasso's
absence. He begins leafing through the stacked paintings until
he finds her. Green-faced, her mouth open and eyes bulging and

tongue jutting. Laszlo steals the *Weeping Woman*. Only the *Weeping Woman*, of all the paintings there.

Stopping at many cafés along the way, talking to the *Weeping Woman* rolled up under his arm, he makes his way to the Palace de Noctambules. By the time he gets there he is triumphant with wine and he unfurls her before the massive mustachioed doorman and nods towards her tortured visage and confides, 'I did this ... with my penis.'

The big man leans down and adopts a similarly confidential tone, 'Have you washed? With turpentine? Or is it still green? I won't allow you in with a green penis.'

The Palace de Noctambules is a nightclub where European royalty rub shoulders with bohemians, a place princes go to fondle courtesans. Everyone is there. Braque is there. Laszlo, having satisfied the doorman that his penis isn't green, enters. He unrolls the canvas before Braque, who is by 1937 handsomely white-haired, the kindly lines around his eyes formed by many years of satisfaction at his place in the pantheon of deathless genius.

'My cock did this,' Laszlo tells him. 'Picasso will tell you it was the Luftwaffe. He will tell you it is Guernica. But it was my cock.'

'Your cock?' Braque asks.

'This is a painting of Dora Maar as I made love to her.'

They are staring at the canvas Laszlo has unrolled on the burn-speckled aquamarine silk of a chaise-longue, its corners weighted with Laszlo's hands and Braque's liver-spotted fists. The massive head of the weeping woman, her face opened and rearranged by Picasso, much as a scientist will use a scalpel to shuttle the parts of an urchin around a Petri dish in order to divine its workings.

'Everyone will blame Hermann Goering. But it wasn't fat Hermann – she isn't weeping. She is climaxing. He will tell you it is an indictment of fascism. But it is his lady in her throes.'

'Dora Maar ... in her throes?' Braque asks.

'Moaning the name of our Lord Jesus Christ in mindless ecstasy.'

Braque is an adenoidal man whose nose hums like an untuned radio as he talks. 'It doesn't look like ecstasy,' he says.

'Ecstasy doesn't.' Laszlo rocks his scotch, ice-cubes chiming above the gurgle of opium pipes. 'You haven't much experience of ecstasy, perhaps?'

Braque tilts his head to see her from another angle, her lime-green flesh, her eyes pressed together, her nose on the left of her head where an ear should be. Could all this deformity be caused by pleasure? An orgasm? Was this his great rival's depiction of ecstasy?

'You want to buy her, or not?' Laszlo asks, in a hurry now.

Braque detects Laszlo's discomfort and wants to continue it, explore it. This young man, this would-be criminal, come here to sell me stolen goods and announce Picasso a cuckold. He lifts a fist and the weeping woman curls inwards, leaving only one triangular half of her still visible. Her horrified, or ecstatic, eyes.

'Why would Picasso let you, his squire, make love to his woman?'

'He is obsessed with her. He paints her endlessly. He wanted to paint her in orgasm. *Le petit mort.* But he couldn't sketch her and make love to her at the same time. So he had me make love to her while he sketched. It was an honour. She is a fabulous beauty. A renowned woman.' Laszlo reaches down and runs a fingertip across her painted hair. 'The old boy sat alongside us in short pyjamas, so close I could hear his nose whistling as I humped her. I gave her ultimate pleasure and he captured it with a stick of charcoal.' His eyes soften and his smile amplifies with reminiscence as he stares at her. 'I had hoped we would have to do it many times before he caught her essence ... the power of her climax. But he is Picasso, he caught it all that first time ... her little death.' Laszlo pouts regret.

'No. It is surely part of his Guernica series,' Braque's lip curls in scepticism. 'His indictment of fascism.'

'Would they call him sick? A pornographer? A pimp? He is scared of what they might say. Even the great Picasso runs in fear of the beau monde. It has sat in his studio for months. *Ecstatic Woman.* Now that the Luftwaffe has bombed Guernica, he sees his chance, he adds a handkerchief, he renames her *Weeping Woman*, he says she is a native of Guernica weeping at the tragedy that has befallen her city. You want to buy her?' Laszlo asks Braque. '*Ecstatic Woman?*'

Braque traces the furrows of his brow with the fingertips of his right hand, reading a braille of his own faked indecision. 'What makes you think I would buy a stolen painting?' He takes a sip of absinthe. His eyes move constantly around the large room, occasionally flashing censure at some acquaintance wandered from the dusk of its outer reaches. Stay away. His eyes move up and down Laszlo. A shabby leather coat, shoes dull-surfaced and wide as gorilla paws, and, yes, a small white dog he recognises as Lisle.

Laszlo shrugs. 'If I had an enemy I would covet evidence of his cuckolding. It would take pride of place in my house, a portrait of my enemy's woman receiving pleasure from his squire.' Braque and Picasso have fallen out by this time, a well-known enmity, each claiming to be the inventor of cubism. So Braque certainly would have enjoyed a proof of Picasso's cuckolding, painted by the man himself. It could be supposed he would have held private showings, laughed at the great Spaniard, spread word of his beloved Dora's ecstasy at the hands of another.

Braque takes a handful of francs from a trouser pocket and Laszlo's face lights with success. He tries to remain calm, counting the native head-dresses on the walls. Sixteen. Braque is poised with the handful of notes held out above her as Picasso enters the Palace de Noctambules searching for Laszlo, searching for Lisle, searching for the *Weeping Woman*. Laszlo snatches the francs from Braque's fist and pushes the canvas at him.

Now comes the great fight between Picasso and Braque of which those of us in the art world have all heard, though the reasons given for it are many and always the person telling of this fight knows the one and only truth: it was a battle in the war over the origins of cubism; it was a fight over an unpaid debt; it was a battle for Dora Maar herself. But ... no. Picasso, who now thought better of painting Dora in orgasm, was desperate to stop Braque owning this painting or hearing the tale of its origin. He wanted to take her back and, eventually, announce her to the world as *Weeping Woman*. Not *Ecstatic Woman*. To paint her in orgasm had been an idea he had given in to under the influence of opium and not worthy of his great artistic soul. He regretted it terribly.

While his dog leaned loose-lipped dreaming in the corner and his climaxing mistress rolled beneath a table he attacked

Braque. The giants of cubism got down on the tiled floor like two *putains anciennes* in a turf war and bit and pulled hair and cursed, Braque calling Picasso a cuckold, Picasso calling Braque a thief, while their sycophants stood glaring at each other. Braque tried to insert a silver Vietnamese opium pipe into Picasso's ear, but had it confiscated by a supporter of the great Spaniard who held such acts lay outside the accepted behaviour of hand-to-hand combat. They wrestled and swore and by the time they had worn themselves to a hyperventilating stalemate of locked and quivering limbs and their respective posses of sycophants disentangled them and laid them gently on a chaise-longue apiece and administered *eau de vie* to their bloodless lips Laszlo had snatched up the *Weeping Woman* and made off with her once more.

So now *Weeping Woman* was stolen from Picasso and *Ecstatic Woman* was stolen from Braque and both owned her and wanted her back and both wanted Laszlo buried in the main Paris sewer.

My mother raises Picasso's marble head from her lap and holds it up before her face and smooths his eyebrows with her thumbs, holding him tightly, not letting him look right or left but only into her eyes.

'After this famous fight word of your cuckolding is out and the only way for you to save face is to pretend you don't love me. To pretend I mean nothing to you. Just another floozy you kept for sex and canapés. A model you kept on-hand. A beautiful mask to express pain, ecstasy or lust, whenever you needed to paint these.'

She lays a palm gently on his cheek. 'I forgive you. You had your duty to the world. You were a slave to Picasso as much as I was – as we all were. You had to protect Picasso. You had to throw me away as if I were a four-francs-a-day model. But it wasn't true, Pabli, was it? I wasn't your model. I was the burning light of your soul.' Here my mother, somewhat unfairly, nods Picasso's head. 'As you were mine.' She nods her own head.

'Unbeknown to you, you also exiled the child I was carrying. Our child. The girl that stands behind me now, just stepped from a lavender bath, listening to us talk.'

I was, perhaps, ten. And freshly from a scented bubble-bath as she said. It was only when she mentioned me I realised she was lucid enough to be talking to the eavesdropping me, rather than the marble Picasso in her hands. That she was using this Alas-poor-Yorick interplay to tell me who my father was and how he was lost to us.

'Your stratagem worked, Pabli. The story of your cuckolding, now that it was with a woman you had no regard for, was worthless and it died. The rumour of a painting called *Ecstatic Woman* died. Your thugs found Laszlo and you got the painting back, it was first exhibited at L'Apache Galleries in 1939. Yes, part of the Guernica series. One of your most compassionate works. *Weeping Woman*. And I forgive you. Every day.'

I heard my mother forgive him face to face many times after that, the smell of pastis on her breath wafting under his marble nose. She knew he had a greater calling than to be a lover to her. That he had to be Picasso to the world. She conversed with his marble likeness nestled in her lap until her dying day. She protected him from me, from my advances into his life, from my claims. Then, after I buried her in 1997, I made my play to stand alongside Paloma as the daughter of Picasso. I announced myself scandalously in *Le Figaro*. The front-page photograph shows my face in a practised clench trying to assume his characteristics and looking most unlike the photo of a lean, young Picasso some malevolent sub-editor had chosen to sit alongside me for its very physiognomic distance. Undaunted, I had my DNA run through the laboratories and law courts of Paris.

I was taking my father to my bosom before the eyes of the whole world. Standing up at last to have my story known and my rank as his daughter acknowledged. It had been a grave weight keeping this secret all these years, and it meant everything to me now to have my exalted place in the world known. I hadn't done much with my life. No lover, no children. I had lived in a cloistered ménage-a-trois with my mother and the marble head of her lover. Dominated and enslaved by the task of being Picasso's secret daughter, I had been a recluse.

Weeks later, as I left the Palace de Justice, my case crushed by the scientific evidence, I stood on the top step with photo-

graphers fanned out before me swimming in my tears and swearing at each other in little territorial battles. For them it was
a circus, but for me a funeral. A dear parent had been killed.
Put to death legally and, most horrible of all, justly. A State-
sanctioned execution. Not only killed, but expunged from my
history, my lifelong love of him a lie. Through my childhood I
had kept a bottle of eucalyptus oil I was going to massage into
his hands to ease his well-documented rheumatism. Through my
teens I kept a valise packed with my most precious possessions so
that on the day he rode into my dull life I was ready to flee with
him to happiness. This Picasso I always knew to be my father was
a cruel joke. This Papa I had lived with … I so wished for him to
be Papa again. My heart was breaking with a loss I hadn't reckoned on and couldn't conceive.

I had had my hair bobbed for the trial, trying, at my age, to
look like a daughter. In expectation of victory I was wearing a
mid-length orange skirt and stilettos. How must I look now in
this cold wind? A sexagenarian gold-digger with blue ankles.
The crouching photographers in their rapper mufti, their ban-
danas and bling, scrabbled backwards before me as I descended
the steps. An egg thrown, I suppose, by an art lover came looping over their hunched backs and landed flush on my glasses,
covering my face. Every one of them was professional enough to
capture this moment for their newspapers. See the front page of
Le Figaro, 21 February 1998. There I am, another weeping woman,
my face bedecked with yolk and shell and shock and the city of
Paris laughing in headlines at the thin gruel of my DNA. I had
come to claim a piece of their man and been trounced.

I hold his dwarfish face at arm's length to talk to him now that I
am losing my close vision. My mother's marble confidante of so
many years, with its eyebrows shined by the outward sweep of her
thumbs.

Papa, Papa, Papa … she loved you so. She would never cheat
on you and there was no one else and I have no other father to
believe in now that you are – debunked. She had no secret lovers
or I would have heard her confess them to you. I heard her confess all her sins to you, one after the other, over and over. Tiny
sins. Sins that weren't sins. Morsels of negligence like forgetting

to light a candle on your birthday. There is little more sense in telling lies to a marble bust than to yourself. So, no. She didn't tell you lies. She believed I was your child.

But if you are not my father, then who? Who? There is only the one known fornication. A liaison that happened at your behest, and brought forth the ecstasy you captured in charcoal and turned into the *Weeping Woman*. It can only be Laszlo Berg. Your squire, the would-be poet who stole your dog and painting and ruined your life with Dora, my mother. And *Weeping Woman* is, then, *Ecstatic Woman*. And the moment of my conception lives on as a denunciation of war. A fact I have tried to be privately happy about.

Patterns

Gillian Bouras

Every morning during the first summer, with Theo sleeping late, Justine walks slowly down the ten stone stairs, crosses the court-yard with its tendrils of jasmine and hesitates at the kitchen door. She knocks once, because it seems to be the thing to do, for one in her particular situation. Nobody else knocks, they simply yell and barge in, but she is the daughter-in-law, the for-eigner, trying her best to do the right thing. She takes a deep breath, puts a smile in place, and enters.

So Justine, whose Greek is reasonable, she's been taking les-sons for long enough, God knows, says *Kali mera* brightly to the bent old woman sitting in the corner by the empty fireplace. The woman, the mother-in-law, *Kyria* Panayota, says nothing. Her eyes, Justine thinks every day, are like flecked pebbles, brown and hard. And every day the ritual is the same. *May I?* asks Jus-tine, taking another deep breath and gesturing towards the breakfast things, the *briki* for the coffee, sitting on its little gas stand, the rusks in their torn cellophane wrappings, and the jar of honey. It glows in the shafts of early light, the honey, all soft and sweet. Panayota, the old woman, makes her own gesture, a brushing of the hand. *Oti theleis. Whatever you like.* And she turns her gaze away.

They do not see or look at the same things, these two women. Not usually. The only time their sightlines run parallel and then bend and converge is when Theo is around. Theo is Justine's husband, Panayota's son, but Justine knows the order is reversed, really. Justine also knows that Panayota never believed her son would return from long years in Australia. But he did. Her prayer was answered. Well, half a prayer. The problem is, Panayota had always wanted her son to return alone.

Theo and Justine talk about his mother. Not a lot, but Theo tries to explain. *She's had a hard life. All that work and hardship and poverty and all those children and the deaths of some of them, the Occupation and the wars and the fear and hunger and the struggle, you can't know what it was like, what really goes on in the heads of people like us.* Justine knows her Australian mother's and her own lists of *ands* are completely different, shorter for one thing. This thought makes her feel uncomfortable. And she notices that Theo's idea of *us* has shifted and changed. Justine is no longer part of *us*.

They are together at the beach, though, speaking English, laughing in the water the way they always have. Except the Greek beach is not like Bronte or Bondi. It's rather like a very large warm bath, thinks Justine, who notices that every time a light breeze ruffles the water, shirring the liquid blue silk, the local women scream softly, ritually, and head at once for the grey pebbles, which are not like Bronte or Bondi sand, either. Not at all. But Theo and Justine stay in the water, so perhaps *us* shifts back again at the beach.

Us changes yet again in the long evenings when Theo does what village men do and goes off to drink coffee and ouzo and play cards in the *kafeneion*. What *Kyria* Panayota does in the evenings is sit out on the front step with two or three of her friends. Usually three: *Kyries* Ariadne, Maria and Eleni. There they while away the time, chatting over the little mounds of snowy crochetwork in their laps. For the light lasts and lasts. The hooks and the threads as fine as a spider's clutched in hands as wrinkled and brown as walnuts somehow make patterns and pictures grow: urns, butterflies, peacocks, pineapples. Justine admires the work, oh yes she does, because she knows something about it and tries to tell the old women so, making comments as best she can about the rows of trebles and double trebles, the fineness of the stitches and the evenness of the tension. Mostly they ignore her, and are never sure how much she understands, how much she can say, or could if she wanted to.

In this way, always the same way, the slow summer evenings pass. Usually Justine drifts off into her own thoughts about her lost world and the mother she has left behind; she moves into her own silence and reverie produced by the rose light on the mountains, the diving and humming of the iridescent green beetles and the scent of the jasmine wafting intermittently in the still air. On one occasion, though, she comes to with a jolt. She is being discussed.

And what about her? Asks *Kyria*-Ariadne-from-across-the-road. *Can she crochet or knit or do anything? Embroidery, perhaps?*

Justine glances quickly at *Kyria* Panayota and sees a struggle in her face. She thinks she knows what the struggle is about: it's one between family honour and malice. Who would want to admit to having a useless daughter-in-law, a *nifi* with no womanly skills? But malice wins. Justine hears her say, *No*, and interprets the tone of voice as one which confirms the idea of poor Theo and poor us, to be saddled with such a one. *No, nothing,* the mother-in-law reiterates, *but what can you expect, after all? She's not ours, is she? She's foreign.*

The eyes, all eight of them, focus on Justine, but she pretends she has not understood, gazes briefly about her, and then suddenly displays intense interest in a clump of gaping, scarlet snapdragons near the stone wall. Then she gazes upwards into the fig tree. In this fashion she lets a moment or two elapse, then pulls herself to her feet and goes inside, leaving a resumed buzz of conversation behind. She has decided.

She crosses the courtyard, mounts the stairs, and opens the two doors that lead to her bedroom, which isn't her bedroom really. The trunk in the corner isn't hers, and neither is the very old embroidered cross on the wall. She kneels by the bed with the crimson and blue cover that Theo's mother wove on the loom that Theo's father made, and then she reaches for the suitcase, and burrows in it. When she finds what she wants she shoves the whole lot, bits, pieces and all, into a plastic bag. She rises and stalks slowly back the way she has come.

The women are still there. Of course they are. Justine resettles herself, slowly and deliberately puts the plastic bag down and extracts the contents. She notices a hush, a definite hiatus, as if all the old *yiayathes* have inhaled simultaneously and have come to some sort of agreement about the business of resuming breathing. Justine takes her crochet hook in her right hand and holds the half-completed Afghan square in the other. It is one of her best, she thinks, brought over for something to do in front of the fire during the long winter evenings she has been told about. Warned about. Good Australian wool, which is now hot to the touch and makes her fingers sweat, but never mind. Totem brand, glowing colours. She bends her head to her task and plies busily.

The silence does not last long. There is an outburst of short staccato babble along the lines of *Fancy that* and *Wonders will never cease. Kyria* Eleni gives a sharp click of the tongue, but it is *Kyria-*Ariadne-from-across-the-road who caves in first, and creeps three paces, half-stooping in order to avoid dropping her spotless white creation in the dust, and lowers herself beside Justine. *Show me,* she commands. Justine does as she is told and the old fingers pat and pull and examine; the old eyes check the pattern and then look at Justine, and then *Kyria* Ariadne's mouth stretches in a toothless grin. Justine can almost hear flesh and bone creaking and cracking. *Oraio, paithi mou. Beautiful, my child. Just beautiful. And what is it going to be?*

Then it is the turn of Justine's fingers to help her brain and tongue in explaining the principle of an Afghan rug. *Kyria* Ariadne beams and shuffles back to her place beside Justine's mother-in-law. And stretches her mouth again. *What is your mother-in-law talking about?* she cackles mischievously, determined to elicit a response of some kind, a strong reaction for preference. And she shoots a glance at *Kyria* Panayota, who will not give anybody any satisfaction: her lips tighten a fraction and her eyes narrow, but that is all.

Justine thinks, and her fingers never stop while she is doing so: *Something complicated is going on here, and it's not just my crochet pattern. Mama has lost, but she's also won. She's lost because she's been proven wrong, but has won because I've proven myself not to be entirely useless. A defeat for her, a win for the family. Or something. And what about me? A victory for me, too. Because, Mama, I've made you realise that there are some things to be learned about me.*

Justine sits and crochets in the way her mother taught her.

Shooting the Dog

Peter Goldsworthy

For Lisa

'Each time the gravel slid off the shovel
it sounded like something
trying to hang on by its nails.'
—PHILIP HODGINS, 'Shooting the Dogs'

He was long in the tooth now, although no one in the district could put an exact figure on the years. His name offered a clue: even this far from the city it had not been possible to call a dog Nigger for at least a decade.

'You get jailed for it these days,' Hedley Stokes liked to joke, ritually, to his daughter-in-law Meg, city born and bred and blamed for all kinds of city nonsense.

Hedley had bought the dog, fully grown and pre-named, years back.

Two droughts back, he sometimes joked – but the worst drought had been the absence of his son Ben at the time, playing football in the city and searching for Meg, or the idea of Meg, and trying to get the farm out of his blood. When Hedley's left knee finally gave way (cack-footed, he had been no mean player himself in his day) and Ben reluctantly returned to take over the place, the name-change insisted on by Meg – 'Nugget' – would not be answered to by the dog. Dogged herself, an English

teacher anxious about the influence of language on impression-
able minds, she tried one more time – 'Nipper' – but even the
softening of a single consonant was stubbornly resisted by the
black dog.

And even more stubbornly by Hedley and his wife, Edna, who
still drove over most days from their retirement unit on the coast.
Hedley gave the notion nothing more than an incredulous snort;
it was Edna who took the young woman aside and suggested that
it might be cruel and confusing for the dog.

Largely retired from farm work, Nigger was allowed to tag
along with his son, Blue, as the younger dog went about its shep-
herding. Blue was an athletic, wide-casting dog – the best in the
district, many thought. If Ben was caught up in the crutching
or drenching he would sometimes leave a gate or two open, and
rely on Blue to bring up the sheep from the bottom paddocks
unsupervised. Nigger was more of a loose cannon now. Slower,
arthritic in the hips, he would break out about the flocks ever
more lazily, much to the younger dog's frustration. The winter
before, while bringing in the Angora goats that Ben had briefly
diversified into, then rapidly out of ('Another get-poor-quick
scheme, son?'), Nigger had cast far too narrowly, dividing the
herd and stampeding half of it through a fence. Half a day's
work went down the drain, and far too much torn hide and
bloodied fleece. The younger dog had taken it upon himself to
admonish his sire's clumsiness, chasing the astonished Nigger
back to the ute, and then directing an equal amount of dog
invective at an even more astonished Ben for his lack of leader-
ship.

Hedley couldn't believe his ears when told the story over that
Sunday's roast. 'Who's running this farm? *You're* the top dog,
Bennyboy. You've got to lead by example – not leave it to the dogs
to sort it out.'

Edna, for good measure, 'It's not fair on Blue, dear.'

'But they do the work,' Meg put in, 'maybe they should have
more say.'

'Votes for dogs!' Ben added.

Hedley allowed himself a chuckle. 'I tell you one thing, girl. A
kelpie-cross or three would do a hell of a better job of running
the country than this mob.' He chewed a little more lamb before

remembering his main theme. 'You can't spoil them, Ben. Next you'll have them sleeping in the house.'

Meg's eyes slid immediately to her husband's, alarmed. He winked, reassuringly. He wasn't about to confess.

'Woof!' he said, and grinned. 'Woof, woof!'

After Blue's rebuke, Ben kept the sire chained in the tray of the ute while working the flocks, often with Hedley – *his* sire, it occurred to him – sitting in the front seat for company. He toyed, briefly, with the idea of moving Nigger to the coast with his parents, but Meg refused to allow it. A working dog would be bored to death inside their tiny, enclosed courtyard, she argued. In fact, she had grown attached to Nigger, and often kept him inside the farmhouse herself, spoiling him with tidbits, enjoying his company, a familiar presence in the corner of her eye.

'Well, if it isn't the house nigger,' Hedley declared over another Sunday roast, as the dog tried to remain invisible beneath the dining-room table.

'Hedley!' his wife warned him before Meg could bite. 'You mustn't say things like that.'

'Sticks and stones, Edna my love. Sticks and stones.'

It was a theme he often returned to, liking to shock his daughter-in-law with his version of straight country talk – but liking, also, her cheek in return, her willingness to give back as much as she got.

'He's not a full-blood nigger,' he announced one morning. 'Look here –' And he ruffled the white patch, roughly diamond-shaped, that stained the dog's black head like a horse's blaze. 'Bentley mark. Know what a Bentley mark is, Meg?'

'Yes, Dad. But don't let that stop you telling me again.'

He grinned, pleased. 'Sign of the true heeler. He's got more than a bit of Queensland blue in him, this feller.'

'I don't follow. You mean they crossed a dog with a cheese?'

Dash of blue heeler or not, Nigger was mostly kelpie. His coat's blackness took on a reddish kelpie sheen in the afternoon light, although Hedley liked to claim it was mostly dust.

Once, after Meg had spent the morning washing the old dog in a plastic washing tub, Hedley had leaned forward from his chair – a sort of cane throne on the veranda – and spat on the dog's coat as it slept in the sun at his feet.

'A working dog should be dirty,' he said, with that glint of mischief in his eye that Meg was beginning to enjoy, and that she knew, also, was his harmless way of flirting with her.

Blue's dam had been a red kelpie from a property further down the Peninsula. The mother's redness had come through almost undiluted in the son, hence his name. He was a beautiful dog to watch at work, prick-eared, sleek as a seal, forever on the move. As a pup he had shown no interest in the sheep, and Hedley had almost given up on him. Then suddenly, at six months or so, watching his sire squeeze sheep into a pen for jetting, some sort of lightbulb had gone on the pup's head. Within minutes he'd been walking across the backs of the penned sheep, up to his hocks in their thick wool. He hadn't stopped moving among them since.

'Gentler than his old man,' Hedley liked to boast. 'The cattle dog hasn't come through. Which is why he's not a biter. Never even nips. Doesn't need to.'

For a time, chained in the ute, Nigger seemed to take a similar pride in watching his son at work. But after a few days the whining started, and then the frustrated straining at the chain. The last straw came with the arrival of the alpacas. Ben bought the small herd against his father's advice, or perhaps because of that advice. ('Rooster one day, feather duster the next in that caper, son.') When the bottom fell out of an oversupplied alpaca-wool market ('Can't say I didn't warn him, Meg. Only the breeders made any money.') Ben offloaded the herd at dog-food prices. The sight of Blue bringing these alien animals – half-goat, half–bonsai camel – in for transport drove Nigger into a frenzy. Maddened even further by Hedley's dressings down, he managed to scramble over the near-side of the ute and almost hang himself on his chain.

'Two things, son. The length of the chain – Jesus! Second – you'll have to leave him at the house in any case.'

'Wouldn't mind leaving both of you,' Ben muttered to himself.

In fact, he and Blue were alone in the top paddock a week later when the dog found the first of the spring lambs. Or found the crows which had already found them.

'What you got there, feller?'

Foxes were his first thought, but the ripped-apart lambs had not been eaten. It looked more like play, or playful torture, than hunting for food. His second thought was Blue – the dog had the freedom of the farm. But Blue seemed as surprised as him at the discovery, and he had never been aggressive with the animals, apart from head-butting the nose of the odd angry ewe.

Meg, back teaching six-tenths, was still in town when he arrived home, but his father was sitting in his cane throne on the veranda and his mother was ensconced in her old kitchen, baking, and chatting to her husband through the open window. Ben stalked straight to Nigger's kennel. As he squatted on his haunches, the dog seemed pleased enough to see him, wagging its tail and innocently offering up its jaws for inspection.

His father limped across the yard. 'Problem, son?'

'A few lambs have been killed.'

'Foxes?'

'They weren't eaten.'

'No sign of wool on Nigger,' Hedley said, peering over his shoulder. 'How fresh was the kill?'

'Yesterday. Maybe the day before. The crows had got stuck in.'

'Then you're not likely to find anything today,' the old man said, and straightened up and limped back to his chair.

'Maybe it was a wedge-tail?'

A chuckle from the older man, 'No chance, son.'

'What about Ted Chambers' dog? I never liked the look of it. Plug-ugly. More pig in it than dog. And always out in the road chasing cars.'

'Big call to make, Bennyboy. You wouldn't want to say anything to Ted without hard evidence.'

Gathering evidence would not be easy, but the chief suspect was waiting for Ben and Meg in the middle of the road – *its* section of road clearly – as they drove home from church that Sunday, alerted by their dust from miles away. The dog's front feet were planted firmly in the dirt, bracing itself less against the oncoming car, perhaps, than against the backward thrust of the force of its own barking. One especially powerful bark seemed to lift the entire dog off its paws, spinning it three-sixty degrees back to its original position. Instead of speeding past, Ben pulled to the side of the road and stopped. Ted and Joan, great talkers, were still back in town on the church steps; he had time for a little sleuthing.

'What are you doing?' Meg asked, alarmed, as he opened the door, but the dog had already stopped its barking, and padded tamely up to the driver's door with its tail wagging, a picture of innocence.

'All bark and no bite,' Ben said, chucking its pale, pig-like ears.

In the adjacent field Ted Chambers' spring lambs were frolicking, and even as Ben inspected the dog's snout for telltale strands of wool, he knew that there was no chance of this dog travelling ten miles across stony country to kill *his* lambs. Behind them, the dust of another car was fast approaching. The Chambers, escaping the church steps earlier than usual? Edna and Hedley, more likely, arriving for the Sunday leg of lamb which Meg always left roasting in the oven before church.

'We need to get home,' she reminded him, and he pushed the blameless dog away and tugged the car door shut.

He made sure Nigger was outside, out of sight, while they were eating, but Hedley warmed to the theme nonetheless. 'It happens to some dogs late in life, son. They turn.'

'Into grumpy old dogs?' Meg suggested.

For once her father-in-law ignored the tease. 'Might be the dingo coming through, of course.'

'He's got dingo in him?' Meg asked, surprised.

'He's got blue heeler in him,' Ben reminded her. 'Heelers are part dingo.'

'Some more than others,' Hedley said. 'Every now and then some genius decides the breed is getting too soft and crosses more dingo back into it.'

'What's this, dear?' Edna interrupted, working with her fork at a white cyst-like pocket in a slice of meat.

'Looks like hydatid,' Hedley pronounced. 'Better not touch that, Mother.'

Meg laughed. 'They're just garlic cloves, Dad.'

Hedley drowned the offending lamb in mint sauce. 'And I thought the meat was off.'

'It's an acquired taste,' she said, but he had already turned back to Ben.

'There's no cure for it, son.'

'What are you saying, Dad?'

'You know what I'm saying. Once they start, they never stop.'

'Then you'll have to have him with you, after all. In town. Where he can't do any damage.'

'It's no life for a working dog in there, son.'

Silence. Meg's eyes met Ben's, pleading. He turned back to his father. 'I'm not going to put him down without definite proof, Dad.'

'Bennyboy – listen to reason. In no time flat you'll have no lambs left. Once a dog acquires the taste …' He turned back to his daughter-in-law. 'Speaking of which – could I pester you for a couple more slices?'

Nigger left his breakfast untouched in its bowl the next morning. After stalking that bowl, and being unrebuked, Blue gobbled it down. Was the older dog sickening? A different explanation waited out in the fields, where three black-feathered undertakers were watching over the bodies of another two dead lambs, one of which this time had been partly eaten.

Even now, finding no wool on the old dog's jaws or blood on his coat, Ben was able to resist the obvious. Although he prudently kept Nigger chained up every night for a week.

Prudently, but sleeplessly: bursts of angry, frustrated barking kept waking both of them. Desperate for a night's shut-eye by the weekend, he left the dog unchained, and found three more lambs ripped apart in the morning. Circumstantial evidence? Only Meg still thought so.

'We have to catch him red-handed, Ben.'

A year or two before he wouldn't have listened. The value of the lost meat and wool would have tipped the scales of justice against the dog. Now the wool mountain was a mile high, everyone wanted to eat beef, or battery chicken, and his monetary losses were negligible. He could afford to bide his time.

'You were thinking of getting rid of the sheep anyway, Ben. Barley prices are up – why not put in a few more acres next year? Or canola – the Chambers are putting in canola …'

'If it's not our lambs, it'll be the neighbours'.'

'I'll keep him in the house then. Or we can put up a higher fence.'

'I can't even afford to fence the back paddock.'

He didn't tell his father about the latest attack. Hedley's trick knee needed replacement, he had enough problems. But when the older man next rode around the farm with Ben he saw immediately that the lamb numbers were down.

'That cold snap,' Ben lied, and Hedley seemed satisfied enough, or too preoccupied with his own health to care.

Meg kept Nigger inside for the rest of the week, and when Ben found the fourth batch of savaged lambs it seemed at first that the dog might be in the clear. But a day later Meg found a leg bone in the dog's basket. She told Ben as soon as he came in that afternoon.

'You let him out last night?'

'He might be able to get out. But I can't see how he could get back in.'

'He must have,' Ben said, and walked to the kitchen door. The flyscreen door was open an inch; he pushed it open, watched it fail to close completely.

'The spring's gone. He could shove his nose in there.'

'No wonder the mozzies were biting,' Meg said, but mosquitos were the last thing on Ben's mind as he stalked outside and chained the dog to the tank-stand.

'Why is Nigger chained up?' Edna wanted to know over the roast that Sunday.

'Just a precaution, Mum.'

'You missing a few more lambs?' Hedley put in.

Ben said nothing; his eyes sought refuge in Meg's, avoiding his father's. But he couldn't turn his ears away.

'You've only yourselves to blame, Bennyboy. Both of you. You can't get close to a dog.'

'A few pats can hardly make a difference,' Meg said.

'A few pats? He has the run of the house. You feed him scraps from the table ...'

'Sometimes.'

'He thinks he's human, girlie. He thinks he's a member of the family.'

'He *is* a member of the family. And he feels things – just like us.'

Hedley spluttered, amused. 'Like you maybe.'

'Like *all* of us. He feels anger. Jealousy. Love …'

'Maybe you'd better get one of these social workers from the city out to talk to him.'

'Hedley,' his wife warned.

'Just trying to help, Edna. The kids have made a rod for their own backs. All I'm doing is offering advice. You have to put the dog down, son. Before you lose any more lambs.'

'We'll think about it, Dad.'

'Well don't think too long. It might be your farm now, but I can't sit by and watch it go down the gurgler.'

Ben, through gritted teeth, 'I *said*, we'll think about it, Dad.'

'And I said, you're running out of time.'

Ben dropped his knife and fork with a clatter. 'Maybe I don't want the fucking farm, Dad. Maybe I never wanted it …'

'There must be someone who would take him as a pet,' Meg interrupted before anything more damaging could be said.

'You could put an ad in the paper,' Edna suggested.

Her son picked up his cutlery again. 'We'll think about that too, Mum.'

The young couple lay awake half the night thinking – and talking. Meg's sleep, when it came, was eased by a sense that nothing had yet been decided. Ben left the house before she woke the next morning, needing an early start. Restringing wires in the top paddock, he waited until he saw her drive away to school before climbing into the ute and heading back to the house. He dragged a stool into the bedroom next to the wardrobe, and climbed up. Three guns had once been kept here, out of his child's reach, until the Anzac Day when Hedley arrived back early from the Club, pulled down his old army .303, carried it out to the woodpile, set it on the block, and took to it with a sledgehammer. He had offered no reasons, then or later, and Ben had never seen him in such a state, before or since. Edna deflected her troubled son's questions by talking vaguely of 'a disagreement at the Club', of someone calling him 'a name that he didn't like'.

Two guns remained. The single-shot .22 Ben had used himself as a boy, spotlighting rabbits and kangaroos and even shooting the odd fox under supervision. The shotgun – a Winchester Type 12 – he had never been allowed to touch. He had been too small the winter his father had bought it. A pair of ducks had settled on the dam, but after breaking a tooth on a pellet while biting into a drumstick, Hedley had gone off duck meat forever. The Winchester had not been used since, except secretly, in play. In his teens, Ben would often take the gun down when his parents were out, and familiarise himself with its workings. He was standing on the stool now, checking the pump action, when his father appeared in the doorway below him.

Startled, he nearly unbalanced. The old man might have been a genie conjured up by rubbing the blue gun metal.

'Jesus, Dad – where did you come from?'

'You can't use a twelve-gauge, son. You'd take his whole head off.'

Hedley turned and limped out of sight as abruptly as he had appeared. Ben placed the Winchester back on the wardrobe and took down the .22, an ancient single-shot Browning, plus a box of shells, and the squeeze can of gun oil. He spread newspaper over the kitchen table, and carefully wiped down the open sights, broke open the breech, and blew out the cobwebs. He oiled the hammer, checked its action, then opened the box of ammo and dropped a single shell into his breast pocket.

He was about to replace the box on the wardrobe when he stopped, and took out a second shell. Just in case.

Outside, Hedley was back on his throne. 'Nigger,' he called, and as always the dog ran instantly to him. 'Sit, boy,' he ordered, and as he leaned forward Ben thought he might be about to pat the dog for the first time ever. 'You've been a good worker, boy,' he said. A pause. 'Well done,' he added, then leaned back again, and turned to his son and nodded. To Ben, unsettled, it felt weirdly like a prison warden's nod to an executioner.

'You coming, Dad?'

'You got to do these things by yourself, son.'

Bullshit, Ben thought. You just don't want to see it. But a lump clogged his throat; his father's terse farewell to the dog had touched him somehow. He averted his face, and whistled Nigger up into the back of the ute. Blue tried to follow; twice Ben had to order the usually obedient dog to stay. The younger dog whimpered, and paced around the yard, agitated. When Ben tossed a spade into the tray, Blue barked frantically up at his sire, as if in warning.

Ben knelt and held the young dog's head for a moment, looking him straight in the eyes. 'It can't be helped, Blue. It's got to be done.'

The condemned dog, its own mind-reading powers apparently diminished by age, showed no qualms at accepting a ride in a ute with a man with a rifle and a spade. The south paddock was three gates away. Each time Ben stopped and climbed out he avoided eye contact with the dog, but Nigger seemed oblivious to this body language, running eagerly from side to side of the tray, tongue lolling, happy just to be out and about. When they reached the stand of uncleared mulga that bordered the south fence, the dog jumped joyfully down, and headed straight into the bleached summer grass. He had killed a brown snake here years before; the patch of scrub was clearly a technicolour mix of nose memories and fresh scents, which was why Ben had chosen it.

Ben took the spade and rifle out of the tray and stood for a time with one implement in each hand, as if balancing them, or weighing something. Should he dig the grave first? Or afterwards? Nosing about in the dry grass the dog still seemed impervious to his fate. Dig first, and work a little agitation out of the system? And if it delayed the inevitable a little longer, so be it.

The work was hard; the stony ground had never been tilled, and no rain had fallen since August. He should have brought a pick, or mattock. He dug slowly and methodically, wanting to take his time, needing to take his time, all the time in the world. He took an unnecessary break, and sat with his legs dangling from the back of the ute, sipping tea from the cap of his thermos. The dog ran to him, expecting a treat, but he was saving the one treat in his pocket till later, and the dog immediately turned and ran back to his explorations, able to read the man's intentions in this respect at least. Ben savoured a second capful of the tea, black and sugary, then returned to his digging. The hole was Nigger-sized in length and breadth, but no more than two feet deep when he decided that enough was enough. The phrase 'a shallow bush grave' came to him, poignantly, from somewhere, another murder story in that morning paper perhaps. He rolled himself a cigarette from a long-abandoned pack in the glove box. Having smoked it to the last few millimetres,

stale tobacco or not, he could delay no longer. How small the .22
shell he fossicked from his breast pocket seemed, not much more
lethal than an air-gun slug. He broke open the old rifle, loaded
the chamber, snapped the breech shut. He took the scrap of
dried liver from his pocket, a treat his father had never approved
of for working dogs, and dropped it into the hole.

'Here, boy.'

The dog came to him, looked down into the hole, looked up
into his eyes, looked down again, then once more up, quizzically.

'It's OK, boy,' he said, and as the dog stepped down into the
hole for its last, small meal, he lifted the rifle to his shoulder in
one quick movement, aimed it into the black crown of the dog's
head, and fired, and the dog collapsed on its own legs without a
sound.

As fast as the shooting had been, the tears that sprang to Ben's
eyes were even faster.

'Sorry, boy,' he said, and knelt and examined the dog through
the film of those tears. 'Sorry, old feller.'

There were no tears in the dog's motionless eyes, or even any
kind of death shiver in its legs. He rose and took up the spade
and began to fill the grave, working rapidly this time. When he
had finished, he found the sight of the small mound – exactly
the length and width and volume of the dog – too disturbing,
and he began to remove dirt from it, and spread it around. He
couldn't bring himself to tread down the remaining heap, not
wanting to further damage the dog, or in any way to squash it.

He drove off immediately to his fencing chores, and buried
himself all day in the physicality of star-dropping, and stringing
and tightening wires. Hard enough work for two, near impossible for one – but he had no distractions. He had drunk most of
his tea while stalling for time at the shooting, and had left home
early without packing lunch. His father's car had gone when he
returned to the house late in the afternoon; he washed down a
meat and pickle sandwich with a bottle of beer then slumped
into the cane throne on the veranda, exhausted.

'Ben?'

'Hmmm.'

A kiss on his forehead. 'You're sleeping in the sun, darling.
Come inside.'

Meg made no mention of Nigger, then or later, over dinner, but she brought Blue into the house, and fed him a choice scrap of meat from the table, whether for her comfort or the dog's or to make some kind of obscure point to Ben he couldn't tell.

He had dreaded facing her, but she seemed especially kind to him also.

His mother rang after dinner. 'You OK, Benny?'

'Fine, Mum.'

'And Meg?'

'She's managing.'

'I know she was fond of old Nigger. But your father was right. It had to be done.'

'I know, Mum. Thanks for the call.'

'Give my love to Meg.'

'Of course. She's right here. You want to talk to her?'

'I'm sure she has more important things to do. Just give a hug.'

Blue nosed his way in through the flyscreen door the next night as they were eating. It was clearly lonely out in the yard, and after the three of them had cleaned the two dinner plates between them, Ben brought the dog's basket inside.

It was Blue tugging at the quilt that woke him in the small hours the following night. He had seen the dog agitated before – the morning of Nigger's execution for one – but he had never seen such a silent, purposeful agitation. Something was afoot. An intruder? The hairs were bristling along the dog's back, but still it made no noise, insisting only with its body language that Ben follow, immediately. Meg, exhausted, slept on as he slipped from the bed. It wasn't until he reached the hall that he heard the scratching at the kitchen door. Blue was already waiting at that door, staring at it, ears pricked, hairs erect, one forefoot raised. Ben pulled his old cricket bat from the hall stand, turned on the porch light, and jerked open the door.

A dog was lying with its head on the doormat, scratching at the flyscreen; it took a moment for Ben to realise, shocked, that it was Nigger. His heart was thumping as he knelt and examined the dog. The entry wound on its crown had congealed into a dark, hard scab. There was no sign of an exit; the slug must still be in there somewhere. Blue was whimpering now, finding his voice, and after some sniffing, and licking of the older dog's nose, began to lick methodically at its wound.

'Nigger,' Ben whispered. 'It's OK, boy.'

The dog had lost the power of dog speech, apparently; it made no noise at all, not even a whimper. It dragged itself an inch or so closer, but skewing sideways, crabwise. Ben saw that it – *he*, he reminded himself – was able to move his right-side legs only, as if cut down by a stroke rather than a bullet. His coat was encrusted with dust and clay; he had clearly been unable to clean away the grave earth. Ben looked out, across the dust of home yard; within the fall of the porch light he could make out the trail of the dog, a dragging, snake-like spoor. A black joke from childhood came back to him, made poignant now; what do you do with a dog with no legs? Take it for a drag.

But what *do* you do? His immediate reaction, through the fog of disbelief, was to take the dog straight back out into the bush and shoot it again, before Meg woke. To put Nigger out of his misery, certainly – but even more, to spare her. But the rifle was in the bedroom; he couldn't get his hands on it without waking her. The cricket bat was still tucked under his arm; he became aware of its weight again. Could he club the dog to death? He baulked at the thought, but the bat seemed to be getting heavier all the time, as if by a sudden surge in gravity. Did he have the heart for it? No – he had the heart *not* to do it. Did he have the stomach for it? He was saved, for the moment, by the padding of bare footsteps along the hall floorboards behind him. He shifted on his haunches to hide the dog, but Meg was already leaning over him, her 'What's the matter, darling?' swallowed by a horrified gasp, 'Oh, my God!'

She covered her mouth with both her hands and in the same movement sank to her knees. 'Oh, my poor boy. My poor Nigger.' She took the dog's head gently in her lap, and its long tongue slid out and licked weakly, lopsidedly, at her hand.

She looked up at her husband, distraught, through wet eyes. 'What can we do, Ben? What can we do? And what are you doing with that *bat*?'

He had no answer. His eyes met hers for a long moment, then he stepped back inside the house, and kept walking through to the bedroom. He climbed the stool, and took down the shotgun.

He slid three plump, red cartridges into the magazine, and loaded one in the chamber. The gun could hold more, but four already seemed like overkill. He pocketed another three cartridges all the same. To be found wanting once was once too many.

'What are you doing?' Meg demanded when he reappeared.

He shrugged, and spread his arms.

'You're going to shoot him *again*?'

'Look at him, Meg. What choice is there? He must be in misery. Dragged himself two miles back to the house. What else can I do?'

'Can't we give him the night at least? Something to eat? Maybe he'll recover.'

He looked at her, unable to speak.

'It's not right, Ben. You put him through this. You and your father. And isn't there some kind of law? If you survive the execution you can't be convicted again ...' How had this nonsense popped into her head? She abandoned it as soon as it popped out of her mouth. 'If you'd done it properly the *first* time ...'

'You think I don't know that?'

The dog was shivering. She took off her towelling robe and tucked it over and around him.

'Get some water, Ben.'

He leaned the shotgun against the wall inside the door, and filled a saucer in the kitchen. The dog ignored it, or was unable to control its head enough to sip.

'I'll warm some milk,' Meg said. 'You bring him inside. Put him on the spare bed.'

At least the dog seemed in no pain. Paralysed down one side perhaps, and unable to speak any dog words, unable even to whimper, but uncomplaining as he was wrapped more tightly in the swaddling of bathrobe, and lifted into Ben's arms. The dog was surprisingly light – dehydration? blood loss? – and by bending his knees Ben was able to grab the shotgun also. Meg had vanished, naked, into the kitchen. For a moment he paused in the doorway, half inside the house and half out. Nigger looked up at him, and licked his hand. Blue was out in the yard, facing them; as Ben stepped down off the veranda the younger dog ran between him and the utility, and turned, crouching, and turned and crouched again, as if trying to herd him back into the house.

'Stand down, boy.'

He laid the bundled dog gently in the tray, then took the shotgun into the cabin with him, placing it carefully across the backrest. He had started the engine and turned towards the grid when Meg walked out in front of the ute. He hadn't seen her emerge from the house; she had pulled on boots and jeans and a thick pullover. Instead of the promised saucer of milk she was carrying the garden spade, cradling it across her chest like a weapon. His pulse flared: was she refusing to allow him to pass? Over my dead body, Ben? Instead she walked around and climbed into the passenger seat, nursing the spade between her knees, perhaps – the thought came to him – to keep it out of sight of the dog. She reached over and squeezed his hand, briefly, but without looking at him. Sensing that she couldn't bring herself to speak, he kept silent himself as the ute rumbled across the grid and into the home paddock. She climbed out to open the first gate and climbed back in after he had driven through, still without speaking. After the second gate, she climbed back onto the tray instead, and sat nursing the dog's head in her lap.

He opened and closed the third gate himself.

He parked facing the same stand of scrub, leaving the headlights blazing. The shallow grave had imploded; he dug it out quickly while Meg remained up in the tray, murmuring soothing sounds at the dog. He worked hard and fast, digging out another entire hole's worth of dirt, wanting to be certain this time, before tossing the spade aside.

'I'm ready,' he finally said.

'You'll need to lift him out,' Meg said.

He took the towelling bundle from her and carried it around into the headlights, keeping the dog's head towards the ute, not wanting him to see the stand of gums, or the gaping hole – although Nigger surely knew exactly where he was.

He set the dog on the ground and, as Meg knelt and fondled his ears again, walked back to the cabin of the ute for the loaded gun. He checked the breech as Meg tugged a corner of the robe over the condemned dog's eyes. Nigger licked her hand once, but as she stood back, the right side of his body, the working side, began trembling, violently.

'He's scared,' she whispered, hoarsely. 'He knows. Do it quickly, Ben.'

Not too quickly, he reminded himself as he aimed the gun with more deliberate care at the masked head. He squeezed the trigger slowly, and with such forced concentration that he barely noticed the hard, bruising kickback of the stock against his shoulder, or the explosion of the shot itself.

Meg's gasp of horror was barely audible to his deafened ears; she had already turned away to lean against the bonnet of the ute as he lowered the gun. He could look no longer than a second himself. He leaned the gun against the wheel of the ute and dragged the dead dog by the hind legs to the edge of the hole, keeping his face averted.

Then he took the spade and cleaned up the fragments of shattered bone and brains, still trying only to look out of the corner of his eye. He had scraped two small mounds of dirt and remains into the hole when nausea overcame him.

'Here,' Meg was saying somewhere, far off, although apparently close enough to take the spade from his hands. He squatted on his heels, with his head between his knees till he stopped feeling faint. He could hear her working somewhere, and by the time he felt safe to rise to his feet again she was banging down the earth on top of the grave.

'You OK, Ben?'

'Getting there. And you?'

A long silence. 'Do you think we're cut out for this?'

'I think you are,' he said, and she offered up the glimmer of a smile.

They drove back to the house as they had driven out, in silence. Blue was waiting at the grid, prick-eared, pacing relentlessly about. As they climbed out, he was already looking past them from the tray to the cabin and back again. Ben left the shotgun in the cabin, but tossed the spade into the toolshed and closed the door; he would hose it down later. Blue followed Meg up the steps onto the veranda, searching her face for a sign, looking back at Ben's face, looking past them out into the night, looking and searching everywhere.

At the door Meg turned, and spoke to him. 'No, Blue. Stay.'
She held the door for her husband to step through, then closed it in the dog's face, slowly but firmly.

Tactics

Karen Hitchcock

In the '80s I was in love with Robert Smith. I also hoped against all rumour that Morrissey's croon was for me. Before then it was the boy from our local grocery store, the one who helped shift the crates of sweating milk between the cool room and the fridges, cap pulled low over frantic blond hair, refusing to look at me whenever I walked past. Once or twice I dropped my school bag and stood right in his path, hands on what was fast becoming a waist. He edged around me like I was just another fridge.

The news about Morrissey, when confirmed in print, hit me and every other girl in 10C hard. That had Mr O'Shaw chuckling to himself. A crush on a homosexual singer, hehhehheh. For a day, his chuckle skirted a sneer. After that, it was something else. He'd stare out the window, blue eyes hovering above the car park, and let out these soft Irish noises we'd never heard him make before.

Then Ben transferred to our school. A boy with lyrical under-standing and the latest personal compact disc technology. It was the start of the-smaller-the-better. A new era. He was everything my family wasn't: a suburban exotic. We shared earbuds over ham and pickle sandwiches. We listened to the entire Cure lib-rary burned onto a plate of shining chrome. He reintroduced me to The Smiths and spoke often of his lust for a Bang and Olufsen stereo with a flat remote control and hidden speakers in every room. He never mentioned his lust for Rosa Mioli, the girl from

11B. She showed me the compilation tape – held it out in front of her two preposterous breasts – proving what she had and that for her he was willing to use the old-fashioned.

My friend Jane and I turned vegetarian. I followed the Moosewood prescription: sprouting my own mung beans for a superior protein; eating tofu as if I liked it. Jane studied for final exams. I hung out at Greville Street Records. The boys who worked there balanced records on their fingertips and polished them like they were the back of a newborn's neck. They took my cash, looking right through me, reluctant to let go of their babies. I bought Bad Brains and Rites Of Spring and Bauhaus, all of them on vinyl. I listened to them at home on Mum and Dad's plywood cabinet turntable. At Nan's house I'd still watch dinnertime TV and eat roast lamb. She promised not to tell. It was almost time for university anyhow.

Jane and I enrolled in our BAs in a university as far-flung from our suburb as possible. We moved in together into a flat above a café. I read Kundera and DeLillo. She read Dworkin and Plath. I worked as a waitress; she cleaned five-star hotel rooms. By then it was the '90s and I was trying different tactics. So when a boy called Daniel showed up in my tutorial, sporting these big brown eyes and a vintage Bowie T-shirt, I acted like nothing had happened. Other girls sat next to him, looked up through their eyelashes and asked him questions about deconstruction; I moved around Daniel as if he were a fridge. One day he cleared his throat and asked me if I had read *The Gulf War Did Not Take Place*. I turned half my face towards him, eyebrows, nose and chin reaching angles Elizabethan. 'Yes,' I said, 'I have,' and I turned back to the front.

Daniel asked me to The Lounge to see a band with fringe-type cultural capital. I wasn't sure what to wear and Jane was no help. She'd recently decided that clothes and boys and Lounges were simply aspects of the patriarchal apparatus. I chose archetypal things dyed black and, before I left, revised *Baudrillard for Beginners*.

Turns out Daniel and I agreed on the big three: *Neuromancer*, *Hunky Dory*, Joseph Cornell. It was the era of the incommensurate.

Our meetings escalated. I went to his place: as small and neat as a converted ATM. I'd never before seen books meet top to toe. He arranged them by form rather than content. He had a titanium computer *and* a turntable. I couldn't beat his arguments so we shared a couple of hamburgers. We smoked imported cigarettes. And all night long we'd make a gentle kind of sense.

He came to my place and precipitated thought experiments: Jane, attempting to will him to death.

'De Beauvoir,' she'd say, slapping overcooked gnocchi into op-shop bowls, 'rejected feminism outright when she crawled into the grave with Sartre.' We sat and listened to the slapping. She took the pan back to the kitchen and threw it at the sink.

'I'm not so hungry,' Daniel would murmur. For a boy he had a sensitive stomach.

Things could have turned nasty but Daniel won a scholarship for a year at UCLA. It was a fantastic opportunity, a once in a lifetime experience, and something he had to do. It was the first time I'd heard him speak in clichés. I pictured blue skies and inordinate suns. I pictured Californian girls with breasts rounder than Rosa Mioli's. I didn't even know he'd applied.

So. I had other things to do. I had books to read, film festivals to attend, papers to write, music to hunt out, clothes to dye. I had Jane. I had a boy called Simon in my postmodern narrative tutorial who was willing to come out and play. I drank macchiatos. Lamented past time. Worked hard to erase history. I was so busy I had to drop down to part-time study. Daniel's aerograms became mournful, then tragic, then frantic. He wrote in tiny clustered letters, between lines, in margins, around the space for the return address. I refused to get email, paced my replies like Tai Chi. *Life is fine*, I wrote to him. *Let's just be rational, philosophic.* I was making the most of my assets.

Daniel came back at the end of autumn. Brown, crisp, beautiful. Towing a degree in cultural studies and a marijuana habit bigger than Texas. At the time these attributes were both considered valuable. His eyes went wet when he saw me, and he said he wanted us to share a house. I played it cool, weighed, then promoted, my options. I knew where I'd come from. Jane called me a fool. The Hungarian man who owned the café downstairs scratched his stubble, mopped his brow and asked me what a 23-year-old was doing with a boyfriend anyways.

I packed my records into crates and my clothes into garbage bags. A vegan named Rosie moved in with Jane and they both set about dreading their hair. Daniel and I moved close to the beach. We both kept separate bedroom-cum-studies and chose where we'd sleep each night. That way Daniel got to order things in his particular way, and I could leave my frocks in bags. I was down to one subject a semester and losing momentum fast. Daniel was planning a thesis on Deleuze. He planned all day, sitting on a Deco couch donated by my Nan, rolling paper and herb between his fingers, between splayed knees. He'd inhale hard, then stare at his thesis on the wall. I was right there with him. We were a duo of vague, ambitious staring, listening to Trance-diluted classics. It was the era of nostalgia.

Jane and Rosie invited us to dinner to announce the inevitable. Jane looked a bit thin but they seemed happy, domestic. After a few mugs of wine Rosie admitted she liked the French Feminists. Daniel said they were philosophically sound. They discussed the dissolution of binary opposition. Words like Kristeva and Helene Cixous floated around us like Méthode Champenoise. Daniel's finger curled around his chin like a question mark. Rosie gently licked a drop of wine from her wrist. I complimented Jane on the lentils. She sat there looking binary.

Rosie moved out within the month. Almost as if the announcement were the whole thing. Jane immediately started a celery-juice diet. She said it was for cleansing her liver. I told her she was the cleanest liver I knew, but her shoulders stayed slumped. We spent our afternoons walking the shore.

'So,' I said to her on one of those afternoons, 'forgetting sexual politics for a moment ...'

She snorted.

'Now that you've been to the other side ...'

We kicked through dirty sand, our hands in our pockets. She said: 'There's nothing else there.'

Daniel's thesis supervisor suggested he commit a few thoughts to paper. Daniel came home and slumped on the Deco. He got up to make a bong out of an apple-juice bottle and a length of plastic tubing. Smoke roared from his open lips. There was no music. Nights were days were nights. For two weeks, his focus stopped before it reached the wall. Then it sharpened. He looked at me sideways. When the phone rang, he would bolt to his feet, point between my eyes, tell me not to pick it up. Then he started talking about the unification of fire and water, about rhizomic thought capable of reinstigating the word, of parabolas reversing to make pathways for death. He didn't recognise me. I waved my fingers in front of his face and asked him if he could see. He said: 'I don't need to see to see.' When his eyes became pinwheels, I called Jane, who called the community mental-health team.

A psychiatrist put Daniel in the locked ward of a state psychiatric institution. He said that in his opinion the problem was drug-related and most likely temporary. Daniel slurred and dozed, slurred and dozed.

Our flat made me think of reversals carving pathways for death, so I stayed at Nan's house for a month, sleeping in the single bed of my childhood weekends, reading the magic realists, watching dinnertime TV on her new velour armchairs. She made us breakfast and lunch and dinner. She urged me to study more and to wear a bit of lippy.

Daniel made no progress. His eyelids were mauve winter quilts. His parents discussed taking him back to their house.

I went to see Jane. What was left of her smiled at me from the open doorway. Her lips pulled her face behind her ears. She said: 'I'll just go for a run before dinner.'

Forty-five minutes later she came back and served herself a level cup of baked beans. 'They're the perfect food,' she said, 'protein and carbohydrate and vegetable, all in one.' She shovelled fried rice and Peking duck from plastic containers onto my plate.

'Aren't you vegetarian?' I asked.

'Yes,' she said and smiled, 'but *you're* not.'

I put food in my mouth. Teeth worked, throat refused. I forced the issue, tried not to cough.

'So,' she said, eating a neatly quartered bean and making the ghoul grin again, 'how's things?'

*

I read *The Aleph* just lately and I thought of Borges recruiting young people to read to him. I thought of the blind, and the golden labradors that lead them. Jane once told me those dogs weren't allowed to bark. She told me they beat the dogs bloody to teach them their silence. She thought the whole thing was wrong. I closed Borges and went online. I looked up the Guide Dogs Association. I signed up as a volunteer.

Griffith Review

Asleep

Kim Scott

Owen washed Pa's feet in a bowl of water. The old man got to
his feet, dropped his trousers, and made Owen understand he
wanted further help.

Owen adjusted the shower taps. 'Hotter, hotter,' the old man
insisted as the steam rose around them.

Towelling the shivering body dry, Owen marvelled again
at the swirling colours of scarred flesh. How skinny the old
man was: like a skeleton draped in such strangely beautiful
skin.

On the back step, in the warm sun, Owen sheared away at the
old man's toenails with a great big pair of scissors. Small half-
pipes of what looked more like ivory or bone fell to the cement
slab at their feet.

It was habit, a routine wordlessly completed by Owen replac-
ing the old man's socks and shoes on his feet. Pa creakily stood
up, leaned on his walking stick, ran the palm of his other hand
over his hair.

'C'mon,' he said, setting off with those brisk, short steps of
his, and Owen padded behind him.

A TV blared sickly and bright in the curtain-drawn gloom.
Someone was asleep on the lounge; a mattress on the floor held
another sleeping adult, and the small child leaning into the
curves of his elder momentarily shifted his eyes from the screen
and smiled at them.

Aunty Heather was at the kitchen table, just the other side of a door. 'Mmm, lookin' deadly, Dad.'

Another woman in the kitchen laughed, and the child on her lap studied Owen, before pushing its face into the woman's shoulder.

'You get paid tomorrow, for the gardening, unna?'

'I think so,' Owen guessed.

'Yes, you do,' she said, 'they wrote it down.'

She went to a drawer, brought back a slip of paper. Owen saw the names, Peter and Corry Wright, an address, and a series of dates.

'Yell out when you're going,' she called as Owen followed the old man from the room. 'I'll walk with you.'

Pa was lowering himself onto a single bed, his shoes neatly placed beneath it. The walls of the tiny room were dull with the grime of years, and stacked along one wall were layer upon layer of paintings and drawings on paper, bark, plywood, glass, and even a few on canvas. Owen thought of his own dishevelled room, the litter of paper there.

He began browsing through the top layers of paintings, and was suddenly *within* a landscape; not looking down at an image, but within it, part of it. Bewildered, he looked up to the sky, and became merely a viewer again, outside, looking down upon.

Quickly, he turned to the next painting.

'You been there,' the old man said. 'Remember?' The bush was full of energy, colour, scents. Owen heard the humming drone of bees, felt the warm sun, the cool shade. The freshly rained-upon earth. 'You been there,' the old man said again, 'but never like that. See, all the flowers coming up together, all the seasons at once.'

Many of the paintings – a paddock of sheep, a large rock among trees, a bitumen road cutting through mallee – had a trail of footprints in them, sometimes wandering across, sometimes away from the foreground, out of the frame altogether, or appearing in the distance. There were other drawings of odd, hybrid creatures: various combinations of machines, plants, animals, humans. There were animated skeletons, skyscrapers crumbling in weak sunlight, a telephone booth leaning at a crossroad …

'C'mon,' the old man said. 'One of our stories. Give it to me in lingo.'

Owen took the empty chair from beside the bed and, reversing it between his legs, leaned his arms across its back and dropped his eyes from the old man's gaze. Pa closed his eyes.

No words came to Owen.

After a few minutes he exhaled his relief. The old man was asleep.

*

Corry paused at the nursery doorway, savouring the backyard before entering it. Our home, our office, our lab and garden, she thought. Our skills. It was as if they – Peter and Corry – were fated to care for the amazing creature they'd found. Who better?

She and Peter had left the creature in a hutch by the balga trees and a clump of granite rocks, hoping to provide shelter, familiarity, even a degree of emotional and psychological comfort, voicing such words and concepts without hesitation.

Now Corry saw that the stem of one of the balgas lay on the ground some distance from where Peter crouched with his back to her, studying what appeared to be the remains of a small fire. There was no sign of the creature.

Peter turned, startled at the sound of her footsteps, and grinned weakly.

'What's wrong?' she mewed.

Peter's hand waved across the broken balga stem, the fire and the set of tracks leading to a hole in the soft soil between granite rocks.

'I think it must've burrowed in there.'

'We'll have to get it out. If it can dig that far …'

'It can't escape. The mesh of the fence goes right down.'

'We don't even know what this is, Peter. We can't lose it, not now.'

'But you've seen it. I've got as much chance of digging out of here with my bare hands.'

'But look, that hole. It's like a burrow. How far …?'

'We'll dig it out. Shovels.'

Suddenly they were wrapped in smoke, each isolated and utterly alone. Coughing, blind and befuddled, they dropped to their hands and knees. Then, just as suddenly as it had come, the smoke cleared. Eyes streaming with tears, grateful to be breathing easily again, they helped one another to their feet. What had happened? Where did that smoke come from?

Peter thought it was the grass tree.

'Must've been smouldering, sparks from the campfire,' Peter suggested. They looked at a tiny pile of ash.

'And the wind.' Corry was workshopping this latest phenomenon, trying to help. 'The wind must've fed it. Thick though, wasn't it, that smoke?'

They dragged their fingers along gummy, charred flakes of wood. 'You know how this stuff burns.'

How fragrant it is.

'When it's dry, anyway.'

'But it went out so quickly.'

'Lucky for us.'

'Yeah, just as well.'

'We'll still have to dig it out, check anyway,' said Corry, and went to get a shovel.

She called out to Peter only a few minutes later. And then a second time, louder. Did she sound distressed?

'What now?' Peter went to her. How strange, he thought, slowing as he saw her at the entrance to the shed. How strange that she should stand so motionless, slumped and with her head down like that. Then he saw the red eyes, the creature staring from beneath Corry's armpit.

Corry had still not lifted her head. 'It's hurting me.'

The creature's face – smeared with yellow pus, eyes foggy and dim – was almost unrecognisable from the day before. It was breathing heavily, phlegm clicking, and muttered something which was, initially at least, incomprehensible. But then Peter and Corry heard, so clear it might have been their own voices, 'Let us be,' followed by what seemed echoes, other voices whispering, 'Allow us,' and 'Listen.'

It grabbed Corry and yanked her to her knees, but as she dropped Peter lunged across and caught the creature by the neck. Immediately it slumped, passive in his grasp, and Peter easily hauled it across Corry's back.

Yet when Corry turned the creature was sitting on Peter's

chest with its hands at his throat, and Peter was gurgling, his legs kicking fitfully.

Corry swung the shovel.

She helped her husband to his feet, and they stood holding one another, looking at the creature she had knocked unconscious. Neither of them mentioned what they'd heard. Each, as they brushed themselves down, adjusted and pulled themselves tighter, dismissed what they might have heard as a fantasy, something heard only inside his or her head, some product of individual imagination and stress.

There were some things you had to do. Just got up and did.

The creature stirred and, silently operating as a single unit, Peter and Corry roped, buckled, shackled the creature so that when it regained consciousness it would endanger neither them nor itself.

'Umm …'

They turned around.

Who?

Ah yes, the gardener: a doughy, soft young man, and his grandfather: dark, all angles and sinew and shabby, formal cloth. The younger held up a hand; in it the key they'd given him to enter the yard, but both he and the old man were staring, their eyes large in their heads and their mouths agape. The old man took a step back.

'Naatj,' he said.

The creature turned its head to him, struggled. Peter and Corry tightened their grip on it. They'd have to give it another sedative. Get the dose right.

'Back in a minute,' muttered Peter and, bundling the creature in his arms, he left the garden.

'What did you say? What did you call it?' Corry asked, as when someone has hidden the answer you seek.

Pa looked at Owen, Owen at him.

The old man grinned. 'Oh, "Naatj." I said, "Naatj nitjak."'

*

'Naatj?'

'Yeah.'

'Did you ask him what he meant?'

Corry's mouth tightened, her face twitched.

'Sorry,' Peter said, hands up to fend off her anger. 'But ...'

'Of course I did, but he wouldn't say.'

'What were they doing here anyway?'

'It was his day. I forgot, didn't ring him to cancel. The old man often comes along with him, sits in the garden. He knows the language names of all the plants, what you might use some of them for, what lives in them. He's his grandfather.'

'Grandfather? You wouldn't think it, not by the look at them.'

*

Owen and Pa were long gone. They'd turned tail; not a dignified exit, what with the old man being so creaky and stiff, so clumsy in layers and layers of clothing and Owen bobbing around him like a balloon on a string. They kept putting their hands on one another, pushing and grabbing, turning in circles. Corry swept past and opened the gate for them. Their motor wouldn't start, but they'd parked on a hill so they let it roll, and with a yelp of its tyres the car jumped to life, snarled and coughed.

The old man's head nodded as the car jerked, the motor stammering and coughing, gathering its rhythm. He'd turned away from Corry, hunched his shoulders and withdrawn into his clothing yet as he was swept away Corry, waving goodbye, saw his dark, almost skeletal hand emerge from the window, flapping, rotating at the wrist as if caught by the wind, by the car's momentum.

Owen's eyes were fixed on the road ahead.

Tjanak. Balyet. Mambera, or *mammari. Djimbar. Woodartji.* The old man intoned the words, his voice almost disembodied, emanating from a bundle of cloth, listing the names of supposedly mythical and spiritual creatures. Owen leaned into the steering wheel, worked the gear shift.

The structure of his own life was returning: him and the old man, the business of driving a car, the gardening job, navigating here and there, the pleasure of being in that garden ... There was a pattern to it, and he found comfort in settling into what must be habitual activities. But it was small, there was not much substance to it, and this talk of tjanak, of djimbar and balyet and woodatji and the old man's consternation threatened to unravel it, to pull it apart.

'None of them but,' the old man said. 'Course some people get 'em all mixed up; tjanak can be any kind, balyet is sort of like a man but not. Mambera – mammari them others say – is the little one. Woodartji too.'

'But it's not none of them, is it?'

Nope, it wasn't.

'We talked about this on those tapes, unna?'

Owen would have to search the tapes to discover that memory.

'Tjanak, some people called wadjelas that early days, cause how they didn't know nothing, or how to behave properly. Some tjanak, they got spears sticking out from their knees, or funny feet, all kinds of tjanak ... Might be like a big dog. Cannibals some of 'em.

'My old girl, my wife (rest in peace), she woke up and a mambera sitting on her. On her hip, she said, she was lying on her side, see. She didn't open her eyes, but put her hand out and it was like, like a hairy thing but been shaved. Prickly, stubble you know. She couldn't walk properly for months after that ...'

Of course Pa was wondering what they'd seen, that strange creature, tied up and unconscious; if it hadn't struggled he wouldn't even have seen it. He was sure it had responded to the sound of his voice.

'Lots of Noongars,' the old man's thin wrists and neck, twigs and stems held in layers of cotton and wool, in shirts and jumpers and coat, 'they're frightened. You know, get back home before dark or mambera'll get you.

'But not me. Lots of times you could say things to 'em if you know the right way to speak, know the language. When I was a little boy, mambera tried to get me to follow him, but I wouldn't go. So you know what? He followed me home. Woke up, and he was sitting just outside our tent. I didn't tell no one. No one else saw him. He was sitting on the bedroom windowsill when I woke up 'nother morning at my wadjela friend's house. Little fella, hairy – not the wadjela, the mambera I mean. I just ignored him. He went away after a couple of days. Never seen him again.

'Not like this one, but. Different from this one here ...'

They'd stopped in traffic, a line of cars before them waiting to move across the intersection. Pa lowered his window a fraction, and breathed deeply.

'I never seen nothin' like it, 'cept maybe one time – I told you, unna – when I was getting gilgie and I saw its reflection, looking at itself same as I was in the water. Standing behind me.' He laughed. 'I took off that time, same as anyone would. Didn't look back. Wish I'd stayed now.

'Go there tomorrow, do their garden, unna?'

'Mmm.' They moved slowly now, only metres at a time, stop and start, caught in traffic. They halted again. Nice car, thought Owen, glancing to one side, changing radio stations, studying people though a series of windscreens.

*

Owen made two large papier-mâché figures, and left them in the sun to dry. Apparently, he'd planned this; Aunty had said as much, and he'd seen his sketches and notes. The lifeless figures slumped now just outside the circle of firelight enclosing Owen, Pa and Aunty Heather.

'When I was a kid,' she was saying, stroking the hair of the sleepy child on her lap, 'there was a TV show. *The Magic Boomerang.*' She mimed throwing a boomerang, and indicated its spinning flight with her hand. 'They musta got the idea from Aboriginal people, cause someone would throw a boomerang in the air, and time would stop. No blackfellas on the TV, though, not then anyway. Not our kind.'

Owen remembered, in a story the old man once told him: a boomerang, spinning in the air, otherwise motionless in the air and just out of reach, looking like a pool of water in the sky.

Memories, thought Owen. I feel so far from home.

He tilted his head back. The moon commanding the sky, clusters of stars at a distance, and all around him the dark pyramids of roofs.

'She rung, said yeah come tomorrow.'

Pa poked at the fire with his walking stick.

*

'"Naatj," I said, "Naatj nitjak, nitjak naatj," like saying, "What," you know, "What's this," cause I didn't know, and I *don't* know, and you may as well say, "Little shit-stirrer," for all I know, cause as for me …'

'Well, but mammari and that, you think they're real …'

'Mambera – well, some say mammari – and yes, well, true. They're real.'

Peter hoped Pa would continue, but muffled in clothes and with gloves covering his scarred hands Pa just repeated 'True,' and looked at them all, one at a time. Owen dropped his gaze, Aunty Heather and Corry smiled, to show all was well.

'Well, there's no doubt about this, this one is real,' and Peter gestured through the observation window recently installed in the wall shared by laboratory and office.

'Naatj.'

Barely conscious, wedged in cushions and blankets in a corner, the creature suddenly looked up, and Owen felt himself recoil a little from the intensity – even from within a veil of drugs – of the creature's brief glance.

'It's real,' Peter repeated. 'We can care for it, help it. It's not just research for us!'

'Fair enough anyway,' said Pa. 'It's a free country, they reckon, since whiteman found it.'

'It's real, but we can't make out quite what. First, we have to heal it.'

'It's my country,' Pa was adamant, 'where you got this, and you don't need to talk to anyone else: no government, no other Noongars, nothing. They know jack shit. I'm the Native Title Claimant down there. I'm the Traditional Custodian.'

Peter and Corry appreciated the convenience of dealing with one man. They'd tried before to establish Indigenous reference groups for their projects, and had consulted various Indigenous bureaucracies, only to be met half-heartedly. However, just as soon as something tangible came up they'd suddenly find themselves swamped with countless and competing claimants and custodians. So yeah, there'd be other stakeholders. Eventually. Sometime.

Peter insisted, 'We want to do this right. You've got your rights, and we want you involved.'

'But just now,' said Corry, 'we need to give ourselves time, keep it sedated, find what it needs to be comfortable. Find out, really, everything we can.'

'And we need to keep it quiet, that it's here, I mean,' Peter added. 'That's part of the fee, the consultancy fee. Confidentiality.'

Pa nodded. Aunty Heather said, 'Yeah, well … That's right, we can do that. And the boy keeps up the gardening, and maybe you can let him help you out with …'

'Naatj,' said Corry, quickly.

'Good a name as any right now,' Peter laughed.

'Naatj,' said Owen, to himself really, as he left the room. Unobserved, the creature lifted its head.

Westerly

Paradise

Jennifer Robertson

In the beginning there is Eden. We all move into the same house. It is a new house. All the houses in this suburb are new. They look alike, too. Our neighbour's house is just the same as ours except the staircase is on the left – a mirror flip. Our house is big and white. It smells of paint and my new mother.

At night, I get out of the sleeping-bag they have set up for me on the floor. My new sister sleeps on the bed. She sleeps lying on her back with her eyes half-open. It seems she has always slept like this – somewhere between death and a sentry guard. She reminds me of a snake. Cold-blooded, too. My walk to his room is all carpet and white doors. Soft white carpet under my bare feet. His room, though, is dark. There is a medicinal smell of acne cream. I can make out the dark blues and greens of his bed-spread and him, lying on his side, feigning sleep. He has been waiting for me. But we both pretend not to know this.

I stand by his bed.

'Eden?'

He rolls over onto his back, sloppy in his false sleep.

'Hey, babe.'

He pulls me on top of him.

In the nights that follow we do not talk about what is going on between us. To talk about such things would be to suggest we have a future. We have no future. Instead we play strip monopoly, smoke reefer and have sex. I have never had sex before and conclude it is painful but necessary. We climb out his bedroom window, sit on the roof and look out on the inky blackness of suburbia.

None of this happens in the daytime. The harshness of the sun makes it implausible. I can't figure out if my nightly visits are dreams. Nobody says anything. But they must know or suspect.

Our family goes on road trips. We sell Bibles for the church and spread The Word. I sit in the back seat between my new sister and Eden. It is summer and I am wearing a short skirt. The car's upholstery sticks to the backs of my thighs. The heat makes me vaguely carsick.

'Praise the Lord, it's time for a lunch break,' my father says, smiling weakly at his feeble joke. We stop at a restaurant on the side of the highway called 'Caesar's'. The toilets are in an outside building separate from the restaurant.

'And praise be, it's time to pee!' my new mother chimes.

They all stomp off. Eden and I are left alone together. I lean on the side of the car. One foot tucked up behind me, knee bent: teen coquettishness. I put my hands palms down on the warm metal.

'Hey.'

'Hey.'

He comes closer to me. He jabs a finger on the exposed skin somewhere between my navel and my crotch.

He smirks.

'Damn, girl, you should put on some weight. You're bones.'

I simper.

'Shut up.'

Pause.

'Bones.'

He rubs his bone against me.

The family re-enters the scene. We go inside the restaurant.

I am achingly aware of him, of the way he sits across the table from me and the amount of his knee touching my knee. I'm so mesmerised by my proximity to him that with an unwitting flick of my hand I overturn my glass of water. It is so appallingly dramatic. The whole family yells, 'Whoa!' Water spills across the table and down into Eden's crotch. Red-faced, I meet his inscrutable gaze. He stands up. The dark circle on his jeans grows. It looks like he's wet himself. He walks off to the bathroom leaving the family laughing.

'If that were me, hon, he would have blew the roof,' my new mother comments.

Again and again I offer myself up as a present to my new brother. He is tender as he puts a pillow behind my head.

'Are you OK?' he asks.

'Mmmhmm.'

But despite this, it still hurts. I try not to flinch. Instead, I put on an expression of fixed ecstasy. The more it hurts the more attachment I feel. I have to stuff my face into the pillow to stop myself from pleading: 'Do you love me?'

I learn my blood is cherry-coloured.

Later we roll onto our sides and hug. Now I feel a real sort of ecstasy – a small patch of paradise in my mind. I feel content. For once, I feel safe. I consider the bruises on my thighs glorious battle scars. Half-asleep, I am happy.

He turns to me and says, 'This is just fun, right?'

'Again, Lord, we thank you for bringing Elfride and her father into our lives so that they might also share in your goodness. And for the glorious food we are about to receive may we be truly thankful.'

It is my new mother's turn to say grace. She likes to ham it up with 'glory glories' and 'blessed bes'. When it is his turn, my father prefers a simple grace. Nevertheless, he smiles at Sharlene now.

What we are eating is something my new mother calls Graveyard Stew – chunks of meat bob up and down in murky brown sauce. It's her specialty. The recipe is supposed to be a secret but I know the secret: cut-price meat from Lucky's Mega-Mart and Oxo cubes.

'How many Daisy the Cows were killed in the making of this?' Eden looks at me with a glint in his eye.

Somehow, Eden can get away with comments like this. Sharlene just smiles benignly.

'The Good Lord created beasts, Eden, so that we, humans, might eat them.'

My new mother seems to regard her son with a mixture of fear and admiration – as if she can't quite figure out how someone like him could have been brought forth from her doughy loins.

We return to eating. My father eats silently, almost apologetically, and with reverence for the food. Sharlene is fast and noisy. She soaks up liquid with slices of bread and plunges them down her gullet. My new sister makes conscious slurping noises and fidgets like the eleven year old she is. Eden sits low in his chair and smirks at me evilly through spoonfuls of the stuff.

'Mum, how long do I have to share my room with Elfride for?' My new sister scowls at me from under lowered eyelids.

Eden is quick.

'Don't be rude. Elfride's the one who's had to move into a new house with all of us and get used to everything and share with you, twerp. Learn some fucking manners.'

'Mum he said "fuck".'

'Eden, I will not have swearing at my table. Baby Girl was just upset, that's all. It's hard getting used to sharing your room with someone new. You weren't offended were you, Elfride?'

My new mother looks at me.

'No, not at all.' I try to efface myself behind my water glass.

'There you go, no harm done,' she says, but her eyes linger on me speculatively. She looks at Eden and then back at me, as if she only now realises the size of what has blossomed before her.

There is no one truth in the memories I have of my mother. My real one, that is, who existed in a time before Eden. I can't separate what I actually remember of her from what I've been told or what I have just imagined. I seem to recall a summer when I was very little before she went away and before my father found The Lord.

The day was impossibly hot and all the blinds and curtains in the house were drawn. The rooms glowed deep orange like the inside of a lung and the walls pulsated as if the house itself were breathing in and out. I had been crying. My mother was sitting in a chair by her bed. There was a blanket across her lap, which seemed strange to me given the heat of the day. I crawled into her lap and lay my sniffily wet face on her shoulder. She smelt of talcum powder, sweat and sweet jasmine, but there was something else – the ripe, unmistakable smell of an invalid.

At church on Sunday, Marcie, from across the street, tells me how she fucks boys up against the church car park wall. Or, rather, they fuck her. 'It doesn't count if you're not lying down,' she tells me.

I make a face.

'Don't be such a prude, Elfride. It's not like I'm a slut or anything. Besides, I take it up the ass so I'm still a virgin.'

I express mild incredulity.

'I'm a Christian for Christ's sake. I'm still saving myself for my wedding night. This is just fun. Everyone has fun, Elfride.'

Sensing my lack of enthusiasm, Marcie changes tack.

'You know everyone's saying you're a godless communist because you won't go to youth group. Your brother goes. He's heaps cute, too. Anyway, everyone thinks you're weird. Is it true you're a lesbian?'

No, Marcie, I think to myself, I'm not a lesbian. I'm just in love with my stepbrother. I sleepwalk into his arms every night and it feels like heavenly drowning. What is happening between us is like dissected fruit. It tastes good but looks obscene. I ache for him like a cut-open pomegranate. In equal measures, I long to dwell in and escape from this imperfect paradise.

I'm standing in the kitchen with my new mother. We peel apples over blue enamelled bowls. She is teaching me to make pies.

'You've never made a pie?' she asks, incredulous.

She has asked me to call her 'Mum' but I resist and continue to call her Sharlene. It is a small act of defiance on my part. It goes along with my other pathetic gestures. My so-called 'dark looks' and my aversion to the church.

'You need to socialise more. Go out with some of Eden's friends. I'm sure there's a nice quiet one that you would get on just a treat with.'

I'm not openly hostile. I'm described as shy and sweet. But they sense, they know, that I have quietly refused to commit to this life. I see it as a temporary condition. The only thing permanent is Eden. I have a vision of him sitting at the bottom of a lake. Quietly waiting. I will rescue him and he will fall in love with me.

The front door opens and shuts. Eden's home. He comes into the kitchen and smirks.

'Women in the kitchen, that's what I like to see.'

'I'm teaching Elfride to make a Graham Cracker base.'

She pronounces it 'gram'. It annoys me to a surprising degree.

By the window I can see the whole street and enjoy the rounded darkness of evening. I can see Marcie naked, walking back and forth in front of her window. She's an exhibitionist but an insecure one. I'm like that. I can identify people's frailties. I pity them. I can see my own, too, but that doesn't stop me from carrying on.

Eden has told me it can't work out between us. I'm his sister; I can't be his girlfriend. It's sick. Besides, if he doesn't go out with other girls it will look weird. But that doesn't stop him coming to the door every night after my new sister has fallen asleep and taking me back to his room. We lie together in the sad brown light of the early morning until it gets so late it's dangerous.

Outside in the street a car pulls up in the driveway. Eden gets out and walks quickly and lightly around to the passenger side to let her out. The girl takes her time fixing her make-up and then slides out, yanking at her skirt. I get into my sleeping-bag and press my body against the wall. I hear them creeping up the stairs.

'Shut up, we'll get caught.'

The girl giggles.

I hear them fall heavily, clumsily, onto the bed and break my heart. I hear her half-heartedly say, 'Stop it, Eden.' It begins with giggling and groans. I cling closer to the wall. My stomach turns to paste. My bowels are water. But I listen intently. I don't move for minutes as they slam against one another and the bed creaks something violent and unhappy. Again, I see Eden at the bottom of a lake waiting for me to rescue him.

It is over eventually. He says goodbye to her in our front yard. The girl is still giggling. He trips up the stairs and back to his room.

Later, he comes for me and I go to him.

Griffith Review

Drive

John Kinsella

He checked the saplings out front and then went back inside.
Eucalypts, they'd made it through the summer, and were looking
sturdy. It was his achievement, his reason for being outside, with
the paddocks spreading around. The place was an island, and
the trees would grow to screen out the unwanted. He looked
through the window at them, vigorous alongside the gravel drive.
Yes, they would survive. He flicked on the television – news, a
game show. He switched it off again and heard the cross-cutting
peals of pink and greys lifting suddenly as a flock: they aren't just
raucous, he thought, they are modern. They work together by
working against each other. They are making new mythologies,
as well as the old. Timeless. Silence.

Then a rumbling, a sound he hasn't heard for years. He looks
outside and jolts. He is suddenly out the door screaming Fuck
me dead! as a dozen horses gallop towards the saplings, halting
just before them, and he sees the eucalyptus leaves tremble. The
horses – mares and geldings – start tearing chunks of dried wild
oats and radishes out of the dirt. Slowly they calm down, they
concentrate on their eating. He sees the shire ranger is on the
drive, and behind her the 'Horse Woman', his neighbour. They
are working around the horses to drive them back up onto the
road.

In a decade he's only talked with the Horse Woman on four
or five occasions. She's always out in the paddocks or on the

road, riding, with her strapper following: a girl of a certain age, always the same age, year in year out, thin and sullen, who can tame the wildest horse. He sees the Horse Woman most days, of course – in the distance, riding past ... calling to her horses, yelling at the strapper ... but they've only spoken those few times. They don't even greet each other as he drives slowly past her riding along the gravel shoulders.

The Horse Woman starts to yell at her horses. Down the road there are cop cars blocking 'exit holes': the T-junction, gateways. This is obviously a *major incident*. It all slows down for him and he looks past the ranger, who is moving cautiously, at his neighbour: she is tough and small. In her riding pants she looks asexual. He has never thought of her as being separate from her horses. Their immensity against her slightness. She has a reputation around town, and no one bothers her. She has trained stayers and bolters. By her house, she keeps the great stallions that service the mares. In the paddocks behind his house most years there are foals gambolling. He finds this soothing.

The Horse Woman gets behind the horses and he walks closer. The ranger calls to him to block the top of the drive – we'll drive them out the other side where the fence is down. He asks what has happened. Someone left a gate open ... He senses the ranger's disgust. We found them halfway to town. Not the first time.

Years ago, the last time he spoke to the Horse Woman, it was after someone had shot one of the horses. Horses bring out the best and worst in people, he thought. Horses aggravate humans like no other animals, strangely ... he wondered why. He had been around horses, vaguely, indirectly, his whole life, and could head them off without a problem. He watched the Horse Woman get behind them. Get on! Get on! Whoowhoowhoo! Whoowhoowhoo! Ya! Ya! she called. Then she whistled like he'd whistled with his brother when they were young, driving the sheep towards the shed. Horses respond like sheep, he thought. They leapt and kicked, then ignored the calls and started eating again. One broke away towards him and he could see it was the leader so the others would follow. So quiet now, so unused to speaking to people ... he found it in himself to call at the horses. Get back! Get back! Ya ya ya! He clapped his hands. He'd always been embarrassed doing this, but he felt good about it now. He yelled louder and louder, so much so the ranger stopped her driving and looked at him. He didn't let it stop him.

The Horse Woman was right behind them now, and he could see the sinews of her neck working hard as she yelled. He noticed she had blonde highlights through her hair. Never thought how old she is ... maybe fifty, but it's hard to tell ... skin exposed to the season, like her horses. Maybe she was younger, or older. The horses stopped dead still, eating, swishing their tails. Then, abruptly, she picked up a paddy melon and threw it at an old mare. The melon – noxious infesting weed in those parts, that he thought he'd removed entirely from the paddock – burst over the flank of the old mare, which kicked and bolted, Ya, get a move on, you old bitch, you old slut ... called the Horse Woman, liquid and pale unformed seeds spilling down the mare's flank, leg. Since she was not the lead horse, the group compacted with the mare's charge, and stood their ground. The Horse Woman picked up another missed melon, and he opened his mouth to say No! but nothing came out. He felt like that statue, *The Caller* ... the mouth shaped, the intention written in the features, but eternal silence. He saw the ranger semi-laughing. The next salvo hit the lead gelding: Move, ya fuckin old whore ... bitch slut ... move ya ball-less wonder! With that, the horses charged onto the road and down the bitumen towards the police cars blocking the town end of the T-junction.

Mesmerised, he was drawn along behind them and caught up to the Horse Woman. Do you still want help? he muttered. Yes, block any holes you see. She didn't look at him. Driving them back towards their paddock under the hill, he worked alongside her, calling and clapping. He noticed that some of the older horses had numbers written on their shoulders: not branded, but something close to that. He feared for them, the old bitches.

He was hot, his heart pumping, and kept calling even as the horses trotted in a mannered way towards their place. Behind him, cop cars that had come from around the district, called in by the ranger as part of a general SOS, rolled slowly as back-up, calling out to the ranger, telling her it was good exercise and that they'd signed up with the force just to witness such occasions. The horses slipped through the gate in single file, and then fanned out at a gallop, all of them suddenly lead horses, looking relieved to be there. The strapper – different face, but same age – was at the gate and closed it behind them. He spoke to the sullen girl, her eyes downcast, conscious the Horse Woman was looking closely. He remembered the story of how the Horse Woman was said to watch her animals mate, and felt uncomfortable. He said quickly to the girl, You better lock it up tight. The girl said something indecipherable back and didn't look at him.

He retreated and stood near the Horse Woman. She turned to one of the cops who had just emerged from a patrol car. Locked it after I was in there this morning. It's been opened. I've lost three gallopers over the years – shot. Found bullet shells up here the other day. He spoke then: I heard a shot a few weeks ago. I rang the police. They said not to worry, it's the country, what do you expect. But I've been here all my life and I know there are places you don't hear shots. Yes, I heard that – it was a high-calibre rifle, the woman said ... thanks for ringing the cops, maybe they'll work out that there's a pattern to this. Don't ask us, said a police sergeant, we're from out of town! The Horse Woman ignored him and spoke to her neighbour again. Spoke to him. Remember, years ago, after one of my horses was shot, you said you heard shots then as well. I did, he said, the horses are in the paddock behind me, my house is closest to them. I listen out for them.

The cops melted away, and the ranger went off to file a report, and the strapper walked into the paddock, wandering nowhere in particular. The Horse Woman looked at her reclusive neighbour – he was dripping sweat and panting. Want a lift back up to your place? she asked. He hesitated, slightly – *she* didn't have a drop of sweat on her, and her breath was the same as always. Took it out of me! he laughed. Jump in then, she said, brushing past him as she opened the passenger door. He felt a different heat rise in him – he stepped back: No, no ... I'll be right ... still a bit of gallop left in these legs. He felt her staring at him as he headed back up to his place. Those horses are a lot of work for her, he thought. But then the saplings, their resilience. Winter was almost there, and steady rains were predicted.

Over the Sea

Sonja Dechian

When the plane begins to fall out of the sky, Simon doesn't take any solace in the fact that he knows the safety demonstrations off by heart. He knows about the brace position. But it seems too late for that. It is too late.

It feels strange to be dying.

Yet, strangely, there is time to recap.

Subtly, every aircraft is different.

The Qantas in-flight safety video. Life jackets, gas masks, deep vein thrombosis. *Subtly,* it says, *every aircraft is different.* Especially this one.

And every time you fly, you will almost certainly be sitting in a different seat. That's why it's important to take a few moments to view our safety demonstration.

Just a few hours and a short nap earlier, Simon ignored the safety demonstration that the flight crew so deftly performed as they all taxied together along the runway. Simon preferred not to watch. He already knew to look out for life preservers under seats and baggage shifting in overhead lockers. But he couldn't remember a day when he had watched all that choreography. Really watched.

Once again, he pulled his dark blue blanket up high, plugged in headphones ready for the start of the in-flight entertainment program, and closed his eyes. He figured the safety information had been repeated and heard so many times that it had probably cemented itself inside some universal consciousness. It would be there if he needed it. He wondered if people in Third World countries who had never flown (or never even seen movies about flying, or even seen *any* movies) knew about the row of lights that would appear and lead passengers to the nearest exit, in the unlikely event of an emergency.

Simon was relieved to be under his blanket with his head-phones on. His legs were tired from three hours of pacing the terminal browsing duty-free, trying to decide whether it was worth buying a bottle of whisky or not. He'd decided it was. Of course it was.

A day earlier, Simon had been pacing the streets of the city, trying to locate the Qantas office, feeling, for once, entirely alive. It was a horrific feeling. Unheard of amounts of sweat smeared parts of his body that he couldn't politely wipe clean. A trail of perspiration made its way along his spine at unpredictable inter-vals, eroding previous layers and building mountains of grime. Meanwhile, he continued to breathe, the angry Bangkok air grat-ing at his insides.

Simon adjusted his blanket to show the flight attendant that yes, his seatbelt was done up. He thought about the young woman in the Qantas office who had changed his flights. He'd tried to tell her about his ordeal, how everyone had given him wrong directions and how the name of the street had been incorrectly translated from Thai.

She was about his age, which was twenty-five. She might have been younger. She was beautiful, but she had no idea what he was talking about. He felt inadequate speaking his own language to her. So he'd imagined what her naked breasts would look like as she tapped away on her keyboard. The slow cool of the tradi-tional Thai (arctic temperature) airconditioning was finally working its way into his sweaty crevices. He enjoyed thinking that this was the same air that made the woman's nipples stand so erect.

It was the physicality of Bangkok that shocked Simon. He'd spent the last six months wrapped inside a Canadian winter. He'd felt safe there. The snow and the whiteness had helped to clear his mind, much like the rhythms of air travel. The comings and goings of flight attendants, their identical outfits, the turning down of lights: all as predictable as the hum of the engines that would lull him to sleep. In comparison, Bangkok burned his senses. Strangers called to him on the street. Desperate, skinny mothers looked him in the eye, demanding compassion. Dirt collected in the cracks of his heels as something in him began to stir. His skin prickled and his eyes watered. He had to get out of there. He'd gone to bed with an erection three nights in a row and had almost forgotten what to do about it.

When the plane took off, the roar of the engine and the welcome force that flattened Simon into his seat swept these things from him. He fought to make himself blank again.

Three days in Bangkok, erased.

Something had happened to Simon.

Not something big, just a smattering of small moments that he had allowed to numb him. People tended not to notice. They assumed him to be sharply observant in only the intellectual sense. It's often impossible to tell what someone is feeling, or whether they are feeling at all. So it was not people's fault if they saw Simon wrongly. Or if they didn't notice when he erased the part of himself that had been overwhelmed by too much feeling.

The compulsion to erase didn't grow so strong as a result of any one single thing. It was a kind of critical mass of shocks and blows that forced Simon to begin to bury parts of himself. It was a necessary kind of suffering, because its ultimate goal was safety.

A summary of the kinds of moments that burned Simon might have three major points.

1. The first thing

Simon was playing with two jars, a rough circle of cardboard torn from the back of a cereal box, and a yellow plastic gardening trowel. He was catching ants and worms and sorting them into different jars, a task which, in his six-year-old mind, served some greater purpose. They would be happier this way.

He was distracted for a moment by the rush of ants across the paving. He loved the way they followed one another, forming long and frantic pathways across all sorts of terrain. He imagined their underground cities and their day-to-day concerns. Simon loved the ants. In the dusk, he squinted at the sunset light and squatted by the edge of the driveway. He sat fully motionless, unaware of the stiffness in his legs because he was too deep into his contemplation of the ants' nest. Just the sound of his own breathing and the sound he imagined ants made when their antennae touched or their feet padded on the grass. It was the most perfect world. So tiny and fast that Simon could oversee a lifetime. He dug his toes into the soft soil at the edge of the paving and felt the happiness of sunshine on his face and the silent turning of the world. On and on.

When the screen door flew open and his mother's voice trailed out, Simon looked up just fast enough to realise his mistake. Being happy was a misleading distraction. Words had not yet formed inside his mother; she had not figured out how to explain these things. But her face showed the type of fear that adults should not know, the fear that children lived with and hoped would be dissipated by age and knowledge and responsibility. He had no name for it. But in the following days, Simon would remember that in the moment his grandfather had a heart attack and died, he had been thinking of ants.

If you forgot the possibility of terror, it would remind you. You had to remember.

2. The second thing, which stayed in his mind for a really long time

Simon was nineteen when he first gained unrestricted access to the Internet. He looked up all the normal things like porn, neo-Nazi websites and blogs written by anorexic girls. He illegally downloaded all sorts of things.

Then he saw the picture.

And it wasn't the fault of technology or the Internet because it was a photo he could have seen in a library or a bookshop anywhere. Or maybe a museum. But something about the unexpected nature of this photo – the way it was linked to a forum about music (so he'd had no idea what it was going to be when he clicked on the link) – made him feel reckless. So he clicked (maybe he had *wanted* to find it all along). Something about it shifted his sense of the world and of himself.

It was a picture of a soldier. It was less than black-and-white, maybe brown-and-yellow. Not because it was old, but because it had been taken in a place where that was the colour of the world. And the soldier was dead. He was so much more than dead, though, because the description beneath the photo read: *This soldier has been run over by a tank.*

He had been alive, and then he was something between alive and mincemeat, and then he was dead. And worse, someone had thought to photograph it, and then someone had thought to post the photo online.

And then: Simon.

He watched the man's body, tried to make out the shape of the dead man's limbs, his insides. He mentally put the man back together and watched him re-die, over and over. He took the man to bed with him that night, blood and guts and mincemeat and all. Simon couldn't erase him. And even if he could have rewound and unclicked and gone to bed that night without that image to keep him warm, Simon would not have changed things. That was the thing about knowledge. Even when it changed everything, it brought you tumbling closer to the truth. And that made it impossible for Simon to wish he could unknow this man.

3. The third thing

Going to the gym wasn't really very satisfying but Simon liked the feeling of keeping his body busy. He joined because he figured he should be fitter and because he liked to keep things moving. Walking on the treadmill occupied parts of him, leaving less of himself to deal with. True, it felt kind of ridiculous because he wasn't getting anywhere, but there weren't many options when it was too hot or cold to be outside.

He was bemused by the other members. Hyper-fit and lycra-clad, or ageing flesh in faded tracksuits. It was all the same. The people didn't change and sometimes he wondered if he should tell them that they all looked just as fat/thin/tired as they had a month ago. He didn't do it. But he thought about it.

There was this one girl. A girl who tied her dark hair back and jogged while reading books he could never see the titles of. Sometimes she wore headphones. She looked his age. Simon started to arrive earlier to coincide with her visits but was too embarrassed to walk beside her, because he walked while she ran effortlessly. But he watched her.

The girl wore dark grey, fleece-lined running shorts. They were slightly too big, so they flapped as she ran.

She had long, smooth legs and Simon quickly got into the habit of imagining the air that ran over them as it circulated around the tops of her thighs, beneath the flapping of her cotton shorts, up over the curves of her hips and under her waistband.

The first time they talked was in the line for the water fountain. A fat man ahead of them guzzled down what seemed like litres of water. Simon and the girl exchanged glances that meant *leave some water in the fucking reservoir*. While they waited, Simon asked the girl what she was listening to on her headphones that day.

'Interpol,' she said, 'NYC.'

Simon was quick to reply, 'So, why is the subway a porno, then?'

And the girl frowned, 'I always wonder that.'

He watched her drink. Then he put his lips to the same water and thought of kissing her. When he finished drinking, he looked up and wiped his mouth and she was still watching. Still standing beside him. They were awkward because it was apparent that of the two of them, no one was not thinking about kissing.

Later, away from the gym and the lycra and the sweat, there was kissing. She was charmed by his vulnerability and he was not afraid to have her see through him.

They'd still meet at the gym, though now they walked on adjacent treadmills. They read one another articles from boring magazines. Simon struggled to walk and read at the same time. But she always laughed when he tripped up on the treadmill and had to catch himself. And the discomfort of looking foolish was worth the sound of her laughter. He might have let himself fall in love with her and with that sound.

One afternoon, he was supposed to pick her up from her house. It was after three p.m. and he was late. He had taken to knocking at the backdoor because no one ever went to the front. He rounded the corner of the house and found her in the backyard, hanging out her washing. Her yellow jumper (two pegs).

A pair of black stockings (one peg). Her brown knitted top (reaching for a spare peg). She had not seen him.

Still in her fleece-lined running shorts, she reached up to peg a pair of black underpants to the line. Her legs, long and pale. Fine blonde hairs glinted on her thighs. Simon felt the breeze that caught the edge of the stockings on the line. They rippled. The same air caught up and around the edges of her shorts, and then traced the edges that his hands now knew. Her pale arms extended and her neck was revealed to the light.

She was so vulnerable. Hair, flesh, blood. Her heart beat. He imagined it pulsing, her blood forced through veins, and tiny cells scrambling like ants in tunnels. He imagined her mortality.

Simon withdrew. He watched her from the end of a long tunnel. She knew him. Yet all her terrible faith in him was wasted because he turned away in silence and he left her that day.

As he walked back along the driveway in silence, Simon focused on not stepping on ants or cracks.

Simon does not think of her – of any of these moments – as the plane hangs in the air somewhere between Denpasar and Darwin. With the evening meal complete and his tray-table safely stowed, Simon turns off his reading light and tries to sleep. He is unconcerned, mainly. He's thinking about the plane touching down in Melbourne and about the number of hours he has to pass between now and then. Simon kicks his shoes further under the seat ahead of him. The woman beside him laughs softly at the in-flight movie. Simon closes his eyes.

And this is when something big happens to Simon.

It feels just like turbulence at first. The way a storm might feel, except that instead of all that side-to-side and up-and-down there's only a sudden shift to the left and then a lot of down. Quite a lot of down. The lights flicker on and babies start screaming. An old woman stands up in her seat and starts to panic in a foreign language. But most people remain quiet because the possibility of a disaster is small and they don't want to embarrass themselves by doing anything they might live to regret.

When oxygen masks fall from overhead, adults give in to panic. Parents hush children and the old woman can no longer stand up. Everyone expects the pilot's voice to reassure them (*Ladies and Gentlemen*, it will begin). But the pilot remains silent. The PA crackles to life and someone tries to say something but then the lights start to flicker out and it's really too late to deny what is happening. They are falling out of the sky.

Now it is too late for epiphanies. The world has changed; it has crumbled and reassembled itself, this time with secret tunnels and ant hills in human size.

People find their life vests folded neatly under their seats. They have a single strap, a light, and a whistle for attracting attention. Some things can always be relied upon.

Simon wouldn't have expected to be afraid. He's afraid of a lot of things. But not dying. He's spent a lot of time contemplating reality from a safe distance. Now, Simon discovers that he does believe in the world after all. With a thud, Simon falls safely out of his tunnel and into the reality that he is about to die. He struggles to release his seatbelt, to find his oxygen mask, to grab his life vest. The woman next to him has begun to pray. He feels a rush of anger and swears at her under his breath. *Fuck!* He feels a rush of sadness. Fear. Fear! He feels just about everything there is. *Fuck!* He yells. He starts to scream. Simon is alive. Simon is about to die. Simon screams.

Fuck!

And no one tells him not to.

When the plane crashes into the ocean, everyone on board clutches the chairs in front of them. They clutch their neighbours. Two women in First Class hold hands and cry, screaming the names and ages of their children (*Kelly, three-and-a-half! Jason, nine-next-Thursday!*). A man in Business Class hyperventilates while two old men in Economy (rows thirty-eight and seventy-two) are already dead. Everyone else clutches at the hope that maybe, maybe they will be the one to survive. And if they do, things will be different. (*Please, God!*)

The water floods in through a hole in the body of the plane.

People scramble. It's dark. People scream. The drowning starts. Most likely, this happens very quickly.

Simon, who is not dead, sits very still with his eyes tightly closed. He listens to his heart beat. The wonderful beating of his own heart. He is alive. He starts to laugh.

It is the most wonderful laughter. All the joy of living. Ants in tiny tunnels hear his laughter. Simon has been wrong.

He opens his eyes and an eerie light has lit the plane's interior. People all around are laughing. Bewildered, they're taking off their seatbelts and laughing. As the water pours in and the air bubbles out, babies hiccup and old ladies perform underwater somersaults. Seatbelts click off. Everyone has been wrong. Simon floats up out of his seat and smiles at the woman beside him, who has let off on the praying and is holding her hands over her heart. (Was she right all along?) Simon basks in this eternal life.

A baby wriggles up over the seat ahead of him and Simon leans over to untangle her foot from the cord of her gas mask. The baby clutches at his hands and giggles. He lifts her and forgets himself for a moment.

Anything seems possible as they float inside that sinking tube. Simon smiles at strangers and thinks about tomorrow.

Sleepers Almanac

Loved Her More than Lettuce

Gavin Carver

I like to throw four balls up in the air and see if they make a square. If they do, I take a photograph of them with my new digital camera. It's so great having a digital camera because now I can take as many pictures as I want of the balls in the air, which improves my chances of getting photos of good-shaped squares. Tonight I've got four good shots already.

Before my new Kodak CX7430 digital camera I had to use an old film camera, which was tricky and expensive. It meant that sometimes, even when I thought I caught the balls making a square in a photo, it would take a long time to find out if I did because of having to get the film developed. I guess the only downside to having my new camera is that I don't get as excited when I get a good square in the picture because now I can get the good pictures more easily.

This is what I like to do when I'm at home, which is a lot. I've always found good things to do by myself. I'm used to being alone. I prefer it because I'm used to it. Not like when she came along and made me unhappy. I've got rid of her now because she made me so angry and upset. She messed me and everything up for a while. I feel like screaming sometimes when I think about her. It was nice for a bit but mostly she made me crazy.

I met her at work and she came on to me so strong. She was new and she looked at me sexily on her first day. From then on I just knew that she wanted to do stuff with me. After she started at the office where I work I would go home and throw the balls in the air and every now and then they would just drop to the ground before I realised I wasn't even looking at them, I was thinking of her. She said hello to me every day. She would say 'Good morning, Dwayne,' and 'See you tomorrow, Dwayne.' It made me feel so good because not many people at work really speak to me.

I'm a Filing Officer and as well as filing I do what's called data entry too. Her job was pretty much the same as mine except she didn't do data entry because she was new and only I knew how to do it properly.

She sat in front of me at work and I used to just look at her all day. She looked heavy and wore long dresses that always had flowers on them. Her hair was curly and brown and I used to imagine myself inside the folds of her arms and kissing her face a lot.

After a couple of weeks of daydreaming about her all the time, I decided to put a note on her desk. I had written it out a hundred times until I got it just right. It was frustrating because even after I worked out what I wanted to say, I would get to the end and realise I'd made a mistake with one of the words and have to start all over again. Then I would make more mistakes and I'd have to keep starting again.

The note said: *Hello. Would you like to have lunch with me? From Dwayne.* I put it on her desk when she wasn't there. I can't tell you how nervous I was! I was *so* nervous. At first she didn't see the note and I thought, *Oh no! She's not going to see the note.* But thank goodness, after a few minutes she unfolded the piece of paper I had put on her desk. She read my message and then folded it over again. I didn't know what she was thinking. I was so, so sure she liked me in that way, but now I was so scared I started to sweat and I could feel my heart just going kakathudoom, kakathudoom.

It seemed like it took forever but it's funny thinking back about it now; funny because it only took as long as it did for her to write her reply, which was only about two-and-a-half, maybe three minutes. Without even looking at me she stood up and walked towards my desk. I watched her, waiting for her to look at me, but she didn't. Then, guess what happened? It was really sophisticated – even though I hate her now, it was sophisticated. She dropped a note on my desk as she walked past. I waited for her to take a few more steps then I read the note. It said: *I would love to. How about tomorrow?*

She wrote the word love, which I read over and over. It felt like we were already having a secret office thingy, just like I know some of the other rude buggers at my work are. I wanted to write something really funny and clever so that she could see how smart I could be, but I didn't have much time because she would be back any minute. So I just wrote: *Yes. I'll meet you in the park at twelve-thirty.* It was really scribbly writing because of how nervous I was, but you could still read it. I put it on her desk. When she came back and read it she turned around and smiled.

That night I couldn't think of anything else but her. I didn't play with my balls at all. I worked out what I was going to wear, which was easy since most of my clothes are the same anyway. And I thought a lot about what we could talk about because I hadn't even spoken to her more than just saying hello.

The next day I could tell she was more done up than usual. We met in the park and it was good. Even though I was nervous, and she was too, we spoke about lots of things. I told her about stuff I like to do, like just pick a place on the train map and go there. I told her how I called the numbers out at bingo and read the quiz questions on trivia night. She thought it was so funny when I told her that I mainly did it because I liked hearing my voice through the speakers. She laughed a lot and I wasn't even *trying* to be funny.

Some people from work saw us at the park and I could see them pointing and laughing. At first I was embarrassed, but when she told me how rude she thought everyone at work was I wasn't embarrassed anymore because I felt the same. Together we didn't care. After that we had lunch together every day for a week, then I took her out for dinner and we came back to my place and did it. It was better than I had ever imagined. The next morning though, I started to get nervous about what it would be like if she stopped liking me. But mostly I was having heaps of fun with her. Most things I liked to do before were on my own and now we were always thinking of stuff to do together, which was really different.

A couple of days later she came on the train with me and let me pick a place on the map the way I normally do, which is by standing with my back to the map and just spinning around with my finger pointed out and seeing where it hits. She laughed so much when I did that. She mustn't have seen anyone do it before. But when we got to where we were going, she started complaining that her feet were sore, even though we hadn't walked very far, and that she was hungry. She was hungry a lot because she was so heavy. I wasn't hungry at all really and she was too ashamed to eat more than me, so mostly she was still hungry and tried to talk me into eating a lot. It wasn't a very good day. She didn't even come back to my place afterwards! I wanted to see what her place was like, but she told me she was embarrassed to take me there because her flatmate was so messy.

That night, even though the day wasn't as good as when I go by myself to new places, I still thought how much I enjoyed being with her. She was funny and made me feel sexy a lot, especially when we were tongue kissing and I was playing with her melons. I told her I liked her melons and she blushed, but I was glad I said melons instead of tits because that would have been ungentlemanly. I remembered all my manners and opened doors for her and stuff like that. We went through one door that you had to push inwards. It was really heavy and I had to try extra hard to open it with one arm while she walked past, and because she is wider than most people, she kind of had to squash through it. She didn't like that I thought it was funny.

I don't know why she didn't want to come back to my place and I was scared that maybe after our day together she didn't like me as much. This really made me mad, because if that was true then it wasn't fair because I was a bit nervous and she didn't see the real me at all. I started to play the balls-in-a-square game again and after getting a couple of good shots I decided to write her a love letter. That's what that game does for me. It makes me think of things and work things out, even though I'm doing something else. This means I can do two things at once. I wanted to tell her how much I loved her and really show her with words. But every time I tried to think of something I would get stuck. All I could write was: *I love you.* I wanted to say more because everybody says that and it's not very original and I wanted to be special. Then I remembered that when we were having lunch I told her how much I loved lettuce. So I wrote: *I love you more than lettuce.* I was so excited that night I couldn't sleep. The next day I was going to tell her I loved her more than lettuce. I hadn't said 'I love you' to her before and I hoped that she would tell me she loved me too, more than something else she really loves – maybe cake.

The next morning I went to work early so that I could be there before she got in and put the note on her desk. I'm so stupid for even doing this, or even thinking I loved her, because I hate her now, hate her more than brussels sprouts. When I put the note on her desk, someone saw but I didn't know someone saw. That someone was that mongrel James Percy but I call him James Penis. He went over to her desk and pretended to put something there for her and picked up the note.

Later that morning everyone was standing around the notice-board laughing. I went over to have a look and saw my note. James Penis had written her name at the top and put my name at the bottom. I was so embarrassed that I just said, 'Very funny, very funny,' and took the note down. I was so mad and she was so embarrassed too. She didn't even look at me that day, but at the very end, when I was getting ready to go home, she walked past and bent down and whispered in my ear. She said, 'I love you too.' Well, I was *so* happy. I had forgotten all about people making fun of us and all I could see were stars and sparkles, just like in the movies. She kept on walking and I sat there, all numb and funny like my bones had turned into rubber. Nobody had said that to me before, not sexily anyway. I felt like a man, and I knew then that as long as we had each other everything was going to be terrific.

She started coming around a lot after that and we spent most of our time together at my flat. We didn't have any privacy at her apartment to fool around and do stuff because her flatmate was usually there. I have my own place which is just one room with everything in it, bed, kitchen, a TV and a table. I don't have much stuff, mainly because it's not that big, and also because I need room to play the balls-in-a-square game. I keep it very clean and she told me that she liked me because I had a tidy place.

Before I knew it we were spending all of our time together. At first this is what I really wanted but then most of the stuff I liked to do wasn't as enjoyable anymore. She started helping me with the balls-in-a-square game and it stopped being as fun because it was getting easier to do. I knew she wasn't really enjoying it either. Then she wanted to come to bingo and trivia night. She used to sit and play by herself and not talk to anyone. She told me it was a bit boring so I asked her if she wanted to read the questions and numbers out with me. She was really good at it, but people liked the way she did it a bit better because she would put in little stories and jokes. She was mucking up the way I did things. I told her I didn't want to go to bingo anymore or the trivia nights either, which wasn't true because I would've liked to go but only on my own, so we stopped going. I was all confused and mucked up. I loved her more than lettuce still but it wasn't as fun anymore.

One night when she was sleeping, and she took up most of the bed, she did a fart, which wasn't a stinker but it made a rumpumpapump sound. She had done farts before but I ignored them. She didn't mean to do them but she told me she had a lot of wind, which I didn't mind. There were a lot of times when I wanted to do farts too, but didn't because of my manners. So when she farted this rumpumpapump fart in my bed I decided enough was enough.

The next morning we had a fight, not about her sleep fart but about what we were going to do that day. I said I wanted to get on a train and go somewhere.

She said she didn't want to.

I said I never asked her to.

She said what do you expect me to do all day then?

I said do what you normally do, nothing!

She said she thought I was weird and that I was a loser who had no friends.

Well I'm sorry, I said, where are all your friends?

She said she was only with me because I was the only sort of guy she could get.

Sort of guy, I said. What do you mean, sort of guy? Do you mean that you can only get loser weirdo guys? Well doesn't that make you a loser? I said she was the hungriest girl I had ever known.

She said she never loved me and that she only told me she did because she felt sorry for me.

I said I hated her and that I was better off without her. Then she stomped out. She wasn't even really emotional but I was starting to cry. I didn't let her see this – and don't tell anyone – but I was.

I hate her now, hate her for mucking everything up, for getting me all sexy and then for leaving me with sad thoughts. I hate her for messing up the way I do things, for making all this stuff come into my head and for fuzzing up my brain. My head was full of fog and I couldn't stop thinking about her. She made me feel all shitty pardon my French. She made me hate myself. First, she made me like myself and then she made me hate myself. I still think bad thoughts about her but I miss her a lot too. She left work not long after that. Now she does filing in a different place.

I'm much happier now. Tonight I'm going to try to make six good pictures and then I'm going to start making new shapes with even more balls.

Making Tracks

Breathing Amber

Matthew Condon

Amber lived for eleven days on sachets of soup and two-minute noodles. When they ran out, and she was too afraid to leave the Elizabeth Bay apartment, she ate rice and vegemite mixed with boiling water. She kept the blinds drawn and grew listless and exhausted with the effort of keeping herself still and listening for signs of Wynter. It was tiring to listen. But Tick's methamphetamines kept her awake, and she needed to be awake.

'It's the next big thing, darling,' he told her of chrystal meth. 'A little birdie in New York put me onto it. They call it biker's coffee, isn't that cute? Or *redneck* cocaine, which has its own appealing connotations. It's recommended by some gentlemen truck drivers I know.'

For a week, a man and a woman next door had been continuing a rolling argument that began very loudly and then went through days of tense silence then slowly built again and ruptured and went quiet again. In the peaceful stretches the slamming of a saucepan on the stove top or the clang of cutlery thrown into the sink released staccatos of abuse that always ended neatly with the slamming of a door. An increase in volume of the stereo or the television always pushed either the man or the woman out of the flat. Sometimes she heard either the man or the woman sobbing through the old plaster walls.

Upstairs they held a party during her eleven days of vigilance, and the deep tribal thud of dance music reverberated through her hollow apartment and skittering around the beat were the sounds of stiletto heels on the wooden floor and smashed glasses. Looking out the sliding doors to the bay she could see all night the dull shooting stars of flicked cigarette butts. Sometimes she heard the long wail of the container ships coming in and out of the harbour. It made her think how big the world was with its ocean traffic of ships full of cars and furniture and timber and coal and wool and sugar and shoes and handbags and washing machines and DVD players. When she thought this her head ached and she craved more of Tick's crystal meth. It made her feel bigger. Invincible. Without it she was smaller and weaker and the flat pressed in on her and she got headaches.

On the eleventh day, with the man and woman barking at each other and the picture on her wall shifting millimetres out of alignment with their door slamming, she did what she promised she wouldn't do, and ordered more biker's coffee from Tick on credit. Within three hours he slid under her door a plain envelope. Inside was one of his sachets, and a pressed flower. She smoked the meth and opened the blinds and in the bathroom mirror could see that some blood had leached onto her tongue from the back of her throat and had turned her front teeth pale pink.

Amber discovered the high of Tick's new drug seemed to last forever, that two smokes could take her through twenty-four hours, and she paced the small flat and talked to herself and relayed to the empty rooms what seemed to be the diary of her life. It was all there, on her tongue, and she heard the story as if someone else were reading it to her.

In the end she didn't have to speak at all. Another voice simply took over, and told her the story.

The voice told her she had to get out, into the world, and this was fucking ridiculous and if he found her and killed her then, so fucking what, you had to die sometime. You've known him for seven years and you know what? You know what? Those seven years were no different from hiding here in this fucking shitbox of a flat. You never had any friends, a proper place to live, a bedroom with your own bed and a garden out the back and a dog and a cat. You never had friends you could call for a coffee or someone to laugh and cry with or just to sit with, someone you could trust, someone normal, because that's the way he wanted it. That's the way he had to live. Now you're here with 4 million people in a box in the city and you may as well be out in the middle of the fucking outback; it's the same thing, the same thing.

For years she'd been living inside Wynter's head. It was small and cramped and lonely and she'd been inside his head since the moment he found her at Central Railway Station. She still had the warmth of the train cabin inside her that night after the trip down from Murwillumbah, and her hair still carried the stale cigarette smoke from the cabin, and she'd barely alighted from the train and he had taken her hand and walked her straight into the dark room of his head. Later, it didn't matter if they were in Goondiwindi or Bourke or Adaminaby, it was always the same dark room. She decided not to inhabit it anymore. And if he found her and killed her, at least she wasn't living there in that room. You don't have to live in that place anymore, the voice said.

Only after several days did she realise the voice she was hearing in her own head was a male voice. It was not Tick's or Wynter's or her father's, but a stranger's. It was like the voice in her bedside radio. As the methamphetamines slowly wore off she'd see she was in different clothes, and that someone had moved her sparse furniture and boxes around, and that her bedhead was against a different wall. She knew, too, she had to work. Now she was in Tick's debt. It would unfold as it always did. He would deliver more meth, and she would be deeper in his debt. He would arrange work for her, and lend her some money so she could get by in the meantime, and there'd be more drugs, and he would own her, and her thoughts of a normal life and a friend to have coffee with and a garden would fade just as the long, low wails of the ships came over the surface of the harbour and bounced and echoed off houses and apartment buildings and tangled on spiky television aerials and were absorbed by the great crowns of fig trees until there was not enough of the sound left to fall into the streets.

Then she smoked more crack and none of it mattered.

On the morning of the twelfth day she found another of Tick's envelopes under her door. There was enough stuff there to keep her awake for another two whole days, and an address and time for the following evening printed neatly on a square of paper. It was her first job for Tick.

It was a Saturday, and she sat on her small balcony that over-looked the bay and beyond it the rarified hilly spine of Darling Point with its millionaires and movie stars. Through its thin canopy of gums and palms and figs she could see the old terraces along the foot of the ridge and higher up the old red-brick flats and Spanish-style villas and breaking through the top of the canopy the gangrenous spire of an ancient church. She could hear the bells of the church, the bells of a Saturday wedding, and she turned Tick's pressed flower around and around by its dry stem. The soft bells continued to ring inside her for a long time as perfect as the tongue-click of a metronome, and she was on her father's shoulders on a Saturday morning in Murwillumbah, holding his hair gently with her small hands, the hair tawny reigns for little Amber, riding through that peculiar white light of a Saturday morning when time stretched forever and everything was so clear and detailed it took an age to travel from the drapery to the Regent cinema, from the river to the rotunda. And life to her was of the second, and one moment she was marvelling at the blood-red poppies splayed across a woman's dress, and the heads of pens in a man's shirt pocket, and the spots of discarded chewing gum down on the footpath, and the infinity of space on a movie poster, and the shaved patch and stitched cut on the crown of a passing boy's head, and the fuse-wire hairs that sprouted from her father's ears.

Amber spun the dried flower in her fingertips.

She was only twenty-five years old and she believed she had lived an entire life. That he, Wynter, had removed the middle of it, cut it out of her, and hooked her childhood onto early middle age. Once she had been the mother of a baby boy, and spent an eternity in motel rooms and in cars and in the unending stupors they had experienced together where it was always dusk or dawn, where there was always new and old light, fresh yellow and old yellow, clear and blurred shadows, but never a moment without a trace of the night. The metronome continued its clicking. Her poor, mad mother had one of polished red wood on the old piano. She never played the little cottage upright. Didn't know how to play it. Just had it there, dusted daily, as if she expected someone to come up the front stairs and into the house and sit down on the fringed stool and start making beautiful music.

Who was she waiting for? Who was it that never came to play music?

Not long before Amber left home she would tiptoe into the house late at night and hear the metronome ticking in the dark. Sometimes it was ticking in the morning. Near the end, she rarely saw the lead weight motionless. Her mother sat and listened to the ticking, and Amber knew she was dying even then, had been dying most of her adult life, because that's the way it was with some families, with some family lines, dying while they were living. Her mother. The face creased with herring-bone lines. The eyes alert, waiting for something. For a bullet, fired a long way away, heading for her, just for her, this small casing of spinning brass, that would eventually find its target.

Amber's mother was old before she had a chance to be young, just like her daughter. Amber only remembered it and pieced it together later. Aches, pains, fussing, pottering. There were always things to do, which were never done, because her mother was dying, and there was no point in doing anything.

She wasn't the type of mother who threatened confiscation, or meted out the wooden spoon. She just said – you'll be sorry when I'm gone. Or, I won't be here for much longer, so do as you wish. Or, I'll no longer be a nuisance to you in five years. I won't exist, and you'll have to cope on your own. It took Amber a long time to see that hers was a family tethered to death. It was in the cane setts in the late afternoon, crouching in the fields. Embedded like dust in the lace curtains. It was in the sound of a whistling kettle. It dulled Amber's father. Wore him down. The ticking entered him and he couldn't get it out. He set the cane fields ablaze and stood back and watched rats and snakes and mice and lizards flee, expunged from the cane, but nothing could cleanse the ticking from him. It had to come from somewhere, Amber thought. This waiting for death, while living. From somewhere upriver. Things that float down to you. They have to come from somewhere.

Bury me, her mother always said. I don't want to be burned.

Just before noon on the thirteenth day Amber finally left the apartment. She wore cheap mules and jeans and a peasant blouse and carried her suede shoulder bag with the suede fringes. She felt, negotiating the hill up Greenknowe Avenue, that she had somehow lost the ability to walk properly. The sloping footpaths seemed to tilt her off balance. By the time she got to the T-junction with Macleay Street she felt an odd tension of fear inside her – not at being spotted by Wynter but being out and among other human beings. She clutched the strap of the suede bag and sweat from her hand stained the suede dark.

This is where Wynter had brought her, several years before, straight out of the great womb of Central Station to Kings Cross. To a second-floor apartment that overlooked an alley and the blue and red and orange glow of a drycleaning store and a tattoo parlour and a kebab shop. If she hung out the window as far as she could and looked over to her right she could see the illuminated aura of the city as huge and imposing as Mount Warning.

As she walked down Macleay Street she recognised nothing. The fish-bowl cafés of modular stools and chrome. 7-Elevens. The new apartment buildings with brass door handles and potted palms in the foyers. The boutique furniture stores displaying wicker chaise-longues like distorted and oversized cannellini beans. Everything was shiny and ill-shaped and round-edged. The cars were all silver coupés. Everyone had small, silver, rounded mobile phones to their ears. The leafy arms of the plane trees shivered over Macleay Street. She continued down the street towards the harbour, past the naval base, and crossed over to the long fence that guarded the military wharf and stretched all the way to Harry's Café de Wheels. A third of the way along the fence she stopped in front of a memorial, open to the thundering traffic of the street, and so gritty and fouled by vehicle exhaust that it was almost impossible to read.

It was a shrine to the men and women who had left to fight in the First World War. There was a little red flame. She read that this was the wharf from which they had sailed for Gallipoli and France. In the heat she heard the ticking of insects in the surrounding shrubbery.

Amber flanked the fence alongside the wharf and passed the wharf building then followed a group of people up the steps at the back of the art gallery. From the steps she looked over and saw two giant matches in a park. She had never seen these matches. One with its red head intact. The other burned and twisted. She thought then of Wynter and the menace of his smile and the burn of his eyes and she became afraid again. She hurried up the stairs then and ignored eye contact with anyone and looked for somewhere to shelter, to get out of the open, and she quickly crossed the bridge over the Cahill Expressway and cut into the Botanical Gardens.

Before they had to flee Sydney, before they broke out for the west and breached the Blue Mountains and then ran north, tucking into towns and hamlets off the highway, stealing bread from the open backdoors of country bakeries, the loaves warm and golden in those cold blue dawns of their months, then years, on the run, she had lived only fifteen minutes' walk from the gardens, up on the foul carcass spine of Darlinghurst Road, and only glimpsed the band of foliage of Hyde Park and the Domain and the gardens through the narrow canyons of hotels and terraces and apartment buildings, as if across a swollen and impassable river. Sometimes the view to the city had stopped her and held her, and she was back home, in Murwillumbah, smoking grass in the park on the Tweed River, and across the river the great looming mountain, just like the city, and the mountain caught threads of cloud at its peak just as the city and Centrepoint caught the clouds, and at the base of both the fortress of trees, and again Amber Day was small, an irrelevance in this big world, another useless one of billions, even smaller than that, imprisoned as she was within someone else. It frightened her. To see the city. The sunlight coming through it at dusk. The thick columns of sunlight between the skyscrapers, the columns hitting the river of trees and shattering into millions of shards, the shards falling and decaying in the ground mulch and cigarette butts and worms and food scraps and cockroach nests.

She had never been awake to see it in the morning. The streets and sidewalks black and freshly washed by the street cleaners. The tyres of the delivery trucks hissing over the wet streets. The city out of sleep, warming up for the day, warm rolls and warm croissants on silver trays, the warm steam exhaling from silver coffee machines into the cool, wet air of the streets. The big and little fountains all over the city clicking on and the sound of the rushing water in concert for a while with the wet black bitumen. The statues taking on their features after a long dark night strafed by the blue of police lights and the red of tail lights and the yellow of the council cleaning trucks. Fresh fish, swimming in their vast, beating universe just hours before, ferried on pallets of ice and into window displays and restaurant cool rooms, their eyes not quite dead in the strange neon of morning, a glimmer in them, as if shocked and surprised that they were dead. The hair of a million heads, the billions of cells of skin of the rush hour, whorling like the Milky Way in the dim tunnels underneath the city. The cubes of buses thundering through the transit lanes, full of coloured and damp showered hair and the tang of different perfumes and aftershaves and soaps. And the towering Centrepoint, the red light at its peak just visible, a flashing, beating heart below translucent skin, just visible through a tiny skein of cloud it has caught like a ragged flag of cloth snared on a barb of wire, before it's burned off by the sun of the new day.

Amber Day had never seen this. Wynter had cut her off from it. Had ensured her addiction kept her within the small grid of Darlinghurst Road and Victoria Street. She had drifted in this small, foul pond of his design. And now Tick was drawing, reeling her in as well. Hooking her gently. At first using the finest grade line. Then thicker, later, when she was past caring. And the biker's coffee, which had hooked her firmly through the lip. She didn't feel a thing.

Amber wandered down the bitumen paths of the gardens. The rich, unexpected rush of oxygen, of plant air, hit her and made her light-headed. It overwhelmed her and she suddenly felt cold in the changed atmosphere of the gardens and became aware of an extreme hunger within her. Stopping to sit on a bench, she felt at once light and heavy, and the sounds of the gardens became very loud. She felt she could delineate the noise of leaves scratching against each other and the groan of trunks and the opening of buds and the hum of incessant bat chatter, their millions of gutteral clicks and throaty growls entering the cool air of the gardens. She could hear teeth grinding up against the shells of her ears.

Amber closed her eyes and took deep breaths and when she opened her eyes again she saw pinpricks of light flashing in front of her and imploding and being replaced instantly by other pin-pricks. Keeping her eyes closed she could smell ripe corn and the pungent odour of wet canvas and animal hide and the excretion of sheep and cattle, and behind it all she thought she could hear the sweep of rushcutter scythes and the tinny echo of axe-fall. She staggered off the bench and tried to retrace her steps out of the gardens to the anchor of some landmark she was at least familiar with, the burnt and unburnt match heads, the towers of apartments at Darlinghurst and Potts Point across Wolloomooloo Bay, but she took a wrong turn and entered deeper into the gardens.

She felt that pure panic of having completely lost her bearings, and that a bore had unexpectedly been sunk to the centre of her loneliness, and she emitted a rhythmic whimper as she strode drunkenly beneath the dark canopy of trees. She had entered a tunnel and the walls were impenetrable and everything within her wanted to cry out. She shook violently and was on the edge of breaking into a run when she saw, in the distance, what she thought was a bright red coat disappear to the left, and she followed the colour, knew instinctively the colour was not part of the darkening gardens, couldn't be, and when she reached the junction of the path where she had seen the coat she looked to the left and saw the fernery.

She stood and stared at the fernery house and her eyes welled with tears of relief, just at the sight of its lines, its resemblance to a man-made structure, a pencil sketch from a human hand in the middle of the wildness of the gardens.

Come inside, Amber, the voice said to her.

She walked towards it and her heart slowed. She dried her eyes with a tissue. She entered the fernery and heard human voices somewhere, behind the ancient interlocking fronds, and she smiled to herself and checked herself and gathered herself and became, again, just another person in the world beneath the canopies of the fronds.

There among the prehistoric plants she felt warm again and safe. Studying the plants she was filled with a type of wonder and admiration for them, for the perfect order of the spores, and the little curled tails of the new fronds growing through. She became entranced by the newly born fronds, poised for unfolding,

unfolding forever, and had tears then, not borne of fear but of wonder, and she thought again of her child. That he was somehow with her. And she had the need, there, to talk to him, in the warm fernery. She hummed nursery rhymes to her boy, and whispered to him, and could see the white fluffy horses of his blanket lift off the blue cloth and prance among the brilliant greens.

Amber cried and laughed at the horses in this place where there was no dawn or dusk, where the baby shoots unfurled around her, and for the first time since she could remember she felt the cool air rush in and out of the tree of her lungs.

Meanjin

The Original Is Unfaithful to the Translation

Marion Halligan

On a summer's day in a house in the Paris suburbs Susan Kaye opened a filing cabinet and took out a diary which she leafed through and looked into. The entries were sometimes in French and sometimes in English, except for the very last words, which were *Ich Liebe Margot*.

She would not have expected to be doing such a thing. She believed she was not a person who did such things. Twenty years after that summer's day in Paris, and another twenty years ago now, she stayed alone in the flat of a friend who was quite famous for keeping diaries. As a form of superannuation, the friend said, one day their gossip and anecdotes about literary people and intellectuals would be worth a lot of money. On a small wooden bookcase underneath a window was a whole row of bulging well-bound books, and Susan knew they were the famous diaries. She could have looked at them but she did not, out of respect. Because she was not a person who read other people's diaries.

But on that day forty years ago in the house in Paris she did. She read *Ich Liebe Margot* and wondered why Gerard had written it in German. He was a French scholar and Margot was a French woman, neat and plain in that handsome way of French women, like a small brown bird. Maybe he wanted the particular music of the German sounds. Susan did not speak German but she knew what the words meant: *I love Margot*. The French *J'aime Margot* did not have quite the same sort of feel; maybe it was this other rich exotic foreignness that he wanted, believing that French was already a kind of mother tongue and everyday. Susan felt the words in her chest, a slight choking feeling as though they were about her.

They were written a long time ago, and Susan wondered if they were still true. They had another quality about them, as though Gerard Percy were making a speech to himself, were watching himself making this declaration and not just observing but constructing a young man in love. She wondered if Margot had ever seen them? Now there was a complicated and ramified bourgeois marriage which Susan had often witnessed but until now only as its protagonists had showed it to her. Now she was examining it for herself, in filing cabinets and bookcases and boxes in the study, in armoires and dressers and chests of drawers, in painted china and brown cooking pots and battered aluminium saucepans. She was a research assistant, not paid really, though there was a small grant subsidising something. She had decided that research in a foreign language should not be confined to the words on the page.

She knew that Margot was really Marguerite, that the diminutive was a family nickname. She knew that they always spoke French together and that the five children were expected to speak this language. Gerard was an Englishman and mostly they lived in Cambridge; that was where Susan had worked with him. He was making a translation of Rimbaud, a scholarly activity, not aiming to turn out English poems which would catch the originals in some way but offering the French on the left-hand side of the page and an English translation on the other, discussing possible meanings in academic prose. Susan would have liked to try writing English poems which would somehow *be* Rimbaud, but Gerard was shocked by that; the French was the poems. You must know, he said, the conflation *traditore / traduttore*? Susan was a bit offended; who could study a foreign language without knowing that? It means translator / traitor, she said. Indeed, said Gerard: *Traduire c'est trahir.* To translate is to betray, said Susan. Excellent, replied Gerard. As you observe, not quite so neat in French. And in English not neat at all. We need the Italian for the sharpness of the connection. So, he went on, our Rimbaud: we will have as little betrayal as humanly possible. He made it very clear that the English was to be a handmaidenly tool.

Like herself, thought Susan. She had a plain brown name but did not wish to be that sort of person. A scholar she had plans to be, but not therefore a sexless woman devoted only to the mind. She aimed to speak French like a native of the country, and longed to be mistaken for one. The nearest she'd got was a man in a train asking her did she come from Belgium, which was a start. Gerard did not ever sound like a French person; he spoke beautiful complexly syntaxed eighteenth-century French with an English accent which in France was considered eccentric and charming, but which sounded odd to other English scholars of the language. One of Gerard's students told her it was what grand Englishmen used to do, speak perfect French but always with English vowels and consonants. It was a way of keeping the frogs in their place. Gerard called up and down the staircases of the tall regency house in Cambridge in this strange hybrid, and Margot answered.

The armoire in the Paris house was full of wedding linen. Sheets embroidered white on white, with garlands and violets and ears of wheat. Pillowslips fastened with tiny pearl buttons. Immense piles of tea towels of heavy linen huckaback with a fine red stripe, monogrammed in red with the initials of Margot's name as a young girl, her *nom de jeune fille*; Susan liked the fact that virginity didn't come into it, as in the term maiden name. Some of the tea towels were quite discoloured with use and in all of them the linen had a slight greyish cast. She needed to examine the cupboards because she would be housekeeping here for a while on her own. Margot had given her instructions to walk down into the valley and up the hill to the next village and collect the laundry. She took a big basket and set off. At the laundry she asked for the linen of Madame Percy – she thought it was clever of Gerard, that both his names were bilingual – and the woman had said in that singing way that always charmed her and which she tried to develop in her own speech, *Ah, la dame Anglaise.* Susan had said, Oh no, she is French, but the laundry woman had insisted, *Ah non, Madame Percy, la dame Anglaise,* in a reproachful manner, and Susan suddenly heard Margot's voice calling up and down the regency stairs, and realised that she too spoke lovely formal French but with an English accent. She felt sad, as if Gerard had in some way destroyed his wife's heritage, so that her countrywoman thought she was an English lady.

He had taken Margot and the children to her family in Burgundy for part of the summer holiday, and would come back shortly and he and Susan would work on the Rimbaud together. It had to be finished before the autumn term started. She put the sheets and pillowcases and tea towels neatly on the lace-lined shelves of the armoire. There were cotton sacks of lavender to scent them. It was very satisfactory seeing piles of ordered linen, the plates and cups in the dresser, the ornate silver cutlery, the curious *batterie de cuisine*. The ancient housewifely satisfactions. Not to mention arcane knowledge. There were strange metal picks, rather like rudimentary forks; Margot had told her they were for eating lobster, getting the meat out of the claws, Gerard was very fond of lobster, she always got them for him in the season, there was a special market in Paris, she took the train in. There was a flat fine metal sieve and an object rather like the wooden mushroom Susan's mother had used for darning socks; it had the same name, it was *un champignon,* and you used it to push cooked vegetables through the sieve to make creamed soups. Do you do that, she asked. Oh yes, of course, said Margot, Gerard is very partial to creamed soups.

Susan wondered if Gerard would expect her to be his handmaiden, while Margot was not there. To run the same high bourgeois household. To shine the floors with the immemorial dance of the polishing cloth: spread it with thick wax, dance it backwards and forwards with quick jumping steps like a polka to coat the old wood, and then again with a plain cloth to polish it in, polish it up. Ah but she was there to help with the translations; running the household was a full-time job.

Did Gerard ever say, these days, *Ich Liebe Margot?* Did he murmur, *Margot, je t'aime?* Say Margot I love you? Or did she as well as he simply assume those words upon which this whole edifice was built?

Gerard was a big man, lean and handsome, with a fine bushy head of dark hair; Margot the little brown bird, smooth-feathered and deft, took his arm when they went out, always on foot; they didn't have a car, they walked to railway stations, and her polished little shoes moved fast to keep up with his long strides, he looked down at her with his proud smile. The proudness not specially for her but of himself. His eyes sparkled, sometimes with anger, sometimes at the comedy of things; he was good at observing folly, and finding a pointed phrase to skewer it.

Susan was tall, and took long strides too; she had long pale hair which hung down her back in the fashion of that time, sometimes held back with a band to keep it out of the books. She was golden-skinned and when people heard she was Australian they said Ah, as though that explained her looks, though they also said, but you don't sound Australian. Yes I do, she replied, my accent is a perfectly ordinary educated Australian accent. She had studied French under an old mentor of Gerard's, which was how she came to be here.

Gerard sent her a postcard, announcing when he would be back, and the time of the train to expect him on. He had a thrifty dislike of the telephone. On a shelf in the study, here and in the Cambridge house, were a set of postal scales and a booklet of prices, so Margot could weigh up the scholarly mail and put the right stamps on it. Gerard did not have a lot of faith in the post office's calculations. Susan went to the market and bought some things to eat; when she thought about it she could form no picture of Gerard cooking. And that turned out to be the case. He made suggestions for possible meals, and praised her, saying she was coming on well, she had the making of an excellent cook. He opened wine, and they had two glasses each for dinner. They worked in the mornings, then ate the sandwiches she had prepared; after lunch he had a small nap – he had been up since very early in the morning, it was before breakfast that he got his reading of fiction done – and then a walk, then more work, dinner, and again reading, scholarly this time. Susan had never led so orderly a life. She was used to working hard, but just as it happened, not in a strict pattern.

How old are you, Susan? he asked her once.

Twenty-two.

Ah. *Une jeune fille en fleurs.*

She knew that was a reference to Proust. She wondered how to put it in English. Blooming? No. In flower? A flowering young woman? None worked as well as the French.

Do you feel homesick here in France?

Not really, she said. I know I'm so lucky; Paris, living here, it's my dream. Home can wait.

Is there *un petit ami*?

No, she said. No one special.

She thought of the boys she'd known. They seemed very young and very far away from the person she was now. Even Mark whom she'd had a longish love affair with, even thought of getting married to, was hard to remember clearly. The boys in Australia seemed like puppies playing on a lawn, endearing but not serious. Not till much later did she realise they were probably the same age Gerard had been when he met Margot.

She did not know if she seduced him. Her hair fell across the page; he stroked it. Your medieval hair, he said. (She knew he would spell it like that, it was the Cambridge way.) She had the same choking feel in her chest as from the words of love at the end of the diary. After dinner she washed her hair in the several inches of water it took so long to gather in the immense old bathtub, and sat in the warm twilight evening of the garden, spreading it out with her hands to dry. He came to her bed where she was reading by the light of a dim yellow lamp, homemade from an old brass candlestick. Will you permit me, he said, in a curious formal manner, and she smiled and turned back the covers to invite him in.

He was considerate, he used what he called an English overcoat.

An English overcoat?

Une capote Anglaise. A French letter. Each language blaming the other for the unmentionable.

After that he came every night. He never said I love you, in any language, though he did offer endearments, in French, and odd scraps of poems some of which she recognised: Mallarmé, Baudelaire, Verlaine; the Symbolistes were his period. He called her *ma belle Suzanne.* She thought I am the mistress, of the man and the house. She wondered if she would want this to go on, to take possession of it all for herself, to become the wife as well as the mistress. Take what was Margot's and make it her own. Women did this, sometimes, these days, it was the beginning of the time when it became common for men to leave one wife and family and begin over again with another, mainly because they could, they wanted to, and not because the old life was unbearable.

Do you keep a diary, she asked, I mean, now? Of course, he said. The unexamined life is not worth living, don't you agree?

She wondered where he kept it. She hadn't found any married ones in the filing cabinet. The current one must be in his satchel.

There was a sale of historical papers at an auction house on the Quai d'Orsay; one of them was a letter from Rimbaud, and Gerard sent her in to look at it. He couldn't afford to buy it, but he wanted her to do as Margot did, go to the preview and read it, memorise it, and write it down for him. He already had quite a collection garnered by this means, no use for publishing but handy for research. She did not do a good job; she thought she had remembered it but when she came to write it down, in a café round the corner, she found she hadn't, properly; there were gaps which spoilt its sense. He sighed when he looked at it. I need practice, she said. Memorisation is not a skill of your generation, he said.

On that occasion she'd bought a handsome bound volume in a paper shop in the Boulevard St Michel to keep a diary in but found she needed practice at that too. She wrote down *Ich Liebe* … but did not know what to put after that. She folded the page over and there was a fresh one. She could not write, Tonight Gerard made love to me, not in any language she knew. She noted the names of the poems they translated and what they had for dinner.

He never stayed all night, always went back to his own bed. Hers was one of those very wide single beds, or a narrow double one, good for a passionate couple but not useful for sleeping. When he left she stirred and stretched and hugged herself with her own arms, feeling beautiful and loved and grown-up.

This went on for some weeks, then Margot telephoned; her parents would put her and three of the children on the train from Burgundy, the others staying behind with their grandparents, and Gerard would meet her in Paris and bring her back from there. He came to Susan's bed and said, Our last time. He called her, *ma traduce et trésoré*, which he said was out of a medieval poem in three languages, Latin, French and English. This is the first verse, he said:

Ma traduce et trésoré
Nicht and day for love of thee
Suspiro

She did not like to ask him what *traduce* meant in the context, it is difficult to say to a lover, what exactly does that word mean? She never did manage to find out and in fact quite shortly supposed that she must have been mistaken in what he said. She looked it up in *Harrap's French and English Dictionary* and in the *Robert French* and the *Complete Oxford* but they were no help. The word *traduce* in any kind of loving meaning did not seem to exist, but still sometimes the phrase echoed in her head. Looking back, she thought how passive she seemed, lying in bed waiting for the desired man to come, dreamily making love; nights of elegant verbal passion followed by days of poetry that she was obliged to analyse and codify, catching its imagination in a strict net of academic prose. In the daytime he would make little barbed corrections, smiling to soothe the sting, and then at night he would take pleasure in her body. My medieval girl, he called her, and she thought now from the vantage point of her own years past of marriages, two, and children, three, that she had been like a maiden in a tower waiting for her fate and evidently Gerard had not been it, or anyway she hadn't made him be it. And that she'd known what she was doing.

The summer passed. The children sat impeccably at meals and made conversation in French, and disappeared between times to play in the garden or down by the pond in the valley. Sometimes Margot took them on excursions into Paris, and once they shut themselves in the attic for some days and then invited everybody to the performance of a play they had written, at which they sold Gerard's superior Spanish sherry to the audience for six centimes a glass. There never was lobster though she supposed it wasn't the season, and not much in the way of cream soups pressed through the fine sieve with the wooden mushroom, but the red monogrammed tea towels got plenty of use. Never by Gerard of course, not with two handmaidens in the house. The night before she left she crept down to the armoire and took one. She kept it carefully, using it only to wrap bread; it was one that had hardly been used and stayed pristine. She looked at its red embroidered monogram and remembered her handmaiden days.

At the end of the summer she went to work as an assistant teacher in a high school in Orleans for the autumn term. She went back to Australia in February for the beginning of the academic year to take up her Ph.D scholarship. The book on Rimbaud came out and was a great success in its own circles and probably the reason why Gerard Percy soon after got his chair. Its brief introductory essay was considered a masterly piece of criticism and the translations were described as conveying every possible nuance of meaning. They say that to translate is to betray, said one review, but in this case there is total fidelity. To everything but the poetry, Susan thought, as she had at the time they were doing them. Poetry is what is lost in translation, she discovered Robert Frost saying, years later.

She'd thought Gerard might send her a copy but she had to order one herself from Blackwell's. She did not think she had expected her name to be on the title page, exactly, but she had supposed it might be somewhere noticeable, if not prominent. She had done a lot of the work on those translations. Finally she found herself in a list of names at the back, including typists and friends and dear readers and a whole lot of unknown people. The book was dedicated to his beloved wife, Margot. Well, Gerard is dead, and so is Margot. The house in the Paris suburbs has been sold, the five children are scattered. Forty years on Susan recalls reading that formal asseveration of love in a diary, and tries to remember what that summer of translation and treachery was like. For she has decided that Gerard betrayed both *la belle Suzanne* and the beloved Margot – not least by schooling her in English French – though she does not wish that she had not let him do it. A necessary treachery, she says to herself. She wonders if Margot knew, if it was his habit to bed the pretty student help, and thinks that perhaps Margot considered that was appropriate behaviour for the great man, a kind of *droit de seigneur. Droit de professeur.* She turns over in bed and cuddles up against the back of her second husband. She divorced the first for Gerard's kind of behaviour.

Meanjin

The title of this story is from a remark of J.L. Borges, *El original es infiel a la traducción.* He was referring to Henley's translation of Beckford's *Vathek.*

John F. Kennedy Is Very Surprised

Jenny Sinclair

It's Resurrection Day. God is making good on His promises. All over the world, graves are opening, shrouds are unwrapping and scattered ashes are flying together on the four winds, assembling themselves into whole bodies like so much Instant Humanity. (Just add water! See limbs form before your very eyes!)

The old are still old and the halt and disfigured are still slow and ugly of course, and there are others who need a little, shall we say, nip and tuck? The victims of torture, of car crashes, of dismemberment, of slow deaths in the desert (including, natch, the crucifixees), come back looking a little better than they did at the exact moment of their demise. Gives them a fair chance in the post-Resurrection world.

And what a world it's shaping up to be. The living haven't quite got their heads around it yet. They tried to kill the first few bodies coming out of the graveyard gates – too many zombie movies, I suppose – what a laugh that was! Murder, in the post-death age!

So far – and it's only been ten hours – the truly religious are taking it best. The very old churchgoing ladies weren't all that surprised to wake from their afternoon dozes to find Fred or George or Henry in the other chair, waiting for a cup of tea.

The devout and suffering mothers of the poor countries of the world turned from their baking or their weaving and ran into the arms of their formerly dead children, little boys and girls who came home to their mothers carrying their even smaller baby brothers and sisters. They're not asking any questions.

The Archbishop of Sydney, however, is having some difficulty. The Second Coming began at three p.m., Australian Eastern Standard Time (adjusted for daylight savings). Now it's one a.m. on 4 January, he's fronting a press conference bigger than any congregation he ever managed to pull, and he's not doing so well.

'Archbishop, do you believe this is God's work? Is it a miracle, or a trick of the Devil?'

'Suzanne Pretty,' he thinks. That bitch. Normally she's a political correspondent, only bothering him when topics like abortion and paedophilia arise in the national debate. But this is one hell of a story and the respectful religion writers have been pushed aside by the gimlet glass and steel eyes of the TV camera and boom mike crowd.

'It's too early to tell ...' he begins.

'Hasn't God spoken to His church?' calls out the *7.30 Report*'s hound, seated front and centre. 'What does that suggest to you, Archbishop?'

'God does not normally speak directly to His ministers,' Archbishop Bell begins. 'Through His works He ...'

'Oh come *on*,' interrupts the *Australian*'s disaster and terrorism specialist. 'We can't talk about normal life while every member of the First Fleet is standing on Circular Quay, can we? Is this one of His works or not?'

'What about the abortions?' jumps in the *Herald*'s health correspondent. 'Can you comment on the fact that Westmead Hospital is only seeing babies past twenty-one weeks' gestation in its birthing unit?'

But Bell's not listening. His father has just walked into the room, followed by his grandfather and grandmother, and they're pushing through the media pack towards him. They look like they'd like a word.

'I'm sorry, I'll have to end this conference now,' he hardly has time to say, providing the cameras with a classic turn-pale-cut-and-run grab that the newsroom editors entirely misinterpret and use out of context, as usual.

By three a.m. Sydney time, everyone in the world – and that's quite a lot of people now – is awake, apart from the very small babies. There are an awful lot of those, too, particularly in Africa, South America and Asia. China, for instance, is suffering what can only be called an embarrassment of baby girls.

In Ballarat, Victoria, the Slattery family is having a reunion of sorts. Six generations of Slatterys have been born in Australia since Frederick and Eustace arrived in 1862. With the various Thompsons, Smiths, Loaders and Murphys who fed the family tree along the way, there are now 127 people in Karen Slattery's three-bedroom brick-veneer home. Most of them want to watch the CNN news on cable, so she's moved the box outside. A few, though, are being difficult.

'Hello? Hello, can you hear me in there? Would you PLEASE unlock the door? Hello?' Karen Slattery yells and bangs, but the bedroom door stays shut.

Inside, Paul Murphy and Tamsin Murphy, nee Slattery, killed together in a train smash on their honeymoon in 1922, are going at it hammer and tongs for only the third time ever. As you would expect after an eighty-three-year dry spell. Sadly for them, their efforts to use their shiny new bodies to expand the Slattery clan will be in vain.

That's the deal: the dead come back, but no new souls will be handed out. It seems unfair, but even the already pregnant are bound by the five-month rule.

In New York, several large publishers and event organisers have just cottoned on to the comeback potential of the Second Coming. Ziggy Green is pacing his velvet-floored eyrie, knocking back whisky like there's no tomorrow – or at least not one that includes death by cirrhosis of the liver.

'Hemingway!' he's shouting. 'Find me Hemingway! And Chandler if you can.' He stops and slaps his forehead. 'WILLIAM BLOODY SHAKESPEARE.' The ears of his agent in Europe ring like a bell.

Across the continent, Martin Sorvino, head of MaxiLab Films, is having similar thoughts.

'Fuckin' Tolkien, I said! Yes I know he was an academic for fuck's sake. But Peter Jackson thinks if we can just get him to a screening room, we might get a sequel out of him. No, forget Monroe. She was washed up anyway. Leave her to the tabloids. Yes, River Phoenix, if you can get him straight.'

Back in New York, John Lennon and Yoko Ono are watching snowflakes fall on Strawberry Fields.

In Vienna, it's just after five p.m. Albert Einstein is having a quiet coffee with Stephen Hawking, nutting out a few adjustments to a theory or two.

In Rome, John Paul II wonders how long he's been napping and whether he's got the energy to shuffle out to the balcony yet again. Really, he thinks, isn't it time for me to meet my maker?

God is saying nothing. He's not making it any easier for His servants and ministers, from Mecca to Salt Lake City. But why should He? The mothers of Somalia and Sri Lanka understand. He took in silence and now He's giving back in the same way.

The President of the United States is doing the numbers and is worried. Four hundred years of the immigrant USA versus tens of thousands of years of the Indian nations. He doesn't know where to start until an aide comes into the room carrying the W-phone.

'Prime Minister of New Zealand, sir.'

'Not now, for God's sake.'

'Sir, she says you might like to hear about their treaty? Signed in 1840? She says it's turned out surprisingly useful.'

He sighs, and picks up.

Jesus Christ, meanwhile, got as far from Jerusalem as the UN staff car He flagged down could carry Him before the gas ran out. Then He started walking.

Did they believe Him when He told them who He was? Hell yes. He just sort of has this way of talking, you know? Like He's for real?

Now He's in a farmhouse on the side of a hill in southern Italy. The 1000 or so residents were pretty pleased to have Him, seeing as the farm could normally only support seventy to eighty people. He'll come in handy, and they didn't even mind Him asking for a room of His own; one big enough to share with His mates Buddha and Mohammed when they arrive on Friday.

Every Italian family needs a papa; what it doesn't need is forty-six of them. The current papa (who remains in charge only because he's the one who knows how to use the Internet; the rest are still working out the telephone and light switches) shows Jesus to His room, the one with the south-facing terrace.

He shows Jesus how to work the dodgy window latch, and where the towels are kept. Just before he leaves, he dares to ask: 'So, what now for us all?'

Jesus shrugs, not unkindly. 'Life, Papa, is what you make it. Eternal life's no different.'

And He sits down on the whitewashed stone bench in the sunshine to watch the teeming masses on the plain below.

Verandah

Requiem

Shane Strange

1.

On 11 March 2004, Fresneda walked down the street outside El Pozo station in Madrid. It was a beautiful spring day and Fresneda was feeling good. He had come to Madrid on holidays to stay with his sister and her husband and children, who lived near the station. He was glad to see them. He hadn't seen them in over fifteen years, since his sister had come back to Spain from Australia.

On his way to the station, he stopped at a small café for a strong, black coffee. He was aware of the workers going by around him, down to the station on their way to work. He watched them tramp by, all briefcases and stockings and ties, but he did not want them to be there; he did not want to recognise the mundane, not here in the city of his birth.

He wondered what he would do today. Yesterday, on the Calle de Bailen in Old Madrid, he had seen the King drive past on his way to the Palacio Real. Today, he thought he would stop in the Bourbon quarter and see the Prado. He wondered if he should come to live here.

His grandfather was a socialist who fought Franco during the Spanish Civil War. He had been imprisoned when Fresneda's father was a baby, and tortured and killed. Fresneda's grandmother died when she was fifty. When this happened, Fresneda's father brought his family to Australia, where he thought they would be safe. Fresneda was just five years old.

When he was seven, Fresneda's mother died of cancer. Franco had died the year before.

Fresneda finished his coffee and walked along with the stream of workers down into the El Pozo metro station. He waited for five minutes for the metro that would take him to Atocha station. On his way there he noticed the people around him in the crowded train and again he was struck by the familiarity of the scene. 'You cannot escape it,' he thought.

It happened when he walked out onto the platform at Atocha. It was 7.30 in the morning. Fresneda died instantly with 200 others as a bomb went off in the train carriage behind him, disintegrating him into nothingness.

2.

Strange was awoken by a call from Fresneda's sister early on the morning of 12 March. Strange hadn't been dreaming anything that he could remember but later, on reflection, he imagined that he'd dreamt about the ocean.

Fresneda had left some things with Strange; she was anxious to make sure Strange knew of the events of 11 March. Strange's only memory of this call was waking suddenly from a deep slumber, and falling completely into a sense of shock. 'Yes,' Strange assured Fresneda's sister, he would help in any way he could.

When he hung up the phone, Strange wondered if he were going mad.

3.

Fresneda had come to stay with Strange for a couple of weeks before he left for Madrid. There was an overlap between the end of his lease and the start of his long holiday to visit his sister, and he had asked Strange if he'd mind putting him up until he left. Fresneda was an old friend of Strange; they knew each other in high school and, through the various turns in their lives, had kept in contact. Strange liked Fresneda and was always glad to see him, and, as Strange lived by himself, he thought he'd be glad of the company for a while.

The first days of Fresneda's stay were good. Fresneda was a great cook and he made fine meals: *paella*, *tortilla Espanola* and *sopa Castellana* – a garlic soup that his mother had made. They would eat the food at the table together and, after dinner, sit on the balcony with a cold beer. Here, Fresneda talked of his hopes for his trip to Spain – the joy of seeing his sister again, of meeting his nephews, of walking in the city of his birth and speaking its language. Fresneda taught Strange how to swear in Spanish. *'Me cago en Dios!'* they would shout into the night. The nature of their talk and the situation itself led them both to pretend an intimacy between them that each knew, in reality, would not outlast the fortnight.

And, in fact, within a few days Strange began to tire of Fresneda's company, and increasingly to regard it as an intrusion on his privacy. Strange would come home from work to find Fresneda lying on the couch, reading a book or watching television, and would feel annoyed and put upon. His small unit suddenly seemed too small and his personal space almost non-existent. But a good dinner would always follow, though the conversation on the balcony would wind down ever more quickly, or be drawn over similar, well-trodden ground.

On the Saturday before Fresneda's plane was scheduled to leave, Strange and Fresneda caught a bus to the ocean. They had a beer and lunch at the Verandah Bar and walked the few kilometres out onto the cliffs overlooking the bay. The day was clear and the view from the top of the cliffs stretched away far into the distance, out across the murky green sea.

After standing there for some time, Fresneda suddenly confessed to Strange that he was afraid of dying. Even though he was only in his mid-thirties, he was approaching the age at which his mother had died. This age, he confessed, was a number that had haunted him for years.

Strange could only look at his friend and tell him that it was only natural that these things should bother him, but that in all likelihood he would live a long time and that he should not worry. He was going to Spain soon, to see his sister, and everything would be fine. Fresneda seemed to take heart from this and he thanked Strange for understanding. But, as they walked back to the village, he turned and said: 'If something does happen to me, you must come back to that place overlooking the ocean and remember me.'

The next day Strange took Fresneda to the airport and wished him luck. Fresneda thanked him and promised to send a post-card. Strange thought, as he saw Fresneda walk down to the departure lounge, that his friend looked happy, like the world had finally converged with his dreams.

Strange walked away from the airport feeling a sense of sadness that he suspected was the mask of his overwhelming relief.

4.

After the Madrid bombing, Strange goes about his normal life while taking care of the business of arranging Fresneda's affairs under the direction of his sister. Often, the whole business seems unreal: he has to check himself to see whether he really exists.

He follows the news of the bombing assiduously on the television and in print. He becomes frightened by the nature of the attack and fascinated by the genius of it. As more news comes to hand about the attacks, he explores the Internet for details of terrorist operations, for bomb-making techniques. He buys a map of Madrid, to pinpoint the location of the bombing. He puts the map on his kitchen wall, with a black circle around Atocha station. He feels that he can protect himself with facts.

At night he often dreams of Fresneda, exploding into pieces on the platform of a railway station, following each piece of his body as it makes its way through the air.

Increasingly, in his waking life, Strange imagines that he is being followed, that his phone calls are being listened to. He begins to vary his routine on a daily basis, to carefully inspect his mail before opening it. On the street, he is cautious of people looking him in the face. He takes to noting down his movements for the day in a notebook.

Strange has dreams of blood, of being locked in a room and of being tortured – of torturing Fresneda, of following him down the streets of Madrid or, because he has never been to Madrid, down what he imagines to be the streets of Madrid. In his dreams he follows Fresneda, watching his every move and noting it down.

Strange takes time off work.

On his kitchen wall now is not only the map of Madrid, but diagrams of explosive devices, and a map of his own city with red lines indicating the various routes he has walked in the preceding days and weeks.

And then there is the notebook: slowly filling up with the carefully compiled details of his day.

He feels himself in a cocoon of information. He has grown a beard. His skin is pale. He has a lingering sense that anything could happen now.

While sitting in his kitchen one day, Strange considers all these things and it dawns on him what he must do.

5.

Strange begins to write a story – a document of his friend in these dangerous times. He feels strongly that this story must be told. As he writes the story in his notebook, he realises that it will be more than that. For the story becomes in a sense a list of facts, the facts of his own life, the facts that have turned into the story that, in turn, has dissolved the facts. It will be a purging of all that has burdened him.

He writes for one week, and each word releases him. His horrific dreams recede into nothingness. He tears down the maps from the kitchen wall and burns them. As he fills his notebook, he feels that he is at last doing something, even if only for himself.

On the final night, he dreams of the ocean and when he wakes in the morning, he realises he must do as his friend asked him. He must go to the high cliff overlooking the ocean. He will take his notebook and read it there. He will board the bus to go to the ocean to do as he has been asked.

Griffith Review

Publication Details

Venero Armanno's 'I Feel So Strong' is an extract from his novel *The Dirty Beat*, which will be published by UQP in 2007.

Margaret Barbalet's 'Running from Right to Left' appeared in *Meanjin*, vol. 65, no. 2, 2006.

Fabienne Bayet-Charlton's 'Twenty Pink Questions' appeared in *Meanjin*, vol. 65, no. 1, 2006.

Tony Birch's 'The Good Howard' appeared in *Sheltered Lives, HEAT 11* (new series), edited by Ivor Indyk, Giramondo, Sydney, 2006.

Carmel Bird's 'The Legacy of Rita Marquand' appeared in *Griffith Review 10: Family Politics*, ABC Books, Summer 2005–2006, <www.griffith.edu.au/griffithreview>.

Gillian Bouras's 'Patterns' appeared in *Hidden Desires: Australian Women Writing*, compiled and edited by Christine Houen and Jena Woodhouse, Ginninderra Press, 2006.

John Bryson's 'Barcelona Honours the Prostitute Maria Llopis' appeared in *Meanjin*, vol. 65, no. 2, 2006.

Gavin Carver's 'Loved Her More than Lettuce' appeared in *Making Tracks*, UTS Anthology, ABC Books, 2006.

Tom Cho's 'Today on *Dr Phil*' appeared in *Sheltered Lives, HEAT 11* (new series), edited by Ivor Indyk, Giramondo, Sydney, 2006.

Matthew Condon's 'Breathing Amber' appeared in *Meanjin*, vol. 65, no. 2, 2006.

Barry Cooper's 'Bean Paddock Blues' appeared in *Meanjin*, vol. 65, no. 1, 2006.

Shady Cosgrove's 'Drop' and 'Train' were published in *Overland*, vol. 181, Summer 2005.

Sonja Dechian's 'Over the Sea' appeared in the *Sleepers Almanac 2006: The Nervous System*, Sleepers Publishing, Melbourne, 2006.

Will Elliott's 'Ain't No Ordinary Ham' was published in *Griffith Review 13: The Next Big Thing*, ABC Books, Spring 2006, <www.griffith.edu.au/griffithreview>.

Catherine Ford's 'Jet Lag' appeared in the *Monthly*, October 2005.

Leanne Hall's 'Rabbit' appeared in the *Sleepers Almanac 2006: The Nervous System*, Sleepers Publishing, Melbourne, 2006.

Marion Halligan's 'The Original Is Unfaithful to the Translation' appeared in *Meanjin*, vol. 65, no. 4, 2006.

Karen Hitchcock's 'Tactics' appeared in *Griffith Review 13: The Next Big Thing*, ABC Books, Spring 2006, <www.griffith.edu.au/griffithreview>.

Patrick Holland's 'Flame Bugs on the Sixth Island' appeared in *Griffith Review 12: Hot Air*, ABC Books, Winter 2006, <www.griffith.edu.au/griffithreview>.

Cate Kennedy's 'Cold Snap' appeared in the collection of stories, *Dark Roots*, Scribe Publications, Carlton, 2006. This story also appeared as 'Black Ice' in *The New Yorker*, 11 September 2006.

Fiona McGregor's 'Indelible Ink' appeared in *Griffith Review 13: The Next Big Thing*, ABC Books, Spring 2006, <www.griffith.edu. au/griffithreview>.

Amanda le Bas de Plumetot's 'The Jesus of Ants' appeared in *Page Seventeen*, Issue 3, April 2006.

Paddy O'Reilly's 'Like the World's an Armchair' appeared in the *Sleepers Almanac 2006: The Nervous System*, Sleepers Publishing, Melbourne, 2006.

Jennifer Robertson's 'Paradise' appeared in *Griffith Review 10: Family Politics*, ABC Books, Summer 2005–2006, <www.griffith. edu.au/griffithreview>.

Eva Sallis's 'Fox Unpopuli' appeared in the *Bulletin*, 20 December 2005.

Kim Scott's 'Asleep' appeared in *Westerly*, ed. Delys Bird and Dennis Haskell, University of Western Australia, vol. 50, November 2005.

Jenny Sinclair's 'John F. Kennedy Is Very Surprised' appeared in *Verandah*, vol. 20, Deakin University, 2005.

Christine Stanton's 'Dangerous Shoes' appeared in *Griffith Review 11: Getting Smart*, ABC Books, Autumn 2006, <www.griffith.edu. au/griffithreview>.

Shane Strange's 'Requiem' appeared in *Griffith Review 13: The Next Big Thing*, ABC Books, Spring 2006, <www.griffith.edu.au/ griffithreview>.

Girija Tropp's 'Rockpools' appeared in *Southword 10*, Literary Journal of the Munster Literature Centre, Ireland, June 2006.

Chris Womersley's 'The Shed' appeared in *Granta New Writing 14*, Granta Books, 2006.

Daniel Wynne's 'Emily' appeared in *Griffith Review 13: The Next Big Thing*, ABC Books, Spring 2006, <www.griffith.edu.au/ griffithreview>.

Notes on Contributors

Venero Armanno is the author of a book of short fiction and seven novels. His latest novel, *The Dirty Beat*, will be published in 2007. He is currently Head of Creative Writing at University of Queensland.

Fabienne Bayet-Charlton is of Bungalung/Belgian descent. Her second novel, *Watershed*, was shortlisted for the 2006 Victorian Premier's Literary Award (Indigenous Writing).

Margaret Barbalet was born in Adelaide and now lives in the United Arab Emirates. She is the author of eight books for both children and adults, the most recent being *The Presence of Angels*.

Tony Birch publishes short fiction, poetry and essays. His recent collection of stories, *Shadowboxing*, was shortlisted for the 2006 Queensland Premier's Literary Awards. He teaches in the English Department at the University of Melbourne.

Carmel Bird's most recent books are a collection of stories, *The Essential Bird*, and a novel, *Cape Grimm*. Her book of inspiration for memoir writers, *Writing the Story of Your Life*, will be published in early 2007.

Gillian Bouras is an Australian who has lived in the Peloponnese, Greece, for twenty-six years. Her journalism has been published in five countries, and she has written seven books, mainly on cross-cultural issues.

John Bryson is the author of four books including *Evil Angels* (1985), his novel about the Lindy Chamberlain case for which he won several literary awards and which was made into a film by Fred Schepisi in 1988.

Anson Cameron is a Melbourne-based author whose books include *Tin Toys, Silences Long Gone, Nice Shootin', Cowboy* and *Confessing the Blues.* His latest novel, *Lies I Told About A Girl,* was published by Macmillan in 2006.

Gavin Carver is a freelance copywriter and lives in Sydney. He has completed a Master of Arts in Professional Writing at the University of Technology, Sydney, and is currently working on his first novel.

Tom Cho is writing a collection of short fiction that explores the themes of identity and popular culture. He is completing a Ph.D in Professional Writing at Deakin University and works at Footscray Community Arts Centre.

Laurie Clancy has published twelve books of fiction and criticism as well as many articles and reviews. He taught in the English Department at La Trobe University for many years and now teaches Creative Writing at RMIT.

Matthew Condon has received two Steele Rudd awards for his collections of short stories. He is the author of several novels, including *The Motorcycle Café* and *The Pillow Fight.* His new novel, *The Trout Opera,* will be published in 2007.

Barry Cooper is an Indigenous Australian and a descendant of the Yuin Tribe from the far south-east coast of New South Wales. He studies Aboriginal Art and Cultural Design at Reid CIT and has been writing for two years.

Shady Cosgrove is a lecturer in Creative Writing at the University of Wollongong. Her Ph.D, from the Australian National University, examined structural and post-structural theories of character.

Patrick Cullen's story 'Dust' – and three linked stories published in *Best Australian Stories 2005* – are from a collection being written as part of a Ph.D at the University of Newcastle.

Sonja Dechian is a television producer for the ABC's international service, Australia Network. She edits the chapbook series *The Mudd Club* (www.themuddclub.com) and is vice president of Australians Against Racism.

Will Elliott's novel *The Pilo Family Circus* won the inaugural ABC Fiction Award and was published by ABC Books in September 2006, and in the UK by Quercus. He has studied law and is currently completing a Bachelor of Arts.

Catherine Ford is the author of *Dirt & Other Stories* and *NYC*. She is currently working on a novel set in France.

Peter Goldsworthy's most recent book was *The List of All Answers: Collected Stories*. The State Theatre Company of South Australia's stage adaptation of his 1992 novel *Honk If You Are Jesus* won the 2006 Curtain Call Award for Best Comedy, and the 2006 Ruby Award for Best New Work.

Leanne Hall is a Melbourne writer, currently working on a novel for junior readers.

Sandra Hall is a film critic for the *Sydney Morning Herald*. She is also the author of two novels, *Beyond the Break* and *A Thousand Small Wishes*, and has written two books on the history of television in Australia.

Marion Halligan has published eight novels, including *The Fog Garden* and *The Point. The Taste of Memory: An Autobiography in Food and Gardens*, was published in September 2004. Her most recent novel is *The Apricot Colonel*.

Karen Hitchcock is a doctor and writer. Her fiction has been published in *Meanjin*, *Griffith Review*, *Psychotherapy in Australia* and in a forthcoming *Sleepers Almanac*. She is a lecturer in Medicine at the University of Newcastle, where she is also completing a Ph.D in English/Creative Arts.

Patrick Holland won the 2005 Queensland Premier's Literary Award for Best Emerging Author. His novel *The Long Road of the Junkmailer* was published by UQP in September 2006.

Cate Kennedy is an award-winning short-story writer who has twice won the *Age* short story competition. Cate is also the author of the travel memoir *Sing and Don't Cry: A Mexican Journal* and the poetry collections *Joyflight* and *Signs of Other Fires*. She is now at work on her first novel.

John Kinsella's most recent publications are *The New Arcadia* (FACP, 2005) and *Fast, Loose Beginnings: A Memoir of Intoxications* (MUP, 2006).

David J. Kramer is a young writer from Sydney whose work has previously appeared in *Voiceworks*.

Amanda le Bas de Plumetot's stories have appeared in *Verandah, Page Seventeen, Taralla* and *Going Down Swinging*. She has been awarded prizes in various competitions including those of Eastern Regional Libraries, Glen Eira and Tarralla.

Fiona McGregor has written several books including *Chemical Palace*, shortlisted for the NSW Premier's Literary Awards. Her novel *Indelible Ink* will be published in 2007.

Alex Miller is an acclaimed Australian novelist. He has twice won the Miles Franklin Award and is an overall winner of the Commonwealth Writers' Prize. His most recent novel is the critically acclaimed *Prochownik's Dream*.

Frank Moorhouse's most recent book is *The Martini Memoir*. He has written fourteen books, five of which have been made into films. His novel *Dark Palace* won the Miles Franklin Award for literature.

Paddy O'Reilly is a fiction and screenplay writer. Her novel *The Factory* was published in October 2005 and a collection of short fiction, *The End of the World*, will be published by UQP in 2007.

Jennifer Robertson's fiction has appeared in *Griffith Review*, *Meanjin* and has been selected for the 2006 UTS Writers' Anthology.

Eva Sallis's novels include *Hiam* (winner of the Vogel and the Dobbie literary awards), *Mahjar* (winner of the Steele Rudd literary award) and *The Marsh Birds* (winner of the Asher literary award).

Mandy Sayer's most recent books are *Fifteen Kinds of Desire*, *Dreamtime Alice: A Memoir*, which won the 2000 National Biography Award, and her childhood memoir, *Velocity*, which won the 2006 South Australian Premier's Award and the *Age* Book of the Year for Non-Fiction.

Kim Scott's most recent book is *Kayang and Me*, a collaboration with Noongar Elder Hazel Brown. His second novel, *Benang*, won the Miles Franklin Award, the WA Premier's Literary Award and the Kate Challis RAKA Award.

Jenny Sinclair is a Melbourne writer. Her work has appeared in *Island*, *Verandah*, *Litmus* and *Woorilla*. Formerly a journalist with the *Age*, she is currently studying writing at the University of Melbourne.

Christine Stanton is a Sydney-based writer and teacher. 'Dangerous Shoes' is an extract from her recently completed novel *Xenoliths*.

Shane Strange is a Queensland-based writer and reviewer. His stories have appeared in *Griffith Review* and *Verandah*.

Girija Tropp's work has appeared in *Agni*, the *Boston Review*, *Best Australian Stories 2005* and *Southword*.

Patrick West is a widely published short-story writer and essayist. He is a lecturer in writing at Griffith University and lives on the Gold Coast.

Gerard Windsor has published nine books of fiction, memoir and essays. The most recent was the novel *I Have Kissed Your Lips.* He was awarded the Pascall Prize for Criticism in 2005. His new book is *Ned Kelly and the Odd Rellie: Fifty Micro Lives of the Great Australians.*

Chris Womersley lives and works in Melbourne. His work has been published in a variety of journals, most recently in *Granta New Writing 14.* His novel *Among the Dead* was shortlisted for the 2006 Victorian Premier's Award for an unpublished manuscript.

Daniel Wynne is a young Queensland writer. His work appeared in 'The Next Big Thing' edition of *Griffith Review.*